THE MASKED CITY

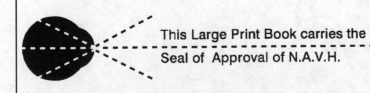

This Large Print Book carries the
Seal of Approval of N.A.V.H.

AN INVISIBLE LIBRARY NOVEL

THE MASKED CITY

GENEVIEVE COGMAN

WHEELER PUBLISHING
A part of Gale, Cengage Learning

GALE
CENGAGE Learning·

Farmington Hills, Mich • San Francisco • New York • Waterville, Maine
Meriden, Conn • Mason, Ohio • Chicago

LIBRARY OF CONGRESS CATALOGING-IN-PUBLICATION DATA

Names: Cogman, Genevieve, author.
Title: The masked city : an invisible library novel / Genevieve Cogman.
Description: Large print edition. | Waterville, Maine : Wheeler Publishing, 2017. |
  Series: Wheeler Publishing large print hardcover
Identifiers: LCCN 2016042963| ISBN 9781410496386 (hardcover) | ISBN 1410496384
  (hardcover)
Subjects: LCSH: Librarians—Fiction. | Secret societies—Fiction. | Large type books. |
  GSAFD: Fantasy fiction. | Alternative histories (Fiction)
Classification: LCC PR6103.O39 M37 2016b | DDC 823/.92—dc23
LC record available at https://lccn.loc.gov/2016042963

Published in 2017 by arrangement with The Berkley Publishing Group, an imprint of Penguin Publishing Group, a division of Penguin Random House LLC

Printed in Mexico
1 2 3 4 5 6 7 21 20 19 18 17

ACKNOWLEDGEMENTS

Thank you, again, to everyone who helped with this book. Thank you to my agent, Lucienne Diver, who helped me find monsters in the depths of London, and my editor Bella Pagan, who is marvellous at her job and to whom this book owes a great deal.

. Thanks to my beta-readers, my friends, my family, my supporters, and the classifications team at work. Your help is very much appreciated.

And many thanks to the beautiful city of Venice, which deserves far better writing than I have been able to give it.

THE STUDENT LIBRARIAN'S HANDBOOK

EXCERPT TAKEN FROM
BRIEFING DOCUMENT ON
ORIENTATION AMONGST VARIOUS WORLDS
SECTION 2.1, VERSION 4.13
AUTHOR: COPPELIA; EDITOR: KOSTCHEI
REVIEWERS: GERVASE AND NTIKUMA
FOR AUTHORIZED PERSONNEL ONLY.

Introduction

By now you will have passed basic training, and will either be working in the field with a more experienced Librarian or be preparing to do so. This confidential document is a more in-depth examination of the Library's position towards both Fae and dragons. It will help you understand why we remain unaffiliated with either side.

The Fae — Their Orientation Towards Chaos and Their Powers

You will be aware of the dangers that the Fae present to humanity. They receive their nourishment from emotional interactions with humans, feeding off us in this way. And they perceive everyone other than themselves, both humans and indeed other Fae, as mere participants — fulfilling background roles — in their own personal stories. And here we have an interesting feedback loop. The more dramatic they can make their personal stories (for example, playing the role of villain, rogue, or hero), the more power a Fae can gain. And the more powerful they are, the more stereotypical this role-playing behaviour becomes. As a result of all this, a Fae's view-point will grow correspondingly more sociopathic[1] over time.

In terms of other dangers, the Fae display powers ranging from the ability to clothe themselves in a basic glamour (in order to affect human perceptions of them) to the capacity to emotionally manipulate those around them. In addition, powerful Fae occasionally display specific magical or physi-

1. The question of whether this is sociopathy or psychopathy is beyond the scope of this briefing document.

cal powers, depending on the personal archetype or stereotype they have chosen to adopt.

The Fae — Their Worlds
The known worlds are ranged on a spectrum from order to chaos. And the farther we journey into the worlds affected by chaos, the more Fae can be found there. In chaos-affected worlds, there is of course the risk of humans being open to chaos contamination. This may affect a Librarian's powers or even prevent them from reentering the Library. In such worlds where Fae dominate, humanity forms a background cast. Their roles range from pets to food, and they are seen as props for the psychodramas, romances, or vendettas indulged in by the Fae around them — these Fae being contaminated with chaos, body and soul. Individual or weaker Fae may be able to interact with single Librarians on a relatively "human" level. The more powerful ones either won't want to or won't be capable of doing this. Beware of forming alliances if what appear to be friendly overtures are made, as they will still have very Fae motivations.

Fae or Dragons — Pros and Cons

So, you might ask, why don't we ally ourselves outright with the dragons? They stand for order, just as the Fae stand for chaos. They represent reality in the same way that the Fae embrace and are empowered by concepts of fiction and unreality. As such, the dragons esteem the "real" and the physical world above all else, having little patience with matters of the imagination. So why shouldn't we want to embrace[2] physical reality? The answer is that, in their own way, the dragons are just as biased and non-human in their view-point as the Fae.

Dragons — Their Orientation Towards Order and Their Powers

Dragons may represent the physical world — the world we can touch, if you like — but physical reality is not kind.[3] It is raw, brutal, and merciless. Dragons' powers are grounded in the physical realm: they can control the weather, the tides, the earth, and so on. Dragons are also highly practical

2. Figuratively speaking. Librarians' personal lives are their own business.
3. Librarians who have other theological opinions are reminded that their personal beliefs are also their own business.

10

in their thinking, and see little need for discussions about democracy, human self-determination, or other such fantasies — they consider themselves demonstrably the most powerful creatures around. They believe they automatically have the right to rule by this token. So in the worlds where a high degree of order is present, the dragons do rule, either openly or behind the scenes.

The Library — How It Maintains Balance

Through connections via its doors to multiple alternate worlds — connections forged by harvesting key books from these worlds — the Library helps maintain the balance. Its links with alternate worlds prevent them from drifting too fast in the direction of chaos or order, and a reasonably stable environment for humans is possible somewhere in the middle.[4] Junior Librarians may be heavily penalized if they are seen to be making unauthorized pacts with the Fae. This is especially the case if these pacts are seen to undermine the Library's all-important neutrality — which must be

4. We are aware that this is extremely simplistic. An in-depth discussion is beyond the scope of this briefing document and requires a high level of expertise in the Language.

preserved at all costs. It should be stressed that we aren't here to make judgements about what is "best for humanity." Humanity should be left to make its own decisions. The purpose of the Library is to preserve humanity from either absolute reality or absolute unreality.

And you will do this by collecting nominated books, to maintain the balance.

PROLOGUE

The London air was full of smog and filth. Kai's senses were better than those of a human, though he tried not to be too smug about it. But even he couldn't see down a dark alley any better than the average Londoner. And even native Londoners walked carefully in the narrow streets behind King's Cross Station.

But where crime flourished, so too did detectives. And he was here to meet Peregrine Vale, friend and fighter of crime.

He paused to inspect a pawnbroker's window, trying to gauge the street behind him. While he couldn't see anyone specifically following him, there was something in the air that set him on edge, a foretaste of danger. But there were very few humans who could challenge a dragon, even in his human form, and he didn't expect to meet any of them in the back alleys here.

Vale was in a warehouse just round the

corner. Almost there, and then Kai could find out what kind of assistance Vale needed with his case.

And then someone screamed nearby. It was a woman's scream, genuinely terrified, cut off in the middle with a coughing yelp. Kai turned abruptly, peering into the swirling fog. Two men and a woman were huddled at one end of a particularly dank passageway. The woman had her arms pinned behind her back by one aggressor, while the other was drawing back his fist to strike again.

"Let her go," Kai said calmly. He could handle two humans easily enough. Even if they were werewolves, they weren't a significant danger. But this would make him late.

"Back off," one of the men snarled, turning away from the woman to face him. "This isn't none of your business, nor your part of town neither."

"It's my business if I choose to make it my business." Kai advanced down the alley towards the group, automatically assessing them as his father's armsmasters had trained him to. The men were muscular in the shoulders, well built, but both showed signs of a paunch and dissipation. He could take them, just as he'd taken others of their kind a few days before.

The free man advanced towards him, fists up in a crude boxer's stance. He was lighter on his feet than Kai had expected, but not fast enough. He bluffed with his right fist, then tried a straight left at Kai's jaw. Kai sidestepped, slammed his hand sideways into the man's kidneys, kicked him in the back of the knee to take him off balance, and ran his head into the wall. The man went down.

"Now, don't be like that," the other man said, backing deeper into the alley and holding the woman in front of him like a shield. Panic was starting to show in his eyes. "You just walk away and nobody gets hurt . . ."

"You just let go of that woman," Kai corrected him, "and *you* don't get hurt." He walked forward, considering his openings. A dodge to the side and a strike to the man's neck might be the least risky option for the woman, and yet —

"Now," a voice said from above.

Doors slammed open on either side of him and behind him, and at the same moment something fell from above, tumbling down towards him in a knot of shadows. Kai dived to one side on instinct, but then there were too many men in the alley with him. A dozen of them, the combat-trained part of his mind noted, and more behind those

15

open doors. He had no room to dodge, and it looked like a trap. They didn't even hang back and let other people take the first blows, in the normal manner of thugs. They came charging in, most of them barehanded, but a couple with knuckle-dusters or small weighted saps.

He had to get back and out. There was no shame to it. Part of a warrior's training was acknowledging superior force and reacting appropriately. An arm came around his neck from behind. He grabbed it, went down on one knee, and flung the man over his head and into the ones closing in on him. Staying low, he pivoted, bringing a foot round and scything another combatant's feet from under him. He used the momentum to turn and rise. Four men were between him and the way out. Four obstacles to remove.

Vale's case must be important to warrant this sort of interference.

Kai noted the coils of the net, which had barely missed him, tangled on the street. It was a nasty piece of work, with metal woven into the ropes. Curious. Why go to this trouble to snare him personally? If they had already caught Vale, they would regret it.

He slammed an elbow backwards, feeling the jolt as it connected with a chin, and started forward at a swinging run. At least one of the men in front of him should back away . . .

He didn't expect them to all come at him at once, like a sudden human tidal wave. He struck high for a throat, and then low to a groin — disabling blows. But they weren't going down. They felt the pain, they grunted, they staggered, but they were still in his path.

A blow took him across the back of the head, causing a sudden burst of pain, and his attempted nerve-strike lost its force as he went down on one knee. He knew that he was a sitting target, but for that moment his muscles wouldn't respond.

Another man hit him in the face. He spat blood.

A man behind him threw himself on top of Kai, bringing him down to the filthy pavement. Kai struggled for breath, sparks still dancing in his vision. He could feel pure fury running through his veins now. How dare these humans assault him like this?

There was no room in him for fear. It was not *possible* that this scum could win.

He felt his natural body assert itself, his hands becoming claws, scales beginning to trace their way across his skin as his true nature rose with that fury. He would call up the river against them; he would scour them from this London; he would make them pay for this *insolence.*

Across London, he felt the Thames and all its tributaries stir in response to his anger. He might be the least and youngest of his father's sons, but he was still a dragon of the royal house. With an uncoiling shove, he thrust backwards, forcing the thug from his back and away, and pushed himself up, teeth bared in a snarl.

More bodies hit him and took him down, heavy hands pinning his wrists to the pavement. His claws left marks in it as he struggled for leverage. For the first time he felt a prickle of doubt. Perhaps it would be wiser to fully take on his true form, one that they could not possibly restrain. It would alert all London that a dragon walked in their midst, but if he should lose . . .

A hand snarled itself in his hair, pulling his head back, and he felt cold metal snap shut around his neck. And now abruptly there was the ferocious, electric tang of Fae magic in the air, locked around him, *binding* him. He cried out in sudden shock as the distant rivers faded and were gone from his senses, as his fingers, now purely human, scraped against the concrete.

"That should do it." That cold voice was the first time that anyone had spoken during the whole attack, and it was the last thing Kai heard. There was one final blow to his head, and then he surrendered to unconsciousness.

CHAPTER 1

The Night Before . . .

It was a pity about the poison in her wine-glass, Irene reflected. The underground room was hot, and a glass of chilled wine would have been refreshing.

She hadn't needed Kai's murmur from behind her shoulder. She'd been watching the crow-masked man in the mirror. His real name was Charles Melancourt, and they'd both been hunting for the same book for the past few weeks. He was the agent for a Russian buyer. Irene was an agent for the Library. They'd run into each other often enough while investigating the same sources, and he had certainly recognized her in spite of her mask, just as she had recognized him.

The bidding finished for the current item, a set of gold-plated dice with rubies as the points, and there was a gentle ripple of applause. Everyone was masked, even the waiters carrying round the trays of food and wine. This auction wasn't exactly illegal, but it was certainly dubious. The patrons included eccentrics, the very rich, and a large number of people who had lawyers just to prove how absolutely not guilty they were. (Of anything.) Ether lamps burned on the walls, casting a white glare on the room. It made the beading on the expensive dresses and military decorations glitter as much as the items up for auction. She'd recognized some of London's Fae too, behind their masks. But Lord Silver, their unofficial leader, wasn't present — a fact for which she was extremely grateful.

Irene had gained entrance with Vale's help. It didn't hurt to be a personal friend of London's greatest detective. In return, she'd promised to make sure that she and Kai were out of the place before midnight, before a scheduled police raid happened. A promise she intended to keep. She'd spent the last few months in this alternate world building a cover identity as a freelance translator, and having a criminal record would be inconvenient.

"Next item," the auctioneer droned. "One copy of Abraham, or 'Bram,' Stoker's *La Sorcière,* based on the book of the same name by Jules Michelet. We are sure that our guests don't need to be reminded that this book was banned by the British government. And the Church denounced it on the grounds of public indecency and heresy. No doubt it'll provide the buyer with something entertaining to read, ha-ha." Her laugh lacked anything resembling humour. "Sold as part of an anonymous estate. Bidding starts at one thousand pounds. Do I hear any bids?"

Irene raised her hand. So did Melancourt.

"Lady in the black domino, one thousand pounds," the auctioneer intoned.

"One thousand five hundred!" Melancourt called out.

So he was going to go for big jumps, rather than take it up by stages. Fair enough. At least they seemed to be the only people interested in this lot. "Two thousand," Irene said clearly.

"Two thousand five hundred!" Melancourt declared.

That got a few whispers from the other bidders. The book was rare, but not hugely so. Certain museums had copies, so Irene was being comparatively virtuous in buying the tome at an underworld auction. She could have stolen it, after all. The thought made her smile. "Three thousand."

"Five thousand!" The sudden jump in price made the room fall silent. People were looking at Irene to see what she would do.

Kai leaned over her shoulder. True to his cover as bodyguard, he'd been standing throughout, refusing food and drinks, and keeping watch on the carpet-bag with their assurance of payment. "We could let him win this, and then visit him later," he murmured.

"Too risky," Irene whispered back. She picked up the glass of wine from the tray he was holding, raising it to her lips, and couldn't mistake the sudden tension in Melancourt's posture. Yes, this *had* been from him. She'd thought so.

"Wine, boil," she murmured in the Language, and quickly set it down again as the glass heated up under her fingers. The wine was already bubbling, and it overflowed onto the tray, hissing and steaming as it evaporated. Kai's hands tensed, but he held the tray steady.

The silence had deepened. Irene broke it. "Ten thousand," she said casually.

Melancourt brought his fist down on his thigh with a curse.

"Do I hear any other bids?" the auctioneer demanded against a rising susurrus of whispers. "Ten thousand from the lady in the black domino, going once, going twice . . . sold! If you will come over to arrange payment with our staff, madam, thank you very much. The next item . . ."

Irene tuned out the next item, rising to her feet. Kai handed his tray to one of the waiters and picked up their carpet-bag, following her as she headed over to the payment desk. She kept a weather eye on Melancourt, but he was slumped in his seat, not trying anything dramatic. Men and women nodded to her with respect as she walked past, and she returned the gesture politely.

"Your payment, ma'am?" the man at the desk asked neutrally. He had several large, well-muscled men behind him to help reluctant customers cover their purchases. But they wouldn't be needed this time.

Irene kept her smile faint as the desk clerk examined her synthetic diamonds with a jeweller's glass before closing the transaction and handing over the book. She'd obtained the gems from a Librarian working in a much more technologically advanced alternate, and they paid the bills nicely. Diamond production there was comparatively cheap, and all her colleague had wanted in exchange was a complete set of first-edition Voltaires from her world.

They made it to the door before Melancourt caught up with them. "I can make a deal," he said, his voice low but desperate. "If you would put me in touch with your principal —"

"I'm afraid that's impossible," Irene said. "I'm sorry, but the matter is closed. You will have to excuse me." She remembered she had a deadline — and it was ten-thirty already.

Melancourt's lips drew into a thin line under his mask. "Don't hold me responsible for what may happen," he spat. "And you will have to excuse me as well. I should be getting on my way." He barged ahead of the two of them, calling to a waiter for his coat and hat.

It was quarter to eleven by the time they were clear of the venue and no longer wearing their masks. The night was comparatively clear, and the ether lamps showed every imperfection of the Soho streets. A few women loitered on street corners, but most of them were in the pubs or operating from indoors, and none of them tried approaching Kai and Irene. Melancourt was already out of sight.

"Do you think he'll try something?" Kai asked, keeping his voice low.

"Probably. Let's head for Oxford Street. We should be safe enough once we're on the main road."

As they headed in that direction, Irene considered how her life had changed in the last few months. Previously she'd been a roaming Librarian on assignment, hopping from one alternate world to another in order to collect books for the interdimensional Library she served. Now she had a steady base here as Librarian-in-Residence, an apprentice she respected, and even friends. World-travelling wasn't the best way to keep friendships, especially when she had to spend half her time in disguise. But now she even had people in this world, like Vale, who knew what she was and accepted it.

And, to be honest about it, she was enjoying her work. It was *rewarding* to fulfil requests from the Library, and to do so promptly and efficiently. Providing unique books for the Library from a particular world helped stabilize the world itself too, balancing it between order and chaos by strengthening its link to the Library. But it was also, for want of a better word, exciting. Last month they'd had to sneak into an automaton-filled labyrinth under Edinburgh to rescue a copy of Elizabeth Báthory's lost *Regina Rosae* narrative. Today they'd slipped in and out of the auction without any trouble. (One little attempted poisoning was a minor detail.) Irene wasn't sure what tomorrow would bring, but it promised to be interesting.

"Ah," Kai said in a tone of mild satisfaction as they turned the corner past a pub and onto a dark stretch of road. "Thought so. We're being followed."

Irene turned her head and caught a glimpse of two men behind them, at the turn of the street. "Good catch. Is it just those two?"

"At least one more. I think they're cutting round to intercept us, if we go through Berwick Street." Kai frowned. "What shall we do?"

"Go through Berwick Street, of course," Irene said definitely. "How else are we going to find out what's going on?"

Kai glanced sidelong at her, the ether lamps forcing his profile into a sharp marble carving. His eyes were narrowed and dark in contrast. "You'll let me handle it?"

"I'll let you take point," Irene said. "You distract them. I'll tidy up."

He gave a nod, accepting the order. She wasn't going to demand to fight side by side with him in a street fight. He was a dragon, after all, and even in human form he could jump in the air and kick people in the head. And this London's ankle-length skirts weren't designed with jumping and kicking

28

in mind.

Kai's being a dragon was complicated. It made him a useful apprentice, with capabilities beyond the human norm, but it also meant that he came with his own share of attitudes and prejudices. He outright loathed the Fae as forces of chaos, which was awkward, given that they had a major presence in this world. And he carried himself with the hauteur of a dragon of royal blood, though he refused to go into details about his parentage. Irene was experienced enough to know that this could — no, probably *would* — mean trouble. But right here and now, he was excellent backup.

At this time of night, Berwick Street's market and fabric shops were closed, and the street was dark apart from the ether lamps. Now would be a good time for their pursuers to make their move.

As if on cue, the two men began closing in as a third man stepped round the corner ahead of them. He was scruffily dressed, his ragged-cuffed coat hanging open to reveal a loosely knotted cravat at his throat over a partially unbuttoned shirt. His cap was pulled down low over his face, shadowing his eyes. "Hold it right there," he snarled.

Kai and Irene stopped.

"Now, we can do this the easy way," the

ruffian said, "or we can do it the hard way. Me and the boys, we wouldn't want to hurt you unnecessarily, right?"

"Oh no!" Irene gasped, in an effort to seem unthreatening. "What is this?"

"Just a bit of necessary violence, miss," the man said. He took a step forward. She could hear the other two coming up behind them, faster now. "Now, if you stand away from this young gentleman here, me and the boys won't have no reason to bother you."

It must be because Kai was carrying the bag. Melancourt couldn't have had time to warn them that she might have unusual abilities. Well, Irene wasn't going to turn down an advantage.

"Then what reason do you have to bother *me*?" Kai enquired. He passed the bag to Irene, and she took a step back, giving him room to manoeuvre as she retreated towards the side of the street. Out of the corner of her eye, she could see lights flickering off in upper windows and curtains twitching open. For a moment she thought she saw something move on the top of the opposite roofline, but she couldn't be certain, and the danger at street level was more immediate. Fortunately she had absolute faith in Kai to handle three street thugs on his own.

He probably wouldn't even break a sweat.

The man in front of them slipped a small heavy cosh from his pocket, weighing it in his hand in an experienced-looking manner. Trained gentlemen of the street, then. A little bit more than recruits from the nearest pub.

Irene turned to look at the two men approaching from behind. Their gait had shifted from a brisk walk to a casual lope. And now that she could see them more clearly in the lamplight, their cheeks were thick with whiskers, heavy eyebrows met above their noses, and their fingernails were definitely not quite right.

Werewolves. She hadn't been expecting werewolves.

There were no actual laws against being a werewolf in this alternate world. However, unless one happened to have money, they were firmly stuck in the social class devoted to manual labour and casual thuggery. Werewolves tended to hang together in extended pseudo-family groups in big cities, fulfilling entire labour shifts in factories or on the docks, or simply running protection rackets. Irene had never tried to find out what werewolves did out in the countryside. Perhaps they pursued a wholesome outdoor life, only hunting rabbits, but somehow she doubted it.

Fortunately it took a great deal of time and slobbery effort at the full moon to transmit the werewolf taint. So the immediate danger didn't lie there. But they were tougher than the average human, and hard to slow down in a fight — unless you were willing to do serious damage.

"We'll be having that bag you just passed to your young miss there," the first man — werewolf, rather — grunted. He licked his lips. His tongue was a bit too long for comfort. "And then you're going to take a little message to whoever it was employed you, if you know what I mean."

"I wouldn't recommend this," Kai said, sliding his right foot forward in what Irene vaguely recognized as an obscure martial arts stance. "If you gentlemen would simply tell me who hired you —"

The two behind him suddenly dashed forward, grabbing for Kai's arms. But Kai had clearly anticipated this. He smoothly reached back to catch their wrists, then swung them violently forward with their own momentum. Then, when he yanked them back again, they both almost fell. One swore. The other was silent, but he licked his lips with a nasty glint in his eyes.

"Oh, we've got a smart rusher here," the

first man said. "Circle him, lads. Let's show him some respect." As he spoke, he shifted to his right, his boots scuffing on the pavement, but he didn't yet move in towards Kai.

"I'd still like to know who sent you gentlemen," Kai said. His posture remained loose and relaxed. He didn't take his eyes from the leader of the three, but Irene was sure that he was watching the others as well. It was easy at times to forget that he'd spent a period as a semi-criminal in a high-tech cyberpunk world. He was probably used to this sort of confrontation. It might even feel nostalgic.

"I'll just bet you would," the one on Kai's left snarled. He sidled farther round, closer to where Irene was standing by the wall, trying to get round behind Kai. "Pity that all you're going to be able to tell them is —"

Kai moved in the instant of his distraction, turning to take a quick double step towards him. His balled fist slid into a straight punch at the man's belly, and the man grunted and staggered. Kai opened his hand to strike with the flat of his palm at the side of the man's neck, his face focused, solely interested in the proper form of the blow. The man staggered back with the force of the impact, spittle flying from his open mouth. The werewolf's breath came hard, and he sagged down onto his knees, hairy fists thumping against the pavement, eyes hazy as he struggled to stay conscious.

The two others rushed Kai, both growling at the back of their throats, one trying to get in close and keep him occupied while the first one used his sap. The whole thing devolved into a scuffle and a number of quick blows. Irene frowned as she saw Kai go down on one knee, and she stepped forward to help. But the first thug came staggering to his feet and made a grab for her, his long-nailed hairy fingers circling her upper arm. "Now, just you squeal nice and loudly so the gentleman can hear you," he began.

Irene glanced down at his feet, quickly. Boots. Boots with long, heavy laces. That would do. **"Your boot-laces are tied to each other,"** she informed him, feeling the weight of the Language in her throat.

She was a Librarian. And in moments like this, that fact was exceedingly useful. The world heard her words and altered itself in response. She could boil wine, open doors, down airships, bring stuffed animals to life — and far worse. Or, in this case, tie a pair of boot-laces together.

"What?" the thug asked, predictably confused.

She grabbed and pulled his arm, hard. But the thug, with a leeringly smug smile, kept his grip on her and stepped even closer — before falling flat on his face. His boot-laces had indeed tied themselves to each other.

Irene chopped his hand away efficiently as he went down, freeing herself. She wouldn't be a very effective field agent if she couldn't handle herself in a fight. The thug meanwhile was flailing wildly on the ground, so Irene kicked him hard in the kidneys. When she did it again, he stopped moving in favour of gasping for breath. *One less to chase us when we make our escape,* she thought grimly.

The sounds of combat had died down behind her as she looked over towards Kai. He was brushing dust from his coat-sleeves in an unnecessary manner, and the two other thugs for hire were slumped on the ground beside him. One of them had his arm twisted at an unnatural angle, and the other had a nosebleed. The curtains in the windows above the street had stopped twitching, and the fleeting shadow had vanished from the rooftops. Melancourt must have decided to cut his losses.

"Perhaps the gentleman with the sap

would be kind enough to do some explaining," Irene suggested.

Kai bent down, pulled the first werewolf to his feet, and propped him against the wall. The werewolf's nails had receded, and his facial hair was back to the level of an extremely unshaven normal man. "Now that we've been through the preliminaries," Kai said, "could we discuss the matter?"

The thug gave a coughing grunt. He moved his hand carefully to his face, and when it was clear that Kai wasn't going to try to stop him, wiped away blood and spittle. "Gotta say, you're a bit more than I was expecting, guv," he muttered. "All right. Long as we understand that there ain't going to be no official complaints and the like?"

"Strictly personal," Kai reassured him. "Now, perhaps you'd answer my friend's question. Who are you? And who sent you?"

"I'll be honest with you, guv," the werewolf said. He probed at his shoulder and winced. "Jesus, but you've got a kick on you. We met this woman in the Old Swan, a pub three streets over. Said you'd be coming down this way with a lady friend, and gave us your description. She told us she wanted your bag, and to give you a warning to stay out of other people's business. But didn't want

36

either of the two of you dead. We were to hang on to the bag and she'd contact us."

Irene nodded. "Can you tell me anything about the woman who hired you?"

He shrugged, then winced again. "Proper lady, full purse, but not anyone's mark for the taking. Carried a parasol and had a knife in her sleeve. Evening coat, hat and gloves, nothing obvious, but top of the line. Her scarf pin looked like gold, but I didn't get to do more than look. She had a man with her watching her back, but she was in charge. Dark hair under the hat, dark eyes. Nobody I knew."

"Was she a foreigner?" Kai asked casually. It was slightly less definite than *Could she have been from the Liechtenstein Embassy, a local den of Fae and the dwelling of a certain Lord Silver, who has an ongoing feud with Vale?* But the thought was there.

He shook his head. "If she was, it weren't obvious. Sounded normal enough. Posh accent, like you both."

"And nothing memorable about the man?" Irene was grasping at straws here. "Or about her scarf pin?"

"Well, I'd know him again, miss," the thug said. "But it's not like I'm your Mr. Vale, is it? Not like I can take one look at him and tell you where the . . ." He visibly moderated his language. "Where the mud on his shoes come from. And her scarf pin was just a pair of hands shaking each other — nothing special."

This had been far too easy. Irene turned to Kai. "He isn't telling us everything. Make him talk."

Kai stepped forward, and the werewolf flinched back. "Wait! You said you weren't going to hurt me!"

"Actually, he never said that." Irene focused. The Language could be used to adjust a person's perceptions. It didn't last long, but it could be quite effective at the right time and place. She addressed the werewolf. **"You perceive that my friend is a truly terrifying person who is willing to do anything to make you tell us the truth."**

Fiddling with people's minds was on the dubious side of ethical, but, Irene reassured herself, it was preferable to actually beating the information out of him.

He folded before Kai could reach him, cringing and baring his neck. "All right, all right!" he babbled. "So we followed her outside, didn't we? And we saw her take a private cab to the Liechtenstein Embassy to meet her husband . . . That's what she told the driver. And he addressed her as 'my lady'!"

Now, that was rather more useful. While the woman wasn't necessarily nobility, there couldn't be that many women at the embassy who'd rate that form of address.

"But are you sure that was for real, and not just to fool you?" Irene asked.

Despite his position, the werewolf looked smug. "Naah, it was for real, and you know why? Because the man who was driving the cab, my mate George knew him. He's a regular embassy driver. Even if she wanted to pull a fast one on us, the driver was for real."

"His name," Irene said crisply.

The werewolf hesitated, looked at Kai again, then gave in. "Vlad Petrov," he muttered. "Don't know no more than that."

That sounded honest enough. And now they had a name to work with. "I think this gentleman has told us everything he can," Irene said to Kai.

"I would agree." Kai turned back to the thug. "But let's not run into each other again, hmm?"

"You said it, guv," the thug agreed enthusiastically. "Least said, soonest mended, like my old mum always used to say."

Kai didn't bother asking what that was

supposed to mean. He stepped back. "Good evening," he said. He offered Irene his arm, and they strolled away together. They weren't followed.

They turned the corner. "What do you think?" Kai said quietly.

"Very low-grade types," Irene replied, and watched Kai nod in agreement. "And careless of whoever hired them. They were lucky their new employees didn't attack the wrong people. And that whole business with the bag and 'Don't contact me; I'll contact you.' She really didn't want them getting in touch."

Kai nodded again. "But I can't quite see it as being Silver. Thugs aren't really his style. Even if he was interested in the Stoker book. Our mystery Fae woman knew we'd be coming from the auction, with the bag — so surely she'd come from there herself. Perhaps she was Melancourt's patron."

Irene had to agree with the first part of that. Silver — or Lord Silver, if she absolutely must — was far more likely to arrange duellists with whips and rapiers, or have assassins descend on their house at midnight, if he really felt the need to express himself in that way. "Another Fae makes sense," she said. "But the timing's off. I'm not sure someone could have been at the auction, left at the same time as us, *and* managed to hire those werewolves to attack us."

Kai frowned, thinking. "She could have left early and then hired the werewolves to intercept us — in case we got the book."

"True." They were almost at Oxford Street now. "But it seems a bit haphazard, and really a very *careless* way of handling matters."

"I know you'd do better, if it was you," Kai said graciously.

Irene gave him a sideways look.

"I mean in terms of a planned operation," he added hastily. "Something well-organized and efficient, without trusting the first ruffians you come across to do a good job or being totally outmatched. It was a compliment, Irene. Really." He couldn't entirely hide his smirk, though.

"Planning now saves trouble later," Irene said firmly. "And there was someone watching from the rooftops. Someone of rather better quality than those men. I couldn't get a good view of him — or her," she added thoughtfully.

"Could it be just a burglar?" Kai suggested.

"It could be." Irene adjusted her veil. "But what if it was the person nominated to retrieve the bag, once the werewolves removed it from *us*?"

"Oh, that makes sense. It's a pity we couldn't question the watcher, then."

"They were gone by the time you'd taken the men down," Irene said. "It looks as if that lady and her agents really wanted to hide their trail."

"But they failed," Kai said with satisfaction. "We have a name."

They stepped out into Oxford Street, and Irene raised a hand to signal a cab. "Everyone's unlucky sometimes," she said. "However good the plan may be."

But she couldn't shake the feeling that perhaps she and Kai had been a little bit *too* lucky themselves tonight.

CHAPTER 2

The next morning, Irene spent a while thanking this civilization for inventing the shower. While in many respects it was similar to the period known as "Victorian" in numerous alternate worlds (featuring smog, horse-drawn carriages as well as "ether"-powered carriages, and a lack of instant communication), in other respects it had managed to hit the important points. It had decent sanitation — barring the smog — adequate clean water, and plenty of tea and coffee. So she had to endure zeppelins, werewolves and vampires, and a lack of telephones (the users kept on getting possessed by demons). It could be worse. The smog killed most of the mosquitoes.

But while she was in the shower, she was thinking. She needed to get the Stoker book to the Library — and the sooner the better, before another theft was attempted. But she and Kai also needed to investigate the woman. Vale would be most helpful there. A sparrow couldn't get stabbed in the back without the detective hearing about it. And while Irene or Kai could go sniffing round the Liechtenstein Embassy (Liechtenstein being a haven for Fae in this world), they might show their quarry they knew where to find her.

Kai was working at his desk in their shared study, scraping away with a fountain-pen on a list of booksellers. He acknowledged her politely, but his attention was clearly elsewhere. A harshly glaring table lamp threw his face into sharp profile, giving an extra gleam to his black hair.

It had been a sensible idea to get lodgings together, Irene reminded herself. It had meant that she could keep an eye on Kai. After they fell foul of the traitor Alberich and London's Fae, via Silver, she didn't want to take any chances. And being a friend of Vale's could be risky in itself — especially when they helped on each other's cases. Kai and she were both adults. They could share lodgings without having to get "involved."

But dragons, when taking human form, apparently took implausibly handsome (or possibly beautiful) human forms. Kai had smooth black hair with blue lights to it, skin pale as marble, deep dark eyes, and cheek-bones that *begged* to be touched. He moved like a dancer, with a physique to match. The dramatic sort of dancer, who could whirl you around the dance floor before bending you by the waist and pressing himself against you, and then . . .

He was also, Irene reminded herself firmly, her student and apprentice and her responsibility. The point wasn't whether he might be willing — though he had strongly suggested that he was, and kept on suggesting it — or whether she might be willing. The point was whether she had the right to take advantage of his offer. For the moment, she was content to have him as a friend as well as a colleague, and to be grateful for it.

Being responsible has a lot to answer for, she thought resentfully. "Are you ready?" she asked.

"I was just . . ." Kai fiddled with his pen. "There was a message," he finally said.

"From whom?" This was clearly going to take a few minutes to sort out. Irene sat down opposite him, settling her elbows on the table. The healing scars on her hands from months ago stood out against her skin and made a criss-cross pattern across her palms and fingers.

Kai plucked a scroll from under a pile of

other papers. The wax seal on it had been broken, and the ribbon untied. Irene could make out what looked like Chinese characters, in black ink, signed in red. "From my uncle," he said. "My oldest uncle, my father's next-oldest brother. He requests my presence at a family ceremony in a few months."

"Well, of course you must go," Irene said promptly. "I can manage without you for a few days. Or weeks — how long a celebration is it?" She knew very little about dragons, in spite of sharing lodgings with one, and possibly they thought that a good family celebration lasted several years.

"Probably a couple of weeks," Kai said without any real enthusiasm.

Irene tried to imagine what the problem was. "Are you embarrassed about your current position?" she asked.

"No!" Kai's answer was gratifyingly fast. "No — I wouldn't have done it without my uncle's permission, in any case."

"So he knows?"

"No, that's a different uncle," Kai said. "My father has three brothers. The youngest was my guardian when I started working for the Library. This is an older brother, the second-eldest in the family. So naturally I owe him my loyalty and should attend."

Irene made a mental note that if this conversation was going to go on much longer, she was going to have to ask for names and draw up a family tree. "I don't see what the problem is, then," she said.

Kai shifted slightly in his chair. "I just hadn't expected them to be able to contact me here. Any invitations should have gone to my former guardian, and of course I speak with him every few years. But for it to arrive like this —"

"How did it arrive?" Irene broke in, before he could edge around the subject any more.

"By private messenger," Kai said.

Irene considered that. On the one hand, it meant that some dragon out there knew Kai's postal address and, by implication, hers. On the other hand, was that necessarily a bad thing? "I still don't understand why you're objecting," she said. "If you'd waited till you next spoke to them, you'd have missed this family event."

"You don't understand!" Oh, maybe they were getting to it now. It was the wail of the teenage prince, or at least the college student prince — away from his family and enjoying a previously unknown sense of liberty. Perhaps, for junior dragons, taking a few years to explore alternate worlds was like a student's weekend away in a foreign

47

country — though possibly involving less drinking. "They know where I am. They might visit at any time. They might even disapprove of what I've been up to."

"Wait. You just said that you're not embarrassed about your job. Now you're saying they might disapprove. Is it because of our recent activities?" Such as going to criminal auctions, infiltrating the Inquisition Cloisters under Winchester, or the time they'd had to run a con game on a visiting Kazakhstan warlord with a Silk Road travelogue . . .

"It's possible my uncles might not understand the full complexities of working with the Library," Kai admitted reluctantly. "I believe they think it's just a job of researching and purchasing books."

Irene wanted to swear at the waste of time. They needed to be on their way to see Vale about the woman, or get to the Library to hand over the Stoker. Having to persuade Kai to confess his family problems was like pulling teeth while standing in front of an oncoming train. Though admittedly with less screaming. "When you were recruited for the Library, weren't you hanging around with criminals and street thugs? Didn't your uncle know about that?"

Kai's back went absolutely rigid, and a high flush flared on his cheek-bones. "Irene, if you were not my superior, you would regret saying that!"

"But you *were* hanging out with criminals and street thugs," Irene said, confused but admiring his precise grammar under stress. That was the sort of thing you had to learn when you were young and impressionable.

"That may be true," Kai said grudgingly. "But it was without my guardian's knowledge. He is above such things."

Irene rubbed her forehead in exasperation. "But you were staying with him . . ."

"He encouraged me to sample local literature and art," Kai said, losing a little of his anger. "The fact that I became involved with local criminals was entirely beside the point."

Irene mentally raised the draconic capacity for hypocrisy by several thousand points and took a deep breath. "We are wandering from the point. Kai, you *will* be attending that family gathering. It would be rude not to, and they might suspect I was teaching you bad manners and relocate you." She saw his face twitch. He hadn't thought of that.

Kai sighed. "You talk like my elder."

"I probably am," Irene said. She'd lived more than twenty-five years outside the Library, in alternate worlds where she aged normally. But at least a dozen more had been spent inside the Library at various intervals, and people didn't age within its walls. "Even if you're a dragon."

"But how do you suppose they found me here?" Kai asked, returning to the point in question like a cat with a favourite toy.

"At a wild guess, my supervisor, Coppelia, had word passed to your people, so that they wouldn't worry about you." Irene rose to her feet and began looking for her coat. She wasn't enthusiastic about Kai's family possibly turning up on her door-step, but she could understand the political necessity of being able to account for where he was. "You won't have any problems getting to your uncle when you visit, will you?"

Kai twitched a shoulder in a deliberately casual way. "Irene, I *am* a dragon. I don't require the Library to travel between worlds. I can do so quite easily myself."

She had to concede him that bit of smugness. It was quite justified. Librarians needed props and protocols; she couldn't simply stroll from one world to another as Kai could. "Can all dragons do that?" she asked, trying not to sound jealous.

"All royal ones," Kai said. "Lesser dragons can make smaller journeys — it doesn't really translate into physical terms," he

50

added hastily when she raised a hand to ask what he meant by *smaller journeys.* "Or they can follow in a royal dragon's wake, if he is leading the way."

"I see." She found her coat and started to button it. "Now we should be moving. It's nearly ten o'clock."

"Irene . . ." Kai hesitated. "You don't want to get rid of me, do you?"

She simply gaped at him for a second. "What?"

"You're sending me off to my family. You're treating me like any other apprentice. You don't seem to care that they might order me to leave. You don't . . ." He looked at her, his face full of yearning and uncertainty. "If you want me to go, then I will go, but . . ."

It wasn't some sort of emotional blackmail. It was sincere and it was honest, and it made her heart clench in her chest. She sighed and walked around the desk — nowhere near as graceful as he was, nothing like as elegant, just a mortal human — to take his hands. They were thin and hot in her grasp, his long fingers curling around hers. "Kai, don't you understand that I am saying all this because I don't want to lose you? You are my friend. You are the person whom I trust to watch my back, to fight werewolves for me. To dangle me out of zeppelins. To stand by with a hammer when I'm staking vampires. I don't know what might make your family take you away. I don't want to give them an *excuse.*"

"Do you mean that?" He rose to his feet and looked down into her face, his hands tight on hers. "Do you promise that you mean that?"

It would be so easy just to say yes and let go of common sense, to slide her hands up to his shoulders and hold him against her. She had been spending months now trying to avoid this sort of thought, this sort of situation. "I give you my word that I don't want to lose you," she said. "You're my apprentice. You're my ally. You're my *friend.* Can't you believe me?"

Yes. And stop asking for more, before I do something I might regret.

"I want to." His voice was rough. "It's just that — Irene, I'm afraid."

"The mugging? If you don't feel safe —"

"Not that!" He very nearly sneered at the idea, and it cooled a little of the heat between them, like a sudden touch of fresh air. "Not of danger. Not for myself. It's . . . everything." His eloquence and his grace of speech had deserted him. "You. Vale. The Library. Everything. I've never disobeyed

52

my honoured father before, never challenged the authority of my elders. What am I to do if they tell me to leave you?"

Irene would have liked to give him some sort of reassurance, but she didn't have any easy answers. She didn't even have any complicated ones. She could only return the clasp of his hands. "We'll find a solution," she said firmly. "There has to be a way. Even if I have to steal examples of poetry from a hundred worlds, to convince them that you're on a valid postgraduate study course. There *will* be a way."

She wasn't going to lose him.

There was a cracking noise from the next room, like pebbles on glass. At the same moment, Irene felt a strike against the wards that she'd placed on their lodgings, a thunder-clap in her metaphysical hearing. It wasn't significant enough to bring the wards down, but it was a firm, carefully placed blow, not an ignorant blaze of power. And it was definitely tainted with chaos. Someone was knocking, and they wanted in.

The noise had come from Kai's bedroom. A dozen unpleasant possibilities ran through Irene's mind, most of them connected with last night's attack.

"What?" Kai released her, ran to the door, and slammed it open. "Who dares?"

His room was surprisingly tidy — a bulging wardrobe, a bare floor, a small table, and an equally small shrine with a twist of incense. The large bow window on the other side of the room was intact, but a dramatic figure stood on the other side of it, his cane raised to beat against the glass. His cloak and jacket fluttered in a wind that certainly hadn't been blowing earlier, and his silver hair cascaded down over his shoulders. A lambent glitter sparkled in his eyes.

"Kai," Irene said with great patience, "why is Lord Silver standing on your windowsill?"

CHAPTER 3

"Let me in!" Silver smashed his cane against the glass. It rebounded with the same cracking noise they had heard earlier, leaving the glass untouched. Fortunately, Irene and Kai's wish to collect a critical mass of books meant this apartment could support a Library-style ward. And such things were anathema to the Fae. Though it was taking her a regular effort to maintain it, at moments like this it was totally worth it.

"Certainly not!" Irene pushed in front of Kai. "Lord Silver, how dare you behave like this?"

Silver clung to the arch of the window with one hand and pointed the head of his cane at Irene. He was wearing perfect morning dress — suit and cloak — and his top hat was cocked rakishly, somehow staying on his head despite his position and the morning breeze. "Are you going to tell me you know nothing about it?"

Irene reviewed her conscience. It was comparatively clean. At least, it didn't bring up any particular crimes with respect to Silver. "Nothing about what?" she demanded. "And why on earth are you standing on the window-sill and yelling through the glass?"

"Because you won't open the window, of course," Silver said, in tones that suggested it was too obvious to be worth mentioning. "I came here for a perfectly simple private consultation, and found your lodgings barred to me. Is it my fault that I chose to approach discreetly rather than by the front door?"

Irene supposed the back first-floor window was more discreet than the front door. But not by much. "And what do you want to discuss with us?"

"Ah. I take it that you're not going to invite me in?"

"No," Irene said, prodding Kai before he could say something more emphatic but equally negative. The clock was still ticking. She didn't have time for all these Fae dramatics. But if Silver could answer some questions about last night's events, then it would be stupid not to ask him here and now. "How about neutral territory, Lord Silver? There's a coffee shop down the road.

56

We'll meet you there in five minutes."

Silver shrugged casually. "I dare say it will do. The name of this place, little mouse?"

"Coram's," Irene said, ignoring Silver's little jab. She'd passed the point where he could irritate her with his taunts. If he thought that was going to put her off balance, he was wasting his time. "Close to the foundling-hospital. We'll join you there."

Silver gestured acquiescence, then leapt from the window-sill, landing elegantly on the pavement a storey below. A waiting footman stepped forward to take his cane.

"Just to check," Irene said. "You haven't been doing anything I should know about, Kai?" She didn't *think* he had, but it was probably a good idea to check first, before they got to any blame-slinging.

"Unfortunately not." Kai found his coat, flinging it over his shoulders. "Do you think it has something to do with last night?"

"It seems likely, given his timing," Irene said. "Let's go and find out."

There were always problems in dealing with the Fae. Despite their human appearance, they were soul-destroying entities from beyond space and time who introduced chaos into alternate worlds. One method they used was to subvert people's usual lives

57

and narratives, drawing them into endless patterns of stories. This weakened reality and the natural order of things, until the native population didn't know what was truth and what was fiction. At that point, the world would drown in a sea of chaos. And, more practically, they constantly tried to play hero or villain of their personal narrative, insisted that you had to be a character in that story, and refused to deal with you in any other way.

The coffee shop was a den of snobs, and it wasn't one of Irene's favourites. Which made it perfect for a possible confrontation that might result in her being permanently banned and never darkening its doorway again.

A cab with the Liechtenstein crest had drawn up outside, the engine turning over and giving off little random flares of ether. The driver sat at his post, still perfectly poised despite the heat and the smog, but Irene saw his eyes follow her and Kai as they approached the café.

"It could be worse," Irene said. "Silver might have arrived by private airship."

Kai nodded. "Vale told me they've got a new model out. It's even smaller than the one-man models the museums use."

" 'They' as in Liechtenstein?"

Kai nodded. "He said everyone was bidding for them, and that levels of spying on this new technology had gone through the roof."

"Much like the airships?" Irene sighed when that didn't get a laugh. "Now remember," she murmured. "Polite. Noncommittal. Don't give him any excuses for dramatics."

"Of course," Kai said. He drew himself up to his full height, stepped behind Irene's shoulder, and let her lead the way in.

All the ladies of leisure had congregated in one corner and were holding their coffeecups under their noses, whispering amongst themselves in a semi-panicked, semi-fascinated hissing. Their attention was undeniably on Silver, lounging at a vacant table on the other side of the room. Not surprising, given Silver's reputation as one of London's biggest libertines. A thin, pale-faced servant in grey stood behind him, holding Silver's cane.

Silver himself was looking casually rakish, with his cravat knotted at his throat, his silver hair loose, and his tanned skin golden against his white cuffs and collar. "Ah," he said on noticing Irene's entrance. "Please join me." Another burst of whispering from the women on the other side of the café followed his words.

They seated themselves as Kai and Silver exchanged guarded glares.

"Coffee?" Silver suggested. "I would recommend a demi-tasse of the Bourbon blend."

Kai looked ready to refuse on the spot, on principle, until he glanced at the menu. "Of course," he said with a thin smile.

Irene looked at the menu card surreptitiously. It was the most expensive brand of coffee listed.

"My treat, of course," Silver began.

"Please, Lord Silver," Irene said, before Kai could be undiplomatic. "We wouldn't wish to put ourselves under an obligation towards you." Such things carried weight with the Fae.

Silver shrugged. "Can't blame me for trying," he said, "although I give you my word there will be no obligation incurred for your coffee. Still, I believe this meeting will serve."

"Serve?" Kai said. "You haven't even said what this is about yet."

"Nor can I." Silver leaned forward, and his attitude of casual melodrama seemed to shift and fall away from him, leaving him quite serious. "If anyone asks, you can tell them it was about something to do with

60

Vale. I have no objection to you linking his name with mine. But I'm here to discuss your future well-being."

"Threats?" Kai sneered.

"Oh, do leave that be." Silver sighed. "I had to get your attention somehow. It wasn't as if I were actually trying to break into your house."

Irene frowned. "Lord Silver, if this isn't a threat, then what is it? Are you here to warn us about something?"

Silver glanced over his shoulder. "Johnson, fetch the coffee." He turned back to Irene. "No, no, of course not, we are just having a pleasant little conversation. Because if I were here to warn you about something, I would be breaking an oath that I have sworn *not* to warn you about something. I trust we are all perfectly clear on this point?"

Irene and Kai exchanged glances. "Of course," Irene said smoothly. "We're just drinking coffee together." She had been told the Fae were obliged to keep their oaths, but she'd never been in a position where it was really tested. If Silver was actually being truthful here, then they had even more to worry about than they'd thought.

"Precisely." Silver looked relieved. "And please don't think that this little coffee-drinking session is due to any actual affec-

61

tion for you, little mouse. You crashed my ball a few months back, you snatched a book out of my fingers, and you quite failed to mention that you were a representative of your Library. Any good guide to etiquette would mark you down on all three points."

Irene raised her eyebrows. "As I remember it, you invited me to the ball, and the book was disputed property in any case."

"Finders keepers, I believe the legal term is," Kai put in smugly.

Silver glanced at him sidelong, the light catching his lavender eyes and making them glitter. "A person like you should be more careful," he said. "This sphere is hardly the most hospitable to your kind."

Irene held up a hand before Kai could answer. "I thought we weren't indulging in threats," she said coldly.

Silver studied her as his servant placed cups of coffee on the table. "It is extremely difficult to suggest that you might possibly be in extreme peril without going to the extent of 'warning' you," he finally said. "I'm simply having a cup of coffee with you, and suggesting that you might both want to be very careful. Why not take a little vacation to that Library of yours?"

Retreat to the Library was a sensible response to overt danger. Of course, this all hinged on Silver actually being reliable, which was far from certain.

"Lord Silver," Irene said, picking up her cup. "You are the ambassador from Liechtenstein, and to the best of my understanding that makes you one of the most powerful of your kind in London. Possibly even in England." Not entirely true. She'd heard stories of other creatures in the wilds of the British Isles — Wild Hunts, Faerie Courts, and all that sort of thing — but it seemed a good moment to pour on the flattery. "But in the past we've been on opposite sides. Have we suddenly become allies and I failed to notice it?"

"Being my ally might have its advantages." Silver bared his teeth in a flashing smile. They were perfectly white, with just a suggestion of sharpness about them. Irene found herself wondering how they would feel against her wrist, the back of her hand, the side of her neck . . . He would be gentle, of course; she could tell from his eyes and his smile that he would be gentle, but at the same time he would be masterful, with the easy grace of control and skill and . . .

And he was trying to throw a glamour over her. Glamour was one of the Fae's most convenient tools, a mixture of illusion and desire that somehow crept past all conscious defences, like the very best sort of insanity. She felt a burning across her shoulders as the Library brand on her skin flared in response, and drew herself up straight in her seat with a little sniff. She hoped she hadn't been staring like a gawping idiot.

"Such pretty skin you have, little mouse," Silver said, his smile broadening.

Irene gave him her coldest glare, summoning memories of particularly frosty and upright teachers from school. "I repeat my question. If this is true, why should you want to help us?"

Silver swayed a hand back and forth. "Let's suppose that it might not be so much that I'm helping you as that I'm hindering someone else."

Irene glanced sideways at Kai. He gave her a very slight nod of cautious agreement. She looked back to Silver. "Which you can't tell us about, of course."

"Precisely," Silver said. He took a sip of his coffee.

There had to be some way Irene could exploit this situation. But the Fae couldn't be trusted. It was practically written into their implied social contract. They weakened any world where they congregated, increasing its tendency towards chaos, and she totally agreed with Kai that they should be stopped wherever possible.

"Your skin is very nice too, sir," she said as blandly as she could. His skin was perfect, actually, with the sort of idealized golden tan that came with an inner glow and a feeling of warmth that invited one to lean over and touch it — damn it, he was trying his glamour on her again. She decided to go on the attack. "Tell me, does the name Vlad Petrov mean anything to you?"

"Vlad Petrov?" Silver looked perplexed. He leaned backwards to murmur to his servant.

Kai took advantage of his distraction to whisper in Irene's ear, "Wasn't that the cabby they mentioned last night?"

Irene nodded in response as Silver leaned forward again. "Well," he said lazily, "I have no idea why I should remember every driver on my embassy staff. I cannot see why you expect me to be aware of the fact that he was assigned as driver to Lady Guantes while she's been staying here, even if she's been monopolizing the embassy network of informants. Goodness knows what she's been doing with them. Guests can be so inconvenient, and so difficult to refuse. Honestly, if this is an example of your pettifogging concerns, I am going to be bored to tears." But there was a glint to his eyes that suggested she was on the right track.

Lady Guantes. And the woman who hired those thugs was a Lady . . . But that's scarcely enough to go on. Something else tickled the back of Irene's mind. *Guantes. Gloves. The woman had worn a scarf pin showing a pair of hands . . . or a pair of gloves?* If Silver was reliable, Irene now had a name to investigate. *If.* This could all be a complicated lure into an even bigger trap. Frustration gnawed at her guts. What she needed was more information about this Lady Guantes.

"Now, to return to our previous subject," Silver said. "What do you intend to do?"

"Ask more questions," Irene said promptly. "Which means that we need to be on our way. I will leave you to your coffee, Lord Silver. Since you haven't warned us about anything, we have nothing to thank you for."

Silver nodded. "In the meantime, you may therefore consider this to be an open invitation to my embassy." He reached into his coat and picked out a card, flicking it across the table towards Irene. It slid across the table's glossy inlay, pivoting round and coming to a stop exactly in front of her.

It was a heavy cream card with a secretive sparkle in every letter of the print. On one side it gave a full list of Silver's titles, in a tiny font, to fit them all in. The other side was bare, except for a scrawled: *To be admitted to my presence at once — S.*

"You think we'll need that?" Kai asked, reading it over Irene's shoulder.

"I plan for the worst," Silver said. "That way, at least I'm dressed for the occasion." He rose to his feet in a swirl of cape. "Johnson! We must not keep Lord Guantes waiting. The bill!"

"Already paid, sir," Johnson murmured.

Silver bowed to Kai. He bowed to Irene. He almost managed to grasp Irene's wrist and kiss her hand, but she successfully stepped back, while thrusting the visiting card into her handbag.

"What do you make of that?" Kai demanded as Silver swept out.

"That he left us to tip the waiter," Irene said. "Typical."

"No, no. Other than that. He's going to talk to Lord Guantes?"

"We don't know enough," Irene said, frowning. "And we've been delayed, in any case. Let's hope that wasn't his objective in the first place. Kai, I'm going to take the Stoker book to the Library and do some digging on Lady Guantes. Or Lord Guantes. If they're a notable threat to Librarians,

67

then something may have been recorded. I want *you* to update Vale, ask questions, and get his advice. I'll meet you at his lodgings. I shouldn't be long." And by that time she should know if retreat to the Library, or a vacation to another continent, would be the best option.

"Irene . . ." Kai reached out to touch her wrist. "Be careful."

She managed a wry smile. "Yes, of course. And you too. Even if we aren't dressed for the occasion."

CHAPTER 4

Kai was still speculating about Silver's possible treachery when Irene pushed him into a cab. He drew a verbal picture of the two of them being goaded into paranoia and turned into serial killers before tragically cutting a loved one's throat. Irene made a mental note to find out where Kai was getting *Sweeney Todd* plotlines from and to take it away from him.

It was certainly true that the Fae liked to construct complicated and melodramatic plots, and they enjoyed drawing everyone nearby into roles in the storyline. Irene had been warned about it, and she'd avoided more than one of these herself in the past. And it was true that, due to the Fae presence, this world had a higher level of chaos than was comfortable, or indeed safe, given the potential for reality distortion. The Fae infested it (as Kai would put it) like worms in a well-seasoned grave.

But the attack last night had been real. And Silver's warning had felt real too. It was reassuring to know that Kai would be with Vale while Irene herself was in the Library. She did trust Kai; she just wasn't sure that she trusted him not to do anything valiant but stupid.

Not being able to saunter between worlds like a dragon, she had to use a nominated Library doorway to enter its halls. And the current main Traverse from this alternate to the Library was situated in the British Museum, in what was the office of the previous Librarian-in-Residence. After a series of unfortunate events, it was now a boxroom, meaning that she had to make a special trip to access it. And special trips could be traced, so it was time for a slightly riskier mode of transport.

All that a Librarian really needed to reach the Library was a sufficiently large collection of books or similar media. For Irene's purposes, she also needed a place where she could be undisturbed for half an hour or more. The Senate House Library in Malet Street was within walking distance of her lodgings and would do the job nicely — and she'd previously enrolled as a student, so all her identification would be in order.

She collected the Stoker book and headed

over. The library was moderately busy, but Irene had no difficulty finding her way to a side corridor, using the Language to open the lock on a "restricted section" with a quick whisper, **"Open, lock,"** and then locking it behind her again. The walls were heavy with ranks of leather-bound volumes, their titles barely discernible in the thin ether light from a swaying bulb. Dust on the shelves and floor indicated that this area was not often used. She'd scouted it a couple of weeks ago.

She walked along to the first storage-room door, put down her attaché case, and took out a small bottle of ink and a fountain-pen. This was a new skill for her, only passed on when she became a Librarian-in-Residence. (She was still a bit resentful about that. It would have been extremely useful. And how many *other* things were still hidden from her?)

Normally, when creating a temporary doorway to the Library, a Librarian spoke specific words in the Language while using a strong access point (such as a large collection of books) to forge a connection. This lasted long enough for the agent to pass through. She must then let the connection close behind her, as the two places dropped out of synchronization. More recently, Irene had been shown that with the written form of the Language, one could make the connection last a little longer. Long enough to go through to the Library, transact some business, and then get back again to the same alternate-world location through the same door.

Carefully she went down on one knee, drawing the characters for **This door opens to the Library** above the handle. It would work just as well to scrawl the words across the middle of the door, but she liked to keep it unobtrusive.

As she finished the last character, she felt the sudden shift in reality, and her energy levels dropped to fuel the connection. She stayed on her knees, focusing on her breathing until it steadied, and put away the pen and ink. The Language characters were visibly drying on the wood and already starting to fade. They'd last perhaps half an hour. She didn't have long.

"Open," she said, giving the word its full inflection in the Language, with the special suffix indicating that the door must open to the Library itself.

And it did.

Irene stepped into a warmer, high-ceilinged room, the walls draped with red-and-white quilts. Multiple incandescent lights blazed whitely in the ceiling, but the soft cotton of the quilts muted the effect, making the room more tolerable.

Curiously she pulled one of the quilts away from the wall. Behind it there were shelves of books, their spines in a mixture of English, Swedish, and German, with titles such as *Little Sod House on the Prairie, Vigilante Stories of New Gothenburg,* and *Runestones of North America.* There was no explanation for why the quilts were covering them. Then again, there was often no reason for the Library's architecture or furnishings.

Outside the room, the brass plaque on its door read B-133 — NORTH AMERICAN LITERATURE — 20TH CENTURY — SECTION FIVE. Not a room she recognized. And she found herself in a corridor both paved and walled in blue-and-white marble, with shuttered windows that would have been too high to see out of anyway. To her right was a flight of stairs, leading downwards. To her left was a simple bend in the corridor.

This was the problem — well, one of the problems — with coming through on a random Traverse. There was no way to be sure where you would emerge. What she needed, as fast as possible, was a room with a computer where she could look up Lady (and possibly Lord) Guantes. She also required a local Library map, so that she could locate a wall slot into which she could deposit the Stoker book and fulfil the request — the Library's version of internal post. She hurried down the corridor, noting the decor in case she came this way again. The blue markings lay within the white marble like midnight blue ink-stains, and she had to restrain the urge to rub one of them to see if it would smudge.

I am still far too easily distracted.

Two turnings later she came to a couple of doorways, with a deposit slot between them. With a sigh of relief she opened her attaché case and dropped in the envelope containing the book. One job done. Now she could get down to some serious research.

The doorway on her left bore a plate: B-134 — BELGIAN GRAPHIC NOVELS — 20TH CENTURY — SECTION ONE. She pushed it open to look inside and was relieved to see a computer on the table. An overweight orange cat was curled up on the chair, feigning sleep. With barely a glance at the thickly shelved walls — and the occasional brightly displayed front page of a moon-bound rocket or a set of dwarfish mummies — she pushed the cat off the chair with a mumbled apology, sat down, and logged in.

She scanned her list of personal emails, rated them all as nonessential, and ignored them. There was nothing from her mentor, Coppelia, and nothing from her parents. Everything else could wait.

Instead, she brought up the *Encyclopaedia* function. It was supposed to be a general compendium of information from Librarians in the field in alternate worlds. In practice, although better than nothing, the information was patchy — Fae and dragons often inconveniently used false names.

Guantes, she typed in.

One record came up, twenty years old. Irene resisted the urge to do a fist pump in the air, and clicked on it.

Moderate-power Fae. Masculine, usually claims to be a member of the aristocracy and titles himself Lord. Capable of travel between worlds. His archetypal aspects include power, manipulation, control, leadership. The reader will have observed that his name is the Spanish word for gloves *and may find this indicative of a tendency to subtlety and manipulation.*

Irene glanced at the name of this entry's author: *Rhadamanthys.* His status was marked as *deceased.* Damn, no way to ask

75

him questions now.

Originally encountered on G-112. [A gamma-type world, which meant it had both magic and technology.] *The world was neutral at the time, with both forces of chaos and order present. Guantes was fomenting an aristocratic rebellion against the Holy Roman Emperor. The latter was supported by another powerful Fae called Argent. During the power struggle between the two, the empire fell, and a Byzantine theocracy backed by a dragon princess came to power.*

"Argent?" Irene could feel her frown growing. It was only a matter of languages, after all: silver, *argent* . . .

At that point, both Fae left that world, and I believe they were disciplined by higher-ranking members of their race. I personally have not encountered the gentleman again . . .

Irene skimmed down the rest of the entry. Nothing useful, just a few notes about Guantes apparently being manipulative but prone to distraction by his own cleverness. The sort of schemer who'd come up with new schemes in the middle of ongoing ones and lose track of his ultimate objectives.

A thought struck her, and she checked the circumstances of Rhadamanthys's death. Died in an accident with a diving-bell in the river Dnieper. This was during a Russian revolution, while he was trying to retrieve some volumes of epic poetry. Probably nothing to do with Guantes. Probably.

She tried looking up obvious translations of *gloves* and *silver.* With Russian she got lucky and found an account of one Fae known as Prince Serebro a hundred years ago. He had an ongoing feud with a Lord Perchatka (Serebro had won). During this, the Librarian who'd recorded the entry had looted forbidden works under the Cathedral of the Black Madonna. Nothing definite on the pair, but certainly suggestive.

She was conscious of time ticking away. Quickly she composed an email to her mentor, Coppelia, including the salient facts and a request whether the older Librarian knew anything relevant. Irene wasn't a daily-report person, but if there was a chance Coppelia might know something, it would be stupid not to ask.

Right. That was all she could reasonably find out for the moment. Tension was prickling at the back of her neck. She had the horrible feeling she'd forgotten something, or failed to notice something important. She needed to talk to Vale as soon as possible. Librarians did face death threats from time to time, and, while it came with the job, it was hardly on her list of One

Hundred Favourite Experiences. However, she didn't know the magnitude of the current threat. And a simple book purchase and an attempted assault seemed to be throwing up all manner of new connections. There was no way of knowing how badly it could go wrong.

She shut down her computer and headed back to her exit — it had already taken her twenty-five minutes. She'd come back later today, or tomorrow, and check for a response from Coppelia.

With a twinge of the brand across her back, Irene stepped out of the Library and back into real time and space. (Or, according to some arguments, unreal time and space, if the Library was the only "reality." But that was something for philosophical disputations.) The door closed firmly behind her, and, as she glanced to check, the last remnants of her painted letters faded into the paintwork. Nothing was left behind, not even the faintest trace of ink or shadow on the wood.

She had successfully made it there and back, with nobody any the wiser. And she couldn't help feeling just a little bit of glee that she had once again — now, what was the best phrase for this? — got away with it. *Here's to being a secret agent of an interdi-*

mensional Library!

The glow of self-satisfaction lasted until her cab turned onto Baker Street. As the vehicle drew level with Vale's lodgings, she could see that no lights shone in the upstairs windows, which suggested that he was out. Even though it was only late morning, the fog meant that street lamps and houses were lit against the gloom. She paid the cab-driver and hurried to the door.

The housekeeper answered it. She was a middle-aged woman of unflappable disposition, her greying hair pinned up in a rock-hard bun. "Can I help you, ma'am — oh, it's you, Miss Winters. Mr. Vale said would you mind waiting, if you arrived while he was out."

Irene's stomach sank. Something had gone wrong. She didn't know what yet, but she just had that feeling. "Do you know where he is?" she asked, stepping inside and closing the door behind her.

"He went out early, on a summons from Scotland Yard, Miss Winters," the house-keeper said, taking Irene's hat and helping her off with her coat. "Then your friend Mr. Strongrock came by, just an hour ago —"

So Kai must have come straight here from their discussion with Silver, Irene calculated.

"— and someone met him at the door. I

did catch a few words, and it was a message from Mr. Vale to meet him in the East End. And off he went. And then, when Mr. Vale was back, I told him all this, and he's off to the East End himself, quick as you like. He told me most particularly that if you were to turn up, Miss Winters, I should ask you to wait for him to come back. Or, and he said it very severely, he couldn't answer for the consequences."

Irene had been nodding along as the woman rattled on, but her throat had gone dry. Kai lured away. Vale gone after him. She wanted to be out of here, right this minute, and hailing a cab to take her to the East End too.

Except, common sense pointed out, the East End was a big place. And Vale had specifically asked her to wait for him. Her hands tightened into fists, but she composed her face to calmness. "Of course I'll wait for Mr. Vale to return. Did he say where in the East End he was going?"

The housekeeper shook her head. "You know how he is, miss. Can I get you a cup of tea while you're waiting?"

The door slammed open. "That will not be necessary," Vale said from behind her.

Irene turned to see Vale standing there, looking down at her from his superior six feet of height. His clothing was, as always, austere, but appropriate for a gentleman, and of the most expensive fabrics. (It was no wonder he'd bonded so well with Kai. They both refused to wear anything but the best.) His dark hair was swept back from his face, and his profile seemed even more hawk-like than usual. "Where have you been, Miss Winters?" he demanded.

"To a library, sir," Irene said. She didn't quite let her tone slip into sharpness, but it was a near thing. "I sent Kai to you. Where is he now?"

"Abducted, Miss Winters — while you were out at your library." Vale managed to put an astonishing amount of accusation and simple anger into the words. "And I would like to know what you propose to do about it."

The worm of guilt in her gut — *I leave him alone for five minutes and he gets himself kidnapped* — collided with a sudden burn of anger at Vale's words. "Why, get him back, of course! How dare you —"

The housekeeper coughed loudly, and both Irene and Vale turned to look at her. "I'll bring your tea upstairs, Mr. Vale," she said firmly. "And some for the lady too. I can see that you've got matters to discuss."

"Oh, very well," Vale said, with no grace

whatsoever, and stamped up the stairs to his rooms, with Irene a pace behind him.

I was wrong, ran through her head. *It wasn't a threat to us. It wasn't a threat to me. It was a threat to Kai, and I left him alone, and they caught him.*

CHAPTER 5

Vale walked across to the bow window, looking down at the street below. His rooms were as cluttered as ever, though a dust-free zone demonstrated where the housekeeper had been making headway before Irene's arrival. He didn't look round at Irene as he said, "I should apologize for that, Winters. My words were unjust." He'd thankfully dropped back to his usual style of address, rather than the more formal *Miss Winters.*

Irene flicked on the light-switch and shut the door. She folded her arms. "I accept your apology," she snapped. "Now maybe we should discuss how to retrieve him."

"You show very little emotion of the softer kind," Vale said. He turned, regarding her thoughtfully in a way that was more disconcerting than his earlier angry glare.

"How would that help the current situation?" Irene asked. Her anger and self-blame manifested as a slow roil in her stomach. But the masked city she was going to use it, not let it control her. "Can we please not waste time? Kai might be in great danger right now."

"Probably," Vale agreed. His anger seemed to have ebbed, just as hers had risen. He gestured her to a chair. "But to take action on the spur of emotion, without full information, would be as unwise as I was a few moments ago. Please, Winters. Sit down. Tell me what you know. It's quite obvious that you know *something.*"

Irene sat, folding her hands in her lap. "Does the name Guantes mean anything to you?" she asked. "Probably in connection with the Fae, possibly in connection with Silver."

"Hmm." Vale strode briskly over to one of his big scrap-books that bulged with newspaper clippings and filed notes, and flipped through it. "Grant: the Covent Garden riot and flood. Guernier: the perfume murderess. Guantes . . . Guantes . . . No, nothing in here. The name is familiar, as a new arrival to London from Liechtenstein, both he and his wife, but I don't have anything definite on them as yet." He slammed the book shut and dropped into the chair opposite Irene, folding his long body forward to focus on her. "Tell me more, Winters."

Irene ran through the events of the last couple of days: the auction, the brawl, the scarcely seen watcher, Silver's warning, and her own investigation. She barely noticed the housekeeper or the tea the woman had brought. She was focusing on providing Vale with every last bit of data, everything that he might be able to use. While she had her own plans for searching elsewhere if necessary, outside this world, Vale was the local expert, and she wanted his expertise.

He listened to her, only interrupting with a couple of questions, until she came to a stop. Then he nodded. His hands were curved around his cup of tea, but he hadn't drunk from it.

"Your turn," Irene said. Her anger had ebbed a little and now focused itself on more long-term planning. "I'm assuming that you've just returned from hunting for Kai. Please tell me everything you know." She was aware that Vale, as London's leading private investigator, was the one who normally made such requests of his clients. He knew it too, and his mouth quirked drily in what was almost a smile.

"You are correct, Winters." Vale put down his untouched tea. "I was called out this morning quite early, on a case that I'm afraid I'm not at liberty to discuss. However,

85

it became clear that my presence was not necessary. Whatever had impelled the inspector to summon me . . ." He frowned.

"A deliberate attempt to distract you, you think?" Irene suggested.

Vale nodded. "Given subsequent events . . . In any case, I returned here to find that Strongrock had come by. He was met at the door by a street urchin, who directed him to an address in the East End. Fortunately, one of the newspaper vendors was close enough to hear the details. I followed." He looked down at his hands. "I was too late."

"What *happened*?" Irene demanded.

"You must understand that I assembled the facts after the event." Vale's tone was corrosive, but this time it was a self-directed bitterness. He was clearly blaming himself just as much as she was, Irene realized, though with less cause. "It was not difficult to follow his trail. Once he arrived at the address where he thought that he'd be meeting me, another man — disguised as a Scotland Yard constable — redirected him to an address half a mile away. This was an old warehouse, where I was supposed to be investigating a murder. On the way, he was lured into a side alley, by an apparent assault on a helpless innocent. He was struck down and rendered unconscious by a combination of superior numbers, Fae magic, and drugs. From there, he was taken — elsewhere."

"That's quite a convoluted trail," Irene said thoughtfully. "Why not just direct him to the location of the kidnapping? Or simply try to overpower him inside a cab, where he wouldn't have had room to manoeuvre?"

"I think the point *was* to make the trail convoluted, Winters." Vale stared thoughtfully into the middle distance. "At any of those points, someone attempting to track him might well have lost his traces." *Except me,* he didn't have to say. "But as it is, I have descriptions of two people at the scene who might be these Guantes. A middle-aged man, slightly shorter than me, with grey hair and beard. He's well-dressed, with a commanding voice. The woman had black hair and was slender. She wore a mantle over clothing that was 'foreign,' though my informant couldn't say precisely how."

"And did both of them wear gloves?" Irene asked.

"Yes," Vale said slowly. "Both of them did. Though, to be fair, most well-off men and women would wear gloves."

Irene nodded. That was true. But it still felt significant somehow. "Where did they take Kai?" she asked.

"That's the problem, Winters." Vale looked annoyed. "The woman was escorted to a cab waiting nearby. I have the address to which she directed it, and I intend to investigate. But the man — apparently he left London by some Fae route. And he took Kai with him."

Irene's hands clenched in her lap, rumpling the folds of her skirt. "You should have said that sooner," she said. Her mind ran in circles. How to trace where he had gone? How to follow and rescue him?

Vale sighed. "Winters, let us leave the blame for some other occasion. What I need to know now is how fast you can find him and retrieve him. We cannot leave him in their hands for any longer than we must."

For Vale, this was high emotion, and the urgency in his voice would have indicated standing up and stamping around the room in any other man. Irene had known that Kai considered himself to be Vale's friend. She hadn't realized quite as much that Vale considered Kai to be *his* friend.

Then again, she was the last person to judge people for keeping their feelings under control. "We have three main routes of enquiry that I can see," she offered, after pausing to think. "One is to trace the

Guantes within London, here. Even if Lord Guantes has taken Kai elsewhere, we may learn something from the woman. The second route is for me to look for more information within the Library — and, if all else fails, I can approach Kai's own family."

"How?" Vale asked.

"I can find out where his uncle, who was his guardian, is based — in the world where Kai was originally recruited — and go and ask for information." Irene didn't like the idea. Nobody liked getting bad news, and she suspected that dragons liked it even less than most. But if anyone could find a lost dragon, it might be another dragon.

Vale nodded, accepting her words. "I take it that your third idea is to ask Silver?"

"It's not an idea I like," Irene said ruefully. "Unless you can think of some way to apply pressure?"

"It's a matter worth considering." Vale rose from his chair to stroll restlessly around the room. "For him to be so vague in his warnings earlier might indicate that he is already under pressure from some other direction. Another matter worth investigation. But —"

There was a knock at the door. "Mr. Vale?" It was the housekeeper's voice. "There's a letter for you."

Vale sighed. "Probably some futile request for my assistance. Excuse me a moment, please."

Irene frowned at her hands, considering options while Vale's steps rattled down the stairs. Being a Librarian didn't give her any inherent abilities to track people across alternate worlds. She could travel from one world to another by going through the Library itself, but she would need to know where Kai had been taken.

There was an exclamation from downstairs. "Winters! Here, now!" Vale shouted.

Irene caught up her skirts and stampeded down the stairs after him. He was standing in the doorway, an envelope and paper held carefully between his fingers. A sandy-haired messenger boy in a hotel uniform was cringing in front of him, clearly wishing he'd got away faster. "This fellow has news."

"What news?" Irene demanded.

"Tell us where you got this note." Vale's hands were tight with tension, the lines of his knuckles and tendons showing — but he held the paper delicately, his fingertips barely brushing the edge.

The messenger boy wetted his lips nervously. "I work at the Savoy, sir. Gentleman guest there wanted it delivered to you."

Vale nodded. "His name and appearance?"

"He didn't give his name, sir," the boy said. Vale bit back a sigh. "He was a gentleman, though. Had a beard."

Vale sighed. "Very well. Here." He fished out a half-crown and tossed it to the boy. "For your time and effort. You may go."

"Should we be letting him walk away?" Irene queried softly as the boy dashed off.

"I can find him if I need to," Vale said confidently. "You saw how that uniform fitted him exactly? It was his own, not some stolen disguise. And the five buttons on his sleeve? He's one of the senior boys at the Savoy, with a possible promotion to valet in the near future. His gloves were clean this morning, and his shoes were freshly polished. But he wasn't able to give us any description, besides that the fellow had a beard and acted like a gentleman, which is probably why he's still at the messenger-boy level. A higher-ranking employee would be expected to notice more than that, even if he didn't talk about it."

Irene nodded. "What's in the letter?" she asked.

Vale held it so that she could see it. "Don't touch it," he advised her. "I am still examining it."

It was clearly expensive paper. The slanting italic handwriting was in black ink:

Kai has returned to his own family. Make no attempt to see him again. This is the only warning that will be given.

Vale held it up to the light. "No watermark," he said. "The same paper as the envelope. I need better light to examine these." He was already heading up the stairs again to his room.

Irene followed. "It's a fake of some sort," she said. "It cannot possibly be from his family."

"Oh? You are certain of that?"

"Absolutely. I saw one of his family's messages earlier. It was on a scroll, and in Chinese. Nothing like this. And if one of his people had come to collect Kai, it wouldn't have been done by abduction." She could imagine Kai arguing, but she couldn't imagine him being beaten to the ground and carried off by force. "Besides, you already said that you had evidence of Fae magic being used in his kidnapping. No self-respecting dragon would cooperate with the Fae. And most of all . . ."

"Yes?" Vale murmured. He'd thrown himself down in front of his laboratory table and was examining the letter and envelope with a magnifying glass.

Irene was pacing the room now, thinking it through. "If this had truly been the action of a dragon — perhaps one who felt that Kai was demeaning himself by associating with human beings, with us . . ." *More than that. Being our friend.* "Any dragon who sincerely held those opinions wouldn't bother to send messages. To you or me." She wondered if there would be a matching letter at her lodgings. There wasn't time to go and check. "We would be beneath their notice."

Vale didn't look up from his scrutiny of the envelope. "Do all of them have that opinion, then?" His tone was academic, but there was something in the way he tilted his head that suggested a similar pride and hauteur of his own.

Of course, he's an earl. And an Englishman. And, most of all, the greatest detective in London. How could merely being a dragon compare to any of that?

"I once met one who did. But he was courteous about it. There was a degree of, I suppose . . ." She looked for the right words as she sat down. "Noblesse oblige. One does not cause unnecessary distress to lesser beings."

"How fortunate for us." Vale spun his chair around. "No watermark." He repeated

93

his earlier comment. "Extremely high-quality paper, but not possible to identify it without further investigation. The handwriting is not one that I recognize. Added to that, I would not claim to be one of those people who reads character through handwriting, but the style is somewhat cramped and muted. I would suggest that the writer was attempting to disguise his or her usual script. The envelope was not sealed, so there is no clue to be obtained there. Your thoughts?"

"My thoughts are more on the content than the context." Irene reached out for the letter, and Vale passed it to her. "And on the end result. Even if we weren't aware Kai had been kidnapped, then we certainly would realize something was dubious when we received this. I think it's a deniable red flag."

"A red flag?" Vale queried.

"An attempt to alert us that something is wrong, without the person in question admitting to giving us a warning."

"Ah." Vale nodded. "Lord Silver, yes. With that rather obvious dispatch of the letter via a bearded man, to point us in that direction."

Irene nodded as well. Her shoulders were cramped with tension. She mentally reviewed possible leads. They'd squeezed everything dry for the moment. Which meant that she could finally act. "We need to move," she said. "I need to enquire at the Library, and to see if I can contact Kai's uncle, if they have a way to locate him. And you —"

"Will get onto the Guantes, of course." Vale rose to his feet, offering her a hand to help her rise. "And Lord Silver, while I'm at it. If the fellow is up to something, then I'll know about it. Where should we meet?"

"They'll probably be watching my lodgings," Irene said with regret. "And they must be watching here as well." She frowned as her thoughts came together. "If Kai was intercepted at your front door, then they are certainly watching here, and they may be aware that we are both here now and comparing notes."

"Oh, without a doubt," Vale agreed. "However, our going in different directions should help somewhat. Will you be able to reach a nearby library, do you think?"

"I certainly hope so," Irene said firmly. There was a thread of satisfaction that he didn't assume he'd need to escort her to deal with any trouble, or offer to do so. Earned respect from him was something she truly valued. "I don't know how long I may be. I know it's urgent. But if it's difficult to reach Kai's uncle . . . Should I look for you at Scotland Yard?"

For a moment Vale frowned, then nodded. "Go to Singh. He remembers you." Irene remembered him too. Inspector Singh, probably Vale's closest ally amongst London's police. "If I have any messages, I'll leave them with him, and you can do the same."

He was still holding her hand. In fact, he seemed to have forgotten that he was doing so. "Do be careful, Winters," he said. "Our enemies seem well prepared. If it were possible for me to accompany you, I would —"

"But what you can find out here is more important," Irene interrupted. She would dearly have liked to have him at her back, and damn the rules about bringing strangers into the Library. But what she had said was true. They needed to know what the Guantes had been up to here. "And there's no time to waste. I'm relying on you."

His smile was thin but present. "Then we had better not keep Strongrock waiting."

CHAPTER 6

Irene was almost surprised, and somewhat disappointed, when nobody tried to kidnap her on the way to the British Library. If someone *had* tried to kidnap her, at least she'd have had more of an idea what was going on.

But there were no mysterious hansom cabs waiting to whisk her off to an unknown location, no masked thugs dragging her into back alleys, nothing at all remotely useful. It left her in a bad temper as she stalked through the rooms to the main Library portal.

The Traverse to the Library opened from a minor store-room, one that used to be an office, and luckily there were no visitors around to see her entering. It was the work of moments to lock the door behind her using the Language, and she hurried across to the Traverse door. It looked like a store-cupboard, and to any other user it *would* have been just a store-cupboard. But it was permanently linked to a specific door in the Library, and Irene had the linguistic key.

"**Open to the Library,**" she said, and felt the connection form as her words rolled on the air. She pulled the door open and quickly stepped through.

The heavy iron-barred door on the Library side clanged shut behind her. On the other side there were still posters hanging on rails around the door, proclaiming: HIGH CHAOS INFESTATION; ENTRY BY PERMISSION ONLY; KEEP CALM AND STAY OUT. Irene frowned at the HIGH on the first poster. Last time she'd been through this entrance, a few months back, it had only been standard chaos infestation.

If this was tied to Kai's disappearance . . . She hoped not.

Someone had been using the room to stockpile other books, and beside the packed shelves there were stacks of yellow-jacketed paperbacks all over the floor. Irene had to pull in her skirts to avoid toppling the piles as she made her way to the exit.

The closest computer room was a couple of doors along to her left. It was empty at the moment, so she threw herself down in the chair and logged on, dashing off a quick email to Coppelia: *Kai vanished. Dubious*

circumstances. Request immediate meeting.
Irene.

The answer came within five minutes. She'd only just looked up *Dragons, negotiations with,* but hadn't progressed much further. The message read: *Rapid shift transfer authorized. First turning on left, three floors up, transfer word is* Coherent. *Coppelia.*

Irene logged off, hoisted her skirts to her knees, and began to run. Rapid shifts called for high energy expenditure and weren't held open for long. The fact that Coppelia had seen fit to authorize one was disturbing in itself.

Three flights of stairs later, the walls were covered with Art Deco wallpaper, making the shift-transfer cabinet blatantly obvious stylistically. Its door was heavy oak and looked very out of place between a couple of plaster statuettes of robed women. And it was just large enough for one person and a pile of books.

She stepped inside and closed the door. There were no lights. There was no sound. There was only the smell of dust. She reached out to either side to brace herself against the walls.

"Coherent," she said in the Language.

The cabinet shook around her, like a

99

dumb-waiter cupboard being yanked at high speed in several directions. She shut her eyes, concentrating on not throwing up.

With a thump, the cabinet arrived. Irene took a moment to catch her breath, before pushing open the door and stepping out into the well-lit room beyond.

It was Coppelia's private study, familiar from many hours spent there as Coppelia's personal student and assistant. The focus of the room was the large mahogany desk, which curved round in a wide U, allowing a full range of documents to be shuffled over its surface. The walls were full of book-shelves, naturally — but several Slavic icons in heavy gold and wood hung from them here and there, breaking up the expanse. Irene noticed it was night outside, and the study lights blazed through the bow window, harshly lighting the snowscape beyond. The usual extra chairs had been removed from the room, meaning that Coppelia sat in the only chair, behind her desk.

Standing before her, Irene wondered if she was meant to feel like a schoolgirl reporting to a teacher, or possibly a penitent reporting to an inquisitor. Whichever way, she suspected that she was meant to feel nervous.

Coppelia herself looked almost as controlled as usual. A crimson coif shrouded her head, and only the edges of her white hair were visible at her forehead. Today she was in a stark sleeveless robe of smooth, dark brown velvet that left the full length of her carved-wood left arm visible. It was the same shade of sallow oak as her natural right arm, but an entirely different texture — all joints and clockwork. "A poor report," she said with a faint wheeze. "Unless you really don't know any more than you've told me."

"I deliberately gave you only the bare bones," Irene said resolutely. "Given the importance of the situation, I assumed you'd want to hear the rest in person."

"As opposed to sending a detailed email that anyone could read, is that it?" Coppelia enquired.

"You're making that assumption," Irene replied. "I didn't." Coppelia had chosen to leave Kai's controversial dragon heritage mostly undiscussed the last time they met. But Irene wasn't sure if it was in fact known by everyone at the appropriate level, or still genuinely confidential.

Coppelia raised her flesh-and-blood hand to rub at her forehead. "Tell me what you know, then."

Irene ran over the details quickly. She had

to mention Vale's involvement, of course. But Coppelia already knew about Vale, and that he knew an uncomfortably large amount about the Library. Coppelia nodded slightly at a few points — the invitation from Kai's family, the warning from Lord Silver, the Guantes, and Vale's comments on the letter (also supposedly from Kai's family) — but otherwise she was silent as she listened.

Finally she commented. "Dubious circumstances. I can hardly argue with that definition. Your thoughts?"

"The letter's a fake," Irene said frankly. "It's not just the format. I would expect more *style* if it was from Kai's people. From what he's said of them, they're royalty. Royalty does not send piddling little *Make no attempt to see him again* warning notes. They either wouldn't bother with the commoners at all, or they'd sweep by and graciously inform us that we will be deprived of his presence. So it's not even very good misdirection."

"And yet you're here," Coppelia remarked. "And you're asking about his family. If you're so sure that it's misdirection, why bother?"

"Because we need to find him," Irene said. She folded her hands behind her back, hid-

102

ing her clenched fists. "If Vale can trace the Guantes, or whoever they are, that's good. But if not, then how do we track him? He's my responsibility." The words hung in the air like a promise. "And since he was kidnapped while under my protection, his family may hold us responsible."

Coppelia steepled her fingers, flesh against wood. "It's true that the Library has absolutely no wish to enter into a feud with Kai's kin," she agreed. "And a dragon's revenge is a serious business. Hurricanes, storms, tidal waves, earthquakes . . . I witnessed a world being destroyed in such a way and was barely able to escape. So what do you want from me?"

Irene put aside some deeply unpleasant mental images. This was taking too long. "I need anything that we have on Lord Guantes that isn't in the public records. And I'm assuming the Library knows more about Kai's family than I do. Is there any chance the abduction *could* be their doing?" A thought struck her. "Or the doing of someone connected to them? A rival faction? Or an over-enthusiastic servant?"

"Hmm. A pertinent question. Nine out of ten." Coppelia considered, not taking her fierce eyes off Irene. Irene didn't dare look away. "It is unlikely that his direct family

103

would abduct him or leave a note to say he'd left. It would probably be beneath them. However, any royal family does have subordinates, junior relations, and in general people who would take on *Will nobody rid me of this turbulent priest?* suggestions with too much enthusiasm. One of them could have . . . And there are factions among the dragons. Not all of them support the royalty."

Irene sighed. Yet another uncertainty. "So I can't be sure of their involvement."

"No," Coppelia said. "You can't. Or rather, we can't. And no, we don't have any secret back channels that we can use to ask about it on behalf of the Library, either."

Irene tilted her head slightly. "*On behalf of the Library,* perhaps not, but how about from a private perspective? Isn't there anyone out there who knows someone who knows someone, who could ask . . ." She let the phrase trail off hopefully.

Coppelia shook her head, a definite no, but she also looked wary. Clearly there was someone who knew someone who knew someone else out there, even if they couldn't handle this particular issue.

"Of course there isn't," Irene agreed bitterly. She could see where this was going. "Even if someone did have access to the dragons, they'd be too high-ranking within the Library to act alone. And the Library can't be drawn into this?"

Coppelia spread her hands. "Precisely. There's only one person in this situation who can ask . . ."

"All right. All *right*." Irene saw Coppelia's eyes narrow at her tone, and she tried to calm down. "All right. It has to be me." *Who puts her head into the dragon's mouth. And who will take the blame if it goes wrong.* "But I would like to ask a question first. A general question, before I get down to specifics."

"You can certainly ask," Coppelia said carefully. "If I don't answer, then it isn't because I want to cause you further difficulty."

Irene nodded. "In the widest of terms, then — why bring Kai into the Library? Seriously. You *knew* what Kai was. Why take him in as a trainee at all? And why assign him to *me*?"

This was a conversation that should have been held behind shuttered windows or heavy velvet curtains. It felt wrong to be having it so openly. Wrong, and far too exposed.

Coppelia looked down at the desk. "There have been other young dragons here before Kai," she said slowly. "None as highly born, but — well, it has happened, and it is politely ignored when it does happen. Even if the people brokering a placement may have thought their deception remained concealed. There are hidden protocols. There are understandings. No dragon has yet chosen to remain and take vows as a Librarian. To be honest with you, I doubt Kai will, either. It will not be in his nature."

Irene nodded, accepting the words. "But why me?"

Coppelia hesitated, then nodded to herself. **"Because,"** she said in the Language, necessarily speaking truth, **"we thought it would be best for both of you."** She dropped back into English, looking up at Irene again. "And that's all I will tell you for now."

"For our own good?" Irene said drily. There was no *time* for all these damned mysteries. She was the child of two Librarians, an unusual combination — was this supposed to make her better suited to handling dragons? She couldn't see how.

Coppelia shrugged. "We make the best decisions that we can. Do you object to him?"

"In what sense, object?" Irene temporized. She knew she was avoiding the question, but she wasn't sure of Coppelia's meaning.

"Has he given you any offence?" Coppelia fired the question at her like a bullet.

"He is courtesy itself," Irene said. "As you know."

"Has he done you any harm?"

Irene thought of Kai's eyes, of his hesitation, his sincerity. He'd wanted to protect *her,* when it was her responsibility to protect *him.* "No, and you know it. Is it really necessary to get into all this, here and now?"

"I'm establishing that you have no reason to want to get rid of him yourself."

"For pity's sake!" Irene exploded. "If you don't trust me, then there's nothing more to be said. Besides, please give me credit for some intelligence. If I was trying to kidnap him myself, I wouldn't be in here telling you about it now."

"I have to be sure," Coppelia said. She shifted in her chair. "You have thought about how this may go?"

"Well, yes," Irene said. She was still furious at Coppelia's dig that she could have been in any way involved in Kai's disappearance, but she managed to keep her temper. If Kai was in danger, then every second mattered. "Quite possibly, messily. As you did just point out, the dragons may be upset — and they might take it out on me."

"And the Library may have to allow it," Coppelia noted. "If it's decided that you were responsible for him, and the dragons take offence, we might have to strip you of your position."

A chill ran down Irene's spine. "You wouldn't," she said. But it had the truth of nightmares, of worst-case scenarios. "And the Library mark can't be removed."

Coppelia's eyes were regretful, but her face was like stone. "My dear Irene, we can't risk war over one dragon. Or over one Librarian. You've done an excellent job as Librarian-in-Residence, but when push comes to shove, *someone* will have to take the blame."

"I'm duly warned," Irene said flatly, ignoring the ice in her stomach. "Let's get down to business. How do I contact his family?"

"The easiest way would be via the world where we recruited him," Coppelia said. "Did he ever give you its designation?"

"Only that it was one of the gammas," Irene answered. "So high-tech and medium-magic, he said. Will I find his uncle there?"

"With any luck. Or his uncle's household, at least. I understand that he maintains an establishment there. The name he goes by is Ryu Gouen." She waited for Irene's nod of comprehension. "Our Traverse to that world

— it's G-51, so you know — opens within the remains of the Biblioteca Palatina in Heidelberg. Ryu Gouen was in Europe at the last report a few weeks ago, so with any luck you shouldn't have too far to travel. I'm told the high-speed rail network in that alternate is very good."

"Who's our Librarian there?" Irene asked. "I'm assuming there is a Librarian-in-Residence?"

Coppelia nodded. "Her name is Murasaki. However, I would prefer you to avoid contact with her — the less we all have to explain about Kai, the better."

"If I walk out of the Traverse and she's sitting there, it's going to be awkward," Irene said. She could see Coppelia's point, but at the same time it would make her life a great deal easier if she could get immediate help with crossing a strange new Europe. And clothing. And money.

"If you do, then make some sort of excuse." Coppelia snorted. "Claim you're on a shopping mission for me if you can't think of anything better. Well? Any more questions?"

"Yes. The Guantes. Do you know anything about him, or them?"

"Unfortunately not." Having to admit to ignorance clearly irritated Coppelia. "I'll enquire further, but it may take time. And I'll see if anyone knows anything about ongoing Fae power struggles. Anything relevant, that is."

There was one more thing that Irene wanted to ask. "Can Alberich reach me there? In G-51?"

Perhaps now wasn't the time for private fears, but she had to know. Alberich was a nightmare figure, the Library's most powerful traitor — also a murderer and an abomination. And a few months back she'd confronted him and won. He been barred from Vale's world as a result, and he couldn't access the Library, but the thought of going somewhere that he could find her chilled Irene to the core. And the scars across her hands ached in response. It was bad enough that he killed people, but what he did to them first was worse.

Coppelia regarded her thoughtfully, and Irene wondered if she was going to to be offered a comforting lie to keep her on-mission. Finally Coppelia said, "It would be physically possible for him to enter that world. But he has no way to track you, no reason to assume you will be there —"

"Unless he's behind Kai's kidnapping," Irene suggested.

"If he *were*" — Coppelia stressed the

word — "then he would probably have kidnapped you as well. Eight out of ten for raising the hypothesis, but four out of ten for failing Occam's razor and multiplying the possibilities too far. Now, as I was saying, Alberich has no reason to assume you'll be there. It's also a high-law, low-chaos world, so it's anathema to the likes of Alberich, who's tied in with the Fae. Though that is probably why the order-loving dragons frequent it. Nowhere except the Library is entirely safe, but it's probably on the safer side of things."

Irene nodded, but a shadow of dread remained. "That makes sense," she said. "Thank you." However, she knew Alberich would haunt her dreams for a long time to come.

"For the moment I think that's one trouble you can leave out of things," Coppelia said briskly. A clock chimed the hour from a hidden shelf, and both she and Irene glanced towards it. Time was moving on. Coppelia turned back to Irene. "What do you propose to do after contacting Kai's family?"

"Whatever the situation demands," Irene said firmly. She took a deep breath. "I'll contact you if it seems appropriate."

"And your desire to make your own decisions wouldn't be relevant here?" Coppelia grinned coldly. It showed her age. Her normally serene face, an example of growing old gracefully, was for a moment a mocking, judgemental skull.

"Kai's safety comes first. And my wish to do things 'my own way' will never get in the way of that," Irene said. She took a step forward. "You put him in my care, so I'm responsible for him. Just let me go and do my job."

The study seemed very quiet after her outburst. Coppelia sat back in her chair, still grinning. "So you're going to fetch him back out of duty," she said. "Rather than for any other reason."

"Is this really *necessary*?" Irene snapped. "I need to get to G-51."

"What would you say if I told you to answer in the Language?" Coppelia asked. Darkness pooled around both of them as the lights flickered, and the night sky outside was covered in clouds.

"That in this time and this place, it makes no difference why I am going to fetch him back, or leave him with his family," Irene said. Because it didn't. **"Now, what would you say if I asked you why you are so determined to test me?"**

The question hung in the air between

them, unanswered. Then Coppelia leaned forward again and tapped a quick command into her monitor. "Use the shift-transfer cupboard again," she said. "It'll take you to the G-51 Traverse door. The transfer word is *Responsibility*. And one last thing."

"Yes?"

"You have reminded me that you're responsible for Kai, and everything that goes with it. I would remind you that I'm responsible for you. We both know that you're putting yourself in danger. Please be careful."

FIRST INTERLUDE
KAI IMPRISONED

Kai came back to consciousness slowly and painfully, his whole body aching in a way that felt actively wrong. It wasn't the pain of stretched muscles and joints, or the throb of an injury. It felt more as if the very air were toxic to him, and this was his body's response.

His position didn't help matters. He was lying face down over the back of a horse, his hands still shackled behind his back, breathing fresh horse sweat with every nauseating gulp of air. The collar around his throat bound his power, restricting him to this human shape. He also had no idea where he was or what was happening. But he could tell that he was in a high-chaos world, one far more repellent to one of his kind than any he had visited before.

His head swam dizzily, and he fought the urge to shut his eyes. He wondered how Irene would handle the situation if *she* were

the prisoner. She would feign unconsciousness, he decided, till she had learnt everything that she could, and then she would
escape.

There was water nearby, all around this
place, and even though it was polluted by
chaos and he couldn't touch it, he could
sense its presence. Right. First fact gathered.
There were people walking past. They were
wearing bright clothing. Another observation. He could hear people talking in Italian. Italian and water: that should mean
something, but at the moment he couldn't
work out what. He managed to lift his head
enough to see what was happening ahead.
Another horse, with a rider seated on it —
the man who had kidnapped him.

Anger tightened in his belly. He would not
endure this. He would — he would . . .

The world began to spin again, and he
lowered his head, trying to breathe steadily.
The horses stopped, and voices came from
ahead.

"My lord Guantes, you are earlier than
expected. May we enquire if there has been
a problem of some sort?"

"Nothing significant." It was the voice of
his kidnapper. Kai's lips peeled back in a
snarl. "We had to accelerate the plan a little.
My wife will be following on the Train. Is

115

the Prison prepared?"

"My lord, it is. We will be glad to take your captive."

"I think not." There was a firm arrogance to his kidnapper's voice. "The dragon remains in my custody until he's in the cell, and I keep the key to his collar."

"Do you doubt the Ten, my lord?"

Kai bit down hard on his tongue, trying to concentrate. There had to be something here he could use. He managed to lift his head again to get another look at his kidnapper. The Fae looked travel-stained, his grey fur mantle marked with dust and rain, but he still held himself with the hauteur of an aristocrat and a leader.

"I doubt everyone," Lord Guantes said. "There is one person in all the worlds whom I trust, and she is not here. Of course, I have the greatest of respect for your Ten. But in the circles we inhabit, it is only natural for great men to suspect one another." His voice deepened, and Kai was conscious that other people were stopping to listen, swept along by the Fae's presence and words. "My friend, we move towards a new and greater future, one where we shall march side by side until ever more worlds rest beneath our dominion. I do not speak of some far-off mystic vision. I am offering you — offering all of the Ten that rule this realm — a firm and concrete land of opportunity." He gestured widely, pointing to a metaphorical distant horizon. "We *shall* move forward. We *shall* wage open war against the dragons. The spheres will fall before the Fae and our allies, like wheat before the scythe. Our current scheme is the first of many victories. Those who obey me shall be exalted, shall be gods!"

He sounded utterly convincing. Even tied up as he was, bound, helpless, and a prisoner, Kai could feel the urge to nod and accept what this man was saying — even to volunteer. This wasn't the seductive glamour that Lord Silver practised. It was something that went directly to the command/obey root of the brainstem. Kai understood obedience to his elders and superiors, and this speech tried to play on the same urges. A dragon could resist it. Humans would be far less capable of fighting back.

The admiring chorus of murmurs that had been rising in the background broke off as an earthquake shuddered beneath them, fuelled by a wave of chaotic power. It shoved Kai back towards unconsciousness as the horses neighed, tossing their heads and stamping. The waters trembled in response, lapping up against their boundaries.

"I do apologize," Lord Guantes said, not sounding at all apologetic. "I get a little carried away sometimes. I hope that your masters appreciate my enthusiasm."

"Of course, my lord," the other man said. "But I think they would prefer you to save your eloquence for its proper targets, rather than wasting it on their common citizens."

"Of course, of course," Lord Guantes said soothingly, that commanding tone back in his voice again.

Kai couldn't breathe properly. The air was thick with chaos, clogging his lungs, and he was trapped in this weak human body. He fought against it, against Guantes's voice, against the chaos permeating this world, which burned him like radiation sickness. But there was no firm place for him to stand, nothing that he could do.

He sank into the darkness again. *Father. Uncle.* He shaped the thoughts like a prayer as he tried to hold on to consciousness. *Where are you?*

Vale.

Irene.

Help me . . .

CHAPTER 7

It was no surprise that Kai had quickly ac-
climatized to Vale's alternate, Irene decided
ruefully. It was just as polluted there as it
was here. The main difference here was that
people didn't go around with scarves covering their faces. Either they were rich and
spent their lives inside private air-
conditioned buildings, cars, heli-shuttles,
and estates, or they were poor and simply
breathed the air — and presumably developed lung disorders. Flashing holographic
advertisements offered transplanted lungs,
force grown from one's own genetic stock.
None of the advertisements mentioned
magic, which Irene found interesting. Possibly there was no way to combine magic
with technology here, or magic was illegal.
She wished she actually knew a little about
this world. Even two minutes with a public
information pamphlet would have been
educational, although she had been in

similar worlds before. She'd have to assume the standard problems with this level of technology: too much public surveillance, and everything done electronically.

There hadn't been anyone on the far side of the Traverse, which had made things easier. The library was old and full of dust, antique furniture, tiled floors, and wooden arches. It wasn't the glorious bibliophile's delight that it had presumably once been. But this was a hazard of old Traverses, which might have started off as an important library or collection of books but then dwindled — leaving the Traverse still lodged in place. And as royalties and aristocracies rose and fell, what might once have been a ruler's showpiece eventually became a faded public library or museum. Like this one. There were enough red velvet ropes and helpful signs to make it clear that this building was open to the public. But there was no sign of any Librarian-in-Residence, and Irene was grateful for that. She wouldn't have to waste time explaining herself.

She followed a convenient group of tourists out of the place, her incongruously too-long-for-this-world skirts fluttering round her ankles. She felt exposed but tried to look as if she were simply unfashionable. And then someone tried to mug her, the moment she stepped into a nearby alley. It put the final seal on her mood, and she glared at the young man in gang colours confronting her. He was pointing a small electrically sparking device — some sort of *Hey, I'm a dangerous Taser* gadget — directly at her.

"Kindly put that thing away," she said in icy German. "Or I will make you seriously regret it. I'm in a hurry and don't have time for this."

"Naah, you've got lots of time for this," the man replied. He looked her up and down. "Let's start with your ID and credit cards, if you can find them under that dress."

Irene took a deep breath. She could just blow up his electronic weapon, but she didn't know its exact name in the Language. There might be other electronic devices within earshot, which would be dangerously affected if she used generic nouns — and it might *possibly* be overreacting. A hand-to-hand fight would also be fast and efficient, but there was the chance she might lose.

As for the third option . . . using the Language in this way was extremely hazardous and very temporary, but five minutes might be long enough. **"Young man,"** she said in the Language, regretting that she didn't have anything more specific to call

121

him, **"you now perceive that I am some-one whom you recognize as incredibly dangerous."**

Irene felt the universe strain around her as it tried to come to terms, within the microcosm of the young man's head, with the way that she'd changed reality. The Library brand across her back smarted like a painful sunburn, and a headache tightened her temples. Blood ran from her right nostril, and she raised a hand to blot it away.

For a single self-indulgent moment, it was so very satisfying to watch the man's eyes widen in terror. She also saw a dark stain appear on the artfully tight crotch of his jeans. "Drop your weapon, your ID, and your credit cards," Irene ordered, returning to German again. "Then run."

He dropped the weapon as if it had burned his fingers, then pulled out a wallet from his mesh jacket with a trembling hand and bent to lay it on the ground. Then he backed away several paces, apparently unwilling to take his eyes off her, before turning to sprint down the alley with the speed of pure terror.

It was easy enough to manipulate physical things using the Language. But sentient minds fought back, and always eventually snapped back to their previous awareness, with the knowledge that they had been changed. As soon as the young man realized that he'd been duped, he'd be after her for vengeance. Irene kicked the weapon to one side. Then she picked up the wallet, flicking it open as she stepped out of the alley again. She ignored the glances of passers-by and wished again for native clothing. This wasn't part of the plan, but she could use it.

After that, it was fairly standard work, made easier by the fact that she didn't need to maintain a long-term identity here. It had been years since she needed to operate in a high-tech world, but she remembered the basic principles. Use the Language to adjust computer surveillance and banking as necessary — and keep moving, before the computer backups reset themselves and noticed that something was wrong.

A few words in the Language with a hole-in-the-wall credit mechanism drained the would-be mugger's account and also created one for her. She left in a hurry before anyone investigated the nonfunctional cameras and security mechanisms. A cheap local shop gave her jeans and a jacket. Then *that* got her into an expensive clothing shop, where she could buy a polite business suit that looked almost smart enough to visit a private millionaire. The would-be mugger didn't show up, though there was a sudden influx of siren-blaring police helicopters. She wondered a little guiltily if she'd triggered some sort of bounty alert by convincing him that she was someone incredibly dangerous. Oh well, not her problem.

But all through it, constantly, she felt a terrible sense of urgency. She should be with Kai's uncle already, to ask . . .

To ask what? Irene wondered, looking at herself in the mirror. Her appearance didn't reflect her inner turmoil at all. She had to look the part, or her chances of gaining access to him would drop significantly. Ryu Gouen, Kai's uncle, was a dragon. From what Kai and Coppelia had said, he was a high-ranking dragon too, set up in this world as an influential private collector and successful businessman. Perhaps there were stories where peasant girls gradually won the attention of dragon kings through their innate humility and sweetness of character, but she didn't have years to spare.

She checked herself over. The hair was neat, the suit was classic, and the small tablet computer fitted nicely into her new handbag. She could have posed for a stereotypical illustration in a child's primer: *B is for Businesswoman who Makes Deals.* The nosebleed had nearly stopped.

124

She could almost taste her own desperation. And she was ready to go.

Ryu Gouen was supposed to be in Marseille, according to the news channels on her tablet. It had been a while since she'd used this level of tech, but it came back to her after a little fumbling. She checked the transport options. A chartered heli-shuttle was expensive, but it was the fastest option to get to Marseille from Germany. And it wasn't her money, after all. Money was the least of her worries at the moment.

Swarms of people buzzed around her as she made her way to the airport. And it was the same there too. Everything was too bright, too noisy, too harsh, and flaring with lights and holograms. She'd spent months accustoming herself to the patterns of Vale's world, and now this place felt all wrong. She navigated through the crowd, a bland smile pinned to her face, and kept her gaze on her tablet computer once she'd made it to the heli-shuttle. She tried to imagine herself as a cool shark cutting through an ocean of people, but the image kept on transforming itself in her mind to something more like a herring. One about to be pickled.

An hour later, still with a headache, Irene exited an auto-drive taxi outside a solitary skyscraper in Marseille's outskirts. It was one of the more elegant skyscrapers in the area, tall but not overpowering, sleek but not aggressively glossy. It managed to convey an aura of permanence and age, even though online records showed that it had been built less than fifty years ago. It was owned by a consortium of firms, which happened to include a particular art-export firm — Northern Ocean Associates. And Ryu Gouen was a non-executive director. It was all very neatly done to suit a dragon who wanted to stay out of the public view, but who couldn't resist just a little touch of grandeur. Even the surrounding streets were clean and mostly empty.

"My name is Irene Winters, and I need to see Mr. Ryu urgently," she told the secretary at reception. She kept to French, not wanting to stand out here. As with most Librarians, languages had been a key part of her education — both for covert operations and for reading and understanding the literature that she'd be collecting.

The man behind the desk was so smooth that he might have been extruded from plastic. His hair was a sleek black cap, which lay against his head as if glued on, and his face was utterly unmoving. Small cybernetic insets glittered along his fingernails, sparking as he ran his fingers along the screen in front of him. "I'm sorry," he said, his voice as flat as his eyes, his French perfect. "Mr. Ryu is busy at the moment. If you would like to send us your details —"

"This is an urgent matter," Irene said, "or I wouldn't be here."

"Mr. Ryu is highly busy at the moment," the secretary repeated. His gaze took in Irene's outfit and levels of wealth and fashion, and just as quickly dismissed her as unimportant. "While he has been known to sponsor investment opportunities, this is on the basis of private recommendation only. I'm afraid I must ask you to leave, madam."

The lobby was empty, an echoing space of dull black marble floor and cold grey pillars. Irene and the secretary were the only two people in it. A few fragile chairs near the door did nothing to break the room's imposing effect. If it was designed to intimidate, it worked.

Irene lifted her chin. "I am a representative of the Library," she said, keeping her voice as calm and unimpressed as the secretary's. "I believe Mr. Ryu has dealt with our group before." *And even if he hasn't, that should get his attention.*

The secretary returned her stare for a long moment, then lowered his eyes and ran his fingers across the screen again.

A pause.

The screen flashed. "I am afraid that Mr. Ryu is not available at the moment," the secretary said. "Thank you for your interest in our company. If you would like to leave a message, we will be glad to contact you at a later date."

Right. Time for the brute-force option, hoping that Kai's uncle would give her a hearing, rather than simply tossing her out of the window. Irene leaned in closer. **"You perceive that you have just been given clearance to send me up to see Mr. Ryu,"** she said softly. Her headache deepened as the Language hummed in the air, but she pushed it to one side with the ease of practice. She was more worried that this wouldn't hold for more than a few minutes, or even seconds. The more reasons a person had to doubt their Language-influenced perception, the more likely it was to slip.

But for the moment it did work. The secretary blinked in surprise at what he believed he'd seen. No doubt he hardly ever sent people up to see Mr. Ryu. "Please take the elevator to the fiftieth floor," he said, fingers tracking over the screen again. "Mr. Ryu's personal assistant, Mr. Tsuuran, will be waiting for you in the office on the right."

Irene nodded politely, withholding a smirk, and made her way to the elevator. There was no sound as it glided upwards, a vast cavern walled and floored in dark opaque glass. It was big enough to hold a small lorry as well as a businessman, his entourage, a set of security guards, and a mob of reporters on top of that. Irene knew as she ascended that there would be security cameras watching her at this precise moment. Even if the secretary still thought she had clearance, the building's security would know better.

Floor after floor flickered by on the overhead indicator. Hopefully Kai's uncle — or at least his personal assistant — would be curious enough to actually hear the speech she'd prepared. Rather that than any of the unpleasant alternatives.

The doors slid open onto a corridor both walled and floored in smooth pale tiles. Huge windows on the left looked out on the city below and the sea beyond. And there was a single anonymous door on the right.

There were also half a dozen men and women surrounding the elevator entrance, anonymous in neatly cut black suits and dark glasses. None of them were actually holding weapons, but they had the easy poise of trained martial artists, and she suspected concealed holsters. Whether she was right or not, they were clearly dangerous.

A seventh person stood beyond. Her grey business suit was an order of magnitude more expensive than theirs and was definitely a man's cut, even given the trend here towards unisex business clothing. Her face reminded Irene of Kai's dramatic handsomeness. It wasn't a fashion model's glossy perfection but the flamelike beauty of something a little too alive to be safe, caught in a temporarily human form. Her long silver hair curved in a part over her right eyebrow and was caught at the nape of her neck, falling down her back in a long tail that reached to her hips. Her cufflinks and tie were matt black. She regarded Irene assessingly, with a coldness that whispered *predator.*

Irene felt horribly exposed without an assumed identity to hide behind. Spies never played themselves, and she hadn't had to do so for — well, at least a couple of decades now. But Kai's life could be at stake. "Good afternoon," she said politely.

"You will explain yourself," the woman in grey said.

"Please forgive my intrusion." Irene gave

a half bow, the sort that showed respect without being an actual obeisance. She was conscious of the increased tension as her hand swung across her jacket. "My name is Irene, and I am a servant of the Library." *Stay calm and self-assured,* she reminded herself. *You're a representative of a greater power. You expect proper respect as a matter of course.*

"Indeed. So you informed the secretary downstairs, and he in turn told you that my lord was busy." The woman tilted her head, giving the impression of scenting the air. "I acknowledge that there's nothing of chaos about you. You aren't tainted in that way. But even so, this intrusion is unwelcome."

"I was not able to give a full description of matters to the gatekeeper downstairs," Irene said equably. "Some matters require more privacy."

"I was not aware that my lord Ao Shun had expressed any interest in a private visit from any member of the Library." The woman took a casual couple of steps towards Irene. "You can, perhaps, explain?"

Describes him as "my lord" rather than "my king," the analytic part of Irene's mind noted, her training kicking in. *A close personal feudal relationship? She seems to be playing the role of Gouen's personal as-*

sistant, for what that's worth. And that must be Kai's uncle's real name, rather than the human alias. "I have lately been in the company of an individual who calls himself Kai, who was studying the Library under my guidance. He mentioned . . ." What title should she use? "His uncle might be found in this world, going by the name Ryu Gouen."

"And you presume on that acquaintance?"

Irene clenched her fists at the sharp-toned question, and had to force her hands to relax, feeling the threads of scar tissue on her palms as control returned. "Not at all." She drew a breath and smiled courteously. Courtesy was paramount for Kai, and it would be no different here. "But I have something unexpected to report, regarding Ryu Gouen's nephew. I thought it best to inform his uncle and ask for his advice. Would you be Mr. Tsuuran?"

"That is correct," said the dragon — Irene decided just to think of the person as *the dragon,* for there was no way this was anything but a dragon. "When you say that something has occurred, what exactly do you mean?"

"Kai has left the world where he was training as my Library apprentice," Irene said, her voice as cool as Tsuuran's. She decided

132

to consider the dragon as masculine. If he introduced himself as "Mr.," who was she to argue the point? "I received a message shortly afterwards claiming to be from his family — saying he'd returned to them. If I have in some way given offence to his family, then naturally I wish to apologize. But if something else has happened, well . . ." She spread her hands, aware that the six presumed bodyguards were tensing again. "My own responsibility towards Kai made me wish to investigate."

There was a long silence. Then Tsuuran made a small gesture with his left hand, and the ring of bodyguards stepped back. "Kindly step into my office," he said.

The room beyond the door on the right was full of space and light, floored and walled in the same tiling as the corridor. But its ceiling rose to twice the height of the corridor outside. *This floor and the one above must be somehow merged,* Irene realized. A black granite desk in the centre caught the eye and dominated the room, as was clearly the intention. On the right wall were more windows, but on the left she was pleased to note a neat set of bookshelves, and a starkly elegant dark filing cabinet. The latter seemed out of place in a world as full of computer technology as this one. In the far wall was a single door.

Tsuuran leaned against the desk. "The message?" he said.

"Earlier this morning" — yes, it was still the same day, wasn't it? — "I returned home from work to find that Kai wasn't there, and we had agreed to meet." She wasn't going to say *our lodgings* until she had a bit more data on dragons cohabiting with humans. "We'd been warned we might be in danger, so I was worried. And then this was delivered." She reached in her handbag and removed the note, still in its envelope, and offered it to Tsuuran.

Tsuuran took it in one long-fingered hand, and a thin line showed between his brows as he read. It was a hint of concern, well hidden but still present.

"A mutual acquaintance then found evidence that Kai had been assaulted and taken away," Irene continued. "I don't know precisely what is going on. But you will understand that I was concerned."

"And if it had been his family's doing?" Tsuuran asked. He didn't give the note back.

Irene stood her ground and looked Tsuuran in the eye. "I didn't think it was. From what I know of dragons, that is not a message his family would have sent."

Tsuuran was silent for a moment, which felt far too long. It gave Irene enough time to speculate whether she had just insulted him in particular, Kai's family specifically, or dragons in general, and what the consequences in each case would be. Finally he said, "Then what is your purpose here?"

Irene shrugged, aiming for nonchalance as the menace level in the room rose. *Despite not being dragon royalty,* she reminded herself, *as a representative of the Library, I'm on a level with his staff.* "If something has happened to Kai, then I wish to investigate. I have a great deal of respect for him." *And friendly affection, and desire, and irritation for the number of times he's suggested we go to bed . . .* She didn't know what would influence Tsuuran. He was a dragon, after all. Not human. In the face of his cool, dispassionate gaze, she found herself running out of words. "I just want to make sure that he's safe. I won't leave him in danger."

Was that actually a suggestion of sympathy in the dragon's eyes?

"You have done the right thing," Tsuuran said. No, it wasn't sympathy as such; it was approval. A wave of relief swept through Irene. "Please do not feel embarrassed for coming to beg our help, young woman. Under the circumstances, it was not only the proper thing to do, it was the intelligent thing to do. Give me a moment and I will speak to my lord."

Irene bowed her head, fighting the urge to go down on her knees as Tsuuran walked across to the far door. His air of authority and raw power was hard to ignore. Even if he was only a servant, he was a high-ranking one. And now she might finally have reached Ryu Gouen himself. Admittedly with a big EXPENDABLE sign on her back.

The door, which had closed behind Tsuuran, opened again. It had barely been a minute. This was either very good or very bad.

Tsuuran stood there, holding the door open. "You may enter. His Majesty Ao Shun, king of the Northern Ocean, permits you audience."

CHAPTER 8

The room on the far side of the door was much larger than a regular office. To Irene's first panicked glance, it was all space and darkness. A moment's composure let her see the boundaries of walls and high ceiling, but that first stunning effect stayed with her. The air seemed to spiral around her like a current, dragging her farther in.

There were no windows here, and the walls were panelled in the same dark metal as the floor, swirled with seamless loose curves, which reminded Irene of visits to museums and pictures of underwater metal deposits. Heavy silk banners hung down at regular intervals, and crystals blazed on the wall like torches. They cast a cold, unfriendly light, which still left much of the huge room in shadow. And there was simply nowhere left to go except towards the figure at the far end, sitting behind a desk on a raised dais.

The door behind her clicked shut as Tsuuran stepped through and closed it. "You may approach," the dragon said, prompting her. He clearly knew when a novice supplicant needed a little hint about proper court etiquette.

Irene began to walk nervously towards the throne and couldn't put off looking at the dragon king any longer. And when she did, she wished she hadn't, as she was just as intimidated as she'd predicted. Because this dragon — His Majesty Ao Shun, king of the Northern Ocean — hadn't bothered to take human form.

His throne was set back from the marble-topped desk, allowing Irene a good view of the dragon monarch. He sat illuminated, despite the lack of a power source here, as his power cast its own light. A few locks of hair, as dark as onyx, fell across his forehead, but most was bound back in a long braid. Twin horns stood out from the hair, each a few inches long, each polished and sharp. And his skin wasn't exactly black; it was the clear grey darkness of fathomless overcast skies. Irene thought that she could make out the tiny patterns of scales across his cheeks, even from her current distance. His nails — no, his claws — were as manicured as Tsuuran's, except that he made no pretence of them being anything other than claws. And his eyes were as red as fresh lava, but cold and frozen. He was wearing a heavy, long black silk robe, bordered with white and rich with embroideries.

Irene tried to memorize it all as she'd been taught, because that gave her some sense of control. And at that moment she was struggling to cope with the crushing weight of the dragon king's presence. The room was full of Ao Shun's power, and he was waiting to see if she could walk towards him through it.

She squared her shoulders as she stepped forward, and her Library brand burned on her back, invisible but acutely painful. She found herself abruptly, stupidly reminded of posture lessons from childhood. And where should she stop? Irene settled for ten feet in front of the throne and bowed from the waist, holding it for three seconds before straightening.

Ao Shun opened his right hand, spreading his clawed fingers towards her. "Irene, servant of the Library. I bid you welcome to my kingdom."

Thank god, I haven't done anything too far wrong — yet. "Your Majesty," she answered, her voice as firm as she could make it, "I am grateful for your kindness. I apologize that I have no suitable gift." She felt a stab of apprehension. After all, gifts were expected on state visits.

Ao Shun inclined his head. "I understand that you have come in haste, and I place concern for my nephew's well-being above any number of gifts."

Irene could take a hint to get to the point. "I have already told" — What honorific should she use? Well, he was a king's personal assistant — "Lord Tsuuran what I know. I may be entirely wrong, Your Majesty, and if so, I apologize humbly. But I could not risk the possibility that the note was a fake and that I was leaving Kai in danger."

Ao Shun gestured for her to continue, and Irene quickly ran through the day's events.

He nodded as she drew to a close. "I see. And your own connection with my nephew is a discreet one, perhaps?"

Irene blinked, and the floor seemed a wonderful thing to examine at this precise moment. Discussing her "relationship" with Kai, with his terrifying and inhuman uncle, was going to be very difficult. *But he's surely not going to have me thrown out for debauching Kai — is he? Especially since I haven't debauched him. I have gone to great effort not to debauch him.* But her cheeks had flushed red, and she could guess how that would look. She had to say something. "We do share lodgings, Your Majesty, but, as you say, we are discreet."

"Mnh." The noise was noncommittal. It wasn't aggressive, though. Irene tentatively relaxed for a moment and hoped she hadn't committed herself to a lifelong relationship.

"Might I ask the names and family lines of your parents?" Ao Shun enquired.

"My parents are both Librarians, Your Majesty," she answered. Ao Shun's eyes abruptly slitted, and she felt something go cold in her stomach. Had she said the wrong thing? "My mother's chosen name is Raziel, and my father is Liu Xiang." A mythical name for the Angel of Mysteries taken from one alternate, and a historical name from another alternate, chosen after the first cataloguer of Han China's Imperial Library — Librarians couldn't resist a meaningful pseudonym. "They have never told me what their names were before they joined the Library."

"You must forgive my surprise," Ao Shun said. It hadn't looked like surprise so much as cold alertness, but Irene definitely preferred it to have been surprise. "I had not been aware that those sworn to the Library took partners and sired children. I had been told your devotion to your duty came above all other things."

Irene could feel a blush crawling over her face again. "Your Majesty, it's because of them that I became a Librarian myself. I have always admired their work."

Ao Shun nodded slowly. She still couldn't read his expressions, and she wished that he were in fully human form like Kai. "In that case, you follow a proper course of action in continuing to serve your Library."

She heard the door whisper open and close again behind her, and Ao Shun addressed Tsuuran. "You have the pictures, Li Ming?"

"Yes," said Tsuuran — or should that be Li Ming? Irene turned slightly, enough to see him standing to one side. He was holding a thin tablet, its screen glowing faintly in the dark room.

"Irene," Ao Shun said, addressing her once again. It seemed strange to hear her personal name from him. Perhaps it was because his voice reminded her of Kai, and that made her uncomfortable. "Two individuals have been seen observing my territory in this world. It would ease my mind if you could tell me that you had not seen them." There was something patronizing about his attitude now, even considering his regal

142

aloofness. *Does he really believe me that Kai is in danger?* She felt a spike of impatience twinned with dread — Kai could be in so much danger right now, while she chatted with his family.

The tablet showed two separate photographs. On the right, a woman, standing. Her long dark hair was clipped back at the base of her neck and fell over one shoulder in loose waves. She had a pleasant smile, with just the faintest touch of reserve in her eyes that made the smile look genuine rather than forced. A navy blazer was slung over one shoulder, and she wore a sleeveless white top and a pair of cropped navy trousers. The backdrop was the dock of an old port or fishing village. Thin white cotton gloves covered her hands, going up her arms to her elbows.

On the left she saw a man, seated, a cigar in one gloved hand. He sat at a table in a restaurant — and a very expensive restaurant, by the look of the decor. He was neatly bearded, with a moustache that framed his mouth. Iron-grey hair receded from his forehead in a widow's peak, and well-defined eyebrows hooded his eyes. His clothing, a business suit and silk tie, seemed as expensive as the setting.

Irene frowned. "I don't recognize either of

them," she said. "And I'm sure that I'd remember them if I'd seen them. But the reports of Kai's kidnapping mentioned a bearded man . . ."

"Are you sure?" Ao Shun asked, leaning forward. "They might have been disguised in some way."

Irene shook her head. "I'm sorry, but they're not familiar. But wait, please." She hesitated. "There was an attack on myself and Kai a couple of nights ago, a petty brawl when we were returning home, late." She paused, and Ao Shun nodded for her to continue. "They were just thugs, not a serious threat at all. They said that they had been hired by a woman in a local pub. At the time, I thought there might have been someone watching from the roof above — but then I supposed it had merely been my imagination . . ." She realized that she was in danger of babbling nervously, and shut her mouth.

Ao Shun gave the matter a few seconds of thoughtful consideration, then shook his head. "There is scarcely a link. But are you frequently subject to such attacks?"

Irene could feel the temperature in the room drop a couple of degrees. It wasn't metaphorical. Ao Shun's regard pressed against her, and she could almost feel a glowing sign above her head: LEADING MY NEPHEW ASTRAY. "Not without some good reason for them, Your Majesty."

Ao Shun finally looked away from her. Irene could hear her own intake of breath, obtrusively loud in the silence of the room. "Very good," he said, though it wasn't clear what he was commenting on. "You have raised points that I must investigate further." He leaned forward and slid open a drawer in his desk, removing a black silk pouch. With a tug to the cords at its neck, it came open, and a small sparkling disc on a bright chain fell into Ao Shun's palm.

He stared at it. The tension in the room thickened further. From outside, a crawling mutter of thunder echoed dimly through the walls.

When Ao Shun raised his head again, his expression was clear. Anger. "When my nephew was committed into my care," he said, the thunder echoing in his voice now too, "this token was made with our mingled blood. By observing this token, I could be sure he was well and safe, wherever he might stray. But now you have given me reason to examine it, I find that he is beyond even my reach. This means he now inhabits a world so deep within the flow of chaos that I may not venture there myself.

Such realms are poison to my kind. And, worse, appearing there would be considered an act of war by those who infest that part of reality — a curse upon their name! And even for my brother's son, I cannot risk such a thing."

Irene felt the blood drain from her cheeks. She'd imagined Kai being dragged off to some other world, but not deep into chaos. Even the Library monitored or blocked its links to such worlds. And if she didn't know which world he was in, then she had no way to find him. "But, Your Majesty, surely —"

Ao Shun rose to his feet. "This is not to be tolerated," he said. The pressure in the room was falling, as though they were miles beneath the sea. "This will not be tolerated."

"Your Majesty." Irene forced herself to take a step forward, struggling against the weight on her shoulders and the buzzing in her ears. She felt light-headed, dizzy, uncertain, but knew she had to make her intentions clear. She went down on one knee. "I intend to find Kai and bring him back. This offence against him is an offence against me as well. I beg for your assistance. If there is any way in which you can help me, then I would be grateful."

She remembered Coppelia's warning that

Irene might become a sacrifice in order to salvage the Library's relationship with Kai's kin, if they were blamed. But she also desperately wanted to save Kai.

Silence flooded the room. Irene forced herself to look up and meet Ao Shun's eyes. And a thousand years of power and anger looked back at her.

"Here." He walked towards her. She could see the item dangling from his hand now; it was a pendant of black jade on a silver chain as fine as thread. The decoration was a twisted intaglio carving of a dragon, done in the Chinese style and coiled around itself in multiple loops. The disc was only an inch or so across, but it had a presence all its own. "You may have contacts that I do not. I suggest that you use them. This token should help you to find my nephew, if you are both in the same world."

He held the pendant before her. Guessing what he had in mind, Irene cupped her hands so that he could drop it into them. His skin did not touch hers, and the pendant, as cold as ice, fell into her hands. "It may also be of some use to you as a sign of my favour, should there be need. But most of all, if you are in danger — or if my nephew is in danger — place a drop of your blood on this and cast it to the winds. Help will be sent."

"Thank you, Your Majesty," Irene said. She bowed her head again.

"You have little time," Ao Shun said. He stepped back from her. "I can perceive he is weak and in distress. And know this, Irene." There was something uncomfortably specific in the way he said her name. "I acknowledge that any specific fault in guarding him may be shared between us. Mine, for not taking better care of him, and yours, as his instructor. But should he perish, or worse, then the world where he was kidnapped will be a lesson for those who would challenge my kin. And my brothers and I will not delay in delivering that warning. Do you understand?"

There was thunder in his voice, and hurricanes, and tidal waves, and all the brutal fury of unleashed nature. "Yes, Your Majesty," Irene murmured.

"Then you may go." He seated himself on his throne again. "You may inform your superiors that we have no complaint about your behaviour. Pray give my compliments to those in authority above you."

Irene rose to her feet and bowed again. "Thank you, Your Majesty. I am grateful for your concern in this matter. I will do my utmost." Urgency to get going buzzed in her, fighting the pressure of his authority.

The door whispered open and, as she walked towards it, the currents of the room pulled around her legs like water, dragging her out with them. It was easy just to follow them, to work on holding herself upright, to focus on putting one foot in front of the other . . .

She stepped out into the light of the exterior office, and the weight abruptly lifted from her shoulders, leaving her suddenly so light and unrestrained that she nearly stumbled. The ache of the Library brand across her shoulder-blades was gone too, though it had only seemed a minor irritation compared to the dragon king's presence. And while great storm-clouds were massing on the far side of the windows, darkening the room, there was still an entirely different quality of light here than in the depths of the throne-room beyond. Irene had never been a great believer in the value of sunlight as a child (as in *Put the book down and go out and play*), but right now she thought her teachers had had a point.

Tsuuran — or should she think of him as Li Ming, if that was his real name? — closed the door behind her. "May I be of any assistance with your return travels?" he asked politely.

It seemed pointless to try to hide her method of travel, and speed was vital. "I need access to a library," Irene said, trying to make it sound commonplace.

"Of course," Li Ming said. "I am sure that His Majesty would not want you to be troubled by any delay. Now, will any library do?"

"As long as it is reasonably large," she said. "A few rooms of books at least, please." The pendant was still in her hand, and she placed it over her head as Li Ming murmured into a small telephone. The jade was cold against her skin and stayed cool, a reminder of its presence. She couldn't sense anything from it, as Ao Shun clearly could. But perhaps if she were closer to Kai, or if she used the Language in some way, she could coax it into providing information.

Half a minute later, Li Ming was escorting her out to the elevator. "A vehicle will be waiting for you downstairs," he explained, striding beside her. She had to walk fast to keep up. "It will take you to the Bibliothèque du Panier."

"Thank you," Irene said. She was running out of polite ways to express her gratitude. "I am very grateful."

"Think nothing of it," Li Ming responded. "It is the least we can do, under the circumstances. I can only apologize for the haste of my behaviour. Now, if you will forgive me . . ."

We both have work to do. The unspoken subtext was so clear that Irene let herself be hurried through polite goodbyes and shooed down and out. In a way, it was reassuring that Li Ming *was* clearly in such a hurry, assuming his pressing business was to do with Kai — or that he wanted Irene to be getting on with her rescue attempt. There was indeed a vehicle waiting, a luxurious chauffeured hover-car, which flicked her off to her destination in minutes, under a sky that was knotting itself into a full-blown thunder-storm.

When Irene reached the Bibliothèque, she created an unobserved passage back to the Library out of sheer instinct, far too busy visualizing threats to Kai to worry about being seen. That urgency stayed with her, even back in the Library. Past the endless bookcases, through the empty rooms, until she found a terminal. And then she had to summarize it all into a quick email for Coppelia, one that she knew might be cited later in evidence against her: *The Librarian responsible for Kai's security when he was kid-*

napped . . .

And what did she have to say? *It's worse than we thought. Kai's deep in chaos, and if it's a world that would poison his uncle, then it may well kill him. He's weak and in distress. Ao Shun may not hold this against the Library, but he will certainly hold it against me. And he's even threatened to destroy Vale's world. As an object lesson.* But all she could do was report the facts.

The pendant was still cold against her flesh.

Irene waited for a reply, tapping her fingers against the wrought-iron table on which the computer sat. An impatient glance around the room confirmed that it was decorated in an outdoors-pastoral style — whitewashed bookcases, wrought-iron painted furniture, rough floorboards.

She didn't bother to check what books were on the shelves.

With half her attention, she summoned up a map of the quickest route to the Traverse back to Vale's world. Astonishingly, it wasn't too far away. An hour's walk. Perhaps half an hour, if she ran.

No answer from Coppelia.

The minutes were ticking by.

I know that you prefer to run to your superiors for orders, Vale's voice echoed in the

152

back of her mind from past arguments.

I needed to gather information and talk to Kai's people, she told herself. It was the right thing to do. And Coppelia had endorsed it. However, going to hunt for Kai was a different thing entirely. Librarians-in-Residence were supposed to stay in the alternate world to which they'd been assigned. Running off on her own would be reckless, unwise, unprofessional. She might lose her position. She might lose more than just her position. New information could arrive at any minute, and she wouldn't be there to see it.

No answer on the screen. No further data about the Guantes. Nothing.

The thought came to her in a sudden moment of terrifying release. What could Coppelia tell her to do that she wasn't going to do anyway? Coppelia knew that Irene would do her utmost to find and protect Kai.

And what if the orders weren't to find and protect Kai?

"Well," Irene said out loud, standing up. She leaned down to turn off the computer. "In that case, I suppose . . . that I didn't receive any orders. What a pity."

The high heels were appropriate business wear. But it was easier to run in stockinged feet, carrying the shoes down shadowed corridor after shadowed book-lined corridor.

Nobody had crossed her path by the time she reached the Traverse. She readied herself, brushing her feet off and slipping her shoes back on, then steadied her handbag under one arm. For a moment she hesitated, as though Coppelia were going to step out of the shadows and offer assistance. But Irene was past needing that. She stepped back through the door and into her current home.

The room on the other side was full of large hairy men. They had guns. And they were pointing them at her.

CHAPTER 9

Irene's first impulse was to freeze. She didn't have the reflexes for action-hero moves — at least, not without preparation. Also, dramatic action heroes were usually taller, fitter, and more athletic than their adversaries. She, on the other hand, was five foot nine in her socks and not overly muscular — unlike her five well-built new adversaries.

Although they were all pointing guns at her, cluttering up the room and backing into display-cases, they didn't look as if they'd actually expected her to emerge from the cupboard. Maybe she could use that to her advantage.

One of the men snorted in surprise, choking off a laugh behind his hand. "So here she is, after all. No wonder someone had this bunny tucked away in his cupboard," he grunted. His gun wavered as he looked her up and down, taking in her anachronistic, inappropriate, short-skirted clothing. "Ain't hard to guess what all them professors round here like keeping under their desks, innit?"

Irene let herself sag back against the wall, lowering her eyes tremulously and trying to guess what was going on. They'd clearly been waiting for her, and there were only two people in this alternate who knew about the Library entrance. Vale. And Silver. No, make that Silver and any Fae he'd told. And she could assume that Vale wouldn't be sending cheap thugs after her . . .

"Now, don't you make any trouble for us, duckie, and you won't get hurt," another of the men said. Like the rest of them, he had thick brows, hairy palms, and unsettlingly yellow eyes. Wonderful. Yet more werewolves. "We're just going to take you for a little walk. There's a gentleman as wants you to stay out of his affairs for a few days. You behave yourself, keep quiet, and nothing bad's going to happen to you."

Irene mentally cringed at the dialogue, lifted straight from Plots Involving Heroines Too Stupid to Live, Unless Saved by the Hero. She must have looked unconvinced, as the man's eyes narrowed. "You don't want us to do this the hard way, duckie," he snarled.

"No," she said, attempting helpless meekness. "I'll behave . . . Please don't hurt me."

"And no saying none of them spells," another said. "We've been told as how you can do sorcery."

Ah, so clearly they'd been warned about the Language, in a way that would make sense to them. But it looked as if she could get away with some speech. Irene let her lower lip wobble pitifully, blinked in a way that suggested imminent tears, and did her best to look helpless. The men relaxed. Unfortunately, they didn't stop pointing their guns at her. What a pity. She could think of half a dozen ways to use the Language, but didn't want to compete with a speeding bullet.

But she was still clutching the handbag containing the electronic tablet. Making it look as casual as possible, she shifted her grip, bringing it up to her chest in a mock-terrified cower. Her fingers slid past the clasp of the handbag and inside. She could feel the edge of the tablet, the power-on switch.

"Drop the bag," the evident leader demanded. "No trying to pull a gun on us, dearie."

"I wouldn't dare," she quavered. Flicking the tablet's power on, she let the bag slip from her fingers to the ground. It landed with a soft thump. The men's eyes followed it, before looking back to her.

Three, two, one . . .

The power-on chime sounded bright and clear through the thin fabric of the bag.

The tablet was a lovely piece of technology, set to look instantly for local wireless communications and check for messages. In a world where there were no wireless communications, and where instead broadcast radio signals attracted demonic interference, it had absolutely no chance. A garbled squeal came from the bag, rising abruptly to a roar of inhuman voices shouting something in a language that Irene was grateful she didn't recognize.

The men reacted as she had hoped. All the guns swivelled away from her to point at the bag at her feet, and a succession of bullets thudded into it. There was a muffled explosion from inside, and smoke came pouring out.

Perfect. Irene was already moving, dodging behind the nearest display-case. **"Smoke, increase to fill the room, and stink!"** she shouted in the Language.

The smoke obeyed even faster than she had expected. The small column of fumes bloomed into a thick white cloud, swelling

158

out in all directions till it touched the walls and ceiling, and carrying an odour of burning plastic that brought tears to Irene's eyes. And she wasn't even a werewolf. The sudden chorus of swearing made her smile viciously. A couple of the men were shouting for her to come back — how stupid did they think she was? But the rest, with their superior sense of smell, were really suffering from the odour, if their swearing was any indication.

Irene sidled quickly through the gloom towards the exit, so familiar with the layout that she could have done this blindfolded — which was pretty much what she was doing now.

Unfortunately, the smoke that hid her from the thugs also hid them from her. Five steps from the door she collided with one, surprising both her and the werewolf. He recovered slightly faster than she did, and she felt his hand fumbling at her shoulder.

She didn't have *time* for this. Irene stepped in closer and brought her right hand forward in a straight-palm strike to where his throat should be. She felt something crunch under her hand as he groaned in pain, and she brought her knee up hard into his groin. His grip loosened and she wrenched herself free, dashing the remaining few steps towards the door.

Behind her, the mauled werewolf found the voice to yell, "The bitch is over here!"

Fortunately, the thugs hadn't locked the door. She dragged it open and stumbled into the clear air of the corridor beyond as unseen feet thundered towards her. Voice raw from the smoke, she snapped, **"Door, close and lock!"**

All the open doors within earshot slammed shut with echoing booms. Locks clicked shut, spinning their tumblers into place. And from beyond the heavy wooden door behind her, she could hear yells and howls, and the crashes of large men throwing themselves against it.

The doors in the British Library were solid, but she didn't plan to wait to see how well they held up against a group of enraged werewolves. Questioning them might have been useful, but comparing notes with Vale came first. Brushing herself off, Irene started down the corridor towards the exit.

A man came running up the stairs, but he stopped when he saw her. "Good god, Winters!" he exclaimed. "What happened to you?"

Irene blinked. The voice was Vale's. The face wasn't. It was different and more heavily lined, and he was in shabbier clothing than usual. But the voice was definitely his. "Vale? Is that you?" She'd always thought people coming out with that sort of line were idiots, but she now realized it was a perfectly sensible response to being addressed by name by a total stranger.

"Obviously," Vale said drily. "You must forgive my appearance. There are a number of people looking for me." He tilted his head, catching the racket coming from the room Irene had just left, and seeing the smoke oozing under the door. "Do I take it that you've encountered some inconvenience?"

Irene shrugged. "Dealt with already. Werewolves — half a dozen — sent to take me prisoner. Do you think we'd gain anything by questioning them?"

"No time, and in any case I doubt we'd discover anything that I haven't already learnt." His gaze took in Irene again — with the shock of a Victorian anthropologist discovering that foreign costumes could reveal a great deal more than just the ankle. "We should continue this conversation elsewhere. I'll drop a word to the police on the way out."

Irene nodded. "Probably a good idea. My discoveries are urgent."

Vale nodded. "I feared they might be. I'll

borrow a coat to hide your" — he didn't quite say *scandalous,* but the thought was clearly there — "outfit, and we'll be on our way."

Twenty minutes later, they were sitting together in a small café. Irene was safely muffled in a spare greatcoat from the British Museum's lost-and-found cupboard, which mostly hid her anachronistic clothing. It was early evening by now, and she felt that they were losing time. But Vale had insisted on a short cab ride to break their trail and had refused to discuss anything further until they were at the café. He'd taken the opportunity to remove some of his make-up in the cab and looked more like the man she knew. They'd ordered tea, and Irene warmed her hands on her cup.

"I reached Kai's uncle," Irene said.

Vale leaned forward impatiently. "And? What did the gentleman have to say?"

"He is extremely displeased," Irene said. Her fingers drifted to her breastbone to touch the pendant under her clothing. "He was able to tell that Kai is in distress, and that he is in a world much more chaotic than this one. I believe he will be making his own investigations, but he can't reach such a world — it would be inimical to his nature, and for a dragon king to go there would be treated as an act of war."

"Winters, kindly give me a *little* more detail," Vale said acerbically. "I cannot work without more information, and you have given me nothing but the bare bones of the matter."

Irene ran through a more precise description of the meeting as Vale listened. His focus was, in a way, as unnerving as the dragon king's own scrutiny. "Can you show me the pictures you saw, of those two people?" he demanded.

Irene shook her head. "I have no way of doing so. And no, I can't draw, so please don't ask me to try."

Vale snorted, and gestured for her to go on. When she finished, he sat back in his seat with a sigh. "I fear that agrees with my own findings. Whatever is going on, the people involved are active here and now, in my . . . world."

"There were werewolves waiting for me. That can't be just a coincidence," Irene agreed.

"More than that." He looked strangely uncomfortable, unusual for a man who could normally be at ease in the middle of chaos. "I have been personally inconvenienced. The police are actually looking for *me*. Complaints have been levelled against

163

me, raised with the police and through legal channels. Singh has also had trouble himself — there are accusations of him abusing his position — so it's a good thing you didn't try going to see him. It's probably due to his association with me. Someone is trying to hamper our investigations by disrupting official channels. I came to the British Library in the hope of intercepting you."

Irene raised a curious eyebrow. Inspector Singh had seemed extremely scrupulous on previous encounters.

"Certain, ah, internal-affairs charges have been raked up against him, as a result of those accusations, so I cannot count on his assistance in this matter. I have contacted his superior, but she informs me that it would be preferable for me to avoid any overt dealings with him for the moment. It will simply make matters worse. The police will be no use in this matter." Vale tapped one thin finger on the table surface, frowned at it, then scientifically scratched at the layers of scrubbed-in dirt that gave it such a unique patina. "And the other reason I came to find you was because I found your lodgings under observation, as I'd anticipated."

Something clenched in Irene's throat. It had been quite a day, and she wasn't used to being so personally targeted. "Ah. Thank you."

"You are quite welcome, Winters. I do not think they actually intended to kill you, but . . ." He shrugged. It was not the most comforting of shrugs. "I felt it better not to take the risk."

Irene took a sip of her tea. It was just as bad as she'd expected. "The two individuals Kai's uncle spotted are an obvious avenue of investigation. And if this is all connected — is there any chance that they're the Guantes?"

Vale was already nodding, with a slight air of impatience. "Yes, that is the logical inference, and your description does seem to fit them. So we have the possible presence of Lord Guantes at Strongrock's kidnapping, together with an unknown woman. I've also confirmed that Lady Guantes was absent from the embassy last night, and that she's been known to wear a scarf pin of the sort your assailant mentioned. A pity we weren't able to question those werewolves who attacked you just now, but it would have been too risky to remain there." He leaned back in his chair, his eyes half closing, fingers steepled. It was a customary pose for him, signalling intense thought.

She took another sip of the tea. Yes,

absolutely disgusting. The ether lights flickered in their niches, and from outside came the screech and rattle of cab wheels. Conversations at the other tables were low and discreet, and the general atmosphere was one of quietly illegal under-the-table paranoia. Vale was probably a regular here, she decided.

Vale threw off his lethargy and leaned forward again. "Let me summarize my own investigations, Winters. To give you a full explanation — since I can hardly do less than you — your description of those two characters is almost identical to that of two recent arrivals at the Liechtenstein Embassy. Two Fae." He put his usual dry distaste into the word. "Though naturally they were properly clad for this time and place."

Something about the cant of Vale's head made Irene remember she was in rather inappropriate clothing under her coat. Surely someone like him would be above judging by appearances, if anyone was. If he could ignore the fact that she was from another world, it was surprising that he couldn't ignore the length of her skirt. "And what did you find out about them?" she prompted hastily.

"The gentleman is known as Lord Guantes. The lady is his wife, or so she says.

They claim that he is a marquis, but evidence is lacking. They — or at least he — are recently arrived from Liechtenstein via zeppelin from Barcelona."

"Are they Spanish?" Irene asked. It was the language that the Guantes alias came from, after all.

"No," Vale said, "but he certainly enjoys playing the part of a grandee. If I may continue?"

Irene shut her mouth and nodded.

"Lord Guantes has been present in London for perhaps two weeks," Vale went on. "I have . . . a contact who keeps abreast of such things. Lady Guantes may have arrived at the same time, but she lacks the customary flamboyance of her kind. It is clear to everyone that Guantes and Silver are conducting some manner of power struggle, which corroborates your own investigation. They hold their parties separately and snub each other in public. Heaven only knows what they may do in private."

"And what does Lady Guantes do?" Irene prompted.

"Very little that I have been able to discover." Vale stared into his drink. "This disturbs me. And now Lord Guantes has vanished, and Lady Guantes is apparently preparing to depart herself."

167

"A connection, then." Irene pondered. "And Lord Silver gave Kai and me a warning that we were under threat. And the Library data suggests a prior history. If they are enemies —"

"Given Fae dynamics, if Silver had wind of something, then naturally he'd want to foil their plans," Vale cut in, continuing her thought. "But in that case, why target Strongrock? I think we can reasonably assume they are indeed responsible for his disappearance."

"The nature of his family," Irene said. Her throat was dry at the thought of Kai at the mercy of creatures who detested him as much as he detested them. She choked down another sip of the tea.

"Is that so important to the Fae?" Vale asked, his dark eyes sharp. "This whole thing seems a somewhat excessive sequence of events."

Irene spread her hands. "Dragons and Fae are ancient enemies. Their feuds go back for generations — their generations, not just human ones. They come from opposite ends of reality. They don't think like humans, Vale. You know Silver and Kai — well, they're comparatively weak. The powerful dragons or Fae are as far beyond them as Kai and Silver are different from us."

"Us," Vale noted. "You speak of yourself as if you were as human as I am."

"Don't you think of me that way?" Irene was stung by his remark. "I assure you, I was born human. I am human."

"Winters," Vale said patiently, "you do very well most of the time, but every once in a while, when you're discussing your Library business, you refer to 'ordinary humans.' I dare say you don't even notice it yourself."

"Well." Irene felt a bit ashamed. It wasn't a good idea for a Librarian to start thinking of herself as *special,* however important her job was, and however strange the worlds she travelled to might be. It led to delusions of godhood and other dangerous things. *Like Alberich.* "Well," she repeated, "whatever you may think of me, to *them* I'm just a human. If I'd done something wrong, it would be simply a matter of swatting me down. But if Kai was abducted by the Fae, then to the dragons it's practically an act of war."

The word hung in the air between them. "You think it would be that important?" Vale finally said.

"Yes." She remembered Kai's own strength — that of even a young dragon — and the power and majesty of his uncle. "I don't know what the consequences might be. We have to stop this, fast. For Kai's own sake. But also because this could destabilize whole worlds. Including yours. When I told you what his uncle had said to me, when he warned me he'd make an example of this world, I wasn't being figurative. They could destroy this alternate if Kai isn't returned. Or if the Fae choose to make a fight of it." She had to make Vale understand just how real the threat to his world was.

She remembered, a little guiltily, that she'd skipped over the details of her own precise position and the trouble she might be in. Well, that wasn't so important at the moment.

"You seem extremely concerned for the safety of my 'alternate,' " Vale said drily. "I suppose, now that you occupy yourself here, it seems more important to you."

Irene felt a flare of anger at his flippancy in view of what now faced them both. "I see no reason not to head off a possible war before it can even become a skirmish. Do you think so little of me that you think I'd just stand by?"

"I think you overrate these . . . people," Vale said. "I have encountered enough Fae in my time, and while they are certainly hazardous, you seem to feel they are world-shakingly dangerous. Strongrock himself may have some unusual powers, but in the end he has his limits, as do we all. And as for Silver . . ." He shrugged.

She took a deep breath. "Dangerous enough to shake worlds," she said as calmly as she could. Facts would be more use than losing her temper. "That's an extremely good way of putting it. Although I have never encountered any of the truly powerful ones myself. That is because they usually inhabit the ends of reality, where chaos is the deepest. There, the Fae take over whole worlds and bind their power to the very fabric of these worlds. In your world we are in the shallow end, Vale, somewhere between the deeps on the one side and the heights on the other. I have never encountered any of the great powers of chaos, and I hope I never do. Librarians are taught very early that one does not go swimming in the deep waters with the sharks, because we'd be eaten alive!"

Vale nodded slowly. "Very well," he said. "I accept your judgement on the dangers, Winters. And please keep your voice down. Someone might hear you."

Irene wasn't entirely sure he did believe her. But if he was exposed to that level of power in person, they'd be in so much trouble anyhow that apologies would be pointless. "Ao Shun confirmed that Kai is somewhere in the chaos worlds," she said, "and your witnesses' testimony from the kidnapping suggests that Lord Guantes took him. But I can't track him unless we're already in the same world. Unless you have any other Fae who owe you a favour, then I think our only source of guidance is . . ."

"Indeed. Lord Silver." Vale pursed his thin lips in an expression of profound dislike. "Like you, I see no other alternative."

"Lord Silver did say I could visit anytime, when we last met," she went on. "But the visiting card he gave me is at my lodgings, and you've confirmed they're being watched. And in any case, if Lady Guantes is also at the embassy, we can't simply walk in through the front door."

"Certainly not looking as we do," Vale agreed. "Besides, there is currently a demonstration in front of the embassy, so it will have to be the servants' entrance. And if I am correct, he will be willing to see us with or without a card. Was his manservant with you when you spoke to him?"

Irene thought back and nodded. "Johnson. A thin man in grey."

"He's our key, then," Vale said with satisfaction. "Let us prepare."

■ ■ ■ ■

And so, later that evening, Irene and Vale were waiting in a line behind the Liechtenstein Embassy. They were swathed in heavy hooded cloaks, which would have been more conspicuous if the half-dozen ahead of them weren't also heavily cloaked and hooded. Two men were leading sets of dogs — a pair of poodles, a pair of Borzoi, a pair of terriers, and a pair of Afghan hounds — all of which played merrily around their legs and caused them to curse frequently and with heavy Russian accents. The Afghan hounds had been bleached white, but the ambient grime of London already lay on their pelts in thick dark smuts. Another man frantically studied a musical score, pausing from time to time to blow a few notes on his long-tarnished flute. And two women — at least, Irene thought they were women — tucked up their cloaks to practise a dance, baring stockinged calves and high-heeled shoes. Behind Irene and Vale, the line stretched farther back along the wall of the embassy. A savvy street vendor had set up his stall and was selling oranges.

"Have you done this before?" Irene asked quietly. The dogs, flautist, and tap-dancers made enough noise to cover anything less than shouting on her part.

"On several occasions," Vale said shortly. "But please remember your part, Winters. You are —"

"Your hypnotic medium," Irene said obediently. "Through whom you can summon up the ancient spirits of the departed pharaohs."

"You are rather glib about this. Have you done anything of this nature yourself?"

Irene wondered if he'd forgotten she was a Librarian by profession and so usually wore a false identity, but he did have a point. This was more than usually exotic. "Not since I was at school," she admitted.

"School?" Vale queried.

"Ah. There was one minor incident. Members of an international criminal gang were hiding out in the nearby chalets, and then there was this flood —"

"Later," Vale instructed. The queue had begun to move forward.

However, they had to endure a brief episode when the dogs suddenly refused to enter the embassy. They had to be lured in by their handlers brandishing beef jerky, prompting several stray dogs to make a determined bid for it. The embassy staff ended up throwing buckets of water over the lot of them. The two handlers were screaming in Russian, and the flautist was yelling that his sheet music was soaked. But Vale and Irene finally made it through the door and into the embassy, brushing wet dog hair off their cloaks.

The small receiving room they were shown into was a disappointment. Irene had been expecting something rather more dramatic from the Fae's inner quarters, but instead the room looked like any shabby below-stairs lounge in London.

Vale leaned forward to speak to the bored-looking maid who'd brought them in, and there was the clink of coins changing hands. "We need to speak to Mr. Johnson," he murmured. The maid bobbed her head and left the room in a rustle of wide skirts.

A long five minutes later, Johnson stepped into the room. "You have a private message for me?" he enquired curtly, his usual civility absent.

Vale nodded to Irene. She took a deep breath and pushed her hood back to show her face. "We need to speak to Lord Silver urgently," she said.

"Ah." Johnson drew a thoughtful breath through his teeth. "Yes. Please raise your hood again. Nobody in the embassy must know you are here. If you and your friend will follow me, Miss Winters, we will take the back stairs. Lord Silver will see you at once."

CHAPTER 10

Silver's private study surprised Irene. It actually looked like a place where a human being might live and work, not like an overdone stage-set. The divan, although it was upholstered in red velvet, showed the scuffs and marks of regular use, and the toothmarks of something small and gnawy marred one of its legs. The large mahogany desk had stacks of paper on it, rather than being dramatically bare, although the manacles at its corners were a little worrying. The ether lights in the corners had been turned down, bathing the whole velvet-curtained room in a rich amber gloom. A bookcase in the far corner made Irene itch to wander over and examine its crowded shelves, but she controlled the impulse, looking instead at their owner.

Silver himself was sprawled coatless in a wide chair behind the desk, his cravat hanging loose at his throat. He looked the very model of raffish disreputability, turning a glass of brandy in his hand. He glanced up languidly as Johnson led Irene and Vale into the room, remarking, "I must say that you have cut it rather fine. I was expecting you and Miss Winters earlier, Mr. Vale."

Vale pushed back his hood to show his face, and Irene followed suit. She had agreed with Vale that he should take the lead in the interrogation. He had known Silver for longer and might be able to prod him into a useful revelation. "I would hesitate before coming to any appointment with you, sir. You should not be surprised that I am late — you should be surprised that I have arrived at all."

"But you received the note, then." Silver sipped his brandy.

"I received it," Vale agreed.

"And you believe I sent it."

"I *know* that you sent it."

"And your suspicions as to my motivations?"

"Hardly suspicions. Certainties."

"Entertain me by explaining them, then. I am surprised by so few things these days."

"Very well." Vale strolled a few steps farther into the room. "Your dispute with the Guantes is well-known. You will not argue that point, I imagine."

"My dear Vale, I take pains to cultivate it. You may go on."

Irene noticed the twitch that passed across Vale's face at being addressed as an intimate. She drew her cloak closer around her, so as not to show off her ankles, and stepped back, fading into the shadows as she watched the men. Silver might be a master of glamour, but while he was focused on Vale, he wasn't watching her. And observing from the shadows was her area of expertise.

"You were aware that Mr. Strongrock might be abducted," Vale said. "And you attempted to give him something that might be charitably described as a warning when you met him and Miss Winters earlier. Possibly you were hindered by observers from telling them more."

Silver shrugged. "I was delivering warnings — I'll admit it — and there are no laws against that. My advice to you would be to cease meddling in my affairs, or you'll come to regret it."

"As will you, if you continue to interfere with mine." There was a whole new quality of iciness to Vale's voice. "Or if you simply continue to play your games with the lives of others."

"But why would I play such a game, do

you think?" Silver tapped one nail against his glass, and the crystal chimed prettily. "Surely that should be your question, under the circumstances."

Vale stopped his pacing for a moment to turn and look at Silver. "The paper used for the note — purporting to be from Mr. Strongrock's family — was tainted with Fae glamour."

Silver waved a vague hand. "Anyone could have done that. Johnson? Couldn't you have done that?"

"No, sir, but I can bear witness that many people in the embassy might have done so," the man murmured.

Vale stalked over to put his hands on Silver's desk, leaning forward sharply, like a hound coming to point. "I suggest that you deliberately intended to involve me in this matter. The note was to alert me that something was amiss about Strongrock's absence. You have deliberately schemed to bring me and Winters here — to you in particular — as the next step in our investigation. The question is why. Is this some perverse game between you and the Guantes?"

"Partly," Silver allowed. He put down his glass on the desk with a click — Irene thought she saw a twitch pass across Johnson's face as the glass touched the bare mahogany — and leaned forward, his eyes suddenly alert. "I'm glad to see you justifying your reputation, Detective."

"And did you set your minions on Winters here as well, to involve us further?" Vale demanded.

"That would be overdoing matters," Silver said. "Lady Guantes set the minions on Miss Winters here. Lord Guantes . . . has already left this sphere."

Confirmation at last. "And he took Kai with him," Irene murmured from the shadows.

"Miss Winters is correct," Silver said, still gazing at Vale. "Lord Guantes has taken the dragon with him. By now they are beyond your reach."

"You underestimate my reach," Vale said.

"Your influence may hold in the East End of London, Detective, but not beyond this sphere."

"His may not," Irene said, stepping forward, "but is Lord Guantes prepared to answer to Kai's father?"

"An interesting question," Silver agreed amiably. "Lord Guantes's actions are his own, after all. I am sure that if his misdemeanour could be proven, he and his beloved wife must admit responsibility." There was a muted undertone of pleasure to his words, the almost gloating pleasure of watching an opponent — or a pawn, Irene reflected — move to a weakened position.

"You are the ambassador," Vale stated. "You have authority over him."

"One that he disputes. And in any case, he is not here."

"Then where is he?" Irene asked. "In what sphere?"

"Elsewhere," Silver said. "Venice. Well, an alternate Venice, in a sphere of masks and illusions. The name of the world would mean nothing to you. It's far beyond your ambit."

"And," Irene said, feeling her way, "no doubt this would be towards the more — well, chaotic end of the universe?"

"Indeed," Silver said. "For one of the great dragons to venture there would be an act of war."

Vale drew in his breath sharply. "Surely you exaggerate. If Mr. Strongrock was taken there against his will —"

"Irrelevant." Silver rose to his feet, as tall as Vale. The light seemed to centre itself around the two of them, drawing the eye. "But even if it is true, it doesn't matter. And his family will know that."

Vale cast an apologetic look at Irene, and

she returned a brusque nod. *Yes, I did try to tell you. And here's your proof — if you can't take my word for it.*

Irene ignored the trick of the light; it was just one more show of Silver's glamour. "To business, Lord Silver. You have said that the great dragons cannot interfere there. You have implied you won't intervene yourself. However, you have deliberately drawn our attention to Kai's situation and made us fully aware of what is taking place." She could hear the ring of certainty in her voice. "You want us to go, don't you?"

Silver's mouth curled up at the edges, into a smile as sweet as ice wine and as sharp as vodka. "Why yes, Miss Winters, my dear little Librarian. That is precisely what I want *you* to do."

"Her?" Vale demanded. He'd caught the emphasis in Silver's voice, just as Irene had.

"You cannot go, Detective," Silver said dismissively. "The chaos of that sphere would be too strong for you. You could not endure its power. But the lady is sealed to her Library. Her nature would be unaffected."

"Let her go alone?" Vale said, at the same moment that Irene said, "You can take me there?"

"Precisely," Silver agreed. He smiled, step-

183

ping back from the desk to stretch. Irene could see the lines of his body through his shirt and had to suppress the sudden treacherous warmth in her own veins. The feelings he provoked were lies. And so were the ease and certainty of his smile. There was something hurried behind it, something uncertain and panicked.

"I would be less inclined to trust you were you not so obviously driven by desperation," Irene said softly.

Silver froze, dropping his arms to his sides. "You are mistaken," he said coldly.

"Hardly. The great dragons cannot reach the world where Lord Guantes has taken refuge. However, they can come here and will take great offence at one of their children going missing." Irene paid out the words like the strokes of a clock in the silent room. "Perhaps his family wouldn't cause a war by destroying this other Venice, but what would they do to *this* world, the seat of your power?"

The colour had drained from Silver's cheeks. "You are merely guessing," he said without conviction.

"I don't need to guess," Irene said calmly. "I've spoken to his family. I know."

"This world means nothing to me!" Silver snarled, but Irene wasn't convinced.

"And what about Lord Guantes? Does he matter — Lord Argent?"

Silver sat down hard in his chair and lowered his head to his hands. "He will destroy me," he said, his voice muffled. "We have crossed swords before, many times. And our own lords have forbidden us to war against each other again. The damage to the others of our kind was too great. But if his power should grow to far outmatch my own, then they will not object to him destroying me. I can imagine the favour he will gain through holding a dragon captive, the power — and even if I escape this world, he will hunt me down. He doesn't even want me as a rival. He wants to end me."

"But why?" Irene demanded. "Why are you two fighting like this?"

"Oh, there was some reason," Silver said vaguely. "I dishonoured his sister, or he attacked my mother, or something of that sort. I can't say that I remember — it was all so long ago. But you must understand that vengeance was *necessary.* He's a plotter, a devious manipulator, and his wife is worse. The two of them have no sense of art, no interest in living. They care about power, nothing but power, but their use of it contains no *style.* We simply cannot understand each other — and I, for one, have no wish to," he added petulantly.

"And thus your desire to send Miss Winters on a possibly suicidal mission, so she can sort out this mess, after you've done nothing to prevent it." Vale snorted. "Pitiful behaviour, even for one of your kind."

Silver lowered his hands and looked up at Vale. "Think what you like," he said slowly. "Insult me as you will. But unless Miss Winters does as I suggest, you, I, and your friend the dragon will all face irretrievable ruin. I give you both my sworn word that I am not doing this out of any intent to trap or destroy Miss Winters. My own interests are paramount, and I need her alive and capable to help me carry them out."

Irene was becoming impatient with Silver's dramatics. Kai was in real and serious danger. She would gladly stand around and trade insults with Silver later, but not *now*. At least if he was willing to give his sworn word, then he was sincere. Fae might stretch their formally given oaths, but they wouldn't break them. "Explain your plan, Lord Silver. How else are we to judge it?"

Silver sighed. "Here it is, then. Lord Guantes has the power to cross between spheres while taking with him one of your friend's nature. My own power is less than his — I could only carry humans at best, or others of my kind — and Lady Guantes is weaker still. Lord Guantes has made bargains to ensure that anyone who wants to witness his triumph can travel to this alternate Venice. He has summoned the Horse and the Rider, who are among the great ones of my kind, so they can carry as many passengers as they wish. They will appear as a train in this world. Yes, that form should provoke the least comment." He paused to consider. "I will be travelling on that train with several servants and shall take the lady along in disguise. She will then pretend to have boarded at a different transit point, posing as another of my kind. When we reach Venice, she may rescue the dragon and escape in whatever way best pleases her."

"You consider that to be a plan?" Vale demanded.

"I am not aware of the Librarian's full capabilities," Silver said loftily. "No doubt she has many strange powers that are unknown to me."

"So I am to go alone," Irene said, checking to make sure she had this absolutely correct, "to a world at *your* end of reality, surrounded by your kind, and will have to rescue Kai with no assistance — I take it you *won't* be able to assist me?"

Silver shrugged. "Only if I can do so

187

without being observed, my little mouse. And, of course, Johnson will be able to provide you with the usual services — coffee, tea, your boots blacked, your mask polished, your revolver loaded, and so on."

Irene nodded. There was a sort of relief in knowing the worst. She very nearly felt light-headed with it. After all, the plan was utterly ludicrous. And if this was Silver's idea of developing a story-form, she didn't like his taste in adventure fiction. But it was still a chance to get Kai back. She smiled. "And then I will have to escape that place, possibly with Kai in less-than-perfect condition."

"I'd keep him drugged, if it were me keeping him hostage there," Silver commented helpfully, "though of course the atmosphere of that sphere will be highly uncongenial to his nature, so he might be unconscious anyhow."

Definitely the worst. There was really nothing Irene could do but try not to laugh. When the course of events became quite so impossibly dangerous, the best thing to do was to ride with it. "And then finally, I must restore Kai to his family. Or at least to a safe place."

"I would have said that this world is safe enough," Vale said. He looked around him, his face weary. He already seemed to have given up. "But events suggest otherwise."

"Well." Irene took a deep breath. "So, when does this train go?"

"Winters," Vale began, "you cannot be serious about going alone —"

"Vale," Irene cut in. He hadn't believed her when she'd tried to explain the danger to his world. It had taken Silver to convince him. But she had to be the one to convince Vale now, to stop him from getting himself killed. He didn't know, couldn't accept, just how dangerous a high-chaos world actually *was.* People who had no protection would be swept along in any current narrative that a Fae was managing, their personalities rewritten to suit the needs of the Fae. And there was no time for debates. "You can see yourself that Lord Silver is desperate." That drew an angry twitch from Silver. "But even despite that, he's said it would be too dangerous for you. He has every motivation to send you along with me, if there's the slightest chance of preserving his own exis-tence."

"Well, yes, *obviously,*" Silver said, as though it were too plain to need pointing out. "But please don't think I'm trying to save you out of any misguided notions of charity. You're simply too entertaining an adversary to waste."

"There you have it," Irene said drily. "Straight from the horse's — forgive me, straight from the Fae's — mouth." She folded her arms, feeling her anger rising. "Look what he's doing to *me*. Why should he lie to *you*? I would . . ." Her next words unexpectedly caught in her throat. "I would have appreciated your help. But I don't want you to destroy yourself, and Kai wouldn't thank me for it."

Vale looked at her for a moment as if he wanted to say something, then turned sharply away from her. "Pray spare me your excuses, Winters. Your decision is quite clear. I have no wish to hinder your expertise or to impede your path. I will merely be sure of the details from Lord Silver here before I leave you to your little games. I can only hope that an innocent such as Strongrock will survive it."

Irene felt the colour flare in her cheeks. Something in her heart shuddered at his words. That hurt. It really, genuinely hurt. She'd hoped that he'd accept her decision, but to have it thrown at her like that . . . She turned back to Silver, choosing to convert her anger into focus. "It seems Mr. Vale is clear on the subject. When is this train? And what sort of disguise will I require?"

Silver touched his fingers to his lips, failing to conceal a smile at Irene's capitulation. "We will leave within the hour, and Lady Guantes will also be waiting at the station. I will take care to have other retainers who are also cloaked, so that we can smuggle you on board amongst them. As to costume — you must dress as a traveller from some other sphere. I will look in my cupboards."

Irene didn't bother answering. She merely drew her cloak open to reveal her anachronistic business suit.

"Yes," Silver said, his eyes stroking up from her ankles to her knees. "That will do very nicely. I will give you a small token of my power — not enough to damage you, my little Librarian, but simply to allow you to pass for Fae. We cannot tell from a mere glance that you are of the Library, and my token will ensure that nobody thinks you are to be played with like a toy. Johnson wears one. Show Miss Winters, Johnson."

Irene turned and saw Johnson slip a large brass watch out of his pocket. Its design was surprisingly intricate, traced over with a pattern that slipped away from the eye. He nodded to Irene.

"And perhaps some minor alterations to the hair, the eyes . . ." Silver went on. "It is a pity that we're taking you rather than dear Vale, my Librarian. He would be so much better at changing his appearance." He rose to his feet and strode over to one of the high cupboards in the corner, opening it to reveal an array of low-cut dresses and hooded cloaks. He seemed to have flipped from despair to manic enthusiasm. "I'll let one of the maids handle it. Blue? Perhaps if I could find a blonde wig? No, perhaps if we dressed you as a maid to start with . . ."

Irene was beginning to suspect why the Guantes' plans worked and Silver's didn't as he fussed over the clothing. "Where does the train leave from?" she asked.

"From Paddington."

"Why Paddington?" Irene asked.

"We must travel towards water, therefore westwards. And that means the Great Western line, which leaves from there." Silver tossed off the answer as though it made sense. Perhaps it did, from the Fae viewpoint.

Vale took a deep breath, then set his shoulders. "I will see you later, Winters — assuming you come out of this escapade in one piece. You know my thoughts on the matter. I will not trouble myself to repeat them. I can only hope that your concern for Strongrock is somewhat greater than your fascination with these politics."

Irene met his dark gaze, feeling furious. She truly had not expected this snideness from Vale. He was behaving as pettily as Silver might have done. "You know perfectly well why I'm doing this. This has nothing to do with politics or the threat of war. Sometimes I do things simply because I don't want to see someone die. Or worse —"

He cut her off with a gesture. "Spare me your histrionics, madam. I suggest that you save them for your play-acting. A good night to you both." He turned, raising the hood of his cloak once again, and swept out before Irene could say anything.

"Johnson," Silver said smoothly, "see Mr. Vale out. Ensure that he comes to no harm."

Johnson sidled past her, as quiet as a shadow. The door opened and shut again in a breath of air.

Now Irene had an amused Silver in front of her, and Kai to worry about. And she didn't like being alone with the totally untrustworthy Silver. The thought of sharing this whole enterprise with him was less than enthralling. Or, rather, enthralling might be the problem if he decided to use his Fae wiles on her again.

Silver was still considering Vale's parting shot. "Charming as it would be if he met with some accident, I fear he will leave untouched. Would you like him to?" He looked at her from under his eyelashes. "He was most crassly rude to you, my little mouse, and you are under my protection at the moment."

"I'm more concerned at Kai's predicament than any offence Vale may have given or taken," Irene said sharply.

Silver sighed. "Would that I had longer to enjoy your company, but we must get ready for the voyage. This is the sort of thing that Lord Guantes has his lady for, besides the fact that she can actually keep him to one plan at a time. I cannot understand how she enjoys the details quite so much." He yawned lavishly. "Johnson will be back in a moment, and he will leave you to the maids while he dresses me. You can carry one of the bags. I trust that you can carry a bag, my mouse?"

"With the utmost decorum," Irene said. Part of her mind was considering the remark about Lady Guantes. The reference to "actually keeping him to one plan at a time" was intriguing. Could it be that Lord Guantes was as distractable as Silver? And could she use that? The rest of her mind was focused on clenching her teeth and keeping her temper. For the moment, she had to play along. "But since you've got your way and I'm accompanying you to Venice, I do have a question. *Why* did they take Kai to this Venice, of all places?"

"Well now." Silver considered a moment. "There are very few places where they could be sure of restraining him while at the same time keeping him alive. It also required a world that a number of Fae could access with relative ease. And it needed to have the facilities to host the big display that is being laid on for us. Hence the train being provided so that we may get there, my mouse, my Librarian, my lady. Hence this little jaunt."

Suddenly all that tension and anger were back again full force, twisting in Irene's belly. It took an effort to keep her voice calm. "I don't understand. What do you mean?"

"Why, Kai's to be auctioned, my pet. To the highest bidder." Silver tossed back the last of the brandy and set the glass down with a clink. "And we must hurry if we are to get there in time."

CHAPTER 11

Paddington station at night was full of sparks and brilliance, and the grumble and screech of arriving and departing trains. The great curve of the steel-and-glass roof overhead was lined with harsh white lamps, which threw people's shadows in black pools on the floor. From time to time, singed pigeon feathers drifted down. Irene huddled with Silver's half dozen other servants, a maid's long white apron and black dress tight and cumbersome on top of her business suit, and tried not to grunt at the weight of the bags she was dragging behind her. In view of the severe lack of time, Silver had abandoned any attempts to restyle and colour her hair naturally, and had instead disdainfully handed her a blonde wig with the tips of his fingers. Hopefully that would be enough, together with a short veil, to conceal her from Lady Guantes at the railway station. Irene would have to work out a better way to hide herself later.

The wig itched. The bracelets that Silver had given her to wear chafed, and the Library brand across her shoulders smarted. No doubt the dragon pendant would be itching shortly as well, just as soon as it identified the worst possible moment to do so.

She wanted to know exactly what Silver had in his bags. Solid gold bars, by the weight of them. Or possibly heavy steel shackles, for use in chaining up dragons, Librarians, and other inconveniences.

No, she wasn't happy about this at all.

The evening crowd could best be described as a screaming mob. Apparently the incoming Fae train had been arranged with the station staff at short notice — where *arranged* meant "informed them it would be arriving, leaving them with the job of preventing a major accident." Half the usual trains had been thrown off schedule, and the other half were arriving at different platforms from normal. Passengers were running in all directions, grabbing guards and demanding directions, or simply throwing public hysterics. One young man had given up, piled his bags in the middle of the floor, and was reclining on them while eating a ham sandwich.

The crowd parted as Silver strode forward, his coat flaring dramatically and a riding crop held negligently in his left hand. The group of servants and maids, Irene amongst them, shuffled in his wake.

Fortunately, the Fae train was due to arrive at one of the closer platforms, and a space was being kept empty there by the strenuous efforts of several thuggish men. All of them had the identifying hairy palms and heavy eyebrows of a werewolf, something that Irene was growing far too used to. She hoped none of them had smelled her previously. And in the centre of her protected circle stood a woman whom Irene recognized from Li Ming's picture. It had to be Lady Guantes. Although she was dressed in the style of this alternate, she was unmistakeable. She might not have the heart-stirring allure of a Fae like Silver, but she had a serenity that translated into its own kind of attraction. Her eyes were mild, her hair was pinned neatly under her hat, and her dress was stylish. It might even be haute couture, yet it wasn't overdone. On top of it all, she looked positively . . . nice. Reasonable. Understanding.

No doubt it was all Fae glamour, Irene thought cynically.

Several others waited around the edge of the protected circle. Possibly other local Fae. But in that case, if they were here to catch this train, how fast must word have spread about it? Just how far in advance had Kai's kidnapping been planned?

Silver advanced on Lady Guantes, who turned from her contemplation of the railway tracks and offered her hand, smiling. He took it and pressed his lips against it in a way that brought audible gasps from a number of onlookers. The nearby crowd had given up on running frantically in all directions in order to watch the show.

"Madam." Silver's voice was as rich as double cream with brandy. "I hoped I might be here in time to meet you."

"Sir." She withdrew her hand and adjusted her veil. "I think it more likely you allowed time to catch the train."

"Such a pity that your husband is not with you," Silver said, his voice redolent with meaning. "It must be a great inconvenience for you to travel this way, lacking his abilities."

Lady Guantes simply shrugged. "I am confident that he will be meeting me very soon."

Was Silver being typically melodramatic, Irene suddenly wondered, or was he trying to draw Lady Guantes out, so that Irene could get some idea of her? While he was technically helping her to reach this "Venice," Irene hadn't expected any real aid from him, short of getting on the train. But she was used to operating alone — and after Vale's little tantrum, she'd written him off in terms of assistance.

One of the thugs strolled casually towards the circle of servants around Silver's mound of luggage. His nostrils flared to an unnatural width. "Rabbits," he mumbled. "I smell a whole lot of rabbits."

Silver raised a brow. "Madam. Control your servants."

Lady Guantes watched as a few other thugs began to drift towards Silver's people, following the first. "Why? Do yours have something to be afraid of?"

Irene's first thought was that she had been personally scented out, and the werewolf was going to drive through the tangle of servants and bags, straight for her. But he didn't seem specifically interested in her. He paused by one of the other maids instead, looming over her, and looked down at the maid's neat cap. "I like pretty girls with yellow hair," he informed her. "They squeak better."

That raised a jeering laugh from his

friends. Who were closer now.

I can't make a spectacle of myself, and I can't be heard using the Language. That'll just draw Lady Guantes's attention, and then she'll guess who I am and . . . Irene's thoughts ran around the hamster wheel inside her head. *But I can't just stand by and let him assault the poor girl.* Well, nothing had actually happened yet.

But why wasn't Silver getting involved? An answer suggested itself. Power politics. *It's his servants versus Lady Guantes's servants, and the first high-ranking Fae to interfere or call off their minions loses prestige.*

She darted a quick glance left and right, assessing the servants as if they were possible threats this time, and feeling foolish for her earlier disregard of them. Now she saw the casual shifts in balance, the downing of bags, the shaking of knives or knuckledusters down from sleeves, and the slipping of hands into pockets.

"C'mere," the thug grunted, grabbing for the maid's arm.

She squeaked and flinched back. Not one of the combat-trained ones, then. But the man standing next to her moved forward, and his punch took the thug straight in the nose. He staggered back, blood spraying out, and his teeth lengthened as he growled.

201

Someone in the crowd was yelling for the police, but both groups of servants ignored it. Irene joined the half-dozen of Silver's servants who were moving forward towards the werewolves, trying to blend in. She slipped an umbrella free from where it had been strapped to a nearby suitcase and hefted it thoughtfully. Good size, good weight, an unusually heavy handle, solid construction, and it put three feet of steel between her and the nearest werewolf.

She wasn't the only woman in the group. The other woman was pulling up her skirts to the knee, baring three-inch-heel stiletto boots with vicious spurs at the ankles. Two of the men were slipping on knuckle-dusters, a third had a razor, and the remaining two were both as muscular as the werewolves themselves.

It dissolved into an unruly mêlée within seconds as the thugs came charging at them, and Irene realized that Silver's people not only had combat skills but also had training in working as a group. The two burly men grabbed one werewolf between them, and one of the men with knuckle-dusters worked him over with several vicious blows to the head and stomach, leaving him groaning on the ground.

Of course, that left Irene and the others

facing five werewolves between them. The maid spun forward in a whirl of legs, kicking high at one werewolf's face. He raised his arm to take the blow, and her spur left a trail of blood down his arm. He recoiled with a strangled growl, quite out of proportion to the size of the injury. Her spurs must have been silvered.

One of the thugs came at Irene, hands gnarled in partial transformation, fur bursting from his cuffs. She went into a fencing lunge, probing at his face with the point of the umbrella, and he recoiled, sidling to the left. The others were keeping their own opponents busy, and while they were dealing the odd blow, her side's principle of "gang up on them one at a time and take them out of the fight" was working better than the thugs' own penchant for one-on-one brawls.

Not really the pack behaviour one would expect from werewolves, Irene reflected as she snaked the umbrella into another lunge at her opponent and danced back from his return blow. *Perhaps it's because there's nobody actually leading them in this fight.*

She was humming with adrenaline, and it was a relief to have an enemy to fight, even if it didn't do anything immediate to help Kai. She jabbed the umbrella point into the werewolf's stomach, then flipped the umbrella in the air as he bent over, catching it by the point end, and whacked the weighted handle hard into his skull. He went down with a thud.

When she looked around, four of the other werewolves were down, but so were one of the heavyweights and one of the knuckle-duster-users on her side. The razor-wielder and the maid with spurs were engaging the remaining werewolf, while the other servants stood guard over their downed opponents. The maid was carrying one arm close to her chest, but both her spurs dripped blood as she spun and kicked.

But this time she was too slow. The werewolf grabbed her foot as it came at him, and twisted. She left the ground, spinning through the air in a fluid ripple of skirts, and landed with a tumble. Her spurs screeched as they scraped against the floor-tiles. With a grunt, the werewolf lunged for the razor-wielder.

I don't think so. Irene threw herself forward, the umbrella still ready in her hand, and brought it down in an overhand swing. The handle slammed into the thug's wrist with an audible crack. For a moment, Irene wasn't sure if she'd shattered bone or umbrella, but the man's choked scream told its own story. He recoiled, clutching his arm against his belly, his other hand coming up in defence.

Lady Guantes snapped her fingers, the sound unnaturally loud. The werewolf took a step back, then another, bowing his head. He and the others limped back towards Lady Guantes, supporting the ones who were having problems walking.

Silver's servants moved just as quickly, without any obvious signal from Silver. Irene stepped across to offer the other maid her arm, and she took it with a nod of thanks, her breath coming in little gasps that suggested a broken rib. "Wondered why his nibs hired you," she whispered as Irene helped her back into the formation of servants. "Let's have a talk later, right?"

Irene nodded, while inwardly resolving to avoid such a thing if at all possible, and slid the umbrella back into its packing. It was hardly bloodied at all. *And damn Silver for not warning me this might happen.*

Suddenly a distant boom shook the station. The glass panes in the high roof creaked and trembled in their setting, and the ether lamps shook, their glare focusing and then fading again. Screams rippled across the concourse as people backed away from the railway tracks.

A low thrumming filled the station. Another boom, closer now.

Silver and Lady Guantes turned to face outwards at the same moment, without a second's hesitation. Several of the others waiting nearby did the same a fraction later. Without needing to be told, the less-injured servants bent to pick up their bags, and Irene mirrored them.

A third boom, and then abruptly there was a glaring light in the darkness as a train came hurtling into the station. The furious beam of its search-light outshone the actinic white of the ceiling-lamps, burning into the eyes. The ferocious churning of its wheels drowned out the screams of the crowd as they pressed backwards.

The Fae train decelerated fast — too fast, faster than should have been physically possible — and drew up gently next to the platform. It was sleek and black, with a sequence of dark-windowed carriages that stretched out past the platform and into the night. And although the front of the train was clearly an engine car, there was no obvious power source. There was a pause, just long enough to set nerves on edge, and then a door in the engine car swung open and a figure stepped out.

Irene squinted until tears came into the

corners of her eyes. The figure was a man. Mostly. His — or her — image shifted like a film reel jarring between images so fast that the eye couldn't follow them, leaving her with a set of impressions, but no definite fixed conclusion. Most of the images were male. A rider with tricorn hat, greatcoat, and high boots. A train conductor, in dark uniform and cap. A biplane pilot, in flying helmet and sheepskin jacket. A motorcycle rider, in black leathers and helmet.

The image finally stabilized on the train conductor, in a uniform that glittered darkly with ebony braid and buttons. The man stepped forward, and Silver and Lady Guantes both moved to greet him.

Silver bowed as Lady Guantes curtseyed, and the man made a small gesture with one hand. It somehow reminded Irene of Ao Shun's casual acceptance of her formality hours ago. He then turned to re-enter the train. Doors in the carriages farther down from the engine swung open, and the train began to softly thrum again, as though building up some infernal head of steam.

"Move it, the lot of you, now!" Johnson hissed. The servants all shuffled forward quickly as Silver and Lady Guantes chose carriages. Lady Guantes stepped up into the closest one, and Silver strolled down the platform to the next one along, as casually as if he'd always had that one in mind. The small group of lesser Fae and hangers-on tumbled into the carriages after them, leaving Irene and the other servants to hastily cram in and drag the bags, with the growing throb of the engine as a terrifying counterpoint.

The interior of the train was pure luxury. Irene had a moment to take it in, before she had to drag another suitcase up into the carriage, through the narrow corridor and into the closed compartment beyond. It was all plush black velvet, leather, and silver. A curtained bed-sized alcove was at the far end of the compartment, with the heavy brocade curtains drawn tactfully closed. Silver had thrown himself down in one of the long seats, and Johnson had opened a case to find a bottle of brandy and a glass.

With a heave, the last case was dragged on board. The engine thrum was louder now, heavy enough to hum uncomfortably in Irene's teeth and bones. Johnson placed the full glass of brandy in Silver's hand, then quickly strode across and slammed the carriage-door shut as the train began to move. It didn't jerk into motion, like lesser forms of transport, but simply slid forward in a cool organic flow.

He's travelled this way before, Irene noted, but she was on edge, her main focus on blending in with the other maids. She just hoped they were too busy to dwell on the fact that she was a total stranger.

"That will do," Silver said, waving a negligent hand. "Into the corridor, the lot of you. There should be another compartment where you can all wait. Johnson will fetch you if I need you."

Irene watched to see if he had any particular signal for her, but there was no little gesture suggesting she should stay behind. She shuffled out with the rest of the servants, crowding together in the corridor as they looked around for the designated compartment.

Irene quietly slipped off in the opposite direction while they were talking and seeing to injuries. It was time to change her clothing and establish an alibi elsewhere in the train — as a newly arrived Fae from some other world. She just needed to thoroughly avoid Lady Guantes's carriage.

She paused for a moment to look out of the window, tensing against some sanity-destroying view into alternate worlds. But there was nothing to see — only shadowy fields and distant lights and the quiet of the unbroken night.

Nothing to see at all? she wondered, the impossibility of it dawning on her. *No travellers on nearby roads? No other trains? Nobody out late at night? None of the other stations near London? You've been on the rails only a few minutes now, and there's nobody at all out there?* The words *uncharted night* drifted through her mind, and she suppressed a shudder, preparing to open the door into the next carriage. She tensed herself for a confrontation, but there was no need. The next carriage held just an empty corridor, running alongside an empty compartment.

Is this too convenient? Irene considered, paranoia prodding at her. It was easy for a lurid imagination to conjure up invisible Fae — if they could turn invisible? She didn't know. She'd never heard of any that could. But in any case, she had to change her appearance fast. If she kept the maid outfit on, she'd have problems passing as a Fae from a futuristic alternate. She would just have to trust to luck.

Irene hated trusting to luck. It was no substitute for good planning and careful preparation.

She ducked into the compartment, slamming the door behind her and pulling the privacy shade down over the door window.

Quickly she shucked off the disguise and shoved it under a seat. The business suit still looked reasonably smart, and a gleam of gold shone at her wrists. These were Silver's bracelets, which he'd promised would show traces of his magic if anyone checked them. So now she had Fae bracelets around her wrists and a dragon's token round her neck. The symbolism of belonging to either order or chaos was unappealing, and she was surprised that her Library brand wasn't itching . . .

Oh. She reached over her shoulders to rub at it. It was smarting painfully and had been for some time — she'd just had other things to worry about. A bad sign.

The itch on her back suddenly seemed to symbolize all the things that she was trying not to think about. Top of the list was Kai's real and present danger. Her fingers brushed the pendant at her throat. If only she could read his health from it, in the way that Ao Shun had done. Her own dubious situation was next in line: running out on her assigned role and going to high-chaos worlds without permission was liable to get her a reprimand at the very least, and might well lead to even worse. *Removed from your position as Librarian-in-Residence,* her innermost self whispered. *Knocked down to journeyman again. Kept in the Library for the next fifty years. Even stripped of your Librarianship . . .*

But worrying wouldn't solve anything. So she viciously stamped down on her fears, forcing them to the back of her mind. Kai would not be saved by fretting over him like a maudlin romantic, or by panicking like a Gothic heroine in a trailing nightgown. He would, by god, be saved by her going out there and actually *saving* him — and her position be damned!

Time to get moving. She began to work her way down the train.

The next carriage was decorated in brassy gold and deep brown. The corridor was empty, but the privacy shades were all drawn on the private compartment. She could hear the sound of flutes and distant singing through the wall. Better leave well enough alone.

The next carriage — this had to be the third one that she'd come to, with Lady Guantes farther behind all the time — was decorated in cream and ivory. The privacy shades were half-drawn, and through the small slice of window she could see pale tangled bodies in the private compartment. She kept on walking.

Abruptly the train shivered, beginning to slow. Irene looked through the outer window and saw that the view had changed. Instead of night-time countryside, she now saw . . . underwater. It was still dark, as they seemed to be far below the surface, but the lights of a sunken city glared on the approaching horizon. Something large and finned drifted past in the gloom on the other side of the window. Irene couldn't see much of it, except for a single flash of teeth.

The train was almost at the sunken city now, and she had a thought. What if someone opened the outer door and flooded the corridor? What might happen?

Panicking, she ran through into the next carriage. She turned to the compartment window, and it looked unoccupied. So as the train slowed, drawing into the station, she stepped inside, closing the door behind her.

There was a cough.

Irene spun round with a gasp. Sometimes even a Librarian could be surprised.

A woman was sitting at the far end of the compartment. She was tall, sitting razor-straight against the padded black leather seat, and was swathed in heavy deep blue silks. A shawl was wound around her head and neck, covering her hair, but baring her face in the style that Irene had seen referred to as a *khimar* in some alternates. The lines of her stern face were as uncompromising as her posture, and there wasn't the least ounce of softness in her dark, kohl-rimmed eyes. Her lips were thin lines, drawn together in disapproval, and while the whole of her face was beautiful, it was a stern and uncompromising beauty, the sort pictured in illustrations of scholarly angels and last judgements.

"You're late," she said as the train stopped and fell silent.

CHAPTER 12

"I'm very sorry," Irene said, deciding to play along. The woman had spoken in Arabic, and Irene realized that she had answered in the same language. It was a pity that her accent was so bad, but she hadn't had any reason to practise it for years.

"No matter," the woman said. "Come and sit down. I will be lenient, since you are at least here before the others, but we have little enough time before we reach our destination. Your name, please."

Irene mentally grabbed for some name that didn't have any sort of betraying hidden meaning, and seized the first that came to mind. "Clarice, madam," she answered. "I apologize for my poor accent." And what did *the others* mean?

The woman waved her impatiently to the seat opposite, hands still hidden in the depths of her sleeves. There were no obvious weapons, no immediate threats or denunciations, and Irene allowed herself to relax a little. Her cover was holding. "It is acceptable. You have an Egyptian accent, I think. Was that where you learned the language?"

Irene nodded, taking a seat and folding her hands in her lap. "Yes, madam." Well, *an* Egypt. Though presumably this woman — a Fae woman — looked at worlds in the same way. *An* Egypt. *A* Venice. No real Platonic ideal, only a thousand different variants.

"You may address me as Aunt Isra," the woman announced. "Now, as you are here, we will begin —"

The door slammed open, and half a dozen young men and women tried to get through it at once, babbling apologies. "Madam —" "We're so sorry —" "We had no idea —" "I would have been here earlier, but a baby fell under the train —"

Aunt Isra simply glared at them all till they shut up. The six of them — three men, three women — were a mixed bag of cultures and clothing, with one woman in skimpy black leathers with a whip at her belt, and the second in cowboy gear. Two men were bare-chested in overalls, displaying Stakhanovite muscles — one was paler and one darker-skinned, but both possessed the same heroic profile and shaven-headed style. The final woman was dapper in a perfect black business suit and perfectly polished black shoes, and the last man wore scarlet silks with a lute slung across his back. They all looked embarrassed.

"Well might you blush," she snapped. Then noting some looks of confusion, she shifted to English. "You *do* all understand *this* language, I trust? When I agreed to take students for this journey, I expected *intelligent* young individuals, ones who would be able to *follow instructions* and perhaps even *understand* them. Your patrons may be powerful, but you are young, petty, mere observers, barely a step up from human! I did not expect to waste my time on those who would not profit from it. Even the one who came almost upon the hour" — she gestured at Irene — "was late. I *abhor* lateness. Tardiness is a prime offence against courtesy."

While she was still staggeringly confused, Irene thought she might just feel the beginnings of solid ground under her metaphorical feet. This was some sort of pre-arranged class. It was *information.* It was *cover.* It was, in fact, utterly perfect.

Perhaps a little too perfect?

She'd think about that later. This would

be a bad moment to try to leave. Aunt Isra didn't look as if she'd appreciate her students walking out on her. "We're very sorry, Aunt Isra," Irene said, bowing her head. "We apologize for our lateness."

The others joined her in quick murmured apologies and excuses. A couple of them threw Irene annoyed glances, of the *Why did you have to get here first and make the rest of us look bad* sort. Irene didn't care. It meant they thought she was simply one of them, not an intruder. A thread of fear ran through her at the thought of them discovering the truth. That wouldn't be a happy ending for her at all.

"Sit down, all of you," Aunt Isra snapped. The train began to move out of the station.

They sat, squashed into the seat opposite Aunt Isra. One of the muscular young men in overalls avoided the struggle entirely by lowering himself gracefully to the floor and folding his legs under himself. Irene was sandwiched between the woman in skimpy black leathers and the one in the business suit. She produced a notebook and silver pen from an inner pocket — and how did she fit that in there, anyhow? Irene wished *she* had a notebook.

"As a favour to your patrons," Aunt Isra began, "I have agreed to conduct a small seminar about proper behaviour in spheres of high virtue, such as the one that we are about to visit. Some of you may have heard of me. I am a storyteller by trade and by nature, and I desire nothing better than a tale and an audience. I am often invited to these great events so that they may be remembered properly after the fact. Perhaps, in the future, I shall remember you."

Her gaze ran along the group. Irene worried that it delayed a little too long on her. *Paranoia only makes you look suspicious,* she reminded herself. She really, *really* wanted a notebook. This was going to have to go into the files at the Library as soon as she had the chance. It was absolutely vital background information for any close dealings with Fae or visits to high-chaos alternates. Of course, you had to be indulging in this sort of hare-brained interaction with Fae in the first place to get this kind of information — which would explain why it wasn't already there.

And providing such information might even soften any reprimands that could be coming her way. No, that *would* be coming her way.

Assuming she survived to provide the information.

"I understand that you have all so far been

limited to one sphere, or perhaps visited some local ones," Aunt Isra went on. "Would this be correct?"

There were general nods and murmurs of "Yes, madam."

"You may address me as Aunt Isra," she said again. "Now, I think it's likely you will only rarely have mingled with the great amongst us."

The man in the red silk raised his hand. His clothing was cut to flatter his body (and it did so very well indeed), and his hair hung in blonde waves over his shoulders, draping elegantly to conceal one eye. "Madam — Aunt Isra — I have been fortunate enough to attend at my patron's court for many years now, in the more median spheres, and he is a great and mighty lord —"

"And by saying as much, you betray its littleness and his weakness!" the woman snapped. Her eyes shone like black diamonds. "Fool of a boy, have you not felt these spheres shake, as the Rider and his Steed passed through them? So tremble all worlds of lesser virtue when the great move amongst them. Those spheres will not — *cannot* — endure the power of the mighty. The sphere to which we travel is one of higher virtue and will be able to withstand their presence. I say again that you will rarely have encountered the great amongst us, because the sphere of your nurturing could not have contained them for long. Boy, your name!"

"Athanais the Scarlet," the man murmured. He rose to his feet and swept a bow.

"Turn and apologize to your brothers and sisters for wasting their time," Aunt Isra ordered him. "Think yourself lucky that I do not whip your hands to help you remember the lesson."

Still standing, Athanais turned to Irene and the others. "I apologize for wasting your time with my folly," he murmured, bowing again. "Please forgive me."

Amid the general embarrassed mutters of *Apology accepted; think nothing of it,* Irene mentally slapped herself. She'd been so preoccupied by Silver's over-the-top libertine persona that she'd never really bothered to think about Fae who liked *other* sorts of roles when constructing their stories. They might still be the centre of their own narrative, but that didn't mean they had to be the "hero" or the "villain" of the overarching tale. There were other roles for them to take, roles that were probably quite not so *immediately* destructive to those around them. (Though she'd hate to make a mistake in any class run by Aunt Isra. It looked as if it would be painful.) But she'd been unconsciously assuming that they'd all play out their games in the same way that Silver did his, always casting themselves as the main protagonist.

Aunt Isra was Fae, but she was also a teacher and a storyteller by nature. There had to be a way in which Irene could use this.

Aunt Isra nodded. "Be seated again. Well now, as I was saying, you will have had little to do with the great amongst us, nor will you have spent time in a sphere of high virtue — or so I was told?" She glanced around the group and, when everyone nodded, Irene joining in, she smiled thinly. "Ah, this will be a new threshold for you all!"

The woman in the suit raised her hand. "Aunt Isra, may we ask questions?"

"As long as they are intelligent ones," Aunt Isra said, not very helpfully.

The woman nodded. "We've all lived in the wake of our patrons, Aunt Isra, and followed their paths. We therefore have some understanding of what it is to be caught in the 'story' of another of our kind — at least, that was the phrasing my superior used. How much . . . um, bigger is the effect when facing one of the great —" She was clearly looking for some diplomatic way to say *how much worse,* and Irene herself dearly wanted to know the answer to this one.

Aunt Isra sniffed. The harsh light now coming in through the windows cast her features into strict lines of contrast and shadow. "Certainly you can flee, young woman, and retreat back to whatever sphere you came from. No doubt there will be humans there who will feed you sufficient adoration to keep you alive. But it will be no *more* than living. Once you have tasted the full wine of following in the steps of the great ones, nothing less will content you. Once I — *I myself!* — was but a humble maiden who bore her sword in the service of the great Caliph al-Rashid. All things seemed possible to me then. I will admit that I had lovers — nay, even *friends* — amongst the humans. I could live within that petty sphere because I did not realize how much was to be had outside it."

Beyond the window was desert, punctuated by cacti, tumbleweeds, and thin stony paths. The sun burned down on it from a cloudless sky.

Aunt Isra's voice had shifted into the rising and falling patterns of a story. "But then I told a tale that set a Djinn free, and I travelled thrice across the shifting sands with friends to answer its questions. I walked the paths that lead from Paradise to Hell, and I made five choices at their doors. I gave a hero the reins to a horse that galloped faster than the wind. I knelt at the feet of an emperor who ruled five worlds, and I told him a story that brought doom on one of them but saved another. I lay in the arms of the ocean and bore her a child. And once I had done all these things, my children, I saw how little it was worth to be — to be merely a person who had the name that I once had. What are humans, compared to the wine of life, which is found by living as we do? I am what I am, and now I have no desire to be less."

Is less *really the word?* Irene wondered, then thought, *It is for her.*

"Cast aside your uncertainties," Aunt Isra went on. "Be who you *are.* It is the way forward, my children, the way to power, the way to life. And the greater the virtue of the place where you walk, the easier this will be. I see from your clothing and your habits that you are all well-established in your own spheres, which is good. But the great amongst us can walk in any sphere and will appear in the dress and style appropriate to their nature. They can speak and they will be understood in any language. They are unchanging, because they have utterly become themselves and will never be otherwise."

Irene tentatively raised her hand.

"Yes?" Aunt Isra said. She seemed a little less brittle now, more lyrical storyteller than sharp teacher. "What have you to say, Clarice?"

"Aunt Isra," Irene said carefully, her stomach clenching at the risk of drawing more attention to herself, "when I entered the train, I noticed the driver. But he was difficult to see clearly. I saw many different faces and styles of clothing, but each one was appropriate in its own way. He is one of the great ones, isn't he?" Nervousness prickled down her back like an echo of her Library brand, as other people in the carriage looked in her direction.

The train came to a smooth stop. Stage-coaches were waiting outside. From the corner of her eye, Irene could see men in white suits and top hats, and women with parasols and ornate gowns, being helped down from the stage-coaches. They were approaching coaches farther down the train.

Aunt Isra nodded. "He is the Rider. He and his Horse share a story. Do all here know it?"

Before Irene had to either admit she didn't or pretend she did, the man in overalls who was sitting on the floor raised his hand. "Of course, Aunt Isra. I'm surprised that Clarice here isn't more fully aware of it."

Snippy, snippy, Irene thought. *Just because I was here on time.* But she also felt a pang of apprehension, in case she'd exposed her ignorance.

"Then you may tell the story, young man," Aunt Isra said, graciously bestowing the task on him as if it were a prize.

Looking smugly content, the young man began. "Once, in a long-distant state, there was a horse that galloped across land and sea . . ."

It was a typical sort of fairy tale, even if the hero who eventually captured the horse was a *heroic servant of the people* rather than the more usual prince or hunter. Irene took care to memorize the details: silver collar wrought from the moon and stars, whip made from the wind, the rider holding on to the horse's mane while it galloped over thrice nine proletarian states. All the usual stuff. And she nodded at the right moments as she repeated it inside her head.

"And then the steed bowed its head and submitted," the young man concluded, "and from that day to this, the hero commanded its power and it galloped at his will, swifter than a thousand rainbows. From land to land he rides, from the gates of story to the shores of dream, until the world is changed."

Aunt Isra sat there for a while, lost in thought, and the carriage was silent except for the thrumming of the train. There were skyscrapers beyond the windows now, their heights lost in smog. Irene was vaguely aware that there were other people in the carriage, crowding in to fill it — other students, possibly? — but she didn't dare look away from Aunt Isra.

"Tolerably well performed," Aunt Isra said. "An acceptable version of the story. I approve. You may attend me later, if you wish, for further teaching."

"Thank you, Aunt Isra," the young man said, and bowed at the waist.

"Now, what conclusion may we all draw from this?" Aunt Isra abruptly demanded, her gaze sweeping over the group.

Irene mentally scrambled to guess what the proper answer might be. Something about how being in archetypal stories made you a powerful Fae, or vice versa? Something about how the same stories persisted across different worlds? Or about how both the horse and the rider were important participants in the story?

"Clearly that both the rider and the horse

are necessary to each other," the woman in the business suit said, her voice clipped. "This may be interpreted as encouragement to be involved with each other, to our mutual benefit."

Even if I'd rather be the rider than the horse, Irene thought.

"You are correct, young woman, though you put it very blandly," Aunt Isra said. "I would not expect you to understand the sheer glory that comes from sharing another's path, except by experience." Her voice dripped with condescension. "Certainly one can refuse such things. One can limit one's self. But those who choose to do so — well, if they are *here,* then they are in the wrong place. We are now amongst the great company who have travelled upon the Horse. Our story has therefore become that much richer, and we are greater because of it. Also, we can see that lesser things within the story have their own strength. The Horse is a mere servant to the Rider, but it is necessary to the tale. No story is ever about the protagonist alone! Other things are remembered — opponents, friends, servants, and obstacles."

Something was nagging at Irene, and she tried to articulate it as a question. "Aunt Isra . . . ," she began.

"Yes, Clarice?"

"You said that the Horse was one of the great ones, as was the Rider," Irene went on carefully, hoping that she'd got the terminology right. Her Library brand was itching again as they moved deeper into chaos with every stop the train — or Train — made. "We are currently within the Horse, as it were. Does this mean that we are currently in a sphere of 'high virtue,' where the great story forms can flourish?"

"Of course," Aunt Isra said. It wasn't quite a tone of *Only an idiot would need to ask such a question,* but it was close. "That was why you have all found it so easy to reach this seminar. Your paths brought you here."

Irene nodded. "Thank you, Aunt Isra," she murmured, lowering her eyes as she thought. So the interior of this Train was by its nature high-chaos, and being in a high-chaos environment took her to where she "needed" to be for the "story" that she was in. She didn't need to be paranoid about this all being a giant trap — at least, not yet. But she *did* need to be paranoid about the possibility of her "path" taking her to a meeting with Lord or Lady Guantes. This would lead to the drama so appealing to the story, but she might be forced to play the victim, not the heroine. Another trap to avoid — if she even could.

"It's hard for us to make a role for ourselves when the great ones already hold the most notable paths," said an American-accented female voice from somewhere behind her.

"Even the great can die," Aunt Isra said calmly. "The path is eternal, but we who walk it are rarely so. Do not be in haste to limit yourself, child. Go forth and act in accordance with your nature. Only the weak will limit themselves to thinking in human terms. Pity them, use them, but do not become them. We are what we make ourselves."

There was greenery outside the window now. The Train seemed to be moving faster and faster all the time, delaying for a shorter period at each stop. Was it just Irene's perception, or were they going more smoothly and more quickly as they went deeper and deeper into chaos?

Aunt Isra kept on talking, and Irene schooled her expression to deep interest, but inside she was turning over the new facts like cards at a Tarot reading. The more obviously a Fae seemed to be playing a role, the more powerful he or she was. Lord Guantes and Silver must be at about the same level, or presumably Lord Guantes would already have destroyed Silver, given their rivalry. Unless the story demanded that they keep at it for a while longer. So did Lord Guantes have his own competing archetype, path, role, or whatever one wanted to call it? And was Lady Guantes less powerful? Silver had said that she didn't have the power to travel across worlds to the extent that Lord Guantes did, and he'd seemed generally dismissive of her. Then again, how far could Silver's judgement be trusted?

A cold thought formed itself. Lady Guantes might be less powerful as a Fae, perhaps, but cunning enough to throw hindrances at Irene and Vale, and to think of innovative ways to do so. She'd even damaged Vale's links to the official police. The roadblocks she'd thrown in their pursuit had been practical and sensible, rather than dramatic, exotic, or the sort of thing that Silver might have tried. (All right, werewolf ambushes weren't *exactly* practical and sensible, but they had almost worked.) Perhaps Lady Guantes's strength was what Aunt Isra was busy decrying at this very moment. What if she thought like a human rather than a Fae, and so wasn't limited by archetypal patterns of thought? It was only a hypothesis, but it made an uncomfortable amount of sense.

Another stop. Glowing crystal towers outside the windows. Men and women in billowing silk and velvet veils.

Perhaps she wouldn't be able to avoid the Guantes pair. But she could take every precaution to stop them recognizing her. And her priority was to find Kai, rescue Kai, and escape. She'd leave the vengeance to Kai's family. She just had to *get there,* and if there was to be an auction, Kai's time was running out fast.

She fretted as Aunt Isra finished another peroration on the glories of becoming a more powerful Fae — by sacrificing all friendship with "common humans" — and then Irene raised her hand.

"Yes, Clarice?" Aunt Isra said. "Your thoughts on the subject?"

Irene blushed, as daintily and modestly as she could. "Actually, Aunt Isra, I was wondering if I could ask about the ongoing situation at our destination, and its possible implications. As you said, we are all from limited backgrounds, and I would be very grateful to have a wider point of view before we arrive."

There was an approving mumble of assent from behind Irene, surprising her by its volume. It sounded as if this were a popular question. The carriage must have grown a lot larger to be holding that many people.

Aunt Isra nodded thoughtfully. The carriage lights now lit the compartment harshly, as outside the window it was dark again — a wind-swept, shuddering ocean of black waters. "It is true that most of you will have little grasp of the wider implications. Did you know that a common toast in some armies once was 'To a sudden plague and a bloody war'?"

A general nodding of heads, Irene's included.

"Lord Guantes, of the seventh-upon-reticulation sphere, has captured a dragon and put him up for auction. Of course, only the greater amongst us will be bidding, and you children are merely observers. What you may *not* realize, children, is that there is a good chance this will lead to open conflict between our kind and the dragons. Everything could change. Certainly Lord Guantes will either find himself raised high or brought down low. So you see, child" — she smiled at the woman in the business suit next to Irene, and there was nothing in her face but simple pleasure — "you need not fret so much. New paths are opening to all of us. At midnight tomorrow, at the La

Fenice opera house, the dragon will be sold off to the highest bidder. And whichever way the path leads, assuredly it will be a great and magnificent tale for this storyteller to relate."

There was a rustle as people checked their watches or other timepieces. Irene glanced at her own wrist automatically, not wanting to look out of place, but inwardly her heart had frozen. She had a single day to find Kai. And if she failed to rescue him, the result would be war. She could barely breathe. She wasn't without skills, but how — *how* was she going to manage this in a strange city, on her own, by midnight tomorrow . . .

The Train shuddered, and Aunt Isra glanced out of the window. Beyond the glass there were lights in the distance, spangled across buildings and domes and palaces. Venice. "You had best prepare to observe events on the platform, children, or find your patrons. Do not keep them waiting."

SECOND INTERLUDE

KAI IN THE TOWER

Kai woke to the taste of brandy, and swallowed on reflex before the thought of poison crossed his mind.

The dreadful constant pressure and burn of chaos had gone. For a moment, that thought dominated all others. The cold stone and cold metal against his skin were gentle caresses by comparison, and the drag on his arms was unimportant. He was able to think clearly again, to perceive, to reason.

Someone was supporting him and holding his head up, tilting the flask of brandy against his lips. Kai let his eyes flicker open for a fraction of a second, just long enough to see who it was and where they were.

It was his kidnapper, the man they'd called Lord Guantes. Sheer fury spiked through Kai, and he wrenched at whatever was holding his wrists, struggling to pull them free so that he could get his hands around the Fae's neck.

Guantes stepped back, rising to his feet. "I take it that means you don't want any more brandy," he said, wiping the neck of the flask with his sleeve. He was in grey silks and velvets now, with a draping mantle over doublet and breeches. "How are you feeling?"

"How dare you ask me that, after laying your hands on me in this way!" In another place and time, Kai's words would have woken storms, brought rivers and seas rising to his command. But here and now they were only words, and they echoed flatly inside the small grey stone room.

"Oh, please." Guantes tucked the flask into his mantle. "You were a pitifully easy target. I'd have thought your father or your uncles would have taught you more caution. A shame for you that they didn't."

The insult to his sire and his uncles made Kai bite his lip, rage clouding his vision. He strained at the manacles that held him to the wall until blood ran down his wrists. "You are going to *die* for this," he snarled.

"Words, words, words. If I'd known that you dragons were so weak, I'd have acted sooner. So, tell me, would you like to sue for ransom? I imagine that we could send a letter to your uncle. In fact, hmm." Guantes began to pace thoughtfully, distracted by his train of thought. "It could be quite interesting to sow suspicion amongst your uncle's servants. We'd have to leave a trail suggesting that one of them compromised you, of course, and then I could even incriminate one of your older brothers, or possibly suggest the Library was behind it all, while at the same time selling information to . . ."

A man who was standing by the door coughed politely. He was wearing the same sort of clothing as Guantes, but cheaper, and in unobtrusive faded black. "My lord, the test?"

"Oh yes, I quite forgot. You may report to your lords that the dragon shows no sign of breaking free from his chains under severe provocation." He turned back to Kai. "You must excuse me. I do get distracted so easily. Tell me, who do you think would make the most plausible suspect?"

"For what?" Kai demanded, confused. He sank back against the wall. There was no point trying to reach Guantes. He could only hope the Fae would come closer again.

"Kidnapping you, of course. Oh, I know that you know I did it, but who else would? There's so much scope here, I wouldn't want to confine myself unduly. Perhaps the best option would be to wait until word gets out about your capture and then suggest that someone was impersonating me. Or maybe that I was an agent for your mother, and the whole thing was the first strike in a civil war against your father. Of course, there isn't actually a civil war yet, but we can work on that." He shook his head. "No, I must control myself. Stick with the current plan until it's fully carried through, as my dear wife keeps on saying."

Kai tried to laugh, his throat still burning from the brandy. He gathered his pride, squaring his shoulders and rising to his feet. "If you go so far as to offend my mother, the fate that I have in mind for you now will pale by comparison. You are a fool, and you are meddling in matters beyond your understanding."

"A very pretty speech," Guantes said. "I'd be proud of it myself. But allow me to point out that *you* are currently in chains, in prison, and far away from anyone who could possibly help you. Also, nobody knows where you are."

"A temporary situation," Kai retorted as he tried to ignore the hollow uncertainty in his belly. "My friends will come for me. My uncle will find me."

"Not here," Guantes said, with a certainty that conveyed absolute truth. "This sphere is deep in the chaos zones. Even if your uncle could find you, he neither could nor would come here, even to save your life. It would be an act of open war. Actually, the fact that you are here yourself could be construed as a provocation. The king of the Eastern Ocean's youngest son, deep in the heart of our territory."

Anger and fear fought with Kai's urge to roll his eyes. *"You kidnapped me."*

"Yes, that's true. I'd just have to make sure you were incapable of incriminating me . . ." Again he shook his head. "I suppose I can always save it as a last resort, if the auction doesn't go ahead on schedule."

"Auction?" Kai asked. Part of him still didn't accept that this could be happening.

"Yes, at midnight tomorrow." Guantes glanced up at the window openings in the wall high above. Thin, pale light shone through them, and it was impossible to determine the time of day. "You're to be auctioned off to the highest bidder. Very elegant, don't you think?"

"I'm going to kill you," Kai swore again. Anger and pride were the only things he had left to give him strength. "And if I don't, my friends will."

"But I've already told you," Guantes said mildly. "Dragons can't reach you here. Even

239

the Library won't help you."

"You know about the Library?"

"I know all the players in the game." Guantes turned and strolled towards the door. "And you, young prince, are in checkmate. Sleep well."

The door closed behind him with a hollow boom, cutting off Kai's last shouted defiance and leaving him alone in the cell.

Was it checkmate? Perhaps not. He had to believe there was still a chance, or he would despair. And if Guantes thought that the Library wouldn't help, then he didn't know Irene. She would still be in the game.

She had to be.

CHAPTER 13

Just as Irene had expected, the scene upon arrival was mayhem, and very nearly bloody mayhem. She stumbled out of the Train onto a long swaying platform, which extended far into the dark lagoon. The Train rested upon steel tracks, but there was no indication as to what supported those tracks, or if anything did at all.

The crowd from Aunt Isra's seminar conveniently surrounded Irene, and she took care to stay in the middle of it. Some elements were peeling off in an attempt to find their patrons or protectors, but others were holding their current position until the mob had thinned out. What with the servants, maids, piles of luggage, pet greyhounds, and a set of white Lipizzaner stallions, there was very little chance to see what was going on or to tell one group of visiting Fae from another. The platform was a riot of different costumes, almost all of them highly dramatic, and in the light of the high street lamps, it looked like a fever-dream: all colour, brightness, and no logic or sanity at all. The Library brand on her back was a permanent low throb of painful warmth, like sunburn, constantly reminding her of its presence. But, from the outside, she was just one more anonymous person in the mob. And, thankfully, nobody looked twice at her.

Theoretically, since this was a high-chaos alternate, she could wander into the crowd and meet exactly the person she needed to meet in order to rescue Kai and save the day. Stories formed easily here, and she would be just one more protagonist with a story to tell. On the other hand, she might wander into the crowd and be met by someone, such as Lady Guantes, who needed to meet her to continue their own story. And that could be catastrophic for Irene.

"Hey." The woman in cowboy leathers poked Irene's arm, taking her by surprise, and Irene suppressed a twitch of shock as she turned warily towards her. *They've caught me! No, wait, she just wants to ask me something.* "Clarice, was it? My name's Martha. Look, some of us are going to get a — what did they call them, Athanais? —

water taxi from here, and find the higher-ups later. I don't have to be with my lady until midnight, and I know where she's lodging. Can you get in touch with your higher-ups later? Where will they be?"

Irene thought back to the few comments Lord Silver had made. "He said the Gritti Palace," she said truthfully. *But it might be useful to have an excuse for wandering . . .* "But he might change his mind. What can you do?" She shrugged.

Martha nodded. Light brown curls the same shade as her leathers foamed round her face and fell over her shoulders, and her skin was tanned to precisely a few shades paler. "I've had a few like that, yes. But something else — you were speaking to Aunt Isra in Arabic earlier, weren't you? Are you good with languages — such as Italian?" Her question was more than a little desperate.

For a moment Irene wanted to laugh hysterically. Of course, being Fae didn't somehow make you omnilingual, though Aunt Isra had suggested the very powerful ones could get round that. The junior Fae here, low-ranking pawns of her own presumed level, wouldn't necessarily be linguists. "I do," she said. "Well enough to get by, at least . . ."

"That'll do. Hey, Athanais! Grab that boat!" The woman seized Irene's arm and began towing her through the mob towards the far side of the platform, where the waters lapped against it. Irene recognized some of the other students from the seminar there. "Clarice here can speak Italian!"

"Oh, thank god for that," Athanais said. Irene suppressed a sigh of relief. They weren't thinking twice about her, weren't even considering enemies in their midst. A sudden burst of distant fireworks shone on his pale hair. "None of us here speak Italian at all. Look, talk to this ferryman — what we want is a good tavern —"

"Bar," the woman in the business suit put in.

"My dear, we *must* have a clothing shop first," a woman in a black bikini said, sitting at the edge of the platform, her legs dangling knee-deep in the water. "I'm called Zayanna, darling," she offered, introducing herself to Irene. "I swear, had I been allowed to bring as much clothing as certain other people . . ."

Several small boats were floating on the far side of the platform. Some were gondolas, large enough to hold half a dozen, but others were slightly larger crafts with several oarsmen. The boatmen — *gondolieri?* — all wore black cloaks, domino masks, striped jumpers, and tricorn hats, as if it were some sort of uniform.

"Excuse me," Irene said, then switched to Italian. "Excuse me! Let me through, please." She edged up next to Athanais and quickly managed to negotiate a price for the six of them. Sterrington, the one in the business suit, was happy enough to pay, as long as she could have a receipt for it.

The idea of taking refuge in a tavern was sounding better and better by the second. She could use a stiff drink, and get her bearings and pick up local gossip before going back on the hunt for Kai. As long as the pack of seemingly friendly Fae didn't turn on her. She finished agreeing to the deal with the gondolier and shifted back to English. "Everyone aboard, ladies, gentlemen. We are getting out of here before someone high-ranking requisitions our craft for their pet elephant and we all have to swim to the bar."

There were chuckles, and the others filed on board the narrow boat. The remaining student was introduced as Atrox Ferox — an Asian Fae in black leather and latex plating. He had a sleek gun holstered at his side, and his face was chiselled and expressionless. Zayanna simply slipped into the water and swam up next to the boat, sliding an arm over the edge to hold on. Sterrington helped Irene on board before following her, and Athanais joined them.

The boatman stood to the rear, oar dramatically poised, and then the boat slid into motion, pushing away from the platform and heading across a lagoon into the city.

It was everything that a fairy-tale Venice *should* be, Irene decided cynically. The buildings were brick and marble, old and beautiful. They reared triumphant and agelessly out of the night fog, blazing with oil lamps and coloured lights. Farther in, she could see other boats — smaller gondolas — darting around with lamps hanging at their prows, and there were distant sounds of music and laughter. Farther away, someone screamed briefly and was silent.

"Look," Sterrington murmured, pointing back towards the platform they had just left. An ebony coach had come to a stop at the head of the platform, pulled by four black horses. A servant was helping a woman into it while other servants loaded her luggage. Even from this distance, Irene could recognize Lady Guantes.

"Do you think we should have stayed and tried for an introduction?" Athanais suggested. "There must have been a dozen ways we could have done her some small service —"

"Invasive," Atrox Ferox snapped. It was the first thing Irene had heard him say. His voice was like his face, sharp and cold. "One does not force one's attentions upon the dependant of a patron."

The woman in the water lifted herself to rest on the side of the boat, propping herself on one elbow. "That would be 'force one's company' rather than 'force one's attentions.' "

"Your correction is appreciated, Zayanna," Atrox Ferox said sourly. "One does not force one's company upon the dependant of a patron without that patron's permission. The sequel of a casual meeting would be more appropriate when it is arrangeable."

As she tried to unscramble his meaning, Irene found herself wondering if dragons had language issues as well. Was there a draconic language that they all spoke? And if so, could she learn it?

"A penny for your thoughts, Clarice," Martha said.

Irene looked for something innocent to say. "I was surprised that so many of us don't have immediate assignments. Could it be that our patrons were more concerned with the size of their retinues than with us being genuinely useful?"

Athanais, Martha, and Zayanna laughed. Sterrington's mouth twitched at the corners. Atrox Ferox stared, unspeaking, into the darkness.

Irene shrugged. "I suppose some things are the same everywhere." She was very aware that every attempt at interaction was a risk. But if she was going to get information out of them, then someone had to start the conversational ball rolling.

"Oh, look!" Zayanna pulled herself up on the side of the boat again and pointed towards the shore they were approaching.

"Yes," Sterrington said calmly, "the buildings are extremely impressive."

"Not that. Look at the people!"

There was a moment of silence. Now that they were closer, it was possible to get a good look at the people loitering along the pavements, even through the shrouding fog. Some were visible through windows, or in other gondolas, and the most obvious common denominator, Irene realized, was that they were all wearing *masks.*

"Is it Carnival?" Irene asked, her voice barely a whisper.

Martha shrugged. "It's Venice. So of course it's Carnival. Why didn't I *think* of that!" She slapped her hand against her thigh. "I need a mask!"

"We all do, or we're going to be obvious and out of place," Athanais said. "Clarice, you've got to ask our boatman to take us to a mask shop first. Please?" He made big soulful eyes at her. Again, she felt relieved that her cover as one of them seemed to be holding. For now, at least.

It's Venice, so of course it's Carnival. Martha's words echoed in her head. Venice as the dream, not as the reality. No wonder the water smelled pleasantly of salt, rather than of sewage or worse. No wonder they'd managed to catch a boat easily, rather than having to wait for ages and then haggle the man down.

Our best dreams — but our nightmares too? No, better not think that, just in case. Because what if thinking makes it real?

Irene informed the boatman of the change in plans, then smiled at the others. "It's nice to know you all trust me to do the talking." She hoped she wasn't pushing the casual nonchalance too far.

"If you can't trust a total stranger whom you meet on the train, who can you trust?" Athanais said lazily. "It's not as if we were plotting to murder each other's enemies, after all." Whatever his origin, he was apparently a Hitchcock fan.

"Of course not," Martha said quickly.

"Definitely not," Sterrington agreed.

"Quite absolutely not," Zayanna murmured.

"Such illegalities would be not thought of," Atrox Ferox said firmly.

The boatman politely waited for them all to finish exchanging quips before murmuring his agreement to Irene. At a very slight increase in price, of course.

"Clarice?" Martha queried. "What did he say?"

"What you'd expect," Irene said. "We'll be there in five minutes — ten at the most."

The others exchanged glances. "We're aware of the favour you do us by translating," Athanais said, his language becoming formal. "While normally we would be glad to owe you a favour, we can't be sure when we'll see you again — would you consider it sufficient payment for us to cover the mask and perhaps a drink or two?"

Just yesterday Irene had been worrying about accepting a coffee from a Fae. Now it seemed the Fae had just as much trouble with favours and gifts between themselves. "I would consider it a fair exchange, at least until we get to a good tavern," she replied. "Besides, we may run into each other in the future." *If I'm unlucky enough.* "We might as

250

well start our relationships on good terms."

Zayanna nodded. "It's funny how we keep on running into people we know, darling, though I suppose Aunt Isra would say it's only appropriate. Athanais and I are from the same sphere, second-upon-reticulation, third-by-response, and I met Atrox Ferox when he was visiting us in pursuit of a law-breaker at the order of his commander. And Athanais met Martha —"

"I think Aunt Isra may have been a little quick to judge us when she considered us all total novices," Sterrington added. Her tone was pure snobbery, but Irene wondered if she'd intended the undertone of sup-pressed violence.

The boat slid into a relatively small canal between two rows of buildings, perhaps five yards wide, with strings of blown-glass lanterns in different shades of blue and green gleaming above. Here, away from the open lagoon and amongst the palazzos, the fog hung in veils. It was enough to tantalize, but not enough to entirely conceal. Irene tried to track her surroundings, wondering how long it would take to get back to the bay if she had to make a fast getaway. Perhaps she could hire a boat and simply flee this particular city with Kai, once she'd rescued him from wherever he was being held. Then they could escape from another town farther down the coast? If there were any other towns down the coast, or anything else in this world except Venice . . . She wished she knew where the nearest library was.

A couple of streets — or canals — later, they were at the mask shop. It was amazing how much time six people could take choosing a mask, but they all managed to find something in the end, as the gondolier waited, no doubt raising the eventual fee higher with every passing minute. Irene's new garb included a pale Columbina half-mask with inset aquamarine glass, tied with blue ribbons. The bit she really appreciated was the big black cloak, with its large concealing hood.

With something hiding her from any wandering Guantes, Irene found that she could relax a little and pay more attention to the Venice around her. The place was far more alive than it had seemed from the train platform, out on the bay. Tiny lamps burned in little shrines along the canal banks, and sounds came from the tall houses and shops they passed — music, singing, talk, the screams of an argument, the barking of dogs. And the smells! Food, wine, wax candles, oil lamps, the scent of the open sea . . .

Zayanna had clambered into the boat and was more than willing to take up Irene's share of the conversation, leaving Irene to listen to the others and fret silently behind her mask and hood. All of this was useful cover, but Kai was still a prisoner — and time was running out.

At the tavern, Irene was delayed at the doorway by Sterrington, who was still happy to pay the boatman's bill, but wanted a fully itemized and signed receipt. By the time she'd negotiated this with the unenthusiastic boatman, the others had all managed to order drinks, despite their lack of Italian.

Probable lack of Italian. Irene wasn't entirely convinced they were all as ignorant as they claimed. It would be stupid to take their word for it.

"It's the local Prosecco," Zayanna said, presenting Irene with a full glass and tugging her towards a table that their group had commandeered. "Bottoms up!"

"You're really enjoying yourself," Irene said. They had all filled their glasses from the same bottle, so it was probably safe. She sipped. No immediate signs of being poisoned. She sipped again.

"It makes a nice change to get away from

253

all my wretched responsibilities," Zayanna said, with unexpected venom. "All those shrines to administer, all those snakes to care for, and when do I ever get the chance to have a few days off for myself? I'm always the one who has to milk the serpents while my master seduces the heroes. It's just not *fair,* darling." She took a swallow of the wine. It obviously wasn't her first glass.

"I wonder if they'd accept requests for a transfer here," Irene said thoughtfully. "From what Aunt Isra said, a sphere of high virtue like this could be quite . . . stimulating."

Athanais patted her hand. "Don't believe a word of it, Clarice. That's what they tell you, to encourage you to give your allegiance, but it never pans out. Look at me." He sighed. "Three times now I've been promised a higher place in someone's household, and has it actually worked out that way?"

"What we need," Sterrington said, tucking her wad of receipts back inside her jacket, "is a local informant. If we're going to parlay this situation to our own advantage, or our mutual advantage" — she glanced at Atrox Ferox — "or our superiors' advantage, then we need better information on how things stand."

Irene wanted to get up and applaud, but she restrained herself. "But would many local people know about — um, the reason for us coming here?" Irene wasn't sure if saying *the imprisoned dragon* out loud would be the proper thing to do. "And where would we find the right sort of people to question?"

She looked around the tavern, trying to answer her own question. As far as she could judge, the boatman had brought them to a good place — containing actual locals — rather than just a tourist trap. The other people drinking here, although also masked and cloaked, were wearing garments showing signs of wear, rather than ones straight out of a shop, like Irene's own.

"One should be careful," Sterrington said. "After all, in a situation like this, they'll have flooded the area with informers, who will be reporting on any suspicious behaviour."

"*They* being?" Martha enquired.

"Whoever is in power," Sterrington said calmly. "It's the sensible thing to do."

"That assumes that *they* have lots of informers to flood the area with," Zayanna said. "Good spies take such a large amount of the budget." She held out her glass for another refill. "Oh gods, it's so good to have something to drink other than mushroom wine! I swear that when our master told us about this trip, we were positively assassinating each other for the chance to go on it. I don't *care* about spies, dragons, or whatever. I just want the chance to be careless for once."

"Zayanna," Athanais started, reaching out to move the bottle away from her. "Perhaps if you took a little less for the moment . . ."

"Oh, let her drink," Martha said. "We've only got a couple of days here, from what I heard. We might as well enjoy it while we can."

"Is it only a few days?" Irene asked, trying to sound plausibly ignorant. "Even if the auction's tomorrow, there will still be socializing afterwards. That's what I was told, at least."

"Some people may be staying later," Sterrington said. "I'm not fully informed. But the Train itself will be leaving in three days. It can only stay that long in any given place. Is your patron going to be travelling back by some other route?"

"He might be," Irene agreed, her stomach falling again. So much for any thoughts of hiding Kai after the auction, then sneaking onto the Train once the metaphorical heat was off. Granted, the auction was the most urgent deadline, but this extra hurdle didn't help. "He doesn't tell me everything. It makes it hard to organize things." She shrugged.

"I'm surprised that you aren't with him, if you're his personal interpreter." Sterrington delivered the statement quite casually, but Irene felt the hackles on the back of her neck rise in warning.

She shrugged again, as casually as possible. "Oh, he doesn't need me when he has someone *else* to meet." She stressed the word to add a suggestion of an improper liaison and heated affairs. "I didn't want to get a flogging for impertinence, so I took myself elsewhere. As long as I'm back by dawn, I'll be safe."

"Oh, you're *that* sort of private secretary," Martha said, suddenly sounding extremely prim and disapproving. "I hadn't . . . realized."

Athanais rolled his eyes. It was perceptible even behind his scarlet leather mask. He'd stayed with a scarlet theme, to the point where Irene was tempted to ask if he was deliberately impersonating the Red Death, or if he was simply colour-blind. "Martha, dear, some of our patrons use a whip as discipline, some use a brand, and some use expense accounts, but let's not pretend that any of us has that much choice in the matter. If we'd wanted choice, then we wouldn't have sworn ourselves to a patron. Let's all just be grateful that we've the evening to ourselves. Clarice, do they do food here?"

"I can smell seafood," Irene said, trying to ignore Zayanna's sagging towards the table, and her muttering that nobody *cared* anyhow and it was all her patron's *fault* and she was going to slice his heart out on the sacrificial altar someday, just wait and see. "Let me go and ask."

Ten minutes later, shrimp with polenta had been negotiated, and the cheerful landlady, Maria (who fortunately spoke English), had brought round another bottle for their table. "Always good to have new customers in during Carnival," she said, with an approving nod towards their masks. "We may as well enjoy ourselves before it's Lent, eh? And I'll have you know that my little place is good enough to host the Council of Ten themselves —"

Martha was opening her mouth to say something, and Irene feared that it wasn't to say, *Yes, please do go on telling us all about your customers,* when the tavern door banged open. A man in plain livery entered, bowing as he did so and holding the door wide open for two more figures, a man and a woman in heavy black velvet drapes and matching silver-and-black masks. They entered together in a drift of fog and stood in the doorway, surveying the tavern.

Irene saw the crest on their mantles and was seized by an unpleasant suspicion. A pair of silver gloves, crossed on a black background. Her hands clenched on the table edge. Could the story have turned against her? Was this the part of the narrative where the heroine in disguise is confronted by her arch-enemies — or possibly where the protagonists find and dispose of the villainous spy, all depending on the reader's view-point? And the power of story had been so *useful* up till now . . .

"Now, will you look at that," the landlady said. She marched forward, dropping a floor-brushing curtsey. "My lord and lady Guantes. Welcome to my tavern!"

CHAPTER 14

"My dear." Lord Guantes led Lady Guantes into the room, seating her at one of the larger tables, before turning to the landlady. "We always enjoy your establishment, Donata. The usual, if you please." His masked gaze swept across the room, taking in Irene's table. He had a deep voice, bass though not basso-profundo, and his English had just a hint of an accent, though Irene couldn't identify it.

Everyone at Irene's table was scrambling hastily to their feet to bow in the general direction of the new arrivals. Irene rose with the rest of them, feeling her heart go through the floor.

That's it. I am totally doomed. Even if they don't call us over, the others are certain to suggest introducing ourselves. And Lady Guantes at least must know what I look like. She might even recognize me through the mask . . .

Her mind was whirring like a nuclear-powered hamster wheel, suggesting and rejecting plans at a speed that would have made Irene's supervisors proud. If she ever saw them again.

If this is really the Guantes' story, and I'm just a minor enemy character within it, this could happen — I get discovered and dragged off in chains, end of chapter. And it all finishes with a triumphant auction featuring a dragon, then a war.

She needed to leave. And for that, she needed a distraction.

Everyone's attention was still on the Guantes. Irene picked up her mostly full glass, murmured, **"Wine, increase in strength ten times,"** into it, and leaned across to switch it with Zayanna's nearly empty wine-glass.

Sterrington was turning to look at her. Had she seen?

Irene quickly picked up her own glass. "A toast?" she suggested.

"A toast to Lord and Lady Guantes!" Athanais agreed. Everyone picked up their glasses and drank. Irene watched out of the corner of her eye as Zayanna swigged with abandon.

"How very polite." Lady Guantes sounded positively mellow. "Donata, do send over another bottle of your best to that table over there."

Hadn't the landlady said earlier that her name was Maria? But she was nodding in agreement, without the slightest complaint. Perhaps, in this place, if you were human, you were a piece of stage dressing — and then your name was simply whatever the Fae chose to call you.

The group resumed their seats. "Should we go over and introduce ourselves?" Athanais said eagerly and predictably. "It would be courteous to thank them for the wine."

And you're on the lookout for another patron, Irene decided, *however much you're trying to put the rest of us off.*

"Proper courtesy would be to drink the wine and then present thanks," Atrox Ferox said curtly. "To thank without appreciation is not to show due regard for the gift."

Thank you, thank you, thank you, Irene thought silently as she nodded in agreement. She was watching Zayanna unobtrusively, but so far the other woman was resolutely upright.

"I'm surprised they came in here," Sterrington said. She glanced around the room again. "It's good, but I wouldn't expect it to be one of the best restaurants in the city."

She was cut off by Zayanna giving a long

gurgling sigh of satisfaction. The other woman carefully put her empty glass down, then slumped forward onto the table. *Damn. Overdid it.*

"I didn't think she'd drunk that much," Martha said, visibly distancing herself from the situation.

"Zayanna?" Athanais laid a long-fingered hand on her shoulder and shook her gently. "Zayanna, sweetheart, my little honey-flower, wake up?"

Irene glanced nervously over to the Guantes. They didn't seem to be paying attention.

"Perhaps some cold water," Athanais suggested tactfully. "Clarice, can you ask the landlady —"

"Stop shaking me," Zayanna slurred. "Gonna be sick . . ."

Perfect. Irene leaned over to slide an arm round Zayanna. "We'll just go outside for a moment," she announced to the rest of the table as Athanais flinched back. Apparently Fae chivalry didn't extend to situations where he might get his lovely new red velvet cloak messed up.

"A good idea," Martha said. She shifted her chair a little farther away, as Irene levered Zayanna upright and swayed under her weight. Over at their table, the Guantes were emphatically not paying attention, and the landlady was pouring their wine. Irene just hoped that meant the story was on her side tonight.

That's right, keep it up — just don't bother looking over here. Don't think of this as anything unusual . . .

"Madam." One of the other drinkers raised his hand to catch her eye, then pointed over at a door on the right-hand wall of the tavern. "That way goes out onto the alley outside."

"Thank you," Irene murmured. She assisted a staggering Zayanna over to the door, trying to ignore the woman's worrying groans. It might be poetic justice, but she didn't want vomit all down *her* nice new cloak, either.

Outside, the cool air was full of fog. It was even thicker now than during their boat ride to the tavern. The temperature seemed to revive Zayanna a little, and she leaned against the wall, swaying, as Irene looked round nervously. There could be anyone hiding here — on the rooftops, around the corner — and she'd never see them coming.

"Wanna go home," Zayanna mumbled.

"That's a bit far, I'm afraid," Irene said. "Take a few deep breaths and sit down. Let me help you." The alley was mostly free of refuse, and it was easy to find a fairly clean bit of paving. "Now just sit here. I'll get you some water."

"Don't want water." Zayanna's dark curls tumbled round her face as her hood fell back. "Wanna go *home.* Wanna be with all my sisters, preparing for dawn sacrifice. Wanna seduce a hero. Are you a hero, Clarice, darling?"

"Of course not," Irene said quickly as Zayanna tried to curl up against her. "I'm just like you. I'm just a woman with a job." She couldn't hear anyone following them from the tavern; the others must be trusting her to handle things.

Zayanna wasn't saying anything.

"Zayanna?"

The drunk Fae let out a soft sigh. Harsher critics might have called it a snore.

Right. This was the perfect moment for Irene to exit stage left and get well away before the Guantes, or indeed anyone else, took an interest. Really, she had to congratulate herself. Textbook stuff. All she had to do was walk off right now . . . And, her conscience pointed out, leave an unconscious woman alone in the street — at night in a dangerous city. A woman whom Irene herself had drugged. Various words came to mind for this sort of behaviour. They were not nice words.

But Irene had a mission, and Kai's life was at stake. Where was her sense of priority?

She bit her lip. "False dichotomy," she whispered, as if hearing the words would make them true. "There is no reason why I can't help both of them."

She shook Zayanna's shoulder. "Wake up, Zayanna. Where are you lodged? Where is your patron staying?"

Zayanna's eyes fluttered open for a moment behind the mask. "Gritti Palace. Like yours." She slumped again.

Well, that could work, for Irene had been planning to talk to Silver anyhow. Dragging Zayanna along and dumping her on the hotel staff would mean a little extra effort, but it would also, she assured herself, be good cover.

She's just a Fae, and you'll probably have to run or kill her if she finds out who you really are, her sense of expediency pointed out.

The thoughts wormed their way into her mind. But with a grunt she crouched down and slung Zayanna's arm over her shoulder before pulling the other woman to her feet. It was what Kai would have done. Probably. Even if she was a Fae.

The nearest canal was down to the left along the street. Hopefully there were frequent gondolas. "Shut up," she muttered to her inner critic, and staggered along, together with Zayanna.

They waited a cold, damp ten minutes that felt like twenty, Zayanna snoring gently against Irene's shoulder, before a gondola appeared. But he did seem amenable to a fare to the Gritti Palace.

"Perhaps the lovely visitor would care to pay first?" the gondolier suggested just as Irene was about to embark. He quoted double what the previous gondolier had charged to get the six of them all the way from the platform to the tavern.

"I was thinking of rather less than that," Irene said flatly. "About half that, to be precise."

The gondolier spread his hands. "Ah, but have you no pity for a poor man, madam?"

"Yes, I'm sure," Irene said. "Nevertheless, that's still what I'm offering."

"I'm sure the beautiful lady could give a little more," the gondolier said. "Otherwise I must leave her alone here in the mists, waiting for some other gondolier." He gestured at the fog meaningfully. The soft noise of waves lapping against the houses mingled with the faint echoes of singing and talking from the tavern. No other gondolas could be seen or heard.

Luckily, a figure two-thirds of his original price was finally sufficient. And she'd seen a purse under Zayanna's cloak. Hopefully there would be enough in it.

Irene supported Zayanna into the boat, and with a sigh of relief dropped her into the far end. Was it a gunwale? She should really do a remedial course on parts of boats one of these days. It would have been very useful if she'd done one before coming here. With a bit of fumbling she detached the pouch from inside Zayanna's cloak and opened it. Gold coins caught the light from the oil lamps along the canalside. She counted a few into the gondolier's hand, then paused when she saw his eyes widen in satisfaction.

"Madam," the gondolier said in his most melting tone, "beautiful lady, no doubt you are new to the city and do not yet know the exchange rates, but you have not yet paid me my full fee."

"You get the rest of it on arrival," Irene said, snapping the purse shut and sitting down next to Zayanna.

The gondolier must have decided that he couldn't milk any more from this tourist cash cow for the moment. With a sigh he pushed away from the alley, sending the gondola out into the middle of the narrow canal. The houses on either side loomed above them, almost frightening in their height and mass, but also oddly reassuring in their slightly ramshackle nature. This part of the city was real. Human beings lived here.

Within a couple of minutes the gondola swung left and out into the middle of a larger canal, sliding along faster now. The mists cloaked the buildings on either side; they were dark masses, huge and semi-visible, with the blurred brightness of lamps or lit windows gleaming like occasional jewels. Zayanna nestled into Irene's arm with a soft murmur, settling her head on Irene's shoulder.

Irene tried to calm herself by mentally framing her eventual report, but it wasn't working. She got as far as *I was planning to seek out my Fae contact and shake some more information out of him,* but thoughts of Kai were becoming increasingly urgent. She only had until midnight tomorrow. And exhaustion was starting to hit.

They passed under a wide stone bridge, and for a moment the lights beyond, few as they were, vanished. Irene's hand tightened on the side of the boat, and she forced herself to relax.

It wasn't the dark that bothered her — it was what might be hidden within it.

The gondolier hummed something that sounded vaguely operatic, and the gondola emerged on the other side. The mist was as thick as ever, but at least now Irene could see the lights in the distance. "Tell me," she began to frame a question to the gondolier, "is it always this foggy —"

Shadows descended from above, plummeting down in whirls of dark cloaks, landing on the gondola and setting it rocking violently. The gondolier swore, then crossed himself, and Irene sat up abruptly, letting Zayanna sag to one side. There were three of them: two in front of her, balanced on either side of the gondola, and one behind. She could see their boots and cloaks out of the corner of her eye. "What is this?" she demanded.

The gondolier crossed himself again, then frantically turned back to his oar, flinching away from the new arrivals. They might have been male or female. It was impossible to tell. They wore black: heavy black doublets and breeches, black scarves around their throats, black tricorns, and plain black masks without any ornamentation at all.

Zayanna cuddled sleepily up against Irene's side, dropping her head in Irene's lap.

"We are the black inquisitors," the one standing behind her whispered in Italian. The voice could have belonged to either gender. It carried the length of the gondola, before the fogs dampened the sound.

"The lords of the night," the one on her right whispered.

"The servants of the Council of Ten," the one on her left murmured.

"We come by darkness to put you to the question," said the one behind her, with a terrifying lack of inflection in that voice. The boat creaked as he — or she — shifted his weight, bending down towards Irene in a ruffle of heavy cloak. "And nobody will ask where you have gone, because they know better than to ask."

Irene swallowed down panic. Her first thought was, *They're just trying to frighten me. What's the best way out of this?* Her second thought was, *There might not be a way out.*

"I didn't do anything," she said, hastily, non-specifically, and untruthfully.

The two dark figures in front of her folded their arms, dark statues at either side of the boat.

A small sound came from the one behind her. It might have been the noise of metal

271

against leather, barely audible over the lapping of the canal. Imagination supplied the image of a knife being drawn. "Nevertheless, you will tell us everything you know — here or when we reach our destination."

Do they know who I am? Or am I just the unlucky tenth tourist who gets threatened by masked secret police? "Please tell me what you want to know," Irene whispered. She let an artistic wobble come into her voice. "I don't know this city — I only arrived today . . ."

"Lord and Lady Guantes entered an establishment." A creak as the figure behind her shifted its weight again. The voice, she thought a male voice, seemed closer now. "A few minutes later, the two of you left by the backdoor. Why? We want answers. You're going to give them to us."

So these were either servants of the Guantes or somehow connected to the city authorities. But the gondolier's reaction suggested the latter.

The canal seemed endless. The fog formed curtains on either side of the gondola, hiding drawn knives and muffling possible screams. They were in a little bubble of silence, in the centre of the canal, where nobody would see or hear what happened to them. Irene hadn't thought it was possible to be so alone in a public place.

"My friend was drunk," Irene said. She felt Zayanna's muscles tense against her leg. *She's awake. Or waking up.* "I had to get her out of there."

The two in front of her shook their masked heads in unison. "Not good enough," the one behind her crooned. "Such a noble lady and gentleman wouldn't be surprised by a little drunkenness. Let's hear something better, or you're for the Prisons." He lingered on the word, caressing it with his voice.

She could have tried knocking him backwards, but then she'd have been vulnerable to the two in front, and vice versa, if she'd lunged at them. They had the high ground, and she had nothing except the bottom of the boat to work with. "My patron and the Guantes have a feud!" It didn't take any effort to sound desperate, and it was almost the truth. "Yes, I admit it, I took an excuse to get out of there before they saw me — but they'd have made an example of me, to send a message. I had to run!"

"Plausible," said the one on her right, "but not proven."

"Notice that she isn't giving any names," said the one on her left. "I think she should tell us some names, don't you?"

"How about it?" Again the sound of metal on leather from behind her. "Tell us some names, woman. Tell us some *secrets.*"

Irene weighed the options. If she gave them Silver's name, then they'd question him, and he'd possibly sell her out to save himself. But if she just made up something at random, they'd probably spot inconsistencies, and she'd be in even deeper.

And she wasn't convinced they were going to let her go, anyhow. Whatever she told them. However much she confessed. "I can't say," she quavered. "I'd be punished."

Zayanna was tense against her thigh, muscles coiled under her cloak.

"Bah!" The one behind her kicked Irene square in the back, sending her sprawling in the belly of the gondola, trapping a suddenly squirming Zayanna under her. "Get the thongs and sacks —"

Tangled in her cloak, her mask slipping loose, Irene tried to get her hands underneath her, but Zayanna wriggled to one side and knocked her off balance again. She banged her head against the planking of the gondola and felt the man behind her plant his foot in her back, holding her down.

What she needed was a quick exit. And the only way out . . . was down.

The struggles, and Zayanna's thrashing,

would cover the noise. **"Boat planks,"** Irene commanded in a low whisper, her lips against the boarding, **"separate and come apart now!"**

It took more out of her than she expected; energy ran out of her like water gushing through a sudden crack in a dam. She barely had the strength left to take a deep breath, but the results were dramatic. The boat came apart, from front to back, with a sudden expelling of timbers in all directions that made her briefly think of exploded diagrams and cut-out-and-make-your-own-gondola pictures.

Briefly.

Then she was in the water.

Irene had been expecting it, which was more than anyone else had been. She was also facing down and ready to dive, while everyone else was standing or fighting. Her hands went to her throat to unclasp her cloak, and she kicked briskly at the water, diving deeper in an attempt to get away from the turmoil on the surface.

The water was cold — the cold of the open sea, fresh from the ocean that fed the city's tidal canals, and it was dark and full of silt. She had absolutely no idea which direction she was swimming in, after a few strokes, and could only concentrate on trying to get *away.*

Then something curled around her ankle.

Irene suppressed a scream, holding her breath, and kicked back at whatever — or whoever — it was, suddenly full of the energy of panic. She was running short on air, and while she was fairly sure she was moving away from the boat, that was where her certainty ended.

The thing — or person — grabbed at her ankle again. At the same moment her left arm hit something solid. She lost her focus, surging up to the surface in a sudden rush and emerging next to a building's foundations. She took a gulp of air, blinking the water from her eyes.

The scene before her was more audible than visual. The fog hid any pursuers from sight, but despite its dampening effects, she could hear the commotion. The gondolier was screaming threats and prayers, ranging from calling on the Virgin to swearing bloody vengeance on the bitches who had destroyed his gondola, but generally focusing on the loss of his gondola. Irene felt a twinge of guilt.

Zayanna popped up next to her, her head and shoulders emerging from the water like a classical statue. Her hair clung wetly to her cheeks and bare shoulders, and her eyes

caught the light and glittered in the darkness, her pupils slitted and inhuman. "Now,
how *did* you do that, darling?" she breathed,
her voice barely audible.

"Is this really the *time*?" Irene hissed back.
"Can we just get out of here first and
discuss things later?" Hopefully much later
— as in possibly never.

"It's you they were questioning," Zayanna
pointed out. "I wasn't involved . . ."

"Oh yes, and they're really going to believe
that, when they're looking for answers. The
only reason they weren't questioning you
yet was because they thought you were
asleep —"

There was a loud clunk and the sound of
running footsteps near where the action had
been taking place. Irene broke off and made
a vague swimming gesture with her hand.

Zayanna nodded, letting herself slide back
down. Together the two of them swam
quietly up the canal, keeping low in the
water, their heads barely above the surface.

A couple of hundred yards later, they'd
crossed two more canals and nearly been
run over by a passing cargo-boat, and Irene
was feeling far more tired than was normal
after a quick swim. "Stop a moment," she
wheezed, trying but failing to make a question of it. She'd lost her shoes somewhere

way back in the water, and she wished she were wearing a bikini like Zayanna. It'd make swimming so much easier.

"Just a teensy bit farther and we can get up onto the side of the street here," Zayanna called back. She easily swung herself up onto the paving stones, sitting on the canalside with her legs dangling in the water, her skin like liquid gold in the lamplight. Her eyes were normal again. "You're not much of a swimmer, are you?"

"It's more of an emergency thing," Irene panted. "At least I don't drown."

"Is that your only criterion?" Zayanna kicked at the water, splashing it into the fog in glittering droplets.

"You'd be astonished how many girls back at my old school *almost* drowned." Irene leaned her elbows on the paving stones, not quite ready to pull herself out yet. She was bone-tired. She wasn't sure whether to blame the exercise, the use of the Language, or the stressful circumstances. Possibly all of the above. She needed to sleep. Just for a little while. She couldn't save Kai if she was collapsing mid-rescue from lack of sleep. Even the cold water wasn't being much help. "There was someone every summer term who thought she could swim and then found out she couldn't. Not to mention the ones who fell through the ice. Swimming well enough not to drown was useful."

Zayanna tilted her head. "It sounds too, too dramatic, darling. Did they train heroes there?"

"Heroines mostly." The language teaching had been world-class too. Literally. "I wasn't one of them."

"So what's actually going on?" Zayanna raised her hands behind her head to wring some of the water out of her hair. "And how did you break the boat?"

This was probably not going to end well. "You probably heard what those men in black said," Irene said cautiously. "It's true that I was trying to get away before Lord and Lady Guantes noticed me. When you passed out, I took the excuse to leave. I admit it."

Zayanna considered, then shrugged. "Well, you *were* going to take me back to my hotel. I do remember that much. That was sweet of you. It would have been even nicer if you'd gone back for me after dropping us both in the canal — how did you do that again, by the way?"

"Trade secret," Irene said firmly. "Sorry."

Zayanna laughed. "I didn't seriously expect you to tell me! Don't be so silly. Clarice, this has been a *wonderful* evening, and as long as I don't actually get into any trouble for it from the Guantes or anyone else, I think it is going to be the beginning of a beautiful friendship."

The heat of exercise was wearing off, and Irene could feel the chill of the canal water settling into her bones. It made everything feel cold and distant, from her body to Zayanna's smile. *Aftershock,* she diagnosed herself. *Don't let it get to you.*

"I wouldn't mind that," she said, pulling herself together. And perhaps it could be true, after this whole business was settled and Kai was safe and everything was sorted out. Perhaps they could find a way to be friends, in spite of everything. *But she's Fae,* her common sense hissed at her as she tried to pull herself together. "But here and now we just need to get to the Gritti Palace." She heaved herself out onto the side of the canal. She was far less graceful about it than Zayanna had been, and she knew that she looked far less attractive too. Her business suit had never been made for this.

"Do look on the bright side, darling!" Zayanna squeezed her shoulder comfortingly. "We got away! Now *all* we need to do is break into one of these houses and convince the inhabitants they should escort us to the Gritti Palace. Maybe they'll even lend us some clothing while they're at it."

All right, Irene thought, *I have officially met someone who makes even more reckless plans than I do.*

"This could indeed be the beginning of a beautiful friendship," she agreed, and she couldn't help smiling.

CHAPTER 15

In the end, sheer exhaustion forced Irene to spend what was left of the night in one of the Gritti Palace's linen cupboards. She'd had to curl up on a pile of blankets, in a stolen dress, smelling of canal water. It was not the most uncomfortable night she'd ever spent, but it was still far from being an ideal Venice vacation.

The sound of bells woke her. The noise came through the walls of the hotel, even penetrating into the tiny cupboard, and she woke up with a start, banging her head against the lowest shelf and blinking in the darkness. It took a moment for her to orient herself. And the bells were still ringing, settling into their own patterns of speed and tone, somehow harmonic in spite of their lack of unity. She tried to count the strokes, in the hope of guessing what time it was, but there was no way of telling how long she had till midnight and the auction.

By the time she and Zayanna had reached the Gritti Palace, after a couple of minor incidents involving the theft of a pair of dresses, she had been so exhausted that it was difficult not to collapse on the spot. The time had been two or three in the morning, but the hotel was still full of lights and people running to and fro down passages. It had only taken a few screams of "Dear God, my husband!" and "Quick, hide behind the curtains!" for Irene to recognize all the ingredients of bedroom farce. Possibly several bedroom farces, all going on simultaneously. She hadn't wanted to go anywhere *near* Silver's bedroom under those conditions.

She and Zayanna had separated, ostensibly to find their respective patrons. Irene suspected that Zayanna had been more interested in finding some more alcohol. She couldn't blame her. She'd have been grateful for a glass or two of brandy herself.

Still. It was apparently morning. Time to sneak out of her little nest and find Silver, and hopefully get some more information out of him.

Once she was out of the linen cupboard, it became clear that, like most depraved aristocrats, these Fae did not rise early. And if there was a literary trope requiring an early start to fit in a full day's worth of debauchery, Irene had yet to encounter it. The only people up so far were maids, man-servants, and lower grades of attendant, who were running around carrying trays of food and piles of clothing. This made it very easy for Irene to scoop up a pile of sheets, look-ing suitably urgent and harried. She blended right in. She *felt* harried. Her dress was dark and battered, someone's Sunday second best, and not even up to the standard of the hotel maids, but her bodice was laced neatly and her hair was finger-combed into a tight braid. She didn't look anachronistic or otherworldly, and that was the most impor-tant thing.

The back stairs were much the same as in any hotel. They were narrow, cramped, and full of overburdened people running as fast as possible. Nobody bothered wearing masks back here.

One woman, blonde hair straggling in rat-tails down her back, grabbed Irene's arm as she staggered past. "Have you seen the sau-sages?"

"No," Irene said.

"Merciful Virgin, the cook's going to kill someone," the woman screamed, and ran down the stairs again.

Rich panoply of human experience, drama

284

of a Grand Hotel, et cetera, Irene decided as she hurried onwards.

She'd noted the servants Silver had brought with him the night before. Enough loitering back stairs enabled her to spot one, and to follow him to Silver's suite on the third floor. Irene waited until there was nobody else around, dropped her armload of sheets in a convenient window-seat, and knocked on the door.

Johnson opened it, and his eyes widened. He grabbed Irene by the shoulder and pulled her into the highly decorated parlour, slamming the door shut behind her. "You'll get my lord into trouble, coming here in public like this! What do you think you're playing at?" he hissed.

"Johnson?" Silver's voice drifted lazily through from the bedroom. "Who is it?"

Johnson took a breath and composed his face. He now radiated only mild dislike, as opposed to severe aversion. "It's *her,* my lord."

"Oh! Well, do bring the mouse in here. I have a few comments on her performance."

Without letting go of her shoulder, as if afraid she'd make a run for it, Johnson marched Irene through into the bedroom. It was a splendid room, even more so than the parlour. The walls were polished white plaster that shone like marble, and the floor was a mosaic of tiny pale wooden tiles. The far wall was all window, opening out onto a balcony that overlooked the canal beneath and the building on the other side. Curtains of thin lace were tied back, and the sun shone in. The fog had gone, and the sky was a clear, beautiful blue. The room itself was dominated by the double bed, which jutted out from the wall into the centre of the room, as if feeling the need to emphasize its presence. Silver sprawled on it amid a tangle of pale blue counterpane and white silk sheets, draped in a midnight blue silk dressing-gown that left him barely decent. Given the way he lay there with the gown falling open to his waist, Irene was tempted to down-grade that to not decent at all.

He shook his head, mock-sadly. "Dear Miss Winters, I thought that I had lost you."

"Rubbish, my lord," she said crisply. "I'm sure you were very glad to get me off your hands."

"The one does not preclude the other." He toyed with a plate that held sugared twists of dough, crispy little things. Cinnamon was involved. Irene could smell them across the room, and she tried to stop her stomach from rumbling. "So — I take it there have been no daring rescues yet?"

Irene hesitated. "That was a joke, I hope?"

"Sadly, yes." He raised one of the edibles to his lips and nibbled at it. "Hmm, very good . . . I do enjoy coming here. Such a safe, reliable place."

Those were not words that Irene would have used to describe this alternate at all. She raised an eyebrow and folded her arms under her breasts.

"Oh no, that won't do at all." His voice dripped with honey, as rich as an opera singer about to drop an octave in a single sweep of sound. "My lady, do forgive me for referring to you as a mouse. We're past such things. I feel that we're failing to establish any sort of proper communication here. I don't feel truly *needed,* let alone desired. This won't do."

Irene stood her ground. "Lord Silver." She tried not to grit her teeth, because if he sensed her impatience, she might never get answers. "If I rescue Kai, it will be of service to both of us, given your feud with the Guantes. I apologize if my manner doesn't please you, but I have some urgent questions."

He licked the remains of the sugar off his fingers. "I know you do, my little mouse. I know they're *very* urgent. I think I want to see just how urgent they are. On your knees,

287

mouse. Over here, please." He gestured to beside the bed.

For a moment all Irene could think of to say was, "What?" He'd flirted with her before, trailed his glamour at her like a peacock showing off his tail. But he'd behaved as he would have done towards any human being, rather than because he'd actually been *interested* in her. So it had felt comparatively safe.

"Now." Silver gestured loosely at the floor. "Oh, don't worry. I won't *do* anything to you, mouse. You're hungry, aren't you? Hiding all night, scurrying down the corridors . . ." He managed to make the words sound both beautiful and depraved at the same time, suggesting unspeakable things about the night and the corridors. "Let me feed you. Let me answer your questions." His eyes glittered — vicious, avid, hungry. "Let me see just how *urgent* your questions are, little mouse. Kneel. Or get out of here."

She was out of options, out of allies, and Silver was making it personal — clearly very deliberately making it personal. Maybe the novelty of humiliating a Librarian fed power to one such as him.

She set her teeth and did as she was told. The hem of her dress rustled on the floor as she spread it out in a dark billow, sitting back on her heels beside the bed. Johnson had moved across to stand by the door. *Standing guard? Or just not wanting to watch?* It was easier to try to analyse his motivations than to think about her own feelings.

"There. Much better." Silver rolled onto one side, bringing the tray of edibles with him, and lounged on one elbow, looking down at her. "It's good to know that you're sincere, my mouse."

Irene looked down at her hands, folded neatly in her lap. It was a matter of some pride that her fingers weren't clasped white-knuckled around one another, but instead lay perfectly still and calm, as though she were all serenity and self-control. The morning light through the windows was sharp and clear enough that she could see the small scars, thin white traceries, that curled up from her palms onto her wrists. They were memories of another confrontation with a monster far worse than Silver could ever be.

Yes. This was simply *petty.* Having her kneel, playing his little games. And why exactly would Silver be wasting his time trying to exert a petty domination over her? People who were actually in control didn't need to do that.

"Now, where were we? Oh yes. You had

some questions. Why don't you ask one of them."

"Where is Kai being held?" Irene asked.

"In the Prisons," Silver said readily. "Or, rather, the Carceri, as they're called here. They are one of the main features of this bijou little sphere, after all. I should have realized *that* was why the auction was being held here, besides just its location. Perhaps a better question would have been a more general one, hmm?"

Irene looked up at him, and she knew that her dislike showed in her eyes. "You can expect a number of things from me, but I hope you don't expect me to enjoy this. And I can't see why you didn't tell me that before."

"I didn't tell you previously because I didn't know," Silver said. "Messengers from the Ten were waiting at our hostelries to give us the news, to add to the drama. I suppose I might have thought of it myself, but it seemed rather extreme. The Carceri were built to hold our own kind. I would have thought that a normal dungeon would be quite good enough for a mere dragon prince. And as for you enjoying this, or not enjoying this, that's rather the point."

He picked up one of the small pieces of sugared pastry from his plate. "You see, my little mouse, I do need *something* from you. I am Fae, after all, and I can't sustain myself on honour and helpfulness alone. It's quite beyond my nature. Much as you'd like me to just answer your important questions. If I can't provoke some utter and absolute desire, then some thorough shame and hatred will do nearly as well. And I'll sense if I don't get it. Now open your mouth and let me feed you your breakfast —" He must have caught the way she flinched back from him. She was hardly attempting to hide it. "Or you can simply walk out of here and try to manage on your own. It's entirely up to you."

Irene had to take a couple of deep breaths to keep herself kneeling next to Silver's bed. Her hands knotted in her linen skirts as she focused on not slapping his face. "Can we make a bargain?" she asked.

"I'm prepared to listen." Silver held the pastry just above the level of her face, looking down at her with such an air of appreciation that he should have been licking his lips.

Irene rose to her feet. "Then I think I'll settle for the shame and humiliation." Anger ran in her veins, hotter than blood, and she looked down on him in disgust. "Yours."

"What?" He had to roll back on his elbow

to look up at her, and his dressing-gown fell open to bare a triangle of chest. Fragmented desire flickered in her as she responded to the power he radiated, but it was easily driven back by her irritation. "How dare you!"

Irene turned her back on him to walk across the room and seat herself in one of the chairs, taking her time about it and arranging her skirts neatly before replying. "Lord Silver. You addressed me as 'lady' earlier. I would prefer you to continue doing so, rather than treating me like a subordinate — and an inferior subordinate at that."

Silver's eyes caught the light like faceted gems as his face drew into an arrogant snarl of offended pride. "You were the one who came here asking questions," he snapped. "I don't like this sort of behaviour, Miss Winters. I don't like it at all." There was that lick of passion to his words again, stronger this time, as he focused on her.

But the fact that he was trying to bargain at all gave Irene the proof she needed. He wasn't in control of the situation at all — not in general, here in Venice, and definitely not here in this room with her. At this precise moment he needed her help far more than she needed his. And all his little games had been to try to keep her off balance, to stop her realizing that fact. She let herself smile. "Lord Silver, I don't care what you like or don't like. Right here and now, if I don't rescue Kai, Lord Guantes will triumph, and you are doomed. You can give me the information I want, and that might just save you. Or you can lounge in bed and eat pastries until the roof falls in on your head. It is entirely up to you. Because, to be honest, whether or not you meet a horrible fate at Lord Guantes's hands really doesn't *matter* to me. Kai matters. You don't."

He stared at her. And then he smiled. It wasn't precisely a nice smile; it was a suggestive curve of the lips, a hint of metaphorical teeth — an expression that left absolutely no humour in his eyes. But it was a smile. "My lady Winters, you are blossoming in the airs of this place, like a rose in spring. Do tell me what else you would like to know."

"Everything," Irene said drily. "But we'll start with these Carceri. I assume the name is more than just the word *prisons* in Italian?"

Silver swung himself upright, dangling his legs over the edge of the bed. "I don't know how much you little Librarians know about my kind," he started. "I will assume that

293

you have all the scandalous highlights, but very little of anything useful. So, to start by explaining this place: you know that as my kind grow in power, we become more true to ourselves?"

As in become walking stereotypes. Irene nodded in assent, choosing to keep her eyes on his face rather than look elsewhere.

"Well." He selected another piece of pastry. "Some of us become so great that we can no longer be confined by a single sphere or world. You know of the Rider, who brought us here?"

Irene nodded again. "And his Horse," she put in, to show that she was paying attention.

Silver shrugged. "That as well. But as we grow stronger, we can walk between worlds. They tremble at our passing." He smiled at the thought, and the morning light made his face beautiful in spite of his words. "At that level we can no longer touch or enter the shallower spheres, or we would break them — still less endure the small worlds that your friend Kai comes from."

Irene shivered, grateful that at least some worlds might be free from these most powerful of Fae.

"I am telling you this, my lady Winters, to explain another power demonstrated by our great ones. At our end of the universe, so to speak, where the forces of chaos dominate, some are so powerful that their power can permeate the very earth upon which they walk. In this way, they can instigate earthquakes, affect the movements of tides, and the like. The dragons think *they* control the elements, but we have our own methods of influencing our worlds."

Irene frowned, trying to understand. And she *wished* she had a notebook, to preserve all of this for the Library, assuming she made it out alive. "So this world — or at least, this Venice — hosts Fae with these types of powers?"

"Yes, you see you *do* understand. I felt I should warn you, in the interests of fair play." He smiled alarmingly. "Out here, in places that are more hospitable to my kind, the laws of the physical world are fluid, and the great ones can take advantage of that to bend them to their will. Even while the Fae here play at mortal politics, don't forget that their power runs through this world like the blood in their veins."

Well, that explains more about why high-chaos worlds are so dangerous . . . Am I contaminated? I managed to use the Language last night — but would I know if I was contaminated? Another thought came to her. "And is that why the atmosphere of this place is so injurious to someone like Kai? Just as you — as a being of chaos — would be hampered if you were in a world relying on order." And why hadn't these rulers noticed Irene herself? Was she too small for their attention?

"And there we have the second matter." Silver leaned forward, regarding her. "This particular sphere has two points that recommend it to many of my kind, including Lord and Lady Guantes in this case. Firstly, it is neutral ground for Fae to some degree, as the rulers of this Venice keep themselves above feuds with others of their kind." Irene would have liked to ask more about that, but he continued. "This is why the Guantes have managed to invite so many of my powerful kindred to their auction. And disagreements amongst those who are invited must be suspended on this territory. The Council of Ten — the great ones who rule here — are not under the orders of the Guantes. They merely assist, aid and abet them, while playing host to the rest of us." He raised a finger to stop words that Irene had not spoken. "But don't assume that this means that the Ten will welcome you too, pet. Quite the contrary. Be careful of whose attention you draw."

Irene suppressed a sigh. Just one more detail that he'd omitted. "This would have been useful if you had mentioned it earlier," she said. *Like when we were planning this.* "But I thought that, historically, the Council of Ten were just advisers to the doge, and he was the actual ruler when Venice dominated the area —"

"Oh, history," Silver said, cutting her off. "You'll be talking about reality next, as if it were something special too. In *this* Venice, the Council of Ten rule the city from the shadows, and all fear them. They play with one another's agents, just for the fun of it, but they always hold together against outsiders."

"And why are the Ten helping the Guantes?" Irene asked.

Silver shrugged. "While the Ten don't necessarily support the Guantes, they certainly aren't going to turn down a possible advantage. If there is a war, they'll be nowhere near it — the dragons can't reach them here. No, the Ten will let matters play out, and will gain from hosting the auction. It's a sensible choice."

"If you say so," Irene responded. It wasn't worth arguing. "But is this explanation going somewhere?"

"It leads directly to my next point," Silver

297

said. He swung to his feet, pacing in her direction. "The prison. Or should that be the Prison? Or the Prisons? The Carceri. They were designed by Piranesi . . ." He caught the look on Irene's face. "You're frowning. Perhaps in some other place and time, this Piranesi fellow spent his life making etchings of Roman ruins and kept his prisons imaginary. Here, they're real. They are the underbelly of this sphere's imagination, the foundation on which this city is built." He leaned in closer. "To create a city in constant paranoia, my pet, where spies watch each other and run around like rats, where everyone fears what lies behind their neighbours' masks, where you can post an anonymous denunciation every morning before the very Doge's Palace . . . Why, for that, my little mouse, you must have prisons. Dark, choking prisons, secreted in the attics or in the cellars. But even worse than that, even more frightening, are the prisons that lie *elsewhere,* in dimensions only accessible via passages leading down into the darkness, to great echoing rooms and long rows of cells."

His eyes held hers, and his voice was like silk against her skin, something trustworthy but tempting, impelling her to drink in his words rather than analyse and think. "In the farther Prisons, the Carceri, nobody will ever find you — because nobody will ever know where you are. There is no sunlight and no wind, only the movement of air from great turning wheels, which seeps down the long passageways and stairwells. There is no fresh water and no tides, only the deep pools of ancient water that will never stir. You'll find old stone, old timbers, old chains and racks, and all of it more enormous than you can imagine — older than time, and more patient than eternity."

His hand cupped her face, and he bent in to brush his cheek against hers, to whisper in her ear. "And if you are caught, my dear, that will be where they will take you, however much you scream and struggle, however prettily you beg, however desperately you fight." His voice caressed the words. "And they will keep you there until they have decided how best to . . . dispose of you."

She was drowning in his closeness, his presence, his hair like silk against her cheek, his voice in her ear, his hands on her face and her neck. Long, cool fingers that traced across her skin and left her shivering and faint. All her responsibilities pulled at her and tried to draw her away — the reason why she'd come here, the Library brand across her back. But all she wanted was to want what he wanted, to let go of the petty discomforts of reality and to fall down into his eyes, to see where that voice and those hands would take her.

Which was *not* going to happen.

She braced herself by holding on to all that she was — *I am a Librarian; I am Irene; I am not anyone's victim* — and dug in her metaphorical heels. Perhaps this was Silver's story. But it wasn't hers. She was not going to play his game. "Lord Silver," she said, her voice grating to her own ears after the soft velvet of his tone, "you haven't finished telling me everything I need to know."

"But do you really care?" He drew back a little, enough to look her in the eyes. "Wouldn't you rather . . ." He let it trail off, but the meaning was clear.

He'd rather spend his time seducing me than let me save him from certain destruction. And that really said everything one needed to know about Fae who had gone too far into their archetype.

Irene put her hands on his shoulders, holding him away from her. "Yes, I do care," she said. "And no, I wouldn't."

Silver drew back from her in a smooth flex of movement that she couldn't help interpreting as *elegantly muscular and seductive,* even if the functioning part of her brain labelled it as a flounce. "I could turn you in," he said. "The Ten would appreciate a Librarian spy to question." It was meant to sound like a casual threat, delivered from a position of power, but she saw the fear in his eyes, and it came out as a petulant complaint.

"And I suppose you'd say you lured me here to hand me over," Irene said. She kept her own tone balanced and uncaring. The one who cracked first was the one who would lose in this Fae game. And the stakes were too high for that person to be her.

"Well, of course." Silver shrugged. "And anything you'd say about me inciting you to rescue the prisoner would be dismissed as lies."

Irene let herself smile. "Then you wouldn't care that I would be accusing you of collusion with the dragons to rescue Kai," she said.

Silver stared at her. "Nobody would believe you."

"Ah, but we're in Venice." Irene shrugged, just as he had done. "You said it yourself. This is a city of spies and prisons. We'll end up in adjoining cells. If I go down, Lord Silver, then so do you. You have *everything* to lose."

301

A threatening silence filled the air between them, louder than any argument. Outside, the lapping of the canals and the distant ringing of bells seemed a thousand miles away as the two of them stared at each other.

He was the first to look away.

"You believe Kai is there," she said. Best to get the information and then get out of there, before he tried to challenge her again. "In those Prisons, those Carceri. Are they part of what this Venice offers to visitors? The ideal prisons to hold one's enemies?"

Silver shrugged. "So I believe. I haven't been in there myself, needless to say. They say that the Carceri could hold ones who are far stronger than me. I am sure your dragon would be a mere flyspeck within them."

"Then where in Venice are they?"

"If I knew, my lady Winters, then I would tell you, but unfortunately I don't know. The Ten consider it, shall we say, *inappropriate* to share that sort of information, and I have to say that I see their point. But all my sources do agree that you can only reach the Carceri from somewhere here in Venice."

Then there was little point wasting her time questioning him further. "So, Lord Silver, to summarize: Kai is somewhere here, in a prison that can be reached only from this city, but you don't know where the entrance is, or how to get in, or what the conditions inside may be — except in terms that a pseudo-Gothic melodramatic author would consider overblown. And you are, I presume, unwilling to be of any further assistance, in case it is traced back to you. Though if I *am* caught, we both know Lord and Lady Guantes will assume that you were to blame anyhow."

"Accurate on the whole," Silver agreed. "Except for that comment on my prose style."

"Well, in that case, Lord Silver . . ." Irene considered her immediate needs. "I require a pair of shoes, a cloak or shawl, some money, a knife, and directions to the nearest large collection of books. Given all that, I will do my best to avoid contacting you again."

Silver frowned. "Is that bribery, my lady?"

Irene rose to her feet. "Merely pointing out our mutual advantage, Lord Silver. You will no doubt be watched, if the Guantes suspect you. If I stay well away from you, it's safer for both of us."

Silver considered, toying with the collar of his dressing-gown. Finally he said, "You may be right, my lady. Johnson! See to all of that, if you please. And one more thing."

He took a step closer. "I wasn't speaking in jest when I said the airs of this place will be antithetical to your dragon. As a Librarian, you are neutral to it, and you're wearing the tokens I gave you, which shield you a little. The dragon is purely antagonistic to this world. Once you release him, you had best make plans to remove him from this sphere as fast as possible. And yourself, too."

"I don't intend to stay," Irene said flatly. "This place may be your ideal holiday destination, sir, but it is hardly mine."

Silver shook his head sadly. "Someday, my lady, someday." He gestured towards Johnson, who promptly filled Irene's arms with a bundle of fabric. "Johnson, is that . . . ?"

"The requested items, sir," Johnson said tonelessly. "And the most appropriate library for this person's wishes will probably be the Biblioteca Marciana — that is, the Library of Saint Mark." He rattled off a list of directions, and Irene frowned as she committed them to memory. It was close — well, fairly close — to the Piazza San Marco, and if she remembered correctly, that was the main city square. This could be good, or it could be bad. At least it should mean large crowds.

"That will do," Silver said as Johnson fell silent. "My lady, kindly excuse me. I have a full morning ahead of me, and you have roused me early, so I may as well take advantage of it." His smile contained nothing specific to which she could take offence, but it managed to imply a dozen things, all of them sensual.

"I'll be on my way, then," she said, as silence filled the room.

"If you truly need me," Silver said, "I will be at the opera later today, at the performance that precedes the auction. Look for me there."

"Let's hope I don't have to," Irene said bluntly. She turned away from him, making for the door.

Johnson held it open for her. He leaned in towards her. "Get him in trouble," he hissed, his tone suddenly sharp, suddenly *human*, "and I'll kill you."

He slammed the door behind her.

CHAPTER 16

The first thing Irene did was get some food and a cup of coffee. Well, that was her initial *objective*. First she had to pad her new shoes until they fitted, wrap her new shawl round her head and shoulders, hide her new knife (small but sharp) and her purse, then make her way to the Piazza San Marco. She'd find a horde of cafés there, and she needed to scope out the area near the Biblioteca Marciana.

Her fingers brushed the jade pendant again. She only had until midnight. The sense of urgency that goaded her on made any wasted time feel criminal, even stopping for food. But, unlike the Fae, she was still human, and had human needs.

The Piazza San Marco was only a few hundred yards from the Gritti Palace. Irene confirmed her status as a new arrival by standing still the moment she entered it, nearly being run over by the people behind her. It was . . . It was so full of *light*. The huge public square had what must be the Basilica at one end, topped with bulbous domes and covered with marble and mosaics. It was imposing and glorious and, yes, utterly beautiful. The light flowed around it as if it had risen from the waves, and it blazed with gold and colour. To the right of and joined to the Basilica there was another huge building. It was rectangular, more prosaic, despite its pastel colouring. It was built from marble in shades of pink and white, which would have looked trite or washed out under English sunlight, but in the Venetian morning light, it glowed, triumphant and powerful. Other buildings lined the sides of the Piazza, and a high belltower stood in the middle, constructed from fluted red brick, topped with marble and bronze. It was also at least a hundred yards tall. Well, it might have been a little shorter, but it *looked* at least a hundred yards tall. Last night it had felt as if she were drowning in the omnipresent water and mists. Today, in the sunlight, it felt as if she were floating on them — as if all of Venice were floating.

The square was full of people. And with this many people, what were the odds on someone spotting her as an impostor? *Too high for comfort,* she thought.

Her destination was just off the main piazza, with the Doge's Palace on one side and the building that should be the Biblioteca Marciana on the other side. There were also plenty of small cafés there, which gave her an excuse to sit down with a cup of coffee and a roll, and think.

Irene could see out onto the lagoon from her table. The wide space of open water was bordered by Venice itself on one side and the Lido islands on the other. The Train was a dark stationary streak in the distance, lying across the water on its impossible track, gleaming like a midnight black centipede in the brilliant sunlight.

She watched the crowd and the people using the Biblioteca Marciana. She listened to the conversations around her as she planned and scoped out escape routes. She couldn't expect anything more from Silver. But, with any luck, she wouldn't *need* anything more from him. The Biblioteca Marciana should give her access to the Library. She then needed to find these Carceri where Kai was being held, then somehow get him out and make a run for it.

She stared into her nearly empty cup, letting herself settle into the ebb and flow of Italian around her. It wasn't one of her best languages, but full immersion was helping. She could already distinguish a discussion about the scandalous goings-on at a local convent, even if the precise meaning of certain nouns was a little vague.

Looking up, she surveyed the Biblioteca Marciana. It wasn't as tall as some of the other buildings, and she could count a ground floor, a first floor, and a gently slanted roof that might hold a second floor, or at least an attic — all of it in smooth pink-and-white marble picked out with gilding. A pillared arcade surrounded the building, and she could see a balcony featuring yet more pillars on the first floor, these connected by arches. Friezes were carved into the gleaming marble, showing heraldic beasts or heads with swags of foliage beneath them. Any attempt to get in through the windows or over the roof would be painfully obvious, which meant using the main door. But, given the crowds doing the same, she shouldn't stand out.

As she walked towards the entrance, she couldn't banish the image of herself as a tiny beetle walking across a human's exposed skin. Learning how far the Ten's power extended throughout the city had given her an extra sense of paranoia. And indeed, as greater Fae, they might perceive

309

her through the very pavements of the city. *How sensitive are the Ten anyway, and can they sense me? Would they care about me, or am I instant anathema to them? Do I itch, and would they scratch?*

Irene shuffled up a huge staircase of gilt and stucco, just behind a group of young scholars loudly discussing Petrarch. She walked past marble pillars and windows that looked out onto the piazza below.

Here and there people sat at desks, carefully turning the pages of manuscripts, or unrolling scrolls and making notes. It comforted her. *This is a place built to store books, by people who wanted to preserve books, and used by people who want to read those books. I am not alone.*

She finally stepped out into a large reading room. The sudden sensation of space and emptiness made her pause, and she looked up to see the ceiling more than two floors above. On the two higher floors, open galleries surrounded the space, fronted with balustrades. But behind these, she could see bookshelves and doors leading farther into the depths of the building. That was what she wanted.

Fifteen minutes later, she had *finally* managed to find a way up to a quiet section

310

amongst those stacks. And to a storeroom. That would do nicely. This was a library; that was a door — all she needed to open an entrance to the Library proper.

She took a relieved breath, forced herself to relax and focus, and said in the Language, **"Open to the Library."**

And nothing happened.

Her first reaction was the basic annoyance that accompanies something as simple as sauce not coming out of a bottle, or a website not loading on the first attempt.

"Open to the Library," she said again, focusing on each individual word.

Her voice fell into nothingness. There was no feeling of change, of *connection*.

This time panic curdled in her stomach. She'd never been in an alternate where she couldn't reach the Library. She hadn't thought it *possible* to be in an alternate where she couldn't reach the Library.

Except that she'd never ventured so far into chaos before. And in the Library itself, she belatedly recalled, doorways to high-chaos alternates were sectioned off and chained. Access was barred because these were simply too dangerous. And if they were blocked at the Library end, did that mean they were inaccessible from this side too?

"Open to the Library!" Irene snapped,

her voice sharp with terror.

There was no answer.

She clung to one of the shelves on her right, and her fingers bit into the wood hard enough to hurt. *I'm trapped here,* she thought. This wasn't a fear that she'd even considered before. It was new and horrifying, an abyss suddenly opening right in front of her feet.

Someone coughed from behind her. "This is an astonishing place," a woman's voice said, "but I do think that you're neglecting the more interesting parts."

Irene's fingers dug even harder into the shelf as she turned to see who had spoken.

Lady Guantes was standing there, serene in a deep green gown, her hands gloved in white. She had Irene covered with a pistol. Like most guns that had been pointed at her, this one looked far too large. It was turning out to be one of those days, after all. Lady Guantes was holding the pistol in what looked unpromisingly like a professional grip, with both hands on the stock.

Should I pretend to be an innocent local? It might be worth a try.

"I should point out that I said that in English," Lady Guantes said. "Any attempt to convince me that you're an innocent local should take that into account, Miss Winters."

Irene had always felt that one of the most important strategic virtues was knowing when to concede a loss. "I just can't stay away from a good library," she said, keeping to English. "It's an addiction with me. Do you have the same problem?"

"Please don't try to be funny. It was only logical that you'd come to the biggest local library to look for help." The gun didn't waver. "And if you try to say anything that sounds peculiar, rest assured that I will shoot."

Which meant that using the word *gun* in any context would probably result in immediate injury. A pity. Saying something along the lines of **May your gun explode in your hand** sorted out so many of life's little problems.

There was a pause.

"It's difficult for me to speak freely when you might shoot me at any moment," Irene pointed out. "But I assume you don't want to shoot me, or you would have done so already."

"You're very casual about your safety," Lady Guantes said. She still had that gracious air of approachability and common sense that Irene remembered from the

313

railway station, but there was something new. *Nervousness? Could she be nervous? Of me?*

"There are degrees of danger," Irene said. If she kept talking, perhaps she could figure a way out. Silver had described Lady Guantes as weaker than Lord Guantes. How did that stack up against a Librarian? "There's immediate peril of death, which is one thing, and then there's immediate peril of a fate worse than death, which is something else again. And then there's the less-immediate fear of potential death. And all scenarios should be handled on a case-by-case basis. I'd rather talk than do something irretrievable. Do you feel the same way?"

"You're a Librarian." Lady Guantes put the same delicate disgust into the word that someone else might have used for *mercenaries, colonoscopy,* or *mad dogs and Englishmen.* "Letting you do so much as talk is dangerous."

"You might at least explain what you want, then," Irene suggested. If the other woman was talking, then she wasn't shooting.

"I beg your pardon?"

"Well, I'm sure you have a motive for being here." Was Lady Guantes keeping Irene covered until backup arrived to take her into custody? Or was she simply opportunistic, with a pistol in one hand and an enemy in front of her, and no idea what to do next? "In my place, wouldn't you be curious?"

Lady Guantes raised an eyebrow. "Are you suggesting you're open to an alliance?"

Irene shrugged. "I want to know what the stakes are, and what's in play. You've heard of us. You know we're usually neutrals and only interested in books. Why *did* you set your thugs on me?"

"On which occasion?"

Irene blinked. "There was more than one?"

"Two, actually. The first time was after the book auction you attended. I wanted to see how you and the dragon would handle an assault. It convinced me that I needed to separate you before kidnapping him. The second time was a bit more off the cuff, I admit."

At least that explained why those hired thugs had been so inefficient. "More casual? It felt quite serious at the time."

Lady Guantes sighed. "That was your own fault. You and the detective moved too quickly. If things had worked out as I'd planned, you and Mr. Vale would still have been trying to find out where the dragon was by the time the auction had taken place here. His family would have arrived to investigate the world from which he was kidnapped, and you, as his superior, would have ended up taking the immediate blame for his disappearance. That would have embarrassed the Library, and kept them off balance and on the defensive when the war started. Of course, the dragons would have known we were ultimately responsible, but my husband and I would have been well out of their reach by then — and they'd have welcomed a scapegoat or two. As it was, I had to hire some muscle in quite a hurry. It isn't the way I like to operate. If I'd known I was going to have to kill you eventually, I could have hired a sniper well in advance. It would have been so much tidier."

"If the dragon's family had come to investigate, that world being his last known location, it would have had very serious consequences for that world — not just for Vale and me," Irene pointed out.

"I wasn't planning to visit it again."

A little trickle of cold fear worked its way down Irene's spine. But it mingled with a growing anger at the implications of the woman's words. Ao Shun had made it clear that they would destroy Vale's world if they held it to blame for Kai's disappearance. And Lady Guantes clearly knew it. Irene could almost admire the woman's thoroughness in covering her trail, but at the same time was revolted by her sheer cold-bloodedness.

And now she had absolute confirmation from the woman's own mouth that she was involved in Kai's kidnapping. *I'm not here for vengeance,* Irene considered. *But I certainly wouldn't mind making sure she never tries such a thing again.* "So you don't want to kill me now," she said, keeping her voice even and biting back her fury.

"Well, obviously not, now that I've got you here," Lady Guantes said. "You're much more valuable alive."

"As an ally?" Irene said hopefully.

"It's not impossible."

"Or . . . ?" She let the sentence trail off, to see if it would get a response.

"As a Librarian, certain people would find you interesting. As yourself, Miss Winters, certain other people would find you even *more* interesting." She smiled in a way that suggested the whole question was far too unpleasant for nice people such as them to discuss.

Irene blinked. "I'm astonished," she said. "I had no idea I had such a reputation. In fact, I had no idea I had any reputation at all." There had been a few encounters with

317

Fae, and there had of course been the whole business with banishing Alberich — who was indeed a dangerous and notable traitor. But she hadn't thought it was the subject of casual gossip. It made her feel rather exposed.

Lady Guantes looked a little embarrassed. "Well, 'notorious' might be more accurate. But please don't take it the wrong way. It's a compliment."

"I'm flattered."

"And it does make me wonder why you're *doing* this." She turned that serene, understanding gaze on Irene again. "Self-defence is one thing, but this spontaneous expedition deep into our territory isn't what I would call sensible. And you do seem a sensible woman, Miss Winters."

Irene shifted her weight a little. It didn't draw any reaction from the levelled gun. *Good, she isn't going to shoot me for twitching.* "So if we both appreciate common sense — what is your motivation in this?"

Lady Guantes didn't hesitate. "A better world for everyone."

"Really? When you may be about to kick off a war?"

"The whole *point* is starting a war," Lady Guantes said firmly. She didn't even try to dress up her reasoning as glamorous or attempt to weave a seduction, as one might expect from a Fae, but simply presented her case as the only obvious solution. "Our side may not win outright. But by the time we reach a truce, many more spheres will be under our influence. This will be good for the humans. It'll be good for us. We're not going to interfere with you — you're welcome to go on stealing books on the sidelines. And do you really care about the dragons? More than caring about this single dragon, that is?"

"I thought we were both going to be sensible," Irene said. "You can't say you're going to start a war and then suggest that I'm only here because I care about a single dragon. Just how immature do you think I am?"

Lady Guantes shrugged. "True, that sort of narrow motivation is really the sort of thing I'd expect from the more *highly focused* of my own kind. Let's consider a wider view-point." The gun didn't waver. "You Librarians are interested in stealing books for your own purposes. Something to do with stabilizing worlds, I've heard. You're not interested in allying with either us or the dragons, as all you want to do is collect stories. Stay out of our way and you won't get hurt. You've got nothing to gain by meddling in this, Miss Winters."

Is she genuinely trying to convince me? And if she's playing for time, what's she waiting for? "I have yet to see how it would benefit humans to live in a world such as this Venice," Irene replied.

"Ask the people out there," Lady Guantes said. "They're happy."

"They're . . ." For a moment, Irene wondered if she really *should* be talking about "humans" as if she were somehow different from them. "But they've just become part of this place's story. The moment one of your kind interacts with them, the humans lose their volition, their freedom. Their *life.* In your world, the humans are just background characters."

"But such happy background characters," Lady Guantes objected. "Oh, I admit that not all stories have happy endings, but people prefer what they're used to. If you were to actually ask them, nine out of ten would prefer a storybook existence to a mechanistic universe where happy endings never happen."

"Really?"

"Would you believe I actually organized a survey?" Lady Guantes looked smug. "Not in this world, but I think my point holds. People want stories. You should know that more than anybody. They want their lives to have meaning. They want to be part of something greater than themselves. Even you, Miss Winters, want to be a heroic Librarian — don't you? And if you're going to say that people *need* to have the freedom to be unhappy, something that's forced on them whether they like it or not, I would question *your* motivation." She paused for a single deadly second. "Most people don't *want* a brave new world. They want the story that they know."

"Thank you for explaining that," Irene said politely. "It really does help to understand your perspective on the situation."

"My pleasure," Lady Guantes said. She shifted and glanced behind her, but too quickly for Irene to take advantage of the moment.

"Basically, you're utterly convinced of your own righteousness," Irene went on quickly. If Lady Guantes was waiting for reinforcements, then Irene was running out of time. "You're a smug zealot who's willing to destroy entire worlds in order to get what you want. And you want to control humanity, and have convinced yourself that they'd be happier that way. And what persuaded *you* to follow your foolhardy plan — was it Lord Guantes?" She took a step forward.

"Stay there!" Lady Guantes ordered, her voice suddenly sharp for the first time. Her hands were rigid with tension through her gloves.

"Why are you so nervous, madam?" Irene gave her best smile of faint superiority, the one that conveyed — in spite of all evidence to the contrary — that she was totally in control. "Are you telling me that you and Lord Guantes aren't equal partners? Where *is* he?"

"Negotiating with the Council of Ten," Lady Guantes snapped. "Don't come any closer!"

"And you didn't get invited too?" Irene probed.

The flash of fury in Lady Guantes's face said it all. The emotion only showed for a moment, but it was there, as corrosive as acid. "My presence was not required," she said.

"Perhaps I should be the one offering *you* a job." Irene shifted her position again, a little closer. She was almost in range now. "After all, Silver said . . ." She trailed off invitingly.

"What did he say?" Lady Guantes demanded.

"We discussed you and Lord Guantes. Your power imbalance, that sort of thing."

Irene spread her hands innocently. "He was the one who told me that you were nothing but a tool for your husband —"

"That piece of vermin doesn't understand, and could never understand!" Lady Guantes cut her off. A high flush of anger gave her face colour as Irene finally hit a nerve. "He sees everything through his own perspective. He doesn't understand that, without me, my husband would never have been able to bring this to fruition. My husband *understands* that and he values me —"

In one quick movement, Irene slapped the gun barrel aside.

The gun went off. And the bullet thudded into a row of books somewhere behind Irene and to her right.

The next few seconds were an undignified scuffle. Lady Guantes might be an excellent formal shot, but Irene had experience in informal fighting-dirty. She was left with the gun, and Lady Guantes was left nursing a wrenched finger and a stamped-on foot. "I could scream," she panted grimly.

"You could," Irene said, "but that still leaves . . ." She glanced down the corridor. No sign of anyone yet. "That leaves me holding *you* hostage. How important are you to the Ten, Lady Guantes?"

Lady Guantes was silent. Not that important, apparently. Finally she said, "You're making a mistake, Miss Winters."

Pure adrenaline was running through Irene's veins. "I think of it more as disaster management," she answered. *I could ask her where the Carceri are. But would she tell me, even if she knew? Even if I threatened to shoot her? It's not worth revealing what I know.* "Don't try to follow me for a few minutes. For both our sakes, if you please."

Lady Guantes stepped back, signalling surrender. There was a very nasty set to her mouth, and the space between Irene's shoulder-blades developed a whole new itch as she walked past the Fae. *Does she have a knife, and is she about to use it?* But there were no knives, no screams of warning, and no shots from hidden second guns. However, every step out of the library took minutes off Irene's life, as she scanned back and forth for pursuit or Fae backup.

Finally she found her way out onto the *piazzetta*. Fantastically brilliant sunlight sprayed down on her and the crowd as she mingled with it, and, just then, the sound of running feet came from the direction of the Doge's Palace. It was easy to turn and look, since everyone else was turning to look, and she saw a squad of black-uniformed men trotting through the crowd, as bystanders melted out of their path. Walking briskly next to a man in gold-trimmed uniform, presumably their leader, was Sterrington.

Irene sighed as she turned away. Well, clearly she hadn't been quite as convincing last night as she'd thought. She couldn't even blame Sterrington; after all, she *was* here to spy too.

And now I'm trapped, if escaping via the Library isn't an option . . . No, she would not *let* herself despair. She had a job to do, and just because one escape route had been ruled out didn't mean that others didn't exist.

The alley rose into a bridge that crossed a small canal, and she looked down the canal towards the open water of the bay. The wide span of glittering water seemed to stretch out forever, but across it lay the black line of the Train and its impossible railway.

I need an escape route. The Rider might not help me . . . but what about the Horse?

CHAPTER 17

At first Irene had expected that people would be shunning the Train and its platform like a plague ship complete with rats. But as she came closer, she saw that a steady stream of visitors was forming a busy crowd around it.

"Do you know what it is?" she asked the middle-aged woman next to her in the crowd. The woman was clutching a tray of lace kerchiefs to her bosom, and her greying hair was pinned back with merciless precision under a cap of the same lace.

The woman shrugged. "Some new ship from out down by the Sicilies, I heard. They topped it with metal because of the volcanoes."

Irene nodded meaninglessly. "And all those rich folk on board must have money to spend."

"Where are you from?" the woman asked. Now that she was actually looking at Irene, her eyes were uncomfortably shrewd. "You don't sound local."

Probably not. Irene had learnt her spoken Italian from an Austrian who'd learnt the language in Rome. The best she could hope for in terms of Italian accent was *unidentifiable.* "My brother Roberto and I used to live in Rome," she invented.

"Rome." The other woman turned up her nose a little. "Well, I suppose people have to live somewhere."

Irene quickly lost her in the press of the crowd, to her relief. That was the problem with asking questions — people asked them back.

It was easy to mingle with the people moving forward to ogle the Train, and a simple matter to file out onto the platform and join the vendors supplying the crowd of curious townsfolk there. It really did seem to be a bit of a tourist attraction. And the Train itself stood quiet and ominous, the sun gleaming brilliantly on its dark steel body and flashing off the windows.

Irene pushed herself forward, insinuating herself through the mob. "Excuse me," she said to a man with a tray full of pastries. "Pardon me." She circled round an elderly gentleman offering a set of supposedly holy relics, and found herself pressed up against one of the Train's doors.

"Excuse me," she said to nobody in particular, and tried the handle. It turned smoothly, and she stepped up inside the Train with a sigh of relief, quickly closing the door behind her.

It had changed. Now the corridor was all smooth ebony panelling and dark pewter metalwork, and the windows were shaded glass — so dark-toned that it was barely possible to see outside. And all sounds from outside were cut off. The flood of people ebbed and surged silently outside, their faces and hands like pale froth on the surface of a shadowy sea.

Irene took a deep breath. It was time to do something thoroughly reckless. **"My name is Irene,"** she said in the Language. **"I am a servant of the Library. I would like to speak with the Horse."**

Her words echoed in the carriage corridor like whip-cracks and left a tense silence behind.

Come on, come on — at least be curious enough to find out what's going on . . .

With a sound like an exhalation, the door at the far end of the corridor slid open, moving smoothly in its grooves. It was probably the closest thing to an invitation that she was going to get.

Irene began walking down the carriage towards it, but she couldn't reach it. The carriage was longer than it should be — not seemingly longer, but *actually* longer, stretching out without any clear markers of distance or space. She always seemed the same distance from the door, but never made any progress.

All right. Perhaps this was a test. Was it like every other Fae she'd had to deal with here, wanting to interact with her on its own terms? Through a fictional lens? As a story? But this time *she* was going to tell the story.

"I know how these tales go," she said, still walking, slipping back out of the Language and into English again. "The woman buys nine pairs of iron shoes, and nine iron loaves, and nine iron staves, and she walks the length and breadth of the earth until the shoes are all worn through, and the staves are as thin as matchsticks, and she has eaten up every last scrap of the loaves, and only then does she find what she is looking for. But this is a different story."

The door was abruptly ten paces closer. Still out of reach. But closer.

"Once, in a long-distant state, there was a horse that galloped across land and sea . . . ," Irene began. She remembered the story well enough from Aunt Isra's gathering. It was a standard myth, and that was part of its power. She kept on walking as she recited the story, and the door still stayed the same distance away: too far for her to reach, but close enough to tantalize.

Finally she came to the end. "From world to world he rides, from the gates of story to the shores of dream, until the world is changed and the horse is freed." She let the words hang in the air for a moment. "Until the horse is freed, the story says, which means that there must come a point when the horse *is* freed. And it must mean that the horse *can be* freed."

The door jumped forward again in another blink of perspective. It was right in front of Irene now, almost close enough for her to walk through, but every step kept it one pace ahead of her.

Cold sweat trickled down her back. *It's listening to me. I'd better be able to give it what I'm promising, or this particular narrative is going to get very messy, very fast.*

"Of course," she went on, "in this story the heroine doesn't necessarily know exactly how to free the horse. But the horse can usually point her in the right direction. Removing a collar, for instance, or undoing a bridle. And of course there's usually a reason *why* the heroine wants to free the horse. You only get a kind-hearted heroine who unties the horse just because it looks unhappy in certain stories. I don't think this is one of those stories."

The door stayed at the same distance from her.

"So, the story . . ." Irene stopped walking. Without the sound of her footsteps, the corridor was even more ominously silent. **"The young woman was in a strange land, and she looked around for help, for . . ."** It should have been *her true love* — that would have been one of the standard modes for a story of this type — but that wasn't true of her and Kai. *Even if there was wishful thinking on that subject. But that didn't matter.* She couldn't risk a lie. Not if she was speaking in the Language.

"The king's son had been stolen, and she had come across land and sea to find him, in borrowed shoes and a borrowed dress, with no true friend at her side." The words stung in her mouth, true in their way, yet also just a story. It was like eating sherbet and feeling it pop in her mouth and rattle in her skull and ears. Her head was buzzing with it. **"And she said, 'I shall rescue him from the prison where they have kept him, and together we shall flee from his enemies and stop**

a war.' But she was sore afraid, for the whole city would rise to pursue them once the king's son was free from his prison."

It was harder now. Irene had never tried this before, never *thought* of trying it before. But the Language was a tool, and her will was behind it, and this place was fragile, weak, easy to force. She wasn't telling any lies. She was just telling the truth in a different way. **"And as she walked down to the sea, she saw a chained and bridled horse, and said, 'Would that I were as swift as you, so that we could escape!' And then the horse spoke to her, saying . . ."**

It was as if she'd been playing a violin solo before, and now the rest of the orchestra came in on the beat, in a sudden weight of music that pushed down on her and shuddered through her body. She flung out her arms to either side to brace herself on the walls of the passage, struggling for breath as the crushing pressure seemed to catch at her chest, forcing her to breathe in its rhythm. The air in the passage shivered like the surface of a drum.

"FREE ME FROM MY BRIDLE AND REINS," the voice shuddered around her, so loudly that she could barely make out the separate words, "AND I SHALL BEAR YOU OVER LAND AND SEA TO YOUR OWN HOME."

Irene was opening her mouth to say yes without even thinking about it, carried along by the flow of the story, but then she dug in her mental heels and struggled to form different words. She had to set up this bargain to get what she needed. Once it was struck, there would be no chance to go back and renegotiate. Although the Train was still and unmoving, the sound of spinning wheels and clanging engines echoed in her ears, as if it were straining to haul some distant weight. **"Most noble horse,"** she finally forced out, **"I thank you for your offer. I beg that you allow me to go and find the prince, and, when I return with him, I will free you. And you will bear us both back to the land from which we came."**

She'd been afraid of chaos contamination before. She'd been touched by it in the past, had it running in her veins, and it had nearly crippled her before she'd forced it out. What would it do to her if she made a bargain with this creature?

"YES . . ." the voice breathed around her, in a vast exhalation that physically tore at her hair and clothing, dragging her forward so she could no longer keep her balance, but went stumbling through the doorway before her and into the next carriage. Her back, her wrists, and the pendant round her neck all seemed to be burning. Her Library brand, Silver's bracelets, and the pendant from Kai's uncle — each an object of power in its own way — were struggling with the new bond she had willingly undertaken. She wasn't in a train carriage; she was falling into darkness, and she was burning . . .

I have to limit this. Irene was on her knees, but she couldn't quite remember why, and she was shaking so hard that it was physically painful. **"And then we will part and go our own ways,"** she rasped, her voice strange even to her own ears, **"free of all obligation, and with no further bonds between us!"**

The pressure lifted a little, and any release was a blessed relief: Irene's perceptions became functional again. She was *almost* in pain, but not quite.

She stole a glance down to her wrists, where the gold chains of the bracelets showed under the cuffs of her dress. No physical burns. The sensible part of her mind hadn't really expected any, but she had to be sure.

There was now a mask lying on the carriage floor in front of her. It was one of the

334

white full-face masks, with the eyes outlined in black and gold, and lips painted on in red.

Irene picked it up. The black ribbons for fastening it trailed limply from her hand. "Why this?" she asked.

"SO THAT THE RIDER MAY NOT SEE YOU," the great voice whispered. It seemed to be making an attempt to modulate its volume, and Irene could only be grateful. "GO NOW, RETURN WITH THE KING'S SON, AND SET ME FREE . . ."

If this goes any further, I'm going to have so much stuff hung on me that I'll look like a Victorian Christmas tree with extra gingerbread. But it would be useful to have a new mask to conceal her face. Without too much hesitation, Irene raised it to her face and knotted the ribbons behind her head.

Nothing unusual happened. It didn't feel strange. Really. At least, no more than any new mask would. No odd prickles or excessive heat or cold. Nothing at all. She was probably just being paranoid.

"I need to get to work," she said, surprised at how prosaic she sounded after all that shouting. "Thank you for your pledge."

Beside her, the carriage-door swung open onto the outside world, and the noise of the crowd and the city came flooding into the carriage like a living thing, with the sound of distant bells tolling the hour making the hubbub seem almost musical.

Irene abruptly realized that the sun had set, and the sky was dark. The crowd was still present, but now it was lit by torches and oil street lamps. She swore to herself. It was *evening.* She'd lost half the day. And she still had to find Kai.

There was one thing she hadn't tried. She sidled through the crowd till she found a shadow to loiter in, then reached into her bodice to pull out the pendant, dangling it from its chain. **"Thing of dragons,"** she murmured, **"guide me towards your master's nephew."**

The pendant began to spin. It was like an unfocused compass needle confused by a magnet, turning without stopping, as if one more revolution would help it find the right direction. As it spun faster, it began to whine: a thin, high noise like a mosquito, but slowly lowering down the octave towards normal hearing. Its motion grew choppier, jerking at the chain, but still unable to settle on a direction, and Irene could feel a growing heat from it.

"Stop!" she whispered hastily, before the pendant could destroy itself due to the place's chaotic nature, or draw attention from the Ten, or both. She let it dangle for a moment to lose its heat before slipping it back into her bodice.

Damn it to hell. *That* wasn't going to work, and hunting across Venice for the Carceri was no longer an option; there simply wasn't the time. She was going to have to intercept Kai at the opera house, and pray she could handle the Fae who'd come to see the show.

CHAPTER 18

Irene strolled away from the crowd, trying to think of options besides the drastically overdone and hideously dangerous. Her preferred form of book heist — or, rather, *borrowing* — involved a significant amount of time scouting out the area first. Book-collecting activities (as opposed to dragon-rescuing undertakings) usually involved befriending people whom she could pump for information. She also regretted the lack of money with which to bribe guards, a good cover identity, an escape route, and all the little things that made life so much easier.

She was just not used to operating on this sort of shoestring basis, and with no *time* to strategize. That was the hell of it. They'd have Kai on the auction block at midnight. And the chances of scoping out a top-secret prison in time seemed slim at best. Oh, perhaps a heroine might manage it, if the story was in her favour . . . but Irene couldn't depend on that.

She watched the crowd and let herself reflect on what she'd just done. She'd made a pact with a Fae. Not just a convenient co-operative arrangement of the sort she'd organized with Silver, but an outright bargain, promised in the Language. She just hoped there wouldn't be consequences from the Library. Young Librarians were always warned not to deal with the Fae at all, let alone make formal deals with them. And Irene hadn't broken the letter of any ordinances — she hoped. She'd just jumped up and down on the spirit of them, then taken them down a dark alley and made some pointed suggestions at knifepoint. Saving Kai and preventing a war might save her — but only if she was successful.

There were bells everywhere, echoing through the streets and along the canals, filling the air with sound. The people around her, both masked and unmasked, crossed themselves at particular notes, and Irene tried to match the action without too obviously copying it. The air was cooler, and decent women had drawn their shawls around their shoulders against the evening chill, while the more indecent women strutted with bared shoulders and nearly bared breasts. The last fragments of sunset streaked the sky with orange and pink, like folds of silk showing through a grey velvet outer layer of cloud. This morning the city had seemed to float on the water, rising out of it like a particularly architectural Venus in pink-and-white marble. Here and now, as twilight gathered and people whispered, it seemed on the verge of sinking into the smoothly shifting reflections.

But there was more to it than that. With the evening came a more definite sense of suspicion within the crowded squares. Perhaps she'd been blind to it earlier, in the brilliant sunlight, surrounded by the daytime sounds of work and enthusiasm. But now, in the twilight, with the bells echoing in a constant susurrus of minor tones, she felt . . . watched. Observed. Spied upon.

Eyes glinted behind masks, and people murmured to one another in corners. And every time she passed someone, she had an urge to look back and see if they were watching her.

Irene paused to buy a penny's worth of sugared nuts from a street vendor and asked casually, "Which way is the opera house from here?"

"Which one?" the street vendor asked, tugging his apron straight with a weary sigh.

"La Fenice?"

Yes, that was what Aunt Isra had said. And it was one of the biggest and most spectacular opera houses in Europe in a large number of alternate worlds. Where else would one auction off a dragon at midnight? "Yes, if you please," she said eagerly.

"Ah, now that isn't far," the vendor said, and rattled off a string of directions. "Say a prayer to the Virgin for me as you pass her church, young lady, and I hope that you have a good evening."

Irene hoped so too, as she smiled behind the mask and continued on, tucking the packet of nuts into an inner pocket. She would gladly have eaten them, as she was feeling famished. But she couldn't eat anything without removing her mask, and she didn't feel like tempting fate that much.

As she came closer, she realized there was no chance of getting lost. She only had to follow the noise.

She heard the roaring crowd outside La Fenice well before she saw it. This was not one of those cities — such as the many versions of London — where people queued up politely before major cultural events. The mob was a heaving, swirling mass of people. *Good. All the more cover for me.* Soon she was lost in its wild enthusiasm, enthusiastic anticipation, and anticipatory friendliness — all of it containing just a hint that things might go over the edge if the crowd became *too* excited. Men in uniform surrounded the opera house and stood along the bank of the canal, and several nicer-than-usual gondolas displaying coloured pennants were moored alongside.

Irene was again grateful for her mask, and she was far from being the only masked person in the crowd. Both men and women, well-dressed or more poorly clad, had covered their faces, and the last of the sunlight turned eye slits into dark, suspicious hollows.

She drifted inconspicuously into the rear of a medium-sized group of unmasked men and women who were sharing bottles of wine and loudly discussing the main singers in the night's performance. "How long till it starts?" she asked one of the men.

He squinted at her a little blurrily, passing his bottle to the woman next to him. "In five minutes, darling. They're already tuning up for the overture. We won't have a chance to get in until the interval. Were you waiting for someone?"

No chance of getting in round the front, then. She'd have to try the stage door around the back, or wait for the interval.

And this must mean an actual *opera* was about to be performed — it was an opera house, after all. Maybe it was a warm-up for the auction to come? A bit of casual eavesdropping made it clear that the group was expecting *Tosca,* and gave her some additional information on the performers, their voices, and their personal habits. "I think I see him over there," she murmured as she sidled away from the group.

It took fifteen minutes to circle round to the back of the opera house and find the stage door. It then took several coins from the money that Silver had given her to bribe her way inside.

The backstage corridors were functional rather than beautiful, and full of people — the chorus, stage-hands, guards, runners, and two men carrying a stage dummy on a stretcher with a dramatic bloodstain over the chest. It was no place for a bystander, and Irene made her way to the front of the house as quickly as she could. It was all marble and expensive wood here, a far cry from the more pragmatic backstage. She could see a wide staircase and a brightly lit foyer with paintings and frescoes, but she stayed in the shadows.

She'd been able to hear the music quite well backstage, well enough to recognize that they were into the first act, but not that far in. She needed to get a sense of the place's layout. And if she happened to overhear guards talking about incoming deliveries of dragons for an auction at midnight, so much the better.

The back of her neck prickled; someone was watching her. She turned slightly to glance unobtrusively over her shoulder, and saw that a man was indeed coming down the corridor towards her. Wait, not just any man. He'd been one of the people at the stage door when she came in, loitering there along with half a dozen others.

Over twenty years' experience kicked in as she began to stroll casually down the corridor away from him. This was not a coincidence. She'd been spotted, which suggested that he'd been at the door to watch for her in particular. This was very definitely not good. She needed to get rid of him — either lose him or get him alone in a dark corner, knock him out, and slip away — then change her appearance as much as possible and stay out of view.

The corridor ahead branched right and left. Irene chose left at random, turned, and nearly bumped into another man. "Excuse me," she murmured in Italian, ducking in a quick curtsey.

"Grab her," the man from behind said, his voice pitched just loud enough to reach them, but not the boxes or the auditorium. He had an unpleasantly professional tone.

Damn. Irene converted her curtsey into a straight punch into the closer man's stomach, stepped past him, kicked the back of his knee as he bent over, off balance, and ran for it as he went down. This was too public a place to stand and fight.

She heard the sound of pursuing feet as she ran down the corridor, mentally plotting the quickest route round to the backstage passages. Left and down should work. She grabbed the door-frame as she swung into a turn, her shoes skidding on the marble floor. There were no convenient doors to lock, no tapestries or carpets to throw in her pursuer's way.

In desperation, she snatched the packet of nuts from her pocket and threw it behind her. **"Nuts, burst!"** She heard a noise like tiny firecrackers going off as fragments of sugared nuts sprayed in all directions, and a curse as the steps behind her stuttered. Even if they hadn't done any damage, having a packet of nuts go off at ground zero must have startled him.

The passage bent farther left, and she saw a stairway just ahead of her. Almost there.

Then Sterrington stepped into a doorway to her right. Irene recognized her business suit and the mask she'd purchased yesterday. She was holding something in her right hand, but it was too small to be a gun and too dull to be a knife. Irene decided to keep running, until the screaming jolt to her muscles took her completely by surprise. She went down in an uncoordinated lump and stayed down, her whole body spasming with shock.

Oh. Right. A Taser. Sterrington must have come from a world with that technology. Irene's mind framed curses, but her tongue and mouth were numb.

"Pick her up," Sterrington said to the two pursuers, who had caught up with them. "Carefully, please."

"Do we need to get her identity checked?" the professional-sounding pursuer asked. "The werewolf said he'd confirmed her smell, but if we take the wrong person to his lordship, he'll be annoyed."

"No need," Sterrington said. "I can confirm her identity, even with a new mask. Bring her this way."

Irene hung like a rag doll between the two men as they draped her arms over their shoulders, supporting her between them. She was unable to raise her head as they trailed Sterrington back along the corridor, and Irene's feet scraped along the floor.

Sterrington was heading towards the entrances to the boxes, rather than backstage. *So I'm being handed over to someone.* Irene's stomach sank. She tried to remember how long recovery from Taser shock took, and wished it were faster.

She could hear the music again. A tenor and a soprano were singing a duet, the tenor swoopingly romantic, the soprano allowing herself to be convinced. It was almost incendiary in its intensity. Irene vaguely remembered that La Fenice had been burned down once or twice in some alternates and wondered if this one had also gone up in smoke and been rebuilt.

It would make such a good story, after all . . .

Sterrington paused outside the door to a box. She reached across to touch Irene's chin, tilting her face so that Irene could see her clearly. "You do understand that this is all professional?" she said politely. "Nothing personal, Clarice."

Really, on the whole, it was one of the nicer things that had been said to Irene when she was drugged, Tasered, or otherwise unable to reply. But her inability to reply prevented an angry response, rather than the polite *Of course, I quite understand,* which Sterrington seemed to expect.

Sterrington nodded. "Later, then." She knocked on the door, a light rap of her knuckles, then turned the handle and held it open for the men to carry Irene in.

The box was dark, of course. All the light in the theatre was on the stage, and the boxes on either side were unlit, each one a secretive little world of its own — thick with curtains and dense with luxury. For a moment the sheer spectacle of the view took Irene's breath away. The opera house was *magnificent.* Even in the darkness she could admire the network of white boxes along the theatre walls, the pale frescoed ceiling so very high above, the blaze of the high chandelier, and the way the seats below were filled — no, *packed* full — with all the citizens of Venice.

There were two wide wing-backed chairs in the box, turned to face the stage. She couldn't see who, if anyone, was sitting in either.

Then the chair nearer the stage turned, and Irene's heart hit rock bottom as she saw who was sitting there. She wasn't stupid; she had been suspecting it, but she would really have preferred for it to be anyone else. It was the Fae whose photo she had seen on Li Ming's computer, the man she'd seen meeting Lady Guantes at the Train and with her at the tavern. Lord Guantes. And she was shut in an opera box with him.

"Miss Winters, I believe." His voice was soft and deep, with a hint of command to it. He spoke in English. "Please come and sit down."

The two men carried Irene across to the other chair and deposited her in it, before bowing to Lord Guantes and leaving. The door clicked shut behind them as a cannon sounded in the orchestra pit and the noise shuddered through the theatre. There were screams from the audience. Irene tried to work her mouth again, and this time she had a little more control as she considered her options. The strategy of collapsing the whole box and trying to escape in the confusion was tempting, but the concept had some obvious flaws in its execution.

Lord Guantes gave her five minutes of peace, watching the action on the stage and listening to the singing. Then he turned to her. His dark grey silks and velvets faded into the shadows of his chair, and his gloves concealed his hands, leaving the impression, for a moment, of a floating face. *A floating skull.* "Please do relax. We have a number of matters to discuss. You are by no means doomed. I don't want you to panic, Miss Winters. Or would you prefer me to call you Irene?"

Should I fake being incapable of speech or movement? Not much point — he'd just wait for me to recover. "I would prefer Miss Winters, at our current stage of familiarity," Irene mumbled, her tongue thick in her mouth.

Lord Guantes nodded. "I am wary of your capabilities, Miss Winters. I hope that you will excuse the conduct of my servants, but frankly, after you managed to reach this world and avoid my men for hours, I would rather not take any risks."

Irene jerked a nod, and felt a momentary pang of sympathy for Sterrington for being described as just "a servant" and being blamed for not taking her prisoner sooner. She could feel Lady Guantes's gun pressing reassuringly against her leg through her skirts, though she knew that she didn't have the motor control to use it yet. *Careless of Sterrington — I'd have searched me, if I'd been the one taking prisoners.*

"My wife sends her compliments, by the way," Lord Guantes said. He was looking at Irene instead of the action on the stage. "She was impressed by your determination. She had been assuming you were the junior partner in your relationship with the dragon."

Which means he probably knows I've got her gun. "And I was impressed by her ability to track me," Irene said politely. Her speech was less slurred now, which was a relief; she could manage the Language if she had to. "Is there any particular reason why she isn't with us tonight?"

"She is keeping Lord Silver under house arrest," Lord Guantes said. "And waiting to see if you'd come looking for him. Now please, Miss Winters, do describe your relationship with Silver." There was that undertone of command to his voice again, resonating unnaturally in her body — like a physical shove, prompting her to speak.

"I intended to blackmail him," Irene said boldly. It was a bluff and she knew it, and he knew it, but the surge of his personality demanded some sort of answer. If Silver's powers lay in seduction and glamour, then Lord Guantes's clearly lay in control and forced obedience.

"Blackmail? Lord Silver?" Lord Guantes blinked. "You astonish me."

The singing on-stage cut off as someone made a dramatic entrance, but all Irene's attention was on the Fae in front of her. "It astonishes you that I could be an expert

351

blackmailer?"

"Not at all. It astonishes me that Lord Silver could have done anything for which he might be blackmailed. I don't suppose you'd care to share it with me?"

"Absolutely not. It's far too useful."

"Hmm." Lord Guantes turned his attention away from Irene, looking back at the stage. "I would say 'a likely story,' but clearly you are going to stick to it. Very well. Would you like to ask me any questions?"

"Well, yes," Irene admitted. "But I'm surprised that you'd be willing to answer them." If all he wanted was to dispose of her, then why sit and chat, and why allow her to regain her voice? It was hardly a sensible way to treat a dangerous enemy.

He smiled. "Miss Winters, I could say that I am in such a position of overwhelming superiority that giving you answers is nothing to me. But I feel like starting our association with honesty." He glanced at her for a moment, and Irene felt her inferiority washing over her like a wave as he took in her shabby dress, her borrowed tokens, her weakness. She knew it was his power bearing down on her, and that helped her to push it away, but even so, it left her feeling small and grubby. "I intend to recruit you — a tame Librarian would be quite a coup

— and you will be far more useful as an informed operative."

She was painfully conscious of the minutes until midnight ticking away, but she'd take any opportunity to gather information. "As I understood it from Lady Guantes, you intend to start a war."

Lord Guantes waved a hand casually. "Either we start a war, in which case we benefit. Or the dragon's family sacrifices him, and then I am owed a favour by whoever purchases him, in which case we benefit again. I have nothing to lose."

"I'm surprised you're so certain of victory," Irene said.

"Of course." Lord Guantes's tone practically patted her on the head. The word *patronizing* could have been invented to describe its nuances. "However, Miss Winters, I have access to substantially more information than you do."

"More than the Library?" Irene tried.

"More than a very junior member of the Library."

She had to admit that he might have a point there. "So why did you target Kai in particular?"

"Because my information showed he was of sufficient rank to serve as a cause for war, and he was in a vulnerable location. I wouldn't have tried to kidnap him from his own father's sphere. Dear me, no. Should he survive this, and one day be returned to his father's care, I don't think he will be allowed to wander so freely again." He reached over to a small table and picked up a glass of brandy, taking a sip from it in a way that closed the question.

On the stage, Scarpia was confronting Tosca. But it was only the first act — onstage and in the box. And she had to make Lord Guantes think she was weakening. "Why do you dislike Lord Silver?" she asked.

He raised an eyebrow. "I hadn't thought *you* liked him."

"I don't. I'm quite happy to blackmail him. But I was wondering what your reasons were."

He chuckled, deep in his throat. Again there was that note of patronization to it, as though she'd said something charming in its innocence. "My dear Miss Winters, I was born to rank, myself." Again that airy gesture of his gloved hand. "And, as befits my status, I have a purpose, Miss Winters. A duty. An obligation . . ."

"To start a war?" Irene suggested before she could stop herself.

"Quite." He favoured her with a thin-lipped smile. "As opposed to Lord Silver, who is a simple dilettante, placed in a position quite outside his capabilities and ignoring it once there. He offends my sense of the proper use of power."

Scarpia's voice rang through the opera house in a grand crescendo, and Lord Guantes's eyes glinted like flint as the light caught them.

"And now, Miss Winters," he said, "we come to the question of you."

CHAPTER 19

"But I believe it's about to be the interval," Lord Guantes said, glancing at the stage and releasing her from the weight of his gaze. "Can I trust you to sit quietly and refrain from making a disturbance, Miss Winters?"

Irene considered the possible chain of events. *I scream and claim assault. He calls in the guard. My identity is revealed. I get arrested and marched away to prison.* "Yes, of course," she said. She tried to make it sound casual, as if she were in control.

It didn't work. She could tell from the way Lord Guantes relaxed as the chorus onstage went into a dramatic Te Deum. *He knows he's got nothing to fear from me.* And he seemed genuinely interested in recruiting her. But why? Kai was far more important than she was.

She looked out over the audience as the curtains closed. The lights around the auditorium flared brighter as the gas was turned full on, and people broke into a low roar of conversation. A flood of those in the lower seats drifted outside, but most of the men and women who could afford boxes stayed where they were.

"Perhaps you would like to go and fetch a drink?" she suggested politely.

"I couldn't possibly leave you here on your own, Miss Winters," Lord Guantes answered. "Who knows what trouble you might get into?"

Irene placed her hands in her lap, feeling the gun through the folds of her skirt. Her motor control was back; she could use the gun if she had to. But with his power beating down upon her, she'd rather play the waiting game as he tried to recruit her, and look for an advantage. Any advantage at all.

Lord Guantes smiled slightly, as if he'd sensed a lack of resistance. "Quite," he said. "I knew that you'd be reasonable. Now I imagine you're wondering what your options are."

He would probably have enjoyed delivering that line even more if she'd been tied down, Irene decided. It was all about the power. "I had wondered," she murmured.

"Well, you must understand that you are a slightly notorious young woman."

Irene wasn't sure whether to be pleased or annoyed at the *slightly.* She settled for saying, "It's so difficult to know when one has overstepped. I didn't think I'd caused Lord Silver any real inconvenience."

"Oh, it's not *Silver* that I'm talking about." Lord Guantes picked up his glass of brandy and sipped again, drawing out the moment. "That would be Alberich."

The name Irene least wanted to hear. She had never *asked* to be a person of interest to one of the Library's worst nightmares. She didn't *want* to be connected with someone who skinned people alive. And she'd barely escaped with her life herself during their last encounter. "Ah," she said, keeping her voice even, and grateful again for her mask. Perhaps making an outcry and getting arrested *would* be the better option. She could make a break for it in the confusion.

"Indeed." He was watching her, his eyes alert for the least sign of weakness. "A most convenient gentleman, for those who want to take advantage of his unique capabilities. Very — what is that word? Useful. Yes, useful. Astonishing, what he's made of himself, and they say that he's still developing. He may have his own schemes, but he is always the utter professional when it comes to cooperation with others . . ."

"And he's the one who told you where you could find a dragon, wasn't he?" Irene said. It made too much sense. Alberich would have recognized Kai's nature after their last encounter, and he was definitely the sort to hold a grudge.

"Exactly," Lord Guantes agreed. "Which is why I'm in his debt. Handing you over would settle the matter quite nicely."

The spike of fear nearly turned Irene's stomach. Her very worst nightmare was coming true . . . *Wait. This is too obvious.* Cold common sense dragged her back from panic to critical analysis. *He's deliberately waving this at me to persuade me to choose a lesser evil. If he wants me in his service this badly, then why?*

"It would, wouldn't it," she agreed, and caught a glint of annoyance in Lord Guantes's eyes. He'd been expecting his words to have more of an effect. *Come on, boast to me. Tell me something useful.* "The local nobility must be very annoyed that all their boxes are taken tonight," she remarked. "And all these people here from different worlds, but nobody seems to notice."

"This is *our* Venice, Miss Winters." Lord Guantes steepled his fingers as he looked out over the crowd with an air of owner-ship. "The world is what we say it is here, and it begins and ends with Venice. There is no land beyond it to interfere. The Ten command, and the people obey them as their masters. Even the very ground beneath our feet obeys their will. Everything is precisely as Venice ought to be. Napoleon will never come to this Venice; it will never be conquered, never be lessened, never be anything else. The Ten wish everyone to see their chosen visitors merely as foreigners, and so therefore they do." He paused. "Their *chosen* visitors, that is. I do not think *you* received an invitation, Miss Winters."

"I consider the kidnapping of one of my friends to be an unspoken invitation," Irene retorted flatly. "Which makes you my official host, Lord Guantes."

He chuckled. "Not bad, but rather lacking in legal support. I don't think you could argue that in front of the Ten."

"Is that what we'll be doing?"

"Only if you push me that far, Miss Winters, and only if absolutely necessary. You know how this sort of thing goes. An anonymous denunciation. Your public exposure. Your arrest. Your . . . questioning." He didn't give the word the same inflection Silver might have done, to make something unwholesome and lascivious out of it. He merely let it roll out, heavy with the weight of darkness and dungeons and hopelessness. "By the time you were standing in front of the Ten, I promise you that you would already have confessed everything."

"I'm surprised you haven't turned me over already," she said as casually as she could. She was aware that she was walking on a razor's edge, trying to find out what he wanted without pushing him too far.

The lights in the house were dimming again, and the audience noise fell to a hush as the curtains reopened.

Lord Guantes waited until the action had begun again before continuing. "Of course, there are other options."

"Yes?" Irene said, trying to throttle back the eagerness in her voice.

"But your options are now very limited, Miss Winters. Limited to who I decide will be your new master or mistress, for you are my prisoner now." His pause was to allow her to agree to that, but she said nothing. He went on regardless. "The Ten would be glad to have you, I'm sure. You could be traded for later advantage. They have no wish to actively start a feud with your organization, so it would probably be a question of wringing you dry for information, then keeping you a prisoner until they had some use for you."

Which tells me more about how you see things than about how they see things. Irene gave a rigid inclination of her head, waiting for him to continue.

"Then again, I might gain advantage by presenting you to one of my allies, or to secure a potential ally." His pause there could have been designed for her to acknowledge the subtleties of high politics, as expressed by the trade in souls. "Some of the powerful of my kind would be glad to have you as a personal enemy in their story, or as a student."

"A student?" Irene said, surprised.

"Eventually. After sufficient training. Or . . . a toy." His tone conveyed sadness at the need to actually mention such unpleasantness, but suggested that he could easily catalogue each possible indignity, torture, or worse — or even perform them, should it become necessary.

Irene swallowed. Her mouth was dry. From a clinical point of view, she knew he was only — *only?* — attempting to frighten her. But the actual experience was indeed frightening, as she felt the compulsion to obey him, and she had to fight with everything she had not to succumb to that power.

Was Lord Guantes already controlling her? Was that why she was sitting so passively, convincing *herself* she was doing it to discover his secrets? She ran mentally through a couple of plans. *Collapse the entire opera box. Shoot him. Threaten him with the gun. Smash his chair and set fire to his brandy. Jump over the edge into the audience.* She thought she could do any of them . . . if she decided to. If she chose to make the effort.

"Or I could offer you to Alberich." Lord Guantes's hand reached across to clamp down on her wrist, pinning it to the arm of the chair.

Irene jerked against his grip, but his hand ground down, hard enough to hurt, and he turned in his chair to watch her. There was pleasure in his eyes, in the way that he looked at her, but it wasn't a sadistic amusement at her pain. It was simply enjoyment of his power over her. *How very like Silver. I should tell him that, if I ever really want to insult him.* "Ah no, Miss Winters. That is *not* an option. You do not leave this box until we have decided your fate, one way or another. Tell me, are you so very afraid of him?"

"Of Alberich?" Sheer disbelief coloured her voice. "Why shouldn't I be?"

"Come now." He was playing with her. The voices on-stage were all male, interlacing in threat and defiance, promising imprisonment and death. "What is there to dislike so much?"

"I'm sure you know the sort of thing he does," Irene snapped.

"I'd like to hear it from your own mouth." His eyes caught hers, and this time she couldn't look away, even if she wanted to. They compelled her. It was his will against hers, and even her Library brand wasn't enough to save her now.

She barely recognized her own voice as she began to speak. "He skins people —"

The sound of her voice broke that moment of control, and she jerked herself back against the chair, her body shaking. Her back ached as if she had been beaten. This was far worse than Silver's attempt to get under her defences. Lord Guantes had *done* it.

She'd lost time somewhere. Tosca was on-stage and singing now, her voice arcing through the opera house in smooth, effortless sweeps of sound, like a silver pendulum counting away the seconds.

"Charming," Lord Guantes said slowly. "Quite charming." His hand stayed on her wrist, his glove smooth and unwrinkled, as though he weren't applying any pressure at all. "I begin to see why Lord Silver likes you so much. You really are quite stimulating, Miss Winters. You are exactly what I want."

"But what do you want?" Irene whispered. Her voice shook, just as it should if he'd managed to cow her. She'd had people try to break her will before now, but none of them had actually *succeeded,* and she didn't want to think about the implications.

"You as my servant, in public, this very night." His smile was the essence of smugness. "We'll already have proven we can strike against the dragons. Having a Librarian in my service too will demonstrate that they will not be a significant threat in this conflict. Wouldn't you agree?"

Irene's heart sank. He was right. Parading her as a trophy might push some of the Fae swing votes towards war. And it was all her own fault for coming here and running her head into the noose . . .

No, that was what *he* wanted her to think. She thought of the pendant around her neck. She had done the right thing — the *only* thing she could have done — in coming here.

It was time to make her move. **"Brandy, boil!"**

The glass of brandy and the bottle both shattered in a gush of steam. Brandy was a volatile fluid, and the bottle went up in a gratifyingly dramatic display. The violence of it took Lord Guantes by surprise, and his attention shifted from Irene as his eyes flicked over to the shattered glass.

Irene slipped the gun from her skirt with her free hand, raising it to point at him. "Your move," she said.

His attention swung to her again, and this time there was no holding back. His eyes were a thousand tons of weight pressing down on her, cold and heavy as lead, and ice seemed to close around her limbs and heart. His hand bit into her wrist, and she gasped in pain. The burn of the Library brand on her back and the weight of the pendant around her throat were once more distant things, far away from the present oppression of his gaze.

Play along; pretend he's won, part of her mind suggested. *Just put the gun down . . .*

She considered that statement. The most important bit seemed to be *put the gun down,* and that was the last thing she was going to do. She couldn't stop fighting now. If she did, she'd lose. But it was taking all her strength and, the moment she lost her focus, her will would break.

She could feel herself losing, inch by inch. The gun was cold and remote in her hand, and she could scarcely feel her grip on it.

Do something.

She couldn't.

"Answer me," he said.

She struggled with the Language for **Break, shatter, fall,** but she could feel her mouth begin to move in a *yes.*

"I believe the lady declines your invitation," Vale said from the darkness behind her.

CHAPTER 20

Lord Guantes turned to look at Vale, cutting his connection to Irene. She breathed in great sobbing gasps of air. There was just enough space in her head for her to think, and the thoughts went, *Keep that gun pointed at him.*

"Peregrine Vale, I believe. This box is locked," Lord Guantes said. "How did you — ?"

"I didn't," Vale broke in. "I arrived before the performance and simply waited behind those curtains. I found your conversation most interesting."

"I see." Lord Guantes's tone was still composed, but Irene detected a sense of simmering anger and uncertainty. He seemed unsure which of the two of them to target, in terms of directing his will and therefore his powers. She wondered suddenly if he *couldn't* control two of them at once.

"And how did *you* reach Venice?" Lord Guantes demanded. "Must I constantly be interrupted when I am busy?"

"An unfortunate by-product of your line of work," Vale said. "Winters, shall we go?"

"I think not," Lord Guantes said, gripping her wrist even harder. "The lady will be remaining here."

"I'm sorry to disappoint you," Irene said. She'd regained her self-control now. "But if you could tell us where to find the Carceri, we would appreciate it."

Lord Guantes snorted. "You seriously think I'd tell you that?"

"I must insist that you answer her question," Vale said. His voice was lethally cold.

Lord Guantes shrugged. "Or?" he said.

"Or I will blow your brains out. I know that your kind have unusual capabilities, sir, but I don't believe you can enchant both of us, or you would already have done so. And I think that a bullet in the head from ten feet away will seriously inconvenience you."

Lord Guantes paused, his hesitation punctuated by a rattle of drums from the orchestra, which carried throughout the opera house. "At least tell me how you reached this place," he said. "If you are working for Silver, perhaps we can come to some arrangement." He wasn't focusing on Irene any longer, but on the more immediate threat of Vale. And was Vale beginning to frown in distraction, now that he had to fight against Lord Guantes's will?

Guantes is playing for time. And Kai was running out of time. **"Chair arms, break,"** Irene murmured.

The arms of both chairs shattered, wrecking what was probably a valuable pair of antiques. Lord Guantes fell forward as Irene's wrist swung loose, and she dragged it free from his grip. She backed towards Vale, keeping her gun pointed at Lord Guantes throughout.

His eyes widened, and for a moment he hesitated. Then he rose from his chair and stepped back towards the edge of the box, raising both his hands as if in surrender.

Irene spared a glance, and saw that Vale was standing near the door. One of the commoner black half-masks hid part of his face, and he was in a plain dark doublet and breeches. She wouldn't have recognized him, or looked twice at him, under any other circumstances. He didn't shift his attention from Lord Guantes. "See to the door, Winters," he said, as casual as ever.

"It's open," Irene replied. She reached out to test the handle, and it shifted in her grasp. "We should get out of here."

The opera house was nearly silent. Tosca was singing. *"Vissi d'arte, vissi d'amore . . ."* Her voice, and the orchestra behind her, filled the air like light through stained glass.

"You can't possibly get away," Lord Guantes said softly. Power seemed to crystallize in the air around him, almost physical and solid, as he drew himself up to his full height. It wasn't a threat. It was a prediction. They would not get away. They were lost. He had already won.

I almost said yes to him . . . The brand across Irene's back burned with her anger, as if etched in live acid. *I almost betrayed the Library.*

Her finger tightened on the trigger.

Lord Guantes caught the motion and took another step back, grasped the edge of the box with one hand, and swung himself over. He dropped out of the line of fire and out of sight, into the audience below.

His action shattered the spell that his power had cast. It was as if a brilliant light source had blinked out, leaving observers dazzled in the ordinary light of day. Irene glanced sideways to Vale and saw that he still had his gun pointed at where Lord Guantes had been standing, his grip so tight that she could see the bones of his hand taut beneath the skin. "Come on," she said urgently, shoving her own gun back into her skirts. "We have to get out of here."

Some inner tension snapped. Vale nodded, slid his weapon back into his doublet, and was pulling her outside and down the corridor almost before the echoes of her words had died away. Fortunately, Sterrington had followed the orders to leave Lord Guantes alone, and the corridor was empty.

I should have shot him, Irene's brain chattered feverishly. *I should have shot him . . .*

"*Move,* Winters," Vale snapped, dragging her along. "I'm astonished that nobody's reacted to a man dropping out of his opera box."

"Well, it was the middle of '*Vissi d'arte,*' " Irene argued. "Nobody's going to stir until that aria's over —"

A burst of shouting and commotion came from the main auditorium, echoing through the walls of the corridor as they scrambled down the stairs.

"Of course, I could be wrong," she allowed. But a more important question presented itself. "How on *earth* are you here? Now?"

"I will be delighted to tell you when we have the time." He steered her through a side-door into the backstage passages. "If we can get out of here and into the crowd before they can cordon off the opera house, we may be safe."

Irene decided that was as good a definition of *safe* as they were likely to get for the moment, and nodded. She grabbed someone's discarded shawl as they ran past it, dropping her own. It might help camouflage her a little. Vale was already anonymous enough.

"Act normally," Vale directed, slowing abruptly to a casual saunter and letting go of her arm. The buzz of voices came from ahead.

"The sad thing is, this is all fairly normal for me," Irene said wryly. "It's spending a few peaceful months in your world that was the unusual experience." She followed his lead, smoothing her skirt down. Then they turned a corner together, to find the corridor nearly blocked by a group of stage-hands and chorus.

"Do you know what's going on?" one of the chorus asked Vale. He was a young man, ready in uniform for the next act, his make-up fresh and lurid in the candlelight. "Someone said there had been a duel."

"No, I heard it was a murder," another man, one of the stage-hands, put in. He was blotting sweat from his forehead and neck with a dirty rag. "The way I heard it, he strangled her in her own box."

"Neither," Vale said. His Italian was clipped, a little slangy, but his body language had changed to the same absent-minded swagger as the men around them. "Someone was about to be arrested by the doge's guard. He jumped from his box to try to escape."

The group fell silent. Most of the men crossed themselves. "The guard is still back there?" one of them asked.

Vale shrugged. Irene shrugged as well, and tried not to look behind her to see if anyone was chasing them.

"So why are *you* trying to get out the back way?" another stagehand asked. "Got reasons to avoid the doge's guard, have you?"

Before Vale could answer, Irene tugged at his sleeve imploringly. "Darling, we must hurry! If Giorgio catches us together, you know what he'll do. These are honourable gentlemen — they won't betray us to him . . ."

Glances were exchanged between the men. "We didn't see anything," one of them said, extending an empty palm.

"Quite right," Vale said. He dipped into an inner pocket, brought out a purse, and dropped a few coins into the meaningfully extended hand. "To drink the doge's health."

With a few more nods they were out through the backstage door, and a couple of minutes later Vale was handing Irene into a gondola. No frenzied mob of guards came after them, and Irene was beginning to think they might actually get away.

"Round to the Doge's Palace and then around a bit, so we can enjoy the scenery. And let's have a song," Vale instructed, tossing the gondolier another coin. He helped Irene seat herself in the main area of the boat (she still didn't know the right vocabulary for it — rather important for a Librarian), settling a cushion behind her before folding his long body down next to her. The posture might have been casual enough — a man and a woman together in a gondola, his arm against her shoulders — but she could feel the tension in his body.

"Thank you." Irene had to make herself say the words. To her disgust, she was shaking in the aftermath of her brush with Lord Guantes's power. Tackling a Fae at his level was way above her pay grade, she told herself as she gritted her teeth. Vale was here. They were safe — for now. And they needed to talk.

She looked up to meet Vale's eyes for a

375

moment, and then she reached behind her head to untie the strings of her mask. Nobody was looking, and hopefully nobody even knew what to look for. She massaged her damaged wrist as Vale began to speak. He kept to English, his voice quiet.

"I apologize for surprising you like that, Winters. When Lord Silver refused to allow me on the Train, I thought it best to make my own arrangements. I regret that this involved deceiving you as well as him, but there was no time to discuss the matter. By leaving as I did, I was able to assemble a disguise and join the Train amongst the minor Fae."

She jerked her head in a nod, remembering his hurtful words as he'd stormed out of Silver's study. "I'm concerned about you becoming chaos-contaminated just by being here," she said. "Silver wasn't lying. It is a risk for humans visiting these worlds. You've exposed yourself —"

"I've felt nothing odd thus far," Vale said briskly. "Perhaps I am already somewhat immunized? You've said before that my world is higher in chaos than in order. And I had no trouble dealing with the other Fae on the Train. The volume of strangers made it easy for me to pass myself off as one of them. But I assume that you've been pursuing your own investigations, Winters? What have you found out?"

Last night Irene had been utterly furious with him. But she grudgingly accepted his reasoning. Perhaps it was his casual assumption that he'd barely done anything that needed apologizing *for* that still galled her. She ran over with Vale the details of the midnight deadline, her bargain to escape on the Train, and Kai's location within the Carceri — wherever they were.

"Ah," Vale said with satisfaction. "That agrees with certain investigations of my own."

"I hope I haven't been wasting my time *too* much," Irene said with some irritation.

"Not at all, Winters." Vale relaxed farther back into the cushions with her, lowering his voice to what might have been taken for a lover's whisper. "It was simple enough. Venice is known as a hotbed of crime syndicates, secret societies, and spies. The Veneziani, the Mala del Brenta, the 'Ndrangheta, the Carbonari . . ."

"I think the Carbonari were a couple of hundred years later than 'now,' " Irene said pedantically. Of course Vale would know about the criminal side of things. "You've probably noticed that the chronological period is different from your world."

Vale sighed. "The point remains, Winters, that people here are used to the concept of anonymous masked individuals asking questions and expecting to get answers. Once I'd grasped that this place is run by a mysterious group called the Ten, all I needed to do was masquerade as one of their agents. It was easy enough to trace the movements of Lord Guantes, once he'd arrived here — together with an unconscious man, who must be Strongrock. I have spent most of the day and last night criss-crossing the city, interviewing witnesses, and —"

"You've been pretending to be one of the Ten's secret agents?" Irene hissed in shock.

"There are advantages to a city of masks," Vale said. Under his own mask, his mouth curled rather complacently in the moonlight.

"I think you underestimate how efficient they are." She had to resist the urge to look over her shoulder. "They were following the Guantes as well last night, watching for suspicious behaviour. They nearly arrested me."

Vale nodded, with a casual acceptance of the fact that of course she'd managed to avoid arrest. It was, in its way, a compliment. "In any case, I know where Strongrock was last seen, right before he

vanished. It must be the entry to these Carceri of yours — or at least incredibly close.
What I can't do is conveniently infiltrate
the place. I'd been planning to kidnap
Guantes or his wife and use them as hostages, but it's possible that I might have
overreached there."

"But, together, perhaps we might manage
something . . . ," Irene suggested. It was
like the swing of a pendulum, from near-
certain failure to an actual possibility of suc-
cess. There were still a few hours till midnight. There might still be time to save Kai.

"If we didn't know where to go, following
Lord Guantes would be a logical next step."
Vale shifted his weight, looking meditatively
down the canal ahead of them, at the glowing lanterns and windows that lined the
dark waterway.

Their gondolier paused in his vocal rendi-
tion (the equivalent of June, moon, et cetera, in a pleasant if not opera-grade tenor)
to call a greeting to a passing gondola. Irene
eyed the boat nervously, but it held just
another reclining couple, much like her and
Vale. No soldiers. No inquisitors. No Lord
Guantes.

She tried to think through Vale's statement, rather than just reject it flat out.
Guantes was on a very short shortlist of

people she never wanted to see again. "You think Lord Guantes will check on Kai, to make sure he's safe, now that we've escaped him?"

"This is very likely, Winters. He's also likely to set a trap. And our own goal will be fairly obvious, unfortunately — to find Strongrock as soon as is practicable."

Irene frowned. "But won't Lord Guantes expect us to follow him, as the only route to Kai? And be ready for us?"

Vale looked thoughtful. "If setting traps is his game, he'll need time to do that and time to double back and display himself prominently, to tempt us to follow. All this leads to what we were trying to do anyway — reach these Carceri first, and hope we are in time to find him, before Strongrock's taken for auction."

Irene was beginning to nod in agreement when it struck her that the sounds of the canal were changing. There was an ambient hush, a silence like a physical thing drifting towards their gondola and swallowing up lesser noises in its wake. She sat upright, pulling out of Vale's protective arm, to see half a dozen shadowy gondolas moving towards theirs. The approaching boatmen were muffled in black cloaks and moved

with inhuman smoothness, their oars barely
stirring the surface.

CHAPTER 21

"About turn," Vale said to the gondolier. "You'll get a bonus, of course —"

"There's no bonus big enough to make it worth crossing the Ten," the gondolier said, his voice shaking. He brandished the oar at them threateningly. "You stay right where you are."

Pleading innocence was not going to help. The question was how much disturbance was Irene prepared to make in order to get away safely.

Quite a lot, she decided.

She scrambled to her feet and took a deep breath. **"Canal water, freeze deep and thick!"** she shouted at the top of her voice.

Her words hung in the silence. Then their gondola came to an abrupt halt, throwing Irene to her knees. Vale grabbed her and pulled her upright again, steadying her. The silence was gone; the air was now full of the creaking of trapped wooden boats, and a bitter chill rose from the suddenly firm surface of the canal. The approaching gondolas were amongst the trapped boats, and the men in them seemed also briefly frozen in shock.

"Will the ice hold us?" Vale asked, getting to the point.

"It'd better," Irene replied as she swung herself over the side of the boat, the ice groaning under her weight but not breaking. She hastily began shuffling towards the canal bank — the surface of the water had frozen in peaks and ripples, giving her feet some purchase. Besides nearly drowning, her boarding-school experiences had included dangerous adventures on semi-iced lakes, so it wasn't the first time she'd done this. She steadied Vale as he nearly slipped. Crashes from the far gondolas suggested that their pursuers were finding it more difficult.

Under normal circumstances, crowds of curious bystanders would have been mobbing the bank, but the presence of the Ten's own secret police had cleared the area very effectively. Irene and Vale scrambled up off the ice without anyone getting in the way. They'd gained perhaps a minute, but not more. And the black-clad masquers were scrambling across the ice towards them with more confidence now.

Time to slow them down a bit more. **"Ice, break!"**

Interestingly, the ice didn't all fracture in the same way. Some of it crumbled into tiny fragments, sinking into the water like dust, while other pieces stayed in large chunks, miniature icebergs drifting downstream on the canal. The men on the ice dropped into the freezing water in eerie silence, but they were still struggling towards Irene and Vale.

Vale grabbed Irene's arm and towed her into the nearest alleyway, cutting across a narrow bridge and between a row of old houses. "We need to evade them," he said, and she wondered if retreating into the obvious was a habit of his.

"So where was Kai last seen?" Irene demanded.

"The Piazza San Marco," Vale answered. He gave her a boost over a stone wall between two houses and into a private garden, then vaulted over himself. "The Campanile."

"Clearly the Ten believe in the principle of hiding in plain sight," Irene muttered. She kicked a free-range chicken out of the way in a squawk of feathers. "Excuse me," she added to an outraged householder who'd opened his backdoor to complain.

Distraction, distraction — they needed a distraction. "Vale, if we were foreign spies, here with sabotage in mind, what would we target?"

"The Ten themselves," Vale suggested, "or we'd want to assassinate the doge, or blow up the Arsenal. But the Arsenal would be easiest, as both it and the Campanile are north-east of here. So can you make our pursuers think that's our aim?"

"I can try." *But how?* she wondered. She remembered the Venetian Arsenal now, a complex of shipyards and armouries, so huge and industrial that it had supplied images for Dante's *Inferno.* And she had enough grasp of the city's geography to know that it was directly on the water, looking out across the scattered islands to the open sea.

Running feet echoed in the distance behind them. And even if Vale had a semi-preternatural ability to find his way through a city's back alleys on only a day's acquaintance, the Ten's servants were still close behind and gaining.

She needed to make a nice obvious trail if this diversion was going to work. "We need to get to the waterside," she said briefly. "I'm going to need a boat, and we'll need something to put in it."

Vale tilted his head, then nodded. He changed direction, leading her down a street to the right, towards the larger noises of the sea-front.

The two of them burst out onto a small quay, in between two rows of inns and shops, with half a dozen rowing boats tied up at the far end. Perfect. Though it was also a dead end, with nowhere to go but the water. So this idea had better work.

"Untie that one," Irene directed Vale, pointing at the closest boat. She dragged an oiled canvas cover from the one next to it and shoved it into the first boat, tossing her shawl in on top for good measure. From where they were standing, she could see the great curve of the Venetian lagoon and the open sea beyond. At this distance, the Train lay across the water on its protruding platform like a chain, but beyond it, she could see the buildings on the other side of the curve, half a mile or more to their east. Now that she knew where to look, the Arsenal was obvious. Even at this time of night, it blazed with forge-fires, its silhouette irregular with flaring chimneys, high walls, and ships' masts, and smoke rose from it into the cloudless night.

Vale stood back with a grunt as the rope came free. "Can you control the boat remotely if you're directing it that far?"

"I can start it going and leave them chasing it," Irene said, forcing confidence into her voice. Freezing and then shattering the canal had left her with a nagging headache and a sense of weakness. She wished she'd had a chance to eat supper. Or even lunch. Or possibly breakfast. She set her hand on the boat's keel as it bobbed in the water. "Right, stand back . . . **Boat that I am touching, move out to sea fast, go around the Fae Train, and head towards the great shipyard to the east, not stopping until you reach it.**"

Energy ran out of her like blood. But Vale caught her before she could topple into the water, as the boat surged forward, cutting through the waves and out to sea. With an arm round her waist, he pulled her towards a side alley between two fish shops, dragging her into the shadows.

They made it just before their pursuers arrived.

Irene pressed against the wall, grateful for the shabby old building's irregular shadows. Together, she and Vale watched the masked men (most of them dripping from their dip in the canal) point at the now-distant boat, gauge its course, and come to the obvious conclusion as it curved round towards the

Arsenal.

It was a nerve-racking wait, once the Ten's servants had gone. She needed to be sure they weren't just waiting around the corner for her and Vale to come out of hiding. Irene imagined two clocks: one ticking down the seconds until she could be sure it was safe to emerge, and the other larger one counting down the minutes until Kai's auction. It wasn't a comforting image.

Once they were moving again, it was early evening and the streets were still busy, but nobody looked twice at them. Without the Ten's servants lurking, there was enough noise to reassure Irene that nobody else was listening in on their conversation. And everyone was masked now. The light from the lanterns made eye sockets into dark hollows and turned unornamented masks into skulls. The sound of wind-instruments drifted from a house's upstairs window, giving a somehow sinister cast to the approaching night. Vale bought a couple of pastries from a vendor and passed one to Irene as they strolled.

They stopped at the edge of the square, and Irene looked across at their target. The Campanile tower stood alone in a corner of the square, a good three hundred feet tall. She could make out the pale marble belfry, the pyramidal spire at the top, and the weathervane glinting in the starlight. A set of thin marble-framed windows marched up one side of the brick of the bell-tower in a dotted line. It was far enough away from any of the surrounding buildings that she and Vale wouldn't be able to get to it over the roofs. And, more important, a squad of eight guards stood by the only gate at the bottom. "Let's hope they don't have a shoot-on-sight policy," she concluded.

"If we get close enough, can you use that trick of yours?" Vale queried. "The one where you convince them they're seeing something else? If not, we'll have to pretend to be bringing a message."

Eight people was more than she'd ever tried to work on previously, but it wasn't as if they had much choice in the matter. "You're going to have to prop me up when I do it." She finished the pastry and dusted crumbs off her hands. "It's going to exhaust me, at least for a few minutes. But you're right, it's the best option. I wish we could see what's inside."

"I could only see stairs when I looked earlier," Vale said. "Disguised as a beggar, of course. It allowed me to get close enough to see through that archway. Any impediments are likely to be farther up."

And likely to be something that I'll have to manage. Irene nodded, bracing herself. "We'd better get on with it, then, before Lord Guantes catches up," she said. She stepped boldly out, Vale's arm still pseudo-affectionately around her waist, and tried not to look over her shoulder or listen for pursuit.

When they reached the guards, two stepped forward, crossing their pikes in front of Vale and Irene. "Not tonight, friend," one of them said. "If you're a stranger to the city, come back tomorrow and you can be in the piazza to hear the bell ring."

Vale glanced to Irene, and she knew that it was her turn. She took a deep breath and stepped forward. **"You perceive me and the man beside me as people who have a right to be here and to enter the Campanile,"** she said, pitching her voice to carry to all the guards.

She felt the compulsion take, tightening like a fishing line caught in reality, and she staggered as the impact hit her. Her nose was bleeding again, the blood trickling down her face under her mask, and for a moment her head was pounding so loudly she could barely hear Vale's voice as he ordered the guards to open the door. Apparently it really was worse when you tried to affect several people at the same time. Good to know. Though hopefully never again. But the way things were going, it would probably be tomorrow morning, without the benefit of coffee.

The guards saluted and stood back, grounding their pikes. "Certainly, sir," the first guard said, his expression abruptly all deference. "We are at your service."

Vale gave a curt nod to the men, and his arm tightened round Irene's waist, straightening her as she swayed. Then he led her forward and into the arched marble entrance. There were gods carved into the stone, and the lantern-light played tricks with her eyes as the figures seemed to leer at the pair of them accusingly. Another pair of guards threw open the delicate bronze gates, letting them into the building proper.

Irene wondered, through the swimming pain in her head, who the guards thought they were. The Guantes? The Council of Ten? Regular Campanile inspectors here to check for bats in the belfry?

It was very dark inside the Campanile. The narrow windows allowed what moonlight there was into the hollow structure. But its slanting light fell only as far as the walls, leaving the central iron staircase in comparative darkness as it spiralled up the centre of the otherwise empty tower. There were no guards in here.

"Can you stand?" Vale asked, releasing her.

Irene wobbled but stayed upright. "I think so," she said. She pulled her mask away from her face enough to blot with her sleeve the blood running from her nose. It had pretty much stopped, but the headache remained.

"Then we had better hurry. That was too easy for my liking."

You aren't the one who had to do it, Irene thought, but she had to agree. They had been incredibly lucky to escape Lord Guantes and get here first. That sort of luck didn't last. Paranoia immediately suggested that it was a trap; but she and Vale headed up the wrought-iron stairs, Vale going first. Each step creaked and rang under their feet, uncomfortably loud in the confines of the bell-tower. The stairs were guarded on the outer side by curving panels of thin, lacy ironwork, but the steps themselves were re-assuringly solid under her feet.

About a hundred and fifty feet off the ground, Vale came to a stop. They both caught their breath for a moment as he pointed upwards. There was a ceiling directly above them, and the staircase spiralled up through it.

Irene listened, but there was no sound from above, and the air had the particular deadness of empty space. While they were both on their guard as they headed upwards, there was nobody in the belfry. But the staircase continued to climb farther up above them still, spiralling through the ceiling. Up there, the bells hung above them from the rafters in great terrifying masses of metal. Moonlight fell through the four deep arches in each wall, picking out the detail in the tiles of the belfry floor, so at least they could see better now.

Vale looked around, frowning. "Now, is it here somewhere, or is it farther up? Winters, do you perceive anything of value?"

"I . . ." Irene hunted for words to try to describe what she felt. "This whole place feels as if it is a nexus of some sort. I can tell that much, but no more. Can you sense anything?"

"I'm only human," Vale said. He caught the look she was giving him, even through her mask. "Frankly, Winters, given our surroundings, I'd think you should be *glad* of that." He stepped through the archway into the small room and began prowling across the floor, casting a professional eye over the tiles. "Unfortunately, the bell-ringers have confused any evidence that might have been useful. All I can be sure of is that some people have ascended farther up these stairs."

Something was pricking at Irene's mind, beyond the place's general aura of power. She had the feeling that she was missing a connection. She looked down at where Vale was prodding at the tiles, then at her own feet on the iron staircase, and it clicked. "Interesting," she murmured.

"I beg your pardon?" Vale said.

"The iron." She gently tapped one toe on the staircase. "Every Fae I've met dislikes the substance. Why put a wrought-iron set of stairs as the main entrance to a private prison?"

"Architectural necessity?" Vale offered, but his heart wasn't in it.

"No." She was thinking about the purpose of the prison. "This, all of it — the location and the guards, and this iron staircase — it isn't just meant to stop intruders. It's meant to stop *Fae* intruders."

"It makes one wonder about the nature of the prisoners." Vale stepped back onto the staircase. "But I don't think there is anything more to learn on this level."

"I agree," Irene said. "We'll have to go on up."

The staircase passed uncomfortably near the bells as they drew level with them, close enough that she could have reached out and touched the dark bronze. They were both climbing more quietly now, after their earlier fast but noisy pace, trying to keep as silent as they could. There was a light on the level above them, the yellow of lantern-flames. But there was no sound of talking or movement.

Then a shot suddenly rang through the air, cracking against the metal of the staircase. Irene flinched back, looking for cover, except that there wasn't any.

"You will place your hands above your head." A voice came from above them in Italian. It was tense, the voice of a man who was going to react badly to surprises. "You will advance slowly and without making any moves that we might misinterpret. Remain on the staircase and don't try to step off it. And we know there are two of you, so don't try to pretend otherwise."

Vale gave a nod, then raised his hands. "We're coming," he called up the staircase. "We won't try anything."

"See that you don't," the voice called back.

The small roof space at the top of the tower was cramped. There was little room for the four guards waiting above them with drawn pistols. Irene, a couple of steps behind Vale and peering around his waist, could see them rather too well. Two lanterns burned on either side of the staircase, hanging from the rafters, and the guards had a good field of fire. They were positioned behind the only exit from the stairway to the roof. And, trapped between the tightly woven iron safety rails, there was no room to hide.

But the staircase itself kept on going up. It didn't stop at the roof, where by all rules of logic and common sense it should have done, but continued its impossible climb. A cool breeze drifted down, laden with the smell of water and stone.

The Carceri, Irene thought. *We must be at the border.*

"Identify yourself," the first guard said. "If you're carrying authorization, show us, but keep your movements slow."

Bribery or intimidation wasn't going to get them past these guards — they were alert and professional. Beguilement was a possibility, but this time there was a simpler resolution. Irene turned her head till her lips were against the protective iron wall of the staircase, and murmured, **"Iron panels, close to encircle the staircase and block all entry from outside it."**

The metal seemed to scream as it moved, creaking and straining against the frames of the outer panels and the rods that held it in place. The sides of the stairway warped out of shape, forming a barrier between them and the guards, wrenching the interior designs of the openwork panels out of true and twisting them into scrap.

But it was protective scrap. Vale jolted into movement, scrambling farther up the stairs — past the guards in their rooftop space and into the part that shouldn't even exist. Irene was just a step behind him.

One of the guards sprang into action, firing his pistol. The bullet bounced off a panel, cracking against the stone wall. Another guard had more sense and ran round the staircase until he found a gap between two warped panels. Thrusting the muzzle of his pistol into the gap, he aimed it up towards Vale and Irene. The bullet winged Vale's upper arm and rang off the iron post at the centre of the staircase, then fell to rattle down the steps in a succession of pings. Blood spattered and Vale cursed, clutching his arm, but they kept running.

The staircase broadened impossibly as it rose and they left the furious guards behind. In practical terms, they should have moved past the roof of the building by now, but the staircase kept on climbing. The walls were farther away now too, barely visible in the darkness, with only the outlines of large blocks of stone being clear.

Irene wasn't sure where even this small amount of light was coming from. She decided not to think about it, except to hope it didn't vanish. Climbing a fragile wrought-iron staircase at an unknown height in near darkness with guards somewhere below them was bad enough. Climbing it in total darkness would be even worse.

A heavy gust of wind came down the staircase, making the metal creak and shiver.

"It's getting darker," Vale called back over his shoulder.

Irene really wished he hadn't said that. "Maybe they usually bring lanterns," she answered. "How's your arm? Is it bad?"

"Merely a flesh wound," Vale said dismissively. "Can't you use your Language to seal it?"

"You're a living thing," Irene explained, in between panting for breath. "I can tell it to close, but it won't necessarily stay shut. I'd need precise anatomical knowledge to hold it together. Bandages are going to be of more use."

And then it was getting light again. The walls were far away now, and the staircase was a single metal spiral in the middle of a frighteningly large space. There was still no clear way to define from where the light was emerging. When she looked out through the spaces in the iron panelling, Irene could see distant walls and a far more distant ceiling, but no sky or artificial lights. She was breathing heavily now, and her legs were aching.

Another stronger gust of wind made the staircase tremble again. This time both she and Vale slowed their pace, and she saw Vale's hand tighten on the central post as he steadied himself. Blood streaked his sleeve and had spattered across his jerkin.

"Wait here," Irene said firmly. "We've enough light. I need to bandage your arm before you lose any more blood."

Vale peered through the panelling. "I can see something a little farther up. Perhaps we should reach that first?"

"If there is danger up there, I'd rather we stopped your loss of blood before we run into it."

"Oh, very well," he said pettishly, and sat down on the stairs, bracing his arm on his knee. "It doesn't feel that serious."

Irene wasn't sure whether to ascribe that to a casual disdain for injuries — being shot might be an occupational hazard — or simple unwillingness to admit weakness. Rather than get into an argument, she sat down beside him and peeled back his sleeve. A thin, sluggish line of blood oozed down from where the bullet had ripped through the muscles of his upper arm. "You're lucky," she said calmly. "It didn't hit an artery."

"I would certainly have noticed if it did," Vale muttered.

"Do you have any brandy on you?"

"No. But I doubt we'll have time for it to go septic in any case."

Time, yes. Time was a voracious clock eating up the minutes and forcing them closer and closer to disaster. "Excuse me," she said, bringing out her knife. A few seconds' work turned Vale's bloodstained sleeve into a couple of pads, one for each side of the arm, and the bottom of her skirt was repurposed into a bandage.

Vale looked at the ungainly wad of fabric. "Did you ever train as a nurse, Winters?" he said through gritted teeth.

"Only basic first aid and life-saving. You know, sprains, fractures, bullet wounds, sulphuric acid, that sort of thing." She tucked her knife away. "I wonder if there'll be more guards at the top."

"Let us find out." Vale started up the stairs

again, going fast enough that Irene wondered if he felt he had something to prove. But then he came to a halt and pointed. "Look, here."

Irene followed his pointing hand, where the stairs finally came to a halt — like the end of a vertical tube, with the ceiling still lost somewhere above. She felt vertiginous just thinking about the distance they'd climbed. And there was another archway in the side of the staircase ahead. From this gap, a bridge of the same iron as the staircase arced out over the circular chasm that surrounded them, spanning a steep drop, to join some paving on the other side.

The staircase was a single point in the middle of a wide emptiness, and beyond that emptiness there was an incredible, impossible architectural landscape. Stone walls with arches set into them rose in the distance, on an inhuman scale, like a cathedral built to cover an entire country. Bridges made of both stone and iron ran between these arches and across small chasms, pale grey and dark grey in the half-light. Staircases curved down along walls or hung from long cables, which in turn were fastened to some ceiling high above. Tiny grilles marked windows in the sides of flying buttresses and towers, minuscule from Irene's and Vale's distant vantage point. The wind soughed through the stonework, humming against the high stairwells and whispering past the rows of arches. It was a maze. There was probably far more of it than they could even see from where they were, and no way of knowing how far it went on. There were no clear walls and no countryside beyond.

And there were no people anywhere. None.

"A very baroque, convoluted method of entry," Vale said in tones of dissatisfaction.

Irene was thinking this through. "Perhaps," she said slowly, "the only entrance or exit to this place, for Fae at least, is through this stairwell. The iron steps would weaken any Fae trying to get in — or out. After all, it wouldn't be much of a prison if they could travel between worlds and just emerge within this space, as they normally would if they were powerful enough."

Vale nodded. "Well, we will have to hope that it is not proof against dragons or Librarians. They must be restraining Strongrock somehow. But if they can restrain a dragon, we'll just have to hope we can remove the restraint."

Irene sighed. She took off her mask, enjoying the feeling of cool air on her face after the climb. "I'm afraid that I'd need a library to open an exit myself, or at least a good collection of books — and that would be assuming it worked here, when it didn't work in Venice proper."

"Ah well," Vale said. He gave her one of his rare smiles. "You did extremely well with that iron plating, when the guards were questioning us. My compliments."

Irene smiled back. "We make a good team." It was unusual enough to have him actually compliment her, rather than simply accept her proficiency. But she didn't want to get too emotional and embarrass him.

"We do," Vale agreed. He turned to the ironwork bridge and started to walk across. It was wide enough for two to walk abreast. Fortunately, there were rails on either side, but even so, it was a worryingly fragile construction — no, Irene corrected herself mentally, it was solid enough. It just seemed flimsy when compared to the sheer *scale* of everything around her.

Vale halted again once they stepped off the bridge and onto the stone paving beyond, looking around thoughtfully. "The area to be searched is unfeasibly large. However, the guards escorting Strongrock must have passed this way within the last couple of days. If we can find their traces —"

"Actually, I have another idea," Irene said. "I tried it below in Venice, but there was too much ambient chaos interfering with it. Since this area is supposed to be a prison for Fae, it may work better here. Give me a moment, please."

Vale nodded and stepped back to watch.

She extracted Kai's uncle's pendant, then looped it a couple of times round her right wrist to make sure that she didn't drop it — wincing as the chain tugged on the fresh bruises left by Lord Guantes. It was a draconic thing. And there was — or at least, there should be — only one dragon in the area.

Irene raised her hand so that the pendant was dangling in front of her face. **"Like calls to like,"** she said clearly in the Language. **"Point to the dragon who is the nephew of the dragon who owns you."**

The pendant trembled, then swung out at an angle, pointing in a direction about forty-five degrees from where they were facing. Poised there, it tugged at her wrist.

"There," she said, and tried not to go weak at the knees with relief. Or possibly exhaustion. This time it had worked. Focusing the pendant had drained her, and it was still draining her, like blood trickling from a small cut. "I think we have it."

"Well done, Winters!" Vale exclaimed. "Will it last for long?"

"I'm not sure," Irene had to confess. "But I can do it again, if we need to triangulate."

Vale nodded. "In that case, let us hope it's not too far away."

Their footsteps echoed on the stone as they set off into the emptiness. It was as if they were walking across some vast stage-set, with an unseen audience watching from the wings.

CHAPTER 22

They had been walking for at least half an hour before they heard any noise other than their own footsteps.

The pendant was holding up nicely, tugging at Irene's wrist like a dowsing pendulum, although it somewhat inconveniently pointed in a general direction, as the crow flies, rather than changing its bearing at each crossroads or staircase.

The whole place had the quality of what Irene could only describe as *deadness* — the sort of deadness that had never been alive. Even where timber or rope was used amid the cold granite and marble, it had a fossilized, unyielding appearance rather than showing any signs of organic life. The enclosed lakes of water that they passed were clear and dark. Nothing swam in them, nothing moved, and nothing disturbed the water. Nothing *lived* in that water.

She had no background in archaeology or

architecture to make sense of the stonework. A few times Vale had pointed at a lion statue, or at the curve of an arch, and muttered something about "Babylonian influence" or "characteristic Saxon work," but she hadn't been able to do more than nod. She wasn't even sure that categorizing the buildings would indicate any *real* history to this place. That would imply that real people had lived here, once upon a time.

There were no helpful footprints on the road, either, and no dirt or dust marks — there wasn't even any dust. Vale had muttered about that as well, before relegating it to "the general impossibility of the place."

The only good thing was that the ache in her Library brand, triggered by Venice's high-chaos environment, had subsided. It had reached the point where Irene had *almost* stopped noticing its presence, but she did notice its absence. It made a degree of sense. If this place was a prison for Fae, then it should weaken them rather than empower them.

They were passing underneath a high bastion when they heard the first sound. It was a deep, penetrating whisper from the other side of the bastion wall. It echoed amongst the stones and set off an answering ripple from the still canal beside them. It was almost . . . *almost* comprehensible, in a way that made Irene want to stop and listen, to try to make out what was being said.

She turned and saw the same urge in Vale's eyes.

She grasped his arm and pulled him on, away from the ebbing whisper, until only their footsteps broke the silence once more. The whisper still tempted her to look back and linger, as if she'd forgotten something important, something that she should really go back and see to.

But the pendant still led them forward. They travelled up a vast flight of stairs, over another soaring bridge, then through a sequence of angled flights of stairs, which always went to the left but somehow didn't result in them doubling back on themselves. As far as she could tell, anyway.

Then a scream broke the silence. It came from a vast metal sphere — no, a spherical metal *cage* — that dangled over empty space. It hung from a set of cables and chains that rose to a ceiling almost out of sight above them. The noise was shocking and sudden, like an owl's screech in the middle of a peaceful night. It was also just as inhuman, just as animal. Whatever was in that cage, Irene did not want it to get out.

She had considered the other inhabitants

earlier as potential allies. She had wondered if she and Vale could liberate some and escape with Kai in the confusion. But the more she experienced the prison's fundamental vastness and coldness, the less she liked the idea. This sort of prison argued for a very dangerous sort of prisoner. Ones who were so strange and insane that they even scared other Fae. So letting them out might be the sort of really bad idea that finished with a scream and a crunch.

"How much farther do you think it will be, Winters?" Vale asked.

"I've no idea," Irene said, shrugging. "I could argue that Kai wouldn't be too far from the entrance, simply on the grounds of convenience. But they might have some form of transportation that is faster than walking."

Vale nodded. "I had hoped at least to find tracks," he said again, gesturing at the pristine stone paving in front of them.

"I think the situation may not be quite as bad as we thought," she mused.

"In what way?" Vale asked.

"Some of the Fae may want a war." She thought over the last couple of days. "But Lord Guantes isn't being treated as a particularly honoured guest here. He needed his own minions to provide security at the opera. He was being watched by the Ten's secret police too. It sounds as if the Ten are giving him only the minimum level of cooperation."

"But why would the Ten cooperate with the Guantes at all, if they're not fully behind them?" Vale said. "If they would rather rule their lands than expand their boundaries, that's their prerogative, but why then meddle with bigger schemes?"

"Because the Ten can't *not* cooperate with the Guantes if they seem to be making a major political move," Irene said. "It'd be like, oh . . ." She tried to remember the political complexities of Vale's world. "As if someone had pulled in a major French spy in the middle of London and announced it to all the papers. The government would have to handle the matter sternly, even if they'd rather just brush it under the carpet and send the spy back to France, or even trade him for one of their own. The Guantes' power play has made it impossible for the Ten here to be neutral, or they'd risk losing face and power. And if the Guantes succeed . . . then the Ten will certainly gain from a war, along with all the other Fae. But if the Guantes fail and embarrass themselves, the Ten will want to disassociate themselves from the Guantes, along with everyone else."

"Plausible," Vale said. "But we're trying to breach the Ten's private prison here, Winters. If we succeed, they'll have every reason to want us as dead as the Guantes do, if not more so. We're striking directly at their power base, even if we blame the Guantes for it —"

Then he stopped and indicated for Irene to stay silent. In the far distance, barely audible despite the oppressive silence, she could just hear the sound of footsteps, carried to them by some trick of the architecture.

Guards. Or pursuers. Or both.

The next flight of stairs was brutal. It went up at an angle of perhaps sixty degrees, each step formed of pale slippery marble and high enough that Irene's legs were aching before they were halfway up. Vale reached the top ahead of her and looked back — but no one was following them yet.

Irene pulled herself up to the top step. Then, gritting her teeth, she checked the pendant again. It was finally pointing somewhere concrete — at an enormous pillar to the right of their staircase. The pillar was vast, around ninety feet across, and as far as she could make out, it ran from the floor to the ceiling of the prison. Bridges protruded from it like spurs at different heights, and it was ornamented with jutting pennants sporting incomprehensible grey-on-grey designs.

But when they reached it, there weren't even any obvious windows or grilles penetrating its interior. Irene walked around it, holding the pendant out hopefully, but while it indicated the pillar from every direction, it didn't favour any particular place to start.

"I could try commanding it," she said dubiously. "Telling it to open or something?" It should work, but it might also open every other closed door within range of her voice. And she really didn't want to meet the other prisoners here.

"Let me examine it first," Vale snapped. He was all alertness now, tense and focused. He dropped to his knees in front of the column, leaning in till his nose was half an inch from the floor. There, he shuffled along on all fours, squinting at it mysteriously. After what seemed an age, he sprang to his feet, running his fingers up the seam between two of the blocks of stone. "I — yes, I believe I have it. Here." His voice was quiet, but as tense as a tuned violin string. He tapped at a particular point, at approximately eye level. "Winters, I believe there is a lock of some sort here, which would normally require a key, but under the circumstances . . ."

Irene nodded. She stepped next to him and leaned in until her lips were nearly touching the stone. **"Lock, open,"** she murmured.

The seam in the column parted, and one of the blocks of stone swung inwards to reveal a short, dark passageway with an open space just visible beyond. It was entirely silent as they both crept inside.

The room at the centre of the pillar was cold and dim, lit by thin shards of light, which fell from slits in the walls high above. And there Kai was at last, chained against the far wall.

It would have been dignified to stand back and make a clever remark, but Irene was past dignity. She threw her arms around Kai, heedless of whether there might be any traps, and simply hugged him for a long moment.

He was in a shirt and trousers that had seen better days, with his waistcoat hanging loose, and bruises showed livid on his face. A heavy, dark collar circled his neck, with no visible lock, and thick shackles of iron bound his wrists to the wall. He looked at Irene and Vale as if they were an impossibility, as if they might not really be here at all.

Irene took a deep breath. Her eyes burned, and for a moment she thought she was going to sniffle embarrassingly. "I am very unimpressed with these lodgings," she said, pushing herself away from Kai with an effort. He was alive — something that she'd doubted in her darkest moments. She slipped the pendant over her head again. "Vale, do you think you can pick those locks?"

Seemingly lost for words, Vale clasped Kai's shoulder for a moment — probably the closest he could come to Irene's own hug — and then turned to examine the iron cuffs on Kai's wrists. "If they were normal locks, I am certain that I could," he said. "Unfortunately, I suspect that they have Fae enchantments on them. Can you give me any information about them, Strongrock?"

Kai opened his mouth, then shut it, then opened it again. "Irene . . . Vale . . ." His voice was rusty and dry. He looked between them desperately. "You are real, aren't you? Not some sort of illusion? If I told you to pinch me, then would you pinch me?"

"Yes," Irene said sharply. "I would. And I would pinch you so hard, you'd wish you'd never asked. Kai, we are here — you aren't hallucinating. We came." She hugged him again, trying to convince him. "And we're probably running out of time. I'll answer questions later. Do you know anything about those shackles?"

"The collar's enchanted, to keep me in this form and bind my powers," Kai said, then stopped, shaking his head. His voice shook. "I'm sorry. I still can't . . . I don't know about the others. Maybe if Irene uses the Language — how did you *get* here? We're down in *the far end of chaos.*"

"We are in the ancient prison of a particularly corrupt group of Fae, whose world bears a resemblance to a romantic seventeenth-century Venice," Vale said, stepping back and almost visibly withdrawing himself from emotional displays. "We arrived by train. Winters, you may deal with the chains. It's impossible for me to open those locks."

Irene wished she could be that short on detail when reporting to Coppelia. Of course, reporting to Coppelia implied that she would get out of here alive . . . "Hmm," she said, bending in close and staring at the chains. "My abilities don't allow me to sense anything specific about these. Vale, we may want to stand back. I'll try the collar first."

She thought for a moment and then, using as much precision as she could, she said,

"Collar around the dragon's neck, unlock and part and open."

Her voice sank through the air like ink into water as the Language echoed in the room. She had meant to speak quietly, but something made the air tremble like a stifled drumbeat. She felt Vale recoil and step backwards, and Kai gasped in pain, his back arching as the collar tightened around his throat.

Irene had a moment to think, *I've killed Kai,* in a heartbeat that seemed to stretch out into eternity. **"COLLAR, OPEN!"** she screamed, throwing all the weight and focus she could into the words.

The collar shuddered, its surface rippling and shimmering like watered silk, and then flew apart. The fragments whirred outwards, a couple of them slicing Kai's upstretched arms, and buried themselves into the stone walls and floor. Kai collapsed, hanging from the chains on his wrists, coughing and gasping. A fresh red band of pressure showed vividly around his throat.

Completely drained, Irene put a hand out to balance herself against the wall, swaying as she stood there. She was conscious of Vale dashing forward to check Kai's pulse and mutter to him, but for the moment she could only concentrate on breathing and

416

staying upright. There had been a purpose in that collar, and it had taken a lot of her strength to break it.

"Irene?" Kai's voice. Ragged, but functional.

"Let me take a look at those cuffs," she said, pulling herself together and walking over to join Vale and Kai. She hoped it didn't look too much like a stagger.

"Let's hope they were meant to hold Fae," Vale observed. "If so, they should be less effective at holding Strongrock."

"For holding Fae?" Kai said, looking at his wrists in disgust.

"This is a Fae prison," Irene said. "You're not the usual sort of inhabitant. All right. Let's do this."

It was an anticlimax when the cuffs came away without drama, after a single phrase from the Language. Kai fell forward onto his knees, but quickly dragged himself up, rubbing at his wrists where the metal had cut into his skin.

There was something else in the room now. It was linked to the growing anger in Kai's eyes and the way he held himself. It was the same pressure that Irene had felt when Kai's uncle had turned his full attention on her, only more raw, more dangerous, and more likely to explode at any moment. *They imprisoned a dragon. What happens when the dragon gets free?* She thought she could hear a distant rumbling outside.

She had to keep him focused. "Kai," she said. "Stay with us. We have a plan to get out of here, but there are men on our trail. We need to get back through Venice to reach the Fae Train, our route in and out of there, but I don't think you can tolerate that world in your proper form."

Kai looked at her, his eyes suddenly all black. For a moment the fern-patterns of scales were visible on the skin of his cheeks and hands, and the lines of his face were something inhuman and terrifying.

Irene returned his stare. "Pull yourself together," she said. It would have been easier to take him by the shoulders and ask him to be the man she had come to trust. But it would have been treating him as a human, and at the moment he was a very long way from that.

"You have no idea what you are asking of me," Kai whispered. There was an undertone to his voice, deep and resonant, like the leashed boom of distant waves.

Irene was conscious of Vale taking a step back, but she would not look away from Kai, would not break their eye contact.

418

"No," she said, "but I expect you to do it, in any case."

Kai took a long gasping breath of air — and then something snapped and he was all human again, staggering forward to throw his arms around her shoulders and lean on her, his whole body shaking. Thunder shook the air outside, closer now. "I'm sorry," he whispered, his voice barely audible. "I'm sorry, Irene, I wanted to believe that someone would come, but I thought there was no way anyone could reach me here."

The ground trembled under their feet. A slow, booming wave beat through the stone like a pulse or, Irene realized, like an alarm.

"We have no time for this," Vale said curtly, a second before she could. "Can you walk, Strongrock?"

Kai pulled himself away from Irene, his breathing slowing. She patted him on the back, trying to be reassuring and mentor-like, rather than showing just how much she cared. "I think we've triggered an alert," she said.

"Then we had better hurry," Vale said.

They stepped outside, and suddenly it became clear that the thunder in the air and the pulse through the rock hadn't been some small atmospheric curiosity. Being inside the pillar had shielded them from the oppressive storm-wind that was now sweeping through the place. Tremors shook the ground. Irene had disliked the sterile quietness before, but this new brewing tempest was not an improvement. She quickly closed the cell door with the Language to cover their tracks, sparing a vengeful moment to hope that Lord Guantes would be shocked to find the cell empty.

Rocks fell in the far distance, and their hollow booming rang out across the landscape of bridges and arches like distant cannons. It felt as if the shaking were getting closer to them. No, she wasn't imagining it. The shaking *was* getting closer to them.

"We'd better run," she said, and they did.

Vale gave Kai a quick briefing on the last couple of days as they made the long trip back to the prison's entrance. Irene put in a word here or there, but on the whole she saved her breath for running. It also gave her a better chance to scrutinize Kai. He seemed in reasonable physical health, with no serious injuries. His bruises didn't look worse than a thug's casual beating (something that had happened to Irene once or twice) — apart from the livid mark left by the collar around his neck. But he was still diminished. He lacked his usual self-assurance, his unthinking certainty that he was the most powerful thing in the vicinity. *Possibly good for his health in the long term, but still . . . I wish it hadn't happened. And I don't know how he'll hold up in a fight.*

As they descended the flight of stairs, Kai spotted something. "Hold on," he said. "Can we pause for a moment?"

Irene followed his gaze. There was nothing there except a still pool of water. She couldn't shake the feeling that it was intensely ominous, probably full of things with too many tentacles and too many teeth. Although nothing had tried to eat them *yet.*

"Only a moment." Vale frowned; the rockfalls were getting closer. "The guards we bested will certainly have raised the alarm by now. And that noise, whatever it is —"

"Either it's an alarm," Irene said, "and we're being pursued. Or I've fundamentally damaged this place's nature by using the Language — so it's tearing itself apart and the ceiling's falling down. I'm not sure that's much better."

Kai knelt by the edge of the pool and cupped water in his hands, pouring it over his head. It ran down over his hair and in trickles down his shirt, plastering the fabric to his body. He sighed in relief, closing his eyes and splashing his face. "It's safe

421

enough," he said, turning back to Vale and Irene as he rose to his feet. "I just needed to clean myself. There's nothing alive in those waters."

"Or anywhere else in this place," Vale said. "Except for the prisoners, I fear. Do you think they could get free, Winters?"

"It'd be stupid to have an alarm system that let all the prisoners loose when it went off," Irene said. A spatter of dust drifted down from the spur of an arch above them, and the pool's surface shifted in long dark ripples. The instability was getting much closer. "Run now, talk later?" she suggested.

The ground shuddered under them as they began running again. Pieces of the upper bridge-work and pillars began to tumble from above, crashing to the ground in great explosions of sound and sprays of marble shards. It was like the slow unfolding of a nightmare, where the falling rocks and rising wind were always just behind them, forcing them to stumble onwards, their muscles aching, panting for breath. They couldn't afford to stop. Stonework was giving way less than a hundred yards behind them now, dropping pieces into the huge chasms. Distant shrieking came through the howling of the wind as unseen prisoners cried their rage into the storm. All Irene could focus on was running, putting one foot in front of the other, and on the exit ahead. They had to get out before the destruction caught up with them, or they were all lost. There should be only a couple of bridges now between them and the exit, and if they could just make it in time . . .

Then a cold realization spiked through her mind. *We're not escaping. We're being driven like panicked rabbits. And where you have a hunter driving rabbits, there's a snare at the other end.*

She forced herself to look up and around, scanning the horizon rather than the path to the bridge directly ahead. And that was how she caught the glint of light on the gun. With an effort that made her legs scream in pain, she pushed herself forward and slammed into Vale, knocking him down as the bullet ricocheted only a few inches from his head.

CHAPTER 23

All three of them hit the floor with varying degrees of style, and Irene desperately hoped the bridge's marble railings and pillars would block any but the luckiest of shots.

Crawling forward on her belly, she peered through the railings in the direction of the shooting and could see a squad of half a dozen disciplined-looking guards. They were on a ramp that curled up the side of a pillar, level with the centre of the bridge, giving them a rather too-convenient firing point. The one who had fired his long gun was reloading with cool efficiency, while the others were kneeling, ready to fire.

"Those look like muzzle-loaded rifles," Vale hissed.

"What do you mean?" she muttered.

"I mean that they are very accurate, Winters." Fresh blood from his exertions had stained his makeshift bandage. "That shot was not meant to hit me. It was meant to frighten us."

"If I hadn't knocked you down, it would've hit you!" Irene snapped, having to raise her voice now for it to carry above the sound of crashing rock. "Vale, they definitely want to take Kai alive, they might even want to take me alive, but I don't think they mind killing *you*! For heaven's sake, stay down!"

"Hells," Kai muttered. He wriggled sideways, lifting himself up a fraction to check the other end of the bridge. "And the railings cut out, once we get to the far end, which means we'd be an open target. But if they're not trying to bring us down, they're here to keep us trapped . . ." He swallowed.

Until someone else gets here to deal with us. Irene's right wrist throbbed from a remembered grip, and she rested it against the cold stone. "Can we go back?" she asked.

"We were less than ten minutes from the entrance," Vale growled. "If we turn back now and take a different route, we may not be able to find the entrance again, and we'd lose more time anyway."

Irene tried to think. They'd made it this far. She would *not* accept failure. "Kai, if you change form —"

"I'd be a sitting target before I could take

flight," Kai said quickly. "And even if they're holding fire on me right now, we can't assume they'll continue to do so."

Irene sighed. She hadn't even reached the part about *and then you escape on your own, while Vale and I make our way out separately,* but she suspected he'd seen it coming and rejected it.

"We are likely too high up to try dropping from the bridge," Vale said, peering round a pillar to see what lay beneath them. "Hmm. Another of those vast artificial reservoirs. It looks like it holds plenty of water, which could break our fall, but there's no way of knowing how deep it is. And the pillar those soldiers have claimed is pretty much touching the far side."

Irene wondered if his calm was a front. They were caught between the destruction behind them and the men in front, with a razor pendulum counting down the time they had left. She needed to run, to hurry, to try *something,* if only she knew what.

"Wait." Kai's voice was suddenly commanding. "Let me have a look." He snaked along to the next pillar, pulling himself up to inspect the water below. "Hmm. A good hundred feet down. That wouldn't do for you, no. But that body of water is huge — it looks big enough. And deep enough."

"Deep enough for what?" Vale demanded.

"To rouse it. There's nothing living there to stop me."

"Kai —," Irene began, but he was already moving.

"Stay down." With a nod to her and Vale, he rose to his feet, swinging over the rail in a single motion. A bullet, fired too late, hit the stone and chipped it.

Irene bit back a near scream, leaning between the pillars and watching as Kai fell. He converted the jump into a dive as gracefully as any professional athlete and plunged into the water. It seemed to rise to receive him, flashing like liquid mercury as he vanished into its darkness.

For a moment nothing happened. Her throat closed up, and she was barely able to swallow. Vale's hands gripped one of the pillars, and she could see his knuckles showing white through the flesh.

Then the water bulged upwards in a dome, and Kai rose within it. He drifted upwards with no apparent effort until he stood on the dome's very tip, the water seemingly as solid as glass. Irene found it hard to watch, as the soldiers suspended against their pillar seemed all too close. But Kai raised his hand as they aimed, and a wave rolled across the vast sunken reservoir towards them. It uncoiled like a serpent's tongue, gathering speed as it rose. It reached up and outwards in response to the movement of Kai's hand, crashing down on the soldiers' small platform with an unnatural weight. The wash of water sent them scattering, and the hollow boom of its falling echoed around the cavern, drowning out the sound of falling rocks for a moment.

"Move, Winters," Vale snapped, as though he hadn't been flat on his face and watching Kai a moment ago. He caught her elbow to pull her to her feet, and the two of them ran along the bridge to the stairs at the far end, clattering down them without any attempt at stealth.

Kai came strolling across the surface of the water, now raised to their level, to greet them. Water streamed down his clothing and hair and dripped from his hands, until a last rivulet rippled around him like a snake and flowed back into the main body that supported him. "The guards are unconscious or injured," he reported, lifting his hands to run them through his hair with a sigh. "Ah, that feels good. I don't think the waters outside will be as pleasant. They will have too much of a Fae touch to them."

"I didn't know you could do that," Irene said, at a loss for words. She was feeling light-headed. Perhaps they even had a chance now. She could have kissed Kai — and then her common sense cut in. This was not the time.

And when is the right time or place? an internal voice put in unhelpfully. *He just saved your life. He's standing there with his clothing clinging to him. It's not as if he would try to stop you. In fact, the way he's looking at you . . .*

"Can you do it again?" Vale said urgently.

"Oh yes." Kai rolled his shoulders, the muscles in his chest flexing. "The waters will obey my will — here, at least. I may have more difficulty outside."

"I don't think that you'll be able to assert your authority against the Ten in Venice," Irene warned him, and the moment passed.

"I was thinking of here, not there," Vale said, beckoning them into motion again. A piece of rock shivered and cracked away from near his feet, and Irene caught his arm to steady him. "Winters, if I remember correctly, there was another large body of water close to the staircase leading into this place?" She nodded in agreement. "Well then, what if Strongrock can move the water from its basin and raise it up to the level of that staircase? And carry us along with it? I know he can keep us safe in the water, as he's done it before. The Ten might be able to stop a few humans coming down the stairs, but they might have more difficulty with an oncoming tidal wave clearing our path."

"I suppose that gravity will take care of most threats," Kai agreed.

Irene imagined it. Water sluicing down the stairs into Saint Mark's Square in a great torrent. She *liked* it. But despite Vale's casual optimism, she couldn't help feeling there might still be some personal safety issues. "We'll still need to exit the Campanile into Venice itself," she said thoughtfully. "It would be astonishing if guards weren't waiting for us outside. But yes, if the momentum of the water is great enough after it's flooded down the length of the tower, they'll be unable to stand in its way. Kai, can you do this while actually keeping us — well, *alive*?"

Kai took a moment to think about it, which wasn't quite as reassuring as Irene would have liked, but then he nodded. "It may be uncomfortable, but you'll be safe," he said.

"Excellent," Vale said. "Ah, we are almost there. Strongrock, once we cross that open area, we will come to that final lake I mentioned. There is a last high bridge across it, which will take us almost to the exit. They might well have armed guards posted there — it's what I would do. You may need to rouse the water to wash them away first. Do you think you can do it?" He turned to meet Kai's eyes.

"It will be my pleasure," Kai said. "But this place is coming apart. What if I end up damaging the exit?"

"It's still our best option," Irene said firmly, deciding to keep her worries to herself. "Besides, have you noticed that the earth tremors have slacked off a little? Maybe their purpose was to drive us into the ambush —"

More rubble fell — nearly on top of them this time — and the marble paving shivered under their feet, cracking into fragments. A huge gust of wind made them all stagger.

"Or maybe not. Let's get this done fast," Irene said hastily. She didn't add, *Because it may be listening,* but she could see it in their faces.

They moved forward together at a run. Caution was pointless now, for the crashing stone and the wind drowned out any noise they made — and there was no sign of guards or snipers as they mounted the last bridge.

Almost no sign. Irene caught a flash of

red, a sleeve hastily pulled back into cover, violently obvious against the colourless marble.

"You think it's clear?" Kai asked, his voice pitched just loud enough to be heard.

"No, look *there,*" Irene said, pointing, her voice equally low. "They'll be sitting on top of the entrance, just waiting for us to come to them."

"It was all too likely," Vale agreed. "Now, as we planned, Strongrock."

Kai nodded. Leaving wet footprints behind, he sprinted to the edge of the bridge and threw himself into the lake below in a running dive, vanishing beneath the surface. Sweeping forward and upwards, the water began to swell into a growing wave, becoming higher with every moment.

The arched length of bridge shook beneath them.

If they went forward, they might be running into an ambush. If they stayed where they were, she and Vale could end up crushed. **"Stone, hold together!"** Irene shouted as loudly as she could. Her voice wouldn't carry to the ceiling, but if it could just keep the bridge together for long enough, Kai could deal with the soldiers.

Screams carried over the noise of falling rocks from ahead of them. Beneath Irene's feet, a long crack ran through the bridge, black against the white marble, tracing across it like a child's scribble. The bridge groaned underneath them in a long roar of fracturing stone, but it stayed in one piece.

Irene and Vale exchanged a glance, then decided that an ambush was the lesser danger. The marble paving was a heaving surface under them as they ran, still holding together but trembling against the forces threatening to shake it apart. It was barely possible to hear anything now, above the shuddering tumble of stone and the scream-ing wind.

"Over here!" Kai roared in a voice almost too loud for human lungs. "I've cleared our path!"

There was a clear *ping* as something rang against the marble rail beside Irene. At first she thought it was a fragment of stone; then she recognized it as a bullet. "Oh no, he hasn't," she muttered.

"It may be the best he can do," Vale shouted through the wind. He had paused at the sound of the bullet, like her, and was looking around desperately. "Winters, there's no other way out of here. We must risk it. Come on!"

It was quite true. But a Librarian couldn't speak fast enough to stop a bullet. They were about halfway across, so the considerable remaining length of bridge was downhill, but that wasn't much help . . .

Oh yes, it was. "Kai, get ready to catch us!" she screamed. **"Marble bridge surface, become a hundred times more slippery!"**

She launched herself into a desperate skid, and the next tremor tumbled her onto her rear. That only speeded her velocity. Like a child coasting down a hill, she skimmed helplessly and unstoppably down the curve of the bridge, far quicker than if she'd been running. The shuddering stone also pitched her unpredictably from side to side. She hoped that would foil the snipers as she shot forward. From the curses behind her, Vale was just as unable to control his motion, and a scatter of bullets cracked against the stone a few yards behind them.

Kai was standing on the now-ruffled surface of the sunken reservoir, where the end of the bridge met the paving. And he was surrounded by a moving coil of water, which had formed itself into a shield around him. Half a dozen guards were strewn unconscious on the ground, or groaning in the aftermath of being hit by the giant wave. No doubt their gunpowder was as soaked as they were. And twenty yards farther on, their goal was in sight at last: the metal stairway that had brought them here from Venice, standing upright within the yawning dark chasm that became the Campanile. The metal bridge that spanned that abyss to join the paving lay before them. Kai nodded as he caught sight of them, his posture braced and ready, and as Irene and Vale came skidding towards him, he flung his arms high in the air.

The water came shooting upwards around him, encasing him in a rising pillar of water. Like an unnatural tornado, the water moved upwards towards the far-distant ceiling with a roar that was audible even against the falling stone. Then it stopped, its power harnessed on the edge of breaking. Within its grip, Kai's hair floated around his head as if blown back by a wind, and the sleeves of his shirt rippled from the strength of the flow.

A wave reached out to engulf Irene and Vale, sweeping them off the ice-smooth marble and holding them in its grasp. Those of the soldiers who could move scrambled for cover, abandoning their guns. Irene screamed as the waters boiled up around them, and struggled to keep her head above the wave, her skirt a constricting mass around her legs.

"Get ready!" Kai's voice rang in her ears, even through the tumbling water. "I'll be able to control the beginning of the descent down the Campanile, but probably not the end, so hold your breath!"

The thought *This is going to hurt* stood out in the chaos. She emptied her lungs and then took in as much air as possible, trying to store as much oxygen as she could. She and Vale were several feet off the ground now, being dragged by the waters towards Kai's waterspout. Hanging above the ground, she felt a new sense of awe. The immense waves Kai had raised were still dwarfed by the immensity of this prison, which was for much larger, much more *powerful* entities than them. Things that, even if they won free, could scarcely fit down a tiny staircase — she hoped.

The pseudo-tornado's waters curved in a high arc over the iron bridge, to rest poised above the staircase where they had originally entered the prison. Then it fell down into the chasm, a twisting stream of liquid darkness that centred on the staircase, making the whole structure shudder and thrum as water hit iron. The sound was so loud that Irene raised her hands to cover her ears, trying to block it out. She could imagine the gush of water as it followed the spiral of the staircase. Jets would spout in all directions through the gaps in the panelling, but the main force of it would surge ever downwards. And as the dark shaft around the staircase narrowed and drew back to the dimensions of the Campanile below, there would be even less room for the water to escape. There would be nowhere for it to go, except down and out.

She hoped that anyone in the way had the sense to run.

Then Kai gestured towards her and Vale, and the waters pulled them towards him, like mere straws caught in an undercurrent. She took a last deep breath, her stomach knotting in pure terror, and then the rush of water swept all three of them giddily up through the air within the water-funnel. She was relieved, because if there was air, Kai was keeping them safe as he'd promised. They swung up and over the chasm in a single smooth arc, like an arrow's flight, and then they plunged down into the stairwell.

At first the momentum was surprisingly smooth. She curled up instinctively, folding her arms over her head and tucking herself into a ball. The light was gone within moments, as the water swept the three of them round the first couple of curves in the stairs. It wasn't as nauseating as it might have been. It felt more like the guided sliding of a helter-skelter than anything else, and Kai clearly had it under control. She clung to that thought like a talisman. She was going down an extremely high staircase underwater at high speed in the darkness. But she could trust Kai. *He has it under control,* she repeated to herself.

Then abruptly it was colder, and the water was no longer cradling her, but simply carrying her along like a fragment of straw. *We've crossed the boundary into Venice,* she thought grimly as she held on to the last of her air. *Kai can't function here, so we'll just have to get through the rest of it.*

The water now thumped her into the outer side of the staircase, banging her downwards like flotsam and spinning her round faster and faster. She hit the staircase again, the panelling, the stairs below her and the bottom of the stairs above her. Most of the blows were to her hips or shoulders, and she kept her head tucked in tightly, her breath burning in her lungs. There was no room for thought, just sheer panic as she crashed downwards in the darkness.

Abruptly it spat her out. The gush of water threw her out through the Campanile's elegant portico and open gates and into the square beyond. Irene tumbled across the paving for several yards before she came to a halt. She lay there in the draining water, still curled up, the parts of her body that had banged into the staircase aching. Cold water washed past her cheek as she gasped for air. Her head was still spinning, and she vomited, throwing up the little in her stomach onto the freshly washed stones.

"Winters!" Vale was shouting at her, his voice penetrating the general uproar. "Over here!"

She looked around, disorientated. It was full night. Lanterns flashed as they swung madly in the wind, and the square was a churning mess. Like her, others were sprawled in the water as the last of it flowed out across the piazza. It drained into the shops and public buildings that bordered it, or ran over the paving and into the sea beyond. Uniformed guards around the Campanile's entrance were also struggling to their feet. The size of the crowd suggested a near mob — or would have, before one added an almighty flood in the near darkness. It was definitely a mob now. The dim municipal lighting, combined with the masks most people were wearing, turned the scene into a nightmare.

Kai was lying on his face, groaning. Vale, looking battered but mobile, had one of

Kai's arms over his shoulders and was trying to haul him to his feet. It said something about Vale's own condition that he hadn't managed it yet. His arm was bleeding again. Irene pulled on her own mask as she staggered across to join them, her joints protesting with every step, and wedged her shoulder under Kai's other arm. "Get — get to the Train," she coughed, tasting bile with every word.

"You need not belabour the obvious, Winters," Vale snapped.

"Get them!" Lord Guantes shouted from somewhere in the darkness, his voice furious beyond any semblance of control.

I don't think I'm going to be invited to the opera again.

Irene hesitated, getting her bearings. "Over there, to the right," she gasped, pointing with her free hand to where the square led down towards the open water. Her body ached as if someone had taken a carpet-beater to it. "Keep to the right, as if we were going to the Biblioteca Marciana."

"Of course," Vale grunted. He was taking more of Kai's weight than she was. "Guantes will think we're headed towards a library . . ."

Irene saved her breath and simply jerked a nod. The mob was all round them now, scrambling to get out of the piazza. She and Vale weren't the only ones supporting a semi-conscious friend. Even if they were some of the wettest.

The yells of the crowd behind them suggested Guantes's minions were rapidly clubbing their way through — so Irene needed to hide their destination. She staggered to a stop with Kai and Vale between two lanterns, just before the square's exit. Then she took a deep breath, bracing herself. **"Lanterns, shatter and go out!"** she screamed at the top of her voice.

Her voice carried, even over the crowd, and the lanterns above blew out in a fusillade of glass, their flames snuffed in a single breath. Other smaller lanterns within the reach of her voice fell dramatically to pieces, crumbling where they hung in shopwindows or on stalls, or as they were carried along by people in the crush.

The area was abruptly that much darker. And the mob that much more panicked and obstructive, but you couldn't have everything.

"Now we run," Irene gasped, and they did.

CHAPTER 24

They fled through the darkness, the three of them staggering together. Kai was barely conscious, his breath coming in rattling gasps in Irene's ear, and Irene herself desperately wanted to collapse for a few minutes. But even if she could have ignored Lord Guantes and his minions in pursuit, there was a feeling in the air that she didn't like, a febrile edge to the turmoil. They were on the precipice of a riot. Or something worse.

The paving stones seemed to drag at her feet, but she gritted her teeth and pushed on. She wasn't going to be the one to get them caught.

"Hurts . . . ," Kai mumbled.

"We're almost there," Irene gasped reassuringly, not bothering to check if this was true. "Just hold on a bit longer."

"No," Kai said, a little more clearly now. There was genuine pain in his voice. "My feet . . ."

Both Irene and Vale stopped, Vale jostling
her to look down. The paving was rising
around Kai's shoes, seemingly grasping at
his feet as it bubbled in an unwholesome
way in the near darkness. Irene looked
nervously at her own feet, but whatever it
was didn't seem to be affecting her or Vale.

Vale took a deep breath. "Let go of him,
Winters," he instructed. "And be ready to
clear our way." With a grunt of effort, he
bent over and swung Kai up onto his shoulder in a fireman's lift. More blood stained
the bandage on his arm.

Right. That might work. If Kai's feet
weren't actually touching the ground . . .
They were nearly at the Train. Perhaps five
minutes. If they could just make it.

She ploughed her way through the crowd,
using her shoulders and elbows to force a
passage for herself and the men. Behind her,
the shouting seemed louder and more
directed, and she tried not to think what
would happen when Guantes realized they
weren't actually heading for the library at
all. They had to reach the Train — and Lord
Guantes was entirely capable of working
that out. *And where is Lady Guantes?* Irene
hoped not knowing wouldn't prove fatal.

The bracelets that Silver had given her

seemed to be vibrating against her wrists, throbbing with their own heat, and her mask pressed against her face like a suffocating hand. *Is it a sign that the Ten are looking for me too?* she wondered. *They could be looking for anything not native to this place. And there's only me and Kai here who aren't Fae or normal humans . . .*

She shoved onwards through the crowd and stumbled into a sudden emptiness as she reached the waterside. Even the crowd had more sense than to push all the way to the edge, where the darkness of the sea stretched into the distance, wave-tops catching the light of lanterns in pale ruffles of foam. The lights of the island beyond were visible as distantly glowing pinpoints, breaking up the long stretch of shadow where night sky was indistinguishable from sea. The Train was a harsh line of light against the darkness, with the bright squares of lit windows shining like an invitation. But, more practically, it was a good hundred yards farther along the quay. At least.

The noise of the crowd was changing, and Irene turned to look behind her as a chill of apprehension ran down her wet back. There was something about the way that they were moving — and speaking . . .

They were all acting in unison. Like a

pack of dogs, all slowly raising their hackles as they focused on an intruder, the crowd was staring at them as if one intelligence animated each member of the throng. The Venetians' eyes shone like cats' eyes in the gloom, and they were even breathing together — in an audible whisper louder than the shifting water. The air was full of an inhuman attention, a *presence* that curdled the blood and froze the mind in panic. *The Ten. The Ten have found us.*

"Winters . . . ," Vale said, very quietly, as though afraid that any louder sound would set off an explosion of violence. *Do something* went unspoken.

Irene quickly rejected multiple possibilities in her head. The Language could freeze water, but she couldn't freeze the whole lagoon, or even enough to get across to the Train. And confusing the perception of so many people was beyond her abilities.

Even the boatmen in the gondolas were turning to stare . . .

She was moving before she could think twice, pulling up her skirts and jumping into the nearest gondola. The gondolier wasn't expecting it, and she rammed her shoulder into his stomach, shoving him overboard while he tottered and struggled for breath. Vale was right behind her and was already hauling Kai into the gondola.

The entire crowd was still staring at them in dead silence. It was paralysing. Irene choked, trying to get her mouth and tongue to work as she struggled with adrenaline mingled with fear, but the words finally came. **"Mooring rope, undo. Gondola in which I am standing, move towards the Train."**

The gondola was moving before the rope (and all other ropes within earshot) came fully undone. For one terrifying moment it strained against its moorings, still tied to the quay as the crowd came rushing forward with a single, multivoiced scream of fury. She could see the whites of their wide, expressionless eyes. Seagulls rose shrieking from the rooftops and eaves, bursting into motion in a flurry of pale wings in the darkness.

Then the rope snapped, lashing free as it broke, and the boat jolted into motion. Vale collapsed in a pile with the semi-conscious Kai, and Irene went down on her hands and knees as the gondola cut through the water like a motorboat towards the Train, the impression so convincing that she could almost believe she smelled smoke.

A nasty suspicion flared in her mind, and she turned to look at Kai. The wood of the gondola was indeed charring and smoking where his flesh touched it, and a matching discolouration was spreading like a rash on his skin. *He's as allergic to this place as it's allergic to him. There was no way I could have hidden him here and escaped later.* She turned back to the approaching Train, with a feeling of mingled dread and irritation at yet one more obstacle — how were they actually going to get into the thing? Still, climbing into a train from a burning gondola, at sea-level, was a minor problem, considering what they were leaving behind.

The gondola crashed into the side of the Train and bobbed there crazily, pitching up and down. In mute invitation, the nearest Train door immediately swung open, and Vale caught hold of it, steadying the gondola against the side of the Train while Irene scrambled into the carriage. Other gondolas, full of wild-eyed Venetians, were surging through the water towards them, in a dead silence that was almost more horrifying than screams or threats. She pulled Kai by the shoulders as Vale pushed, dragging him into the Train with adrenaline-fuelled strength. She'd barely levered him part-way in when the burned gondola gave way under Vale. He threw himself forward, clutching at the lip of the doorway as the planks sank beneath him.

"Vale!" Irene screamed, dropping her hold on Kai's shoulders to reach for him.

Vale spat out sea-water. "I can manage," he gasped, kicking to raise himself in the water and push himself into the carriage. "See to Strongrock!"

Irene tugged frantically at Kai. He was a dead weight, his eyes closed and his body limp, but she managed to drag him fully inside the carriage just as Vale finished pulling himself in too. From the corner of her eye, she could see the crowd banging on the platform-side doors. She ignored them. She didn't think the Train would let them in.

The interior of the Train was silent, and they found themselves in a luxurious carriage, all ivory velvet and fittings, which made their soaked, dishevelled clothes seem even more inappropriate. But the challenge now was to flee this Venice before the Rider, or the Ten — or anyone else — could stop them.

It was time. Irene took a deep breath, rose to her feet, and said firmly, **"Train, Steed, Horse . . . or whatever I should call you, I am here to free you so that we can escape together. Show me how."**

A scream shook the carriage, too loud to be human, and Irene clapped her hands to her ears before she belatedly recognized the Train venting steam. The noise settled down to a barely tolerable shudder, the wheels trembling in place, but not quite moving yet as the pistons shook in their housings.

"Why isn't it moving?" Vale demanded. He pushed back wet hair from his face.

"I don't think it can until I've freed it," Irene said. She looked round for any obvious indications and hoped it wouldn't involve going outside again.

Vale frowned. "What did you try before — telling a story?"

Irene suppressed a moment of irritation at Vale telling *her* how to use the Language, and nodded, assembling a narrative. Right, that was it. **"And the princess returned from her quest, with the prince with her"** — well, on the floor — **"and her knight by her side."** She couldn't risk leaving Vale out of the story, in case the Train left him behind. **"And the princess said to the horse, 'Where are your bridle and reins, that I may free you from them?' "**

Their carriage-door swung open into the corridor. And, with a sigh, Vale swung Kai onto his shoulder again, staggering under the weight.

Irene was first through the door — and it

slammed shut behind her, nearly catching her fingertips. She could see Vale and Kai on the other side through the carriage-windows, but she couldn't prise open the door, however much she wrenched at the handle. *"Let them go!"* she shouted, seeing faces in the darkness behind Vale, on the platform outside the Train.

The humming of the engine steadied into a regular *shook-a-shook,* a trembling eagerness to depart. Maybe in this story the princess had to free the steed on her own. She'd trusted it so far — she'd just have to keep on trusting it.

With what she hoped was a reassuring gesture through the window, Irene headed down the corridor.

The door at the end of the passage led into darkness. Not the kind of darkness where one could just about see one's way, but total pitch darkness of the sort that suggested underground abysses or hidden cellars. She didn't think a demand to turn the lights on would be much help.

With an inward sigh, Irene stepped through.

She was abruptly in the Train's engine car, which was dark too, but she could now see a little farther. It was filled with complex dials and levers, a coal-powered boiler to supply steam, and a lot of gleaming oily pistons. She looked around for any obvious clues to take things forward.

There. A heavy silver padlock and chain were fastened around one of the largest levers, holding it in an upright position. It looked more ornamental than functional, something that anyone could easily lift off the handle and remove. But, she reminded herself, the symbolism might be important here. The memory of another chain months ago, and the trap that had been woven into it, made her hesitate. That time she'd been infected with raw chaos, and she'd only survived because Kai had broken her free. He wasn't here now.

The machinery hummed around her. Then another scream was ripped from the steam whistle, as if — no, she was sure of it — the Train was impatient with the delay. But how was she supposed to protect herself in a high-chaos environment, when anything she might do could infect her with the stuff?

Well, perhaps she might try protecting herself in advance this time . . .

She scooped up a fingerful of oily grease and hastily scribbled her own name in the Language on the palm of her left hand, then repeated the process on the right. Hopefully defining herself in this way would help keep the chaos out. It had better; she was out of ideas.

"And the princess saw the horse's bridle and reins," she pronounced, flexing her fingers. The words hummed in her mouth and echoed in the engine car as she spoke them. **"And she said to the horse, 'Now I shall free you from your captivity, and you in turn will help me and those with me to escape.' "**

The hum around her rose, throbbing loud enough to hurt her ears. **"And the princess took the bridle and reins . . ."** She was having to shout now to hear herself over the sound of the engine. The Language tore at her throat and weighed on her lungs. Her body was moving as she spoke, and she could not, even for the sake of her sanity, be sure if she was moving of her own volition or because the Language was forcing the movements from her.

Her hands closed on the chain, and the bracelets that Silver had given her shattered, flying into fragments and cascading to the floor in a scatter of links. The mask covering her face dissolved, crumbling into dust that clung to her wet skin. She could feel her own name in the Language burning into her skin, but the metal of the chain itself was cold and as normal as anything here could be. **"And she drew it from the horse's neck . . ."** Her arms rose upwards, dragging the chain from where it hung over the metal handle like a noose. For a long moment it seemed to cling to the top of the lever, dragging against it as if unwilling to be released.

She set her teeth. **"And it came free!"** she shouted.

The small metal *ting* of the chain coming loose rang through the cabin, even louder than the pulsing of the engines. The metal links were slick against her palms now, like oil made solid. They snaked around her hands, curling about her wrists almost affectionately.

The Train shuddered lengthwise, the movement jerking along the carriage like the crack of a whip. Irene lost her balance, falling to her knees. And as if it had been waiting for its moment, the chain lunged for her neck. She cried out in shock, holding her now tightly bound hands as far away from her as she could, and clinging desperately to the chain to stop it getting any closer. The chain's ends brushed coldly against her skin, trying to get nearer to her throat.

Suddenly it slipped between her fingers, freeing her wrists, but flinging itself around her neck. She managed to get her fingers between the chain and her skin, but it tightened against them, cutting into her flesh in a vicious, deliberate attempt at murder. Her pulse rang in her ears even louder than the screaming of the Train's whistle.

She shut her eyes, forcing back panic, holding on to a last thread of consciousness. There was still air in her lungs. **"Chain, slacken,"** she wheezed, the words coming out in a barely audible whisper. **"Slacken enough for me to breathe."**

The chain relaxed its stranglehold, and the flashing lights in front of her eyes receded. It shifted and flexed against her fingers, writhing around her neck as if trying to find a new avenue for attack. If it was somehow alive, then the Language wouldn't have a lasting effect on it. She could throw it out of the window, perhaps? Or, better still, destroy it? Tell it to come to pieces? But what if it rejoined itself?

The boiler door drew her eye, and she staggered across to it and threw the door open. Heat came rushing out, searing her face and making her choke again. The chain tightened as if in response, grinding the fingers of her other hand against her neck and dragging her head back.

"Fae silver chain," she gritted out, being as precise as she could, **"loosen! Be quiescent! HOLD STILL!"**

The chain went slack enough for her to wrench it over her head and get a firm hold of it with both hands. She balled it up and flung it into the furnace, and it clattered and twisted as it left her hands, trying to move and lunge at her. She slammed the boiler door on it, her hands aching from the scorching heat. It hammered at the door, but after a few seconds its last desperate clangs died away.

Then the great lever came down of its own volition.

The steam whistle screamed, but this was a cry of joyous liberation, wild freedom finally allowed to run loose. The whole engine car shook, and the Train began to move.

CHAPTER 25

For a long moment, all Irene could do was lean over, rest her hands on her thighs, and breathe. The wet fabric of her skirts soothed her scoured palms, and there was a great aching numbness in her mind. She'd done it. The Train was moving. All three of them were safely on board.

They'd *done* it.

Outside the window she could see nothing but dark water, shivering and tossing, with distant lights catching the foam-caps. Hopefully it would be a quicker journey back to Vale's London than it had been to get here in the first place. The atmosphere on the Train must be nearly as toxic to Kai as Venice was.

She opened the engine car door, then hesitated. The carriage beyond was *not* the one that she had just left. The Train must somehow have readjusted itself, to bring her so quickly to this end of its structure. "Ah

. . . ," she started, feeling a bit foolish addressing the Train in so conversational a way. "Please can you return me to the carriage containing my companions?"

The carriage was silent.

All right. That was probably a *no,* so she had a walk ahead of her. Shouting at the Train would be a waste of time — but slamming the door did make her feel better.

Just as before, each carriage was different and displayed new heights of luxury. The only shoddy element here was her. And as she travelled the length of the Train, it seemed to be moving more erratically than before, with the juddering and shaking of a regular steam train. Each step had Irene swaying in order to keep her balance.

The sixth compartment also seemed empty, until she spotted someone lounging on a black velvet sofa with a glass of pale green liquor. It just wasn't the person she'd been expecting to see.

"Zayanna?" she said blankly.

"Clarice!" Zayanna attempted to hide the glass of liquor under the sofa, but some of it spilled, and the scattered drops left hissing marks on the carpeting. She was back in her bikini, her long bronzed limbs artfully displayed against the sofa's darkness, hair tumbling down over one shoulder. "I was just about to get back to searching . . ." She frowned. "Wait a moment. It was you that I was supposed to be searching for."

"It was?" Irene tried to think of a plausible lie. "Well, you've found me now, so you don't have to worry about it —"

Then her brain cut in. Zayanna was on the Train, apparently searching for her. Which meant that others would be seeking her too. And Vale and Kai . . . Her stomach dropped.

"Why were you looking for me?" She desperately wanted any answer except the one she expected.

"Well." Zayanna was absently twisting a tendril of hair, but she was also watching Irene closely from under lowered eyelashes. "There was this rumour that you'd rescued the dragon and were escaping with him. Darling. And we were with you earlier, so we were tagged as potential conspirators — until we agreed to help with the search, just to prove how non-involved and non-traitorous we are. Darling."

Irene spread her arms wide. "Do I *look* as if I've got a dragon hidden anywhere?"

"No," Zayanna said readily. "That'd be because he's now being held farther down the Train."

Irene took a deep breath. "Well then," she

said, and was surprised at how normal her voice sounded. Where was the utter stomach-churning, headache-inducing exasperation — no, *fury* — at yet one more obstacle in her way, one more damned interference by the damned Guantes? "I'll just have to do something about that."

Zayanna frowned. "Are you absolutely sure you should be telling me that, Clarice?"

"Look at it this way," Irene said. Her hand sought the butt of the gun that was still somehow concealed in her soggy skirts. The gunpowder would be thoroughly soaked by now, but Zayanna didn't know that. "Is it really in your best interests to get into a confrontation with an armed, dangerous, dragon-rescuing type like me? Seriously, Zayanna, I thought you were complaining earlier because you never managed to interact with heroes."

"I was complaining that I never got to *seduce* heroes, darling." Zayanna smiled. She twirled her hair again, her teeth gleaming and more than a little pointed. "But it's very sweet that you were actually listening."

"Hand me over to the Guantes and you won't even get that chance," Irene said, mentally resigning herself to a potential inconvenient seduction routine. Still, if Zayanna was anything like Silver, she'd probably get just as much out of Irene turning her down — as long as it was melodramatic enough. But first she had an escape to organize. "Is anyone in the next carriage?"

"Atrox Ferox and Athanais," Zayanna said. She frowned. "Are we talking a serious seduction here? A really truly thing of passion?"

"A sporting chance at one, if we get out of this alive," Irene said. She might be laying it on a bit thick, but Zayanna seemed to be buying it. But how far could she push the other woman? "Do you know if Atrox Ferox or Athanais have patrons who are inclined to stability, or to war with the dragons? And what of your own?"

"The Lord Judge is Atrox Ferox's patron, and he's inclined to stability," Zayanna offered without hesitation. "So Atrox Ferox is here to report on events, rather than because of any alliance with the warmongering Guantes. No question, darling, the Lord Judge is one of those known quantities you can depend upon. But I don't know about Athanais. Or his patron. If he has one."

"And what of yours?" Irene pushed. She had no idea who the Lord Judge was, but his neutrality sounded encouraging.

Zayanna sighed, and the droop of her shoulders looked entirely genuine. "Darling, he doesn't *care*. That's why he sent someone like me along rather than one of the proxies he actually trusts. He'll just end up going with the majority, as usual. Of course, he doesn't want me compromising his interests, so I don't want to be caught doing anything I shouldn't, but otherwise he couldn't care less."

Which meant no opportunity for Zayanna to advance . . . unless *Irene* offered her a chance to play a role. "From what you're saying, he's not interested in losers," she said casually. "If the Guantes should fail, then he wouldn't want to know them — he'd deny ever even knowing them in the first place."

"Well, naturally," Zayanna said. Her eyes narrowed again. "Wouldn't anyone?"

"Right," Irene said, conscious of the enormity of the risk. But if it paid off, she'd actually have a chance. She hauled the wet gun out from her dripping skirts and offered it to Zayanna, butt-first. "I need your help, Zayanna. As my ally. As my *friend*. I want you to stand behind me and use my body to hide the gun while I'm talking. And if the talking doesn't work, then I'm going to need you to threaten people with it." Perhaps a slight hint at emotional involvement might be a good idea. *"Please?"* she

461

added hopefully, batting her eyelashes in what she hoped was an appealing fashion.

Zayanna's eyes widened. "You want me to stand behind you with a loaded weapon?"

"Yes," Irene said firmly.

"Oh, *darling*." Zayanna threw herself against Irene, nestling her head against her chest and wrapping her arms around her, ignoring Irene's wet rags. "Nobody's ever said anything so *romantic* to me in all my life."

Irene gently prised her off, somewhat inconvenienced by the gun in her hand. "Let's do this," she said, mentally crossing her fingers that Zayanna was right about Atrox Ferox's neutrality. He was, after all, the other one with a gun.

He and Athanais were standing in the corridor of the next carriage when Irene opened the door, and he immediately raised his gun. It looked futuristic, sleek, and unnaturally large — though that might have been due to it being pointed at her.

She raised her hands above her shoulders, conscious of Zayanna right behind her. "Good evening, gentlemen," she said pleasantly.

"Clarice." Atrox Ferox eyed her levelly, his dark eyes narrowed. "Or would some other name be more appropriate?"

Marvellous, I'm being typecast as a master spy in this story. I think I preferred being underestimated. "My real name is unimportant," she said, aiming for a note of authority. "What matters is why I'm here."

"A matter of grand treason, I heard," Athanais put in. He was wearing a lute slung across his body, and his hands tensed above the strings as if it were a weapon too. "Is there another way of seeing it?"

Irene lowered her hands slowly. Atrox Ferox wasn't making any move to shoot her, and it was tiring to hold them up. "Personally, I'd call it trying to stop a war. Whether or not you'd call that grand treason probably depends on your politics."

"Clarification would be useful," Atrox Ferox said. He wasn't lowering his gun, but Irene decided to count the lack of gun-fire as promising. "Truthful explanation even more so."

"Kidnapping a dragon king's son to auction him off to the highest bidder is an audacious move, I'll give them that," Irene said. She turned to face Athanais, but kept Atrox Ferox just within sight. "It could start a war. It might even start a war you could win. Though let's not go into the consequences for ordinary humans throughout the spheres, shall we? That would just be depressing. But kidnapping a dragon king's son and then managing to lose him in the middle of Venice, in the Ten's personal territory? And allowing him to escape? I'm not terribly impressed with Lord and Lady Guantes, not impressed at all. If someone was going to start a war, I'd hope it was someone a bit more efficient. Truly great leaders shouldn't be so easily foiled. If I were you, Athanais, I wouldn't call interfering with their schemes 'grand treason.' I'd call it a minor action that will save you a great deal of trouble further down the line."

"I'm not interested in winning or losing a war," Athanais said. His fingers drifted lower, brushing the strings. "Maybe just being involved is enough? For the fame, for the story . . . So I'm not sure that I really care about your argument. It's a nice effort, I'll give you that. But it's not enough to save you."

"Maybe it isn't," came Zayanna's voice from behind Irene, before Irene could work out a new line of reasoning. "But this is. If you play a single note, then I will shoot you."

Athanais swallowed. "Atrox! She's gone traitor too — shoot her!"

"Shoot her," Irene said blandly, "and you'll bring her patron into this as well. Do you really want that?"

"She's the one pointing the gun at me, not the other way around," Athanais snapped. "And as for you — we don't even know who or what you are. For all we know, you're another dragon in disguise."

"I'm just incognito," Irene said, wondering how long she had until Athanais called for reinforcements. If there were guards in the next carriage, it might only take a single shout. "This isn't worth your time. The best thing you can do is step aside and stay well out of the Guantes' failure. People remember fame and stories, Athanais, but they remember failure too. Get out while you can."

She saw Atrox Ferox tense, and she braced herself to duck, but he moved in the opposite direction, bringing his gun round to slam the butt into Athanais's head in a whirl of black steel and leather. The other man slumped, his eyes rolling up in his head, and the lute fell against his body in a squawk of jangling strings.

Irene took a deep breath before saying, "Thank you."

"Your argument is sound," Atrox Ferox said crisply. He gathered Athanais under his left arm, holding the unconscious man against his body. "Why expend energy on a lost cause? Even now, if the prisoner were returned, too much power has been lost. The name of Guantes is no longer what it was."

"Oh yes," Zayanna agreed. "He jumped out of his opera box, was washed halfway across the Piazza, and had to run to catch the Train — it's not what one expects of a patron. They ought to be above such things." She paused. "Clarice, did *you* have anything to do with any of that?"

"A little bit," Irene admitted as casually as she could, enjoying the image of Lord Guantes being flushed across the Piazza like a wet rag.

Atrox Ferox didn't quite crack his impassive facade, but his eyes widened and he seemed visibly impressed. "When last seen, the Guantes were in the carriage four down. They had two prisoners — the dragon, and another whose powers aren't known to me. The carriage is guarded. Also, the Train is pursued."

"Pursued?" Irene said in alarm. She hadn't thought things could get any worse, but here they were. Just another cherry on the cake.

"Others among our great ones are involving themselves," Atrox Ferox said. "Even those who had no interest in the dragon would wish to take the Train for themselves — then bind it anew. And the Rider himself comes in force, to reclaim what is his. Thus it flees."

"Can they catch it?"

"Perhaps within the hour." Atrox Ferox shrugged, the light catching the steel plating in his bodysuit. "Perhaps less, if luck favours them."

Irene repressed the urge to run her hands through her hair. "So, correct me if I'm wrong. The Guantes are on board. They have two hostages. They are in the carriage four down from here with — how many other guards?"

"Two armed guards," Atrox Ferox said. "And Sterrington. I will momentarily place Athanais where he will not be disturbed." He opened the compartment door and deposited him on a cream sofa.

"And how many guards in each carriage between us?" Irene was trying to gauge her opposition, but however she did this, the words *YOU LOSE* seemed worryingly inevitable.

Atrox Ferox shrugged. "Half a dozen in each carriage, and the same in the carriages beyond them. You must have made quite an impression." His speech was significantly less formal now, coming and going, and

Irene wondered how much of it had been a deliberate pose.

Zayanna sighed and leaned against Irene's back, draping her arms round Irene's neck. "Darling, I hate to say it, but this isn't sounding good. Can you enchant their eyes?"

"Probably not," Irene admitted. There were just too many. Her mind raced through other tactics instead. She *had* read Sun Tzu, after all, and she knew her enemy. Assuming Atrox Ferox wasn't preparing a trap — to say nothing of Zayanna, whom she could only trust so far, if at all.

She needed to think outside the box somehow. Having Atrox Ferox and Zayanna escort her through as a "captive" was a possibility, but she could think of far too many ways it could go wrong.

Something was prodding at the back of her mind. *Outside the box.* The Train was basically a set of boxes. So she needed to get outside the Train. But could she . . . ? She looked up at the ceiling of the compartment. There were two unobtrusive trapdoors in the ceiling, one at each end of the compartment.

All *right.*

"Clarice?" Zayanna prompted, and Irene realized they were waiting for her to speak.

"I think I have an idea," she said. *A really bad one.* "I need to shorten my skirts, I need a lift, and I need a gun. Atrox Ferox, may I borrow yours?"

He considered for a moment, then handed it over. "If any ask, I will say you overcame me and took it from my body," he warned.

"That sounds very reasonable," Irene said. She took it from him and gauged its weight in her hand. "How many shots does it hold?"

"Fifteen. You will find there is little recoil."

"What do you mean, a lift?" Zayanna asked. "And where do we come into it?" She brought out a knife from somewhere — Irene decided not to wonder how she'd hidden it in her bikini — and offered it to Irene.

Irene tucked the gun under one arm and began to roughly shorten her skirts to knee-level with the knife. "I mean that I'm heading for the roof of the Train."

There was a deadly silence. Finally Zayanna said, "Darling, are you completely and utterly insane? I mean, it's tremendously brave of you, but —"

"The Train hasn't tried to stop me so far," Irene said. The knife ripped through her sodden skirts, baring her stockings and shoes. "I'm counting on that to mean I can move along the roof. I'm grateful for what you two have done, but I don't want to get you into further trouble."

That was a lie, but it was more polite than trying to get rid of them. "Though if you could manage a bit of a diversion, I would be grateful."

"Such is within the bounds of propriety," Atrox Ferox pronounced.

Zayanna pressed her knuckles against her mouth, her teeth showing white as she gnawed on them. "I'll scream," she promised. "We'll draw some of the guards out of the way. Oh, do be *careful,* Clarice."

You're following the Distressed Maiden archetype rather than the Dark Seductress mode right now, Irene mused drily. But all she said was, "Just be careful," as she tucked Atrox Ferox's gun into her sash. "Both of you. Please."

They nodded. Then Atrox Ferox went down on one knee under the nearer trap-door, offering her a convenient step.

Irene balanced on his shoulder, looking up. The round trap-door was large enough to fit her comfortably, with a heavy bolt on one side and two thick hinges on the other. The mechanics were obvious enough. Adrenaline was fuelling her again, and so, before she could change her mind, she quickly tugged on the bolt and pushed,

470

hard, on the cold metal. It swung past her with a loud screech from the hinges, and with a howl the noise of the wind filled the compartment. It wasn't exactly quiet — something to remember at the other end.

She looked up at the night sky, full of stars and darkness. "Now, please," she said.

Atrox Ferox rose to his feet underneath her, boosting her up smoothly. She wriggled out onto the top of the Train, fingers groping for a handhold.

The wind nearly ripped her off the roof before she could even get her balance. She flattened herself desperately against the metal, sliding across the roof of the Train as the trap-door thudded back into place underneath her. Its momentum slammed her into the ornamental rail on one side of the roof, and she latched onto it with the strength of panic. The polished metal was freezing cold, and for a moment her hands began to slip. She forced herself to grip more tightly, her lips shaping silent wind-blown curses, the Language no use to her here. Finally, she managed to wedge her hip into the narrow gap between rail and Train roof to steady herself.

Endless pale dunes of sculpted sand whipped past under the cold stars as she tried to make herself move again. Her very practical and very present fear of death warred with her need to rescue her friends. But time was running out. She pushed herself onwards.

The slip-stream pressed her against the roof as if she were on an extreme fairground ride, but as long as she kept flat to the metal surface as she pulled herself along, it was manageable. The sound of the wind and the Train's wheels filled her ears, shaking her down to her bones.

Then as she came to the end of the carriage, before the covered section that joined it to the next, she raised her head briefly to look down the length of the Train. It seemed to stretch on for dozens of carriages, a near-endless stream of mercury and darkness crossing the desert. Beyond that, right at the edge of her vision, she saw followers, and her stomach clenched. She couldn't make them out clearly, but some were dark, some were bright; some might have been hounds or wolves, while others might have been riders or motorcyclists, or even cars. But they were spread across the horizon, all inexorably tracking the Train. And in the lead was a single figure on his own, running along the track. The Rider, come to take the Horse back and fulfil his own story.

She saw failure in that moment. Unless

she remembered something.

Abandoning one precious handhold, she raked her fingers against a join in the roof's metal panelling until she felt a raw edge snag her skin and draw blood. Then she reached into her bodice, finding the pendant that Kai's uncle had given her, and dragged it over her head. The chain caught in her tangled, matted hair, and she had to tug to get it free. What had he said?

Place a drop of your blood on this and cast it to the winds . . .

Irene folded her grazed hand around the pendant. But nothing happened. There were no dramatic changes of temperature, no glowing lights — nothing. Some sort of sign would have been nice.

Please let this work, Irene thought, and threw the pendant out into the darkness beyond. It glinted for a moment in her vision, perhaps a spark of brightness from the silver chain, and then it was gone.

She continued to crawl down the Train.

CHAPTER 26

Four painstakingly counted carriages later, each one of them a dance with death as the Train swayed and bucked, Irene decided she must be there.

Now she needed to check the interior of the carriage. But fortunately the old cliché was true: people never did look up. And they wouldn't be able to hear her up here, either. She positioned herself over the nearer trap-door, locked her grip firmly, and shouted, **"Trap-door, turn transparent."**

The steel complied. Inside it looked positively cosy, in a dark, steely sort of way. Possibly it was the warm light of the gas lamps, and the contrast from carriages' worth of cold, dark crawling. Her angle of vision also, most importantly, gave her a clear view of Vale and Kai. Both had been tied hand and foot, with their wrists behind their backs. They were on the floor at her end of the carriage, and they both seemed unconscious. Sterrington was standing over them, a naked pistol in her hand, in a posture suggesting that she'd shoot them at the least provocation. She looked, for want of a better word, ruffled. So Irene's first move must be to neutralize Sterrington, and her gun.

The Guantes were farther down the carriage, towards the far end. Lord Guantes was seated, frowning intensely at the hostages, his focus on them almost palpable. *Look away,* instinct prompted Irene, and she forced herself to watch Lady Guantes instead. The woman was pacing slowly from side to side of the compartment, placing one grey-slippered foot deliberately in front of the other. She was entirely dry. (Unlike Lord Guantes, whose fine velvets showed traces of damp.) Her silk gown swished around her ankles as she walked, and her fur cape was drawn tightly around her shoulders; her gloved hands tightened on its edges as she said something that Irene couldn't hear.

"Trap-door, return to your normal state. And thank you," Irene shouted as quietly as she could. She didn't know how much licence she'd been given to use the Language, but she wasn't taking any risks. She flexed her hands one at a time, to get some feeling back as she readied herself. All right. Her situation was pretty dire. But she had the element of surprise, and the Language. And a gun.

Although Sterrington also had a gun. And Lady Guantes and Lord Guantes might be armed too.

Perhaps she should make sure that nobody had guns . . .

Irene inched backwards to where two carriages met. The join was walled and roofed with canvas, swaying alarmingly with each movement of the Train. Fortunately, she didn't need to navigate it, as there was actually a ladder down the side of the carriage. She was out of the wind as she clung there, and she scraped her tangled hair back from her face so that she could see clearly.

The connecting sections opened onto the carriage corridors, rather than the interior compartments. And the corridor would be filled with guards, according to Zayanna and Atrox Ferox. But they wouldn't expect her to burst through the compartment wall — if she had enough adrenaline left to muster the appropriate Language. The butt of Atrox Ferox's gun was cold in her sweating hand.

"Train wall in front of me," she shouted, **"open like a door and allow me**

476

to enter the carriage beyond. Then close."

To her relief, the metal in front of her swung open compliantly, and she stepped into the carriage, just a yard behind Sterrington and the prisoners. She stumbled at the sudden cessation of pressure and wind. But Sterrington was already turning and raising her gun, Lady Guantes was whirling, her hand moving beneath her cape, and Lord Guantes was standing. Irene bowled Atrox Ferox's gun down the compartment, straight at the Guantes.

"**Guns,**" she shouted as Sterrington levelled her pistol at her, "**explode!**"

The carriage rang with the thunder-clap, and the Train shook.

It was messy. There was no way it couldn't be. Sterrington shrieked in pain as the gun in her hand shattered in a bloom of flame. She clutched at her bloody wrist, trying to stop the flow of blood, bone showing white through the bleeding flesh of her savaged hand.

Lord and Lady Guantes were both getting up from the floor. Atrox Ferox's gun had exploded much more violently than Sterrington's, but they weren't as close to it. All that was left of the weapon was a charred patch, like an exotic stain, which stood out

477

against the grey-draped back wall. Fragments of metal had ripped into the cushions of the chairs and into the thick carpet and had scarred the dark panes of the windows.

But both the Guantes looked unharmed, beyond some damage to their clothes. Whatever Lady Guantes had under her cape, it wasn't a gun. A knife, perhaps. Irene didn't think she was the sort of woman to go unarmed.

"Doors, bolt." There were clicks as the two compartment doors into the passage locked themselves, keeping any minions firmly out. "Try anything," Irene said quickly, her ears still ringing from the explosion, "and I'll do even worse. Sterrington, go and stand with them." The woman stumbled down the carriage towards the Guantes, her face deathly pale.

"My dear Miss Winters," Lord Guantes said. "You would appear to have exhausted your resources already." He spoke with casual arrogance, but the sheer fury in his eyes and the snap in his voice betrayed his fragile self-control.

"Lord Guantes," Irene cut in, before he could catch her off balance again. Lady Guantes also had her full attention on Irene, neither of the pair making any move to help Sterrington, who was probably in shock. "If

I want," Irene continued, "I can shatter the windows on you, break the floor and ceiling, set fire to the furnishings, and break each bone of yours as I name it." And it was a good thing that she wasn't saying all this in the Language, because it wasn't entirely true. But some of it was. Her hand went to Zayanna's knife, still stuck in her sash. "I have absolutely no compunction about using my full powers."

"And should we assume you're as dangerous as Alberich?" Lady Guantes asked Irene sceptically. She edged to her right, farther away from Lord Guantes.

There was banging on the compartment door.

"You should assume that I am very dangerous indeed," Irene replied.

Lord Guantes took a step to his left. *They're trying to split my attention.* "Then why aren't you using these incredible powers?" he said in tones of polite curiosity.

"It would endanger everyone in this carriage." The banging on the doors was getting louder. She took a deep breath; she had to look in control here. "But being your prisoner would be worse, so I'll act if pushed. So come on, Lord and Lady Guantes. I'm asking you to offer *me* a better alternative. Call off your men. Let's talk."

"And if we don't?" Lady Guantes asked. Her hand slid under her cape again.

"Then I start by ordering this knife through your husband's eye." Irene pulled the knife from her sash. "And whatever you try, madam, I'll get there first."

Her absolute sincerity must have shown, as Lady Guantes slowed, her hand now still under her cape, and Lord Guantes gave his wife a little nod.

From the corner of her eye, Irene saw Vale move. His eyelid flicked open, then closed again — not the pained blinking of someone slowly regaining consciousness, but a clear signal. He was awake.

"Guards, stand down!" Lord Guantes said sharply, raising his voice so that it would carry through the door. "That is an order. All stand *down.*" His voice echoed in Irene's bones, and she had to stiffen her arm to prevent her hand from trembling. "I will call if there is any additional trouble."

Silence fell in the corridor, and the Train rattled as it raced on, the shadows of great trees moving beyond the windows. Lord Guantes looked at his wife, then turned back to Irene. "Convincing, Miss Winters, but I am hardly about to surrender."

"I'm not asking for surrender," Irene said, her mind racing as she tried to figure out what she *should* be demanding. "There must be some way that we can both walk away from this. You may already have touched off your war. This dragon's family" — she prodded Kai with her foot — "they already know that he was kidnapped by you."

Lord Guantes raised his brows. "By me?"

"And by Lady Guantes, of course," Irene said fairly. "His uncle showed me pictures of you both. You don't need Kai any longer — you've already made your point."

Lord Guantes frowned. "You say you identified us personally to him?"

"You're well-known," Irene said. "He had photos of you. The Library had records on you. I'm hardly the only person who pointed the finger. And even if something does happen to me, you'll still be on record as the people responsible."

"So releasing you would make no difference. And if we let you go, you'll have even more to report," Lord Guantes said pleasantly.

Irene found herself lulled by his speech, and bit her tongue as she felt a wave of his compulsion roll over her. The longer she allowed him to speak, the more opportunity she gave him to use his magic. "But he can't touch you if you stay in high-chaos worlds, can he?" she pressed.

"You'd be surprised how far a dragon king can reach —," Lord Guantes began.

"My love, let us stay with the essentials," Lady Guantes said, cutting him off. "Suppose we make a bargain that lets you walk away. What do we get out of it?"

Irene almost sighed in relief. "Well, *I* let *you* walk away." She smiled, gesturing with her knife.

"That's all?" Lady Guantes said.

"You can spin it however you want," Irene said flatly. "I'm only interested in getting out of here and putting Kai under his uncle's protection. I want your oath on our safety. Say we begged, we grovelled, you twisted us round your little finger — say whatever you want to the other Fae — we won't contradict it. Claim that you got the better of us all the way down the line. I won't argue. I won't *be there* to argue."

"That might be worth something," Lord Guantes said thoughtfully. "Oh, do stop whimpering and tie your hand up, Sterrington. But I'd need more."

"You've given sufficient provocation for war," Irene said bitterly. *Unless I can persuade Kai's family that his safe return is suf-*

ficient to keep the peace . . . "You've chased me out of Venice. And you exposed a Librarian spy who was trying to infiltrate the Fae, if you want to put it that way. And you can easily say we're too petty to waste time pursuing, or alternatively take the credit for making us flee. Your choice."

"And what vow do you want us to swear?" Lady Guantes demanded. She took a step towards Irene, both hands empty now, her eyes on the knife in Irene's hand.

Irene knew it could undo everything she'd worked for if she didn't get this right. If the wording allowed for any wiggle room, it was the Fae way to take it. "I want you both to swear that you permit us — myself, Vale, and Kai" — she gestured at them as she spoke — "to leave this place here and now, in safety, without let or hindrance by you or others under your command or allied to you, by action or inaction, to return in safety to the world from which Kai was kidnapped." At which point she would hustle Kai, and Vale too if necessary, through the nearest Library entrance. They might have to spend the next few years undercover or visiting other worlds, but they'd be alive.

"That is quite a thorough undertaking, Miss Winters," Lord Guantes said. He took a step back to stand beside Sterrington, glancing down at the woman's ruined hand. "Hmm. And what would you pledge in return?"

"To leave this place without taking any further action against you and yours," Irene said. "And I and my two allies here would undertake not to seek revenge against you, by action or inaction." Kai wouldn't like it, but he'd owe her. However, what his family did would be their own business. Irene hoped they'd keep the Guantes running scared for the next few centuries.

"No offers of service?" Lady Guantes suggested.

"Absolutely not," Irene said. "My prior oaths to the Library forbid it."

"Do you speak for the Library?" Lord Guantes asked. "You seem to be negotiating on your own behalf here, Miss Winters. I'm surprised to hear you make such sweeping suggestions without any real authority. What would your superiors say?"

Irene felt the pressure of his will again and knew he'd found a weakness. She *was* here on her own. She *had* run off to rescue Kai without orders. If she came to a private deal with them, on top of her bargain with the Train, she might be in even further trouble when she returned — if she escaped at all . . .

She pulled herself back from the brink of self-doubt. "Garbage!" she said crisply. "That is complete and utter garbage. I *know* my superiors don't want a war, and that's what it all comes down to. Make all the insinuations you like. But understand that here and now, **I speak for the Library**."

The words hummed in the air of the carriage like a high-tension wire in a thunderstorm. And she waited for the Language to punish her for her lies, but the words held true. Both the Guantes flinched, and even Sterrington, distracted by her pain, curled in on herself.

"The bargain is still grossly in your favour," Lord Guantes said, his aura of power too close for comfort. Irene deliberately glanced away from him, to Lady Guantes, who was also uncomfortably near. "But maybe we can negotiate. With a player like you on the other side, one might even consider long-term arrangements —"

"It will do," Lady Guantes said, cutting him off. She took a deep breath. "My love, we must do what we can, with the options available. I recommend taking Miss Winters's deal."

"Perhaps . . . ," Lord Guantes began.

And then Sterrington moaned in pure agony. Irene glanced at her automatically — and saw that Lord Guantes had leaned down to grind his thumb into Sterrington's mangled hand. That was when Lady Guantes made her move. The woman slammed into Irene, covering the space between them faster than Irene would have thought possible. She knocked Irene to the ground, pinning her there with her body weight. Irene fought to keep a grip on her knife as Lady Guantes stretched across her, but was viciously elbowed in the stomach, and struggled just to breathe. Then Lady Guantes slammed her head against the floor, effectively gagging her with a forearm across her mouth. Her left hand held Irene's right wrist down, keeping the knife out of play.

Irene bit down and tasted Lady Guantes's blood.

Lady Guantes grimaced, her face barely a foot away, triumph flaring in her eyes as she pushed down harder. "Stop wasting your time, Miss Winters. You're no better than everyone else — all too easily distracted. My love, could you please come and knock her out?"

Irene bit down harder and brought her left hand up, wrenching at Lady Guantes's right arm. But the other woman had the advantage in strength, weight, and leverage. Irene could hear Lord Guantes's unhurried steps as he approached, above Sterrington's moaning. She struggled furiously, but she just couldn't loosen the other woman's grip. Then Lord Guantes stood above her, choosing his moment. Irene tried to jerk her head sideways, to free her face so that she could speak, but Lady Guantes held her pinned.

But at the edge of Irene's vision, Vale moved, jack-knifing his legs around to slam sideways into Lord Guantes, rolling with the motion to put his weight into it. Lord Guantes fell forward with an indignant grunt, slumping against Lady Guantes and Irene. Lady Guantes pitched off balance, and Irene managed to wrench her head to one side. Blood from Lady Guantes's arm ran from her mouth, and Irene spat it out as she screamed, **"Fae, get off me!"**

The words came without thinking, from a place of fury and terror, but they worked. The Language caught the Guantes and flung them both off Irene — knocking them away, to leave her sprawled on the carpet, trying to get her breath. She saw Vale struggling to his knees, having somehow manoeuvred his bound hands in front of him, but Kai was still unconscious. Irene's hand tightened on the hilt of her knife as she pushed herself to her knees. Then Lord Guantes was suddenly in front of her and had her by the throat. He gripped her neck where the chain had attempted to strangle her, its marks still raw, and dragged her to her feet, forcing Irene's head back so that she had to meet his eyes, but she couldn't get a word out. And she couldn't get any breath in. She could feel her pulse hammering in her brain, rattling faster than the Train's wheels — as his gaze held her like a pin spearing a butterfly. He had all the power now.

Yet she still had a knife.

Irene brought it up and forward, not fighting the grip on her throat, but moving into it instead. It was a sharp knife, a good one, and she slid it up and into Lord Guantes's chest, under the ribs and towards the heart. It was as if someone had drawn her a chart to follow. It was the way this particular fairy tale ended.

His grip loosened and she fell forward again, every breath painful. She heard Lady Guantes screaming, but it was merely a background to her own panting for air.

Then Vale was beside her. She could see the bindings on his wrists. A spark of common sense brought her back to herself, and she rasped painfully, **"Bindings, leave the wrists and ankles of Vale and Kai."**

Lady Guantes was kneeling on the bloodied floor, cradling her husband in her arms. His eyes were closed and he wasn't moving, the hilt of the knife still protruding from his chest. It looked as if it shouldn't be there. Undignified. Somehow human.

Irene rose to her feet, with Vale supporting her. She wanted to disclaim responsibility, say *I tried to offer him a deal,* but she couldn't deny the reality of the scene before her. She had blood on her neck from Lord Guantes's glove, and blood on her hand from her own fatal blow. She could feel it, wet and sticky.

Lady Guantes slowly rested her husband's head on the floor and eased his right glove from his hand, folding it and tucking it into her bodice. Tears ran down her face, but she was too calm — calm enough to make Irene's stomach clench in revulsion. "I'm not going to fight and get myself killed," she said, "but this is not over."

Irene wanted to say something that would somehow ease those tears and that dreadful calm and stop a private vendetta. But even the Language wasn't enough. "Leave," she said. "We won't stop you."

Lady Guantes nodded. She rose to her

489

feet. "Sterrington?"

"Ah, no, madam." Sterrington was crouched in the seat at the back of the compartment, looking incapable of action either for or against anyone. "I regret I must withdraw my service. This game is too rich for my tastes."

Lady Guantes nodded. "*Au revoir,* then. Miss Winters. Mr. Vale. Dragon." She stepped across to the door, her gloved hand on the handle. "I won't bother setting my guards on you. There seems little point now, and I'd rather leave you to far more lethal pursuers. And they'll be upon you very soon." She smiled then, and it was chilling. "If you survive them, then we will certainly meet again."

"**Door bolt, open,**" Irene said. The last thing she wanted was to keep Lady Guantes in the carriage.

Lady Guantes stepped out into the corridor, closing the door behind her.

"Are we pursued?" Vale demanded.

"Yes," Irene said shortly, "by the Rider — and multiple other Fae. They must be almost upon us now." She felt suddenly exhausted, her resources almost gone. She remembered the other person in the room. "Sterrington, are you a danger to us?"

Sterrington was clutching her wrist again,

trying to stop the trickle of blood. "I'm scarcely your friend," she said. Irene could see her struggle to remain civil. "But I'm not going to hold a grudge because I involved myself in someone else's affairs."

Irene nodded. "Then we'd better just hope the Train gets us to our world before it's too late."

"We've reached the disputed spheres," Sterrington offered weakly. "You might do better to jump from the Train — flee by foot. They know you're here, after all."

"Winters?" Vale questioned.

Irene shook her head. "They were close enough for me to see them. So if we jump now, they'd notice us. We'd never make it."

"Ah well," Sterrington said.

There seemed nothing to say to that, and Irene lowered her head wearily. Her whole body ached.

There wasn't any noise from the corridor outside. Lady Guantes must have taken her guards with her. There was just the hammering of the Train. She was out of ideas. There was only hope left.

Sterrington's words jogged a memory. "The disputed spheres?" she asked, raising her head again.

Sterrington nodded. "Those spheres that fully belong neither to us nor to the dragons.

Both sides can act within these lands."

Irene had sent one distress call. Perhaps it was time to shout once more, in case someone was listening. "Excuse me," she said, and levered herself up from where she'd collapsed on a couch. "Just to make sure we've done our utmost."

She limped towards the windows, bracing her hands against a frame. **"Window, open,"** she said, her throat still sore and bruised. The window slid down in its frame, revealing the passing landscape. It was a wind-swept forest now, full of dark trees and blowing leaves. She wondered if their pursuers would look like a Wild Hunt if she could see them now.

She focused her mind as her hands curled tightly around the window-frame. **"AO SHUN!"** she shouted at the top of her voice into the night beyond. **"DRAGON KING OF THE NORTHERN OCEAN!"**

The Train shook with a noise like thunder as a greater darkness than night or forest came roaring down on the wind, great wings outswept as it circled the Train. It was a long torrent of shadow, with a black serpentine body and ebony wings. Pale eyes shone coldly even from that distance, and it hovered above the Train as it ran along its track between worlds. Behind the Train, their pursuers fell back, the figure in the lead slowing as the dragon spread his wings.

Sterrington stumbled to her feet to stare out, her face white and her eyes wide with shock — and Vale moved forward to put a supportive arm around Irene's shoulders. She needed it.

Irene could barely hear her own voice. What was left of her strength was scraped empty, and only Vale's arm kept her upright. But she managed, "I think we have safe escort."

CHAPTER 27

The Train pulled into London with a screech and a shudder, just as it had arrived. Irene had watched through a window as people fled along the platforms, guards frantically waving flags. It was the pre-dawn rush, and the pale sky was split with the first streaks of light, with the remains of the dying moon drifting in and out of the clouds.

Kai had recovered consciousness about half an hour before, but he moved and spoke like a man suffering from a bout of influenza — leaning forward as though his joints ached and constantly rubbing at his forehead. His skin was marked with bruises and red burn-like weals. Vale had filled him in on Lord Guantes's fate. Kai had only nodded, but his eyes had become inhuman for that moment, savage and satisfied.

Irene herself had tried to sleep, but ironically she was too exhausted. The idea of a hot bath hung in the future like the promise of Christmas or a new book in a favourite series. She could imagine brandy too. But first they needed *safety.*

The Train's guiding shadow had left it ten minutes before London, when the landscape had dissolved from an unfamiliar urban cityscape into long shadowy fields, and then into the gasworks and factories that marked the outskirts of the city. Irene had seen those distant silver eyes again, as the long draconic form had pulled loose and lifted away, spreading vast wings that seemed to dissolve into rain-grey clouds at the edges. The future would contain an interview with a dragon king, and she wasn't looking forward to it, even if she had managed to save Kai.

"I will be staying with the Train," Sterrington said. Vale and Irene had finally bound up her hand during the journey, and she held the bandaged limb protectively against her chest. "There's nothing for me in this sphere."

Irene nodded. No doubt Sterrington would be passing on the full details of what had happened to some other Fae, but for the moment Irene couldn't bring herself to care.

Vale had opened the door onto the platform, and London air flooded into the compartment, with all its smells of oil and humanity. "We should leave this conveyance while we still can," he said.

Irene followed Kai out of the compartment, with a final nod to Sterrington. "Thank you," she said to the Train as they left — not sure whether it was listening, but it had served them well in the end.

The Train blasted steam again and instantly began to move, its wheels shuddering against the rails as it slid out of the station.

Irene turned to look at Vale and Kai. They hadn't vanished the moment she turned her back on them — and they were all alive and somehow in one piece. Then she noticed the stares in their direction. They were indeed battered, filthy, and bloodstained. And a guard was approaching, looking scandalized at her shortened skirts, already opening his mouth to complain.

"Yes, yes, quite," Vale said impatiently. He turned to Irene, effectively cutting the guard off mid-expostulation. "Winters, I suggest we take a cab."

"A wonderful idea," Irene said warmly, conscious of all the eyes upon them. "And we should use it to get Kai back to the Library at once."

"Oh, come now —" Kai started.

Irene was suddenly furious. "Look. I don't know how many other Fae know where you are. I don't know what they might do. Until I do know, the Library is the only place I can keep you safe." She realized that she was shouting and lowered her voice. "Or do you have any other ideas?"

"Perhaps I may be of assistance," said a familiar voice behind her.

Irene turned, readying herself to deliver a cutting retort.

But Li Ming was standing there. He — or she, (Irene still wasn't sure what the proper pronoun was) — was impeccably attired for this world in silver-grey with a black tie. He gave a formal bow to Kai, and then a half bow to Irene and Vale. "Your Highness, I have a local transport waiting outside and have arranged a place where you can attend upon my lord your uncle. There are matters of war to discuss."

Kai drew himself up straight and returned a polite nod. "Thank you, Lord Li Ming. That is most kind of you. My friends, however —"

"Naturally the offer of hospitality extends to all of you," Li Ming said. Irene wondered if their attendance was compulsory. The words *matters of war* were echoing in her

497

head like thunder. *No, no, no.* She'd thought they were past that. Were she and Vale witnesses? Or was this invitation actually a sort of protective custody? But there didn't *seem* to be any immediate threat to his words — or at least not a threat to them — or even the suggestion of official displeasure. "My lord your uncle would wish due courtesy to be given to your associates. Miss Winters and Mr. Vale are very welcome."

"Thank you," Vale said. "You are most kind."

Kai looked at Irene for approval. *Putting the responsibility on me again,* she thought acidly. When she gave him a half nod, he turned back to Li Ming. "Then we shall be glad to accept," he said.

The cab trip was full of tension. Li Ming refused to discuss the question of Fae/dragon hostilities, claiming that it was a matter for Kai's uncle, and instead questioned Kai about recent events. Vale brooded in the corner, from time to time sweeping Li Ming with that speculative gaze that suggested he was amassing data. Kai gave a cut-down version of what had happened, unconsciously rubbing at his bruises.

And Irene sat in the opposite corner from Vale and thought about war. Surely Ao Shun would be prepared to accept a peaceful solution? They'd rescued Kai. Or did some dragons want war just as much as certain Fae did?

If he did, then this world, and hundreds of others like it, might be doomed.

Li Ming had a suite reserved at the Savoy Hotel. The trusted lackeys of dragon kings presumably had big expense accounts, Irene thought grudgingly — she certainly couldn't have afforded accommodation on this scale. The room was very pretty, though, all white and gilt, with a light green carpet so spotless that it seemed a crime to walk on it. The heavy white velvet curtains were drawn back in swags from the window, and the morning light made the whole place far too bright. She, Vale, and Kai were untidy blotches on its expensive elegance. Blotches with coffee, though, which helped.

Then Li Ming interrupted her thoughts with the announcement she'd been secretly dreading: "His Majesty the king of the Northern Ocean honours you with his presence."

Irene rose, then stooped into a full curtsey, conscious of Vale bowing as the door swung open.

Kai brought his right fist to his left shoulder and quite unselfconsciously went down on one knee, bowing his head. "My lord uncle," he said. "Your presence is undeserved. I ask your pardon for any inconvenience I may have caused you."

Irene looked up through her lashes, waiting for a cue to rise, and praying it would come before her legs spasmed and she lost her balance. Like Li Ming, Ao Shun was dressed for this London, but his spotless jet-black suit, complete with white silk scarf, could only have come from a royal tailor. He also appeared in a fully human guise this time, Irene saw to her relief, though the sheer impact of his presence was only slightly less overpowering as a result.

"You have my thanks for your actions in defence of my nephew," he said, at last gesturing for them to stand. "I have come to discuss what took place, before raising the matter of war with my brothers."

"Your Majesty," Irene said, and saw Kai suppress a twitch. No doubt it was Not the Done Thing for anyone other than the king to take the conversational lead. "I ask your permission to speak."

Ao Shun levelled his gaze at her, and she felt as if she were in a cannon's sights. "Your actions have earned our consideration," he said. "What concerns you?"

"Your Majesty, the kidnapping was due to two people alone," Irene said. She watched

him as she spoke, trying to gauge his reaction to her words, looking for any hint of
emotion. "One of them is now dead at my
hands. And the other acknowledged her
defeat and fled. Your nephew has returned
to you. We were also helped by others of the
Fae who didn't seek war. Your Majesty, I
am not asking for lenience to benefit the
Fae. But I entreat you to consider all the
humans in all the worlds between you and
them. I beg you, do not make this a matter
of war. It would be disproportionate." She
looked for words that might sway a dragon.
"And, I think, unjust."

Ao Shun's eyes flared red at the word
unjust, and the sky outside darkened in
response as gathering clouds hid the sun.
"Your words are heard," he said. "Your
perspective is natural, as one from the Library."

Irene felt the pressure of his displeasure,
as it lay dangerously heavy in the air, and
had to force herself to continue. "Of course,
Your Majesty," she said, "I am loyal to the
Library. And, as such, I can and must speak
for its interests. But I would also say that
the Fae have suffered a severe setback, prov-
ing that it's unwise to kidnap any dragon,
let alone one of your royal bloodline. Please
consider this to be sufficient, Your Majesty."

Ao Shun turned his head slightly, looking away from her. "You have done your duty to my nephew as your student," he said. "Your responsibilities in this matter are ended. There is no need for you to take further action."

Irene could see Kai looking at her, with a *Please, please shut up now* expression on his face. On her other side, Vale was impassive. "I have fulfilled my duty to my student," she said. "I also have a duty to the Library, and to the people in the worlds that it touches."

"And what of you, my nephew?" Ao Shun's voice took on a distinct edge as he addressed Kai. The room was suddenly full of thick tension — it pressed against Irene, and she could see that Vale was having to square his shoulders to stand firm against it. Thunder shuddered in the air outside. "Have you any thoughts on this matter?"

Kai's throat worked as he swallowed. "My lord uncle," he faltered. Then his voice grew stronger. "My teacher speaks truly. It would be unjust for harm to come to humans who have had no involvement in these hostilities. Those Fae who were responsible have paid for their actions. Time will prove the rightness of our way and the weakness of theirs. If there must be retribution, then blame me for my folly in allowing myself to be captured."

"Your folly, or your teacher's carelessness," said Ao Shun, and the air trembled slightly at his words.

"I will answer for any fault of mine," Irene said firmly. The taste of fear was sour in her mouth.

"Surely his friends must also take some of the blame, Your Majesty," Vale said. "Those like me, for instance."

Ao Shun looked between the three of them. Scale patterns were showing across the skin of his cheeks and hands, and his nails were longer and darker than they had been a moment ago. Rain broke against the window with a slap of wind.

There was a knock at the door.

Li Ming moved to answer it. "I'm afraid you have the wrong room —," he began.

"I don't think so." It was Coppelia's voice. Coppelia, *here*. Irene felt as if she could suddenly draw a breath. "My name is Coppelia, and I am an elder of the Library. I request audience with His Majesty the king of the Northern Ocean."

"She may enter," Ao Shun said before Li Ming could even turn to consult him. "I welcome the advice of an elder of the Library."

Coppelia stepped into the room, neatly dressed in a dark velvet gown and cape suitable for greeting royalty, the wood of her hand hidden by her gloves. And though she was rigidly straight-backed, she leaned on a silver-topped cane as she walked. *Her arthritis is playing up again.* Inside the Library, she was a teacher and friend. Outside the Library, it was harder to forget that Coppelia was an extremely old woman, who'd accumulated years of injuries as a Librarian in the field.

"Your Majesty." She gave Ao Shun a half bow, having to support herself on her cane. "Please forgive my lack of formality. I'd have curtseyed properly if I were as young as these children."

"No forgiveness is necessary," Ao Shun said. The rain outside was slacking off. "Your presence is most welcome. Will you be seated?"

He's treating her as a respected ambassador, so definitely a step above me, Irene decided. *But thank god that Coppelia showed up.*

"I'm only here briefly, Your Majesty," Coppelia said. "I've come to collect my colleague to answer a formal inquiry. I hope that won't be inconvenient?"

Irene felt the colour drain from her cheeks.

So she had to face a penalty for what she'd done. She tried to convince herself that she'd expected it all along, but it rang hollow. She wasn't ready at all.

"I have no reason to complain about her actions," Ao Shun said. "She has acted properly throughout, and I owe her my gratitude for what she has done."

"Madame Coppelia, you can't do this!" Kai had his jaw set, and the metaphorical bit between his teeth. "Irene did everything she could to get me out of there. It wasn't her fault that I was kidnapped. If anyone should be blamed for this, *it's me.*"

"Kai." Ao Shun slapped his open palm on the arm of his chair. "Silence!" But he seemed more astonished than angry that Kai should actually have had the nerve to speak. "If this is an internal matter, then it is not your place to interfere."

"I'm still an apprentice to the Library," Kai said, his skin starting to take on a draconic cast too. "Unless and until I am removed from that position, which was agreed by my father himself . . ." He let it trail off meaningfully.

Irene tried to interpret the sudden look of baffled frustration on Ao Shun's face. Kai's father was his *older* brother. In terms of the draconic respect for hierarchy that she'd seen, this suggested that Ao Shun couldn't contradict *his* orders. The situation was rapidly degenerating into a no-win one.

Someone had to take responsibility.

"Of course I'll return to the Library," she said. Ao Shun and Kai broke their mutual glare to look at her. She addressed Coppelia. "I admit I broke Library rules in visiting a high-chaos world without permission. I also acknowledge that I failed to properly supervise an apprentice who was under my charge, which resulted in him being kidnapped by individual Fae, and might even have led to war."

"These are serious charges," Coppelia said. Her voice was as severe as a hanging judge's, but there was a glint in her eye that Irene recognized as approval. "Your Majesty, I must ask for your permission to leave. Irene and I need to return as soon as possible."

Ao Shun was frowning. He had Kai's trick of glowering, now that Irene thought about it. "Is it necessary for her to return? Perhaps some detached duty could be arranged? I would not see her punished for her actions. I would even be glad to have her in my own service."

"Your Majesty is too generous," Coppelia said. "Her actions are very serious. I'm sure that she herself wouldn't want to avoid due process. Would you, Irene?"

She could throw herself on Ao Shun's mercy and take up his offer. But then she'd also have to say goodbye to the Library — just as devastating as if the elder Librarians cast her out. Either way, she lost. She might retain Kai as a student that way, but she still lost.

Or maybe there was a way out of this that wasn't *quite* losing. It depended on whether Ao Shun really did feel some sort of gratitude for her actions, and just how far that extended.

"I'm not going to abandon my duty now," she said firmly. "My actions and my neglect could still cause war, threatening hundreds of worlds. I submit myself to whatever punishment is required."

Vale seemed about to say something. She caught his eye and desperately stared him down, with a tiny shake of her head. If this huge gamble was going to work, then the threat to her had to be genuine.

Coppelia nodded. "I would expect nothing else. Come, then."

For a moment the room was silent; then Ao Shun said, "Wait."

"Your Majesty?" Coppelia enquired.

Ao Shun's expression could have been

carved from stone. "I request, as a favour and in the interests of *justice,* that this Librarian not be judged too harshly. I can say with some confidence that there is no immediate risk of war."

Irene took a deep breath of relief for those human worlds — and for herself. The sudden lifting of weight from her shoulders was dizzying. There wouldn't be a war. She could survive a penalty — and it might not even be that bad, given what Ao Shun had just said. But then she considered the unbending nature of Library discipline, and her heart sank.

Coppelia gave a dignified half bow. "Thank you, Your Majesty. This will be taken into account in judgement of her. Irene, if you have any farewells to make to your friends, please do so."

Irene turned to Kai and Vale. "I'll be back if, and when, I can," she said. "Don't do anything stupid." It might not be quite the language that one should use in front of a king, but her control was slipping. And the shadow of the inquiry still hung over her.

Kai took her hands in his. "I will be waiting here for your return," he promised. "With my uncle's permission, of course." The last bit was added hastily, and didn't sound particularly sincere to Irene. Judging by the frown on Ao Shun's face, it didn't sound very sincere to him, either.

Vale touched her shoulder briefly. "I'll keep an eye on Strongrock in your absence," he said. "I hope you won't be too long, Winters. Your expertise with languages is surprisingly useful."

Irene's throat tightened. She was *not* going to embarrass herself. "Thank you both," she said clearly. "I hope not to be too long, either."

And she did still have hope. Because Ao Shun hadn't removed Kai from the Library, and because Coppelia had come to help her — and because, whatever the punishment the Library might level, she didn't think they were going to cast her out. She was still part of the Library, and she'd spoken for the Library when things were at their worst. And, with the Library's help, they had stopped a war before it could begin.

And because, in spite of everything that had been set against them, she and Vale had saved Kai.

She dropped another curtsey to Ao Shun and followed Coppelia out of the room — back towards the Library.

■ ■ ■ ■

Secrets from the Library

Insider Information on the Library and Its Spies

■ ■ ■ ■

IRENE'S TOP FIVE
BOOK HEISTS

As a junior Librarian spy, Irene is sent far and wide to collect famous, rare, and dangerous books and bring them back to the Library. This might be to doom a dangerous faction or to save a world — a Librarian may not be told. Sometimes a book is exactly where it's supposed to be, in a well-laid-out library on an orderly world, so it's a simple matter to retrieve the required tome. Sometimes a mission goes badly wrong, and the spy barely escapes with their life, never mind the target acquisition. Needless to say, Librarians all have their favourite book-heist tales and horror stories. So we asked Irene to share her top five.

AGAMEMNON
BY WILLIAM SHAKESPEARE
I suppose the first text that comes to mind would be Shakespeare's *Agamemnon* — everyone wants to boast about retrieving a

unique Shakespeare, don't they? It was one of those jobs where you know exactly where the text is (in a reclusive billionaire's private collection), but the problem is getting it out of there. The world containing the book was still in the middle of a long-running set of wars, dating far back to some crusades in the eleventh century, and the Byzantine Empire was the dominant power. More obstructively, it was one of those worlds where women have a very defined second-class position in society. I ended up "borrowing" a copy of Shakespeare's *Love's Labour's Lost* from yet another world (it had never existed on the target world). Then I let that come to the billionaire's attention. I allowed him to swindle me out of it in order to get at *his* collection. I felt quite good about myself afterwards, since he had at least got his hands on a Shakespeare he'd never read before. As for the play itself . . . well, I found that Shakespeare had borrowed most of the basic plot from Aeschylus, the ancient Greek tragedian. But as usual, Shakespeare had added in some bits of his own. I wonder if he had intended to borrow the rest of Aeschylus's *Oresteia* sequence too and make a trilogy of it . . .

The time I was sent to fetch a copy of the Skjöldunga saga is one of my worst memories. I was posted to a moderate-chaos, high-magic world, and there were idiots waving large weapons every time you turned a corner. Think flying longships, spell-singing skalds, and lots and lots of omens and feuds. Anyone who was anyone was trying to start new wars. It was as if they expected Ragnarök to be happening tomorrow and wanted to make sure they'd slaughtered everyone they could before it got apocalyptic. There was no helpful Librarian-in-Residence on that world. There were barely any libraries. And there were plenty of Fae. Worse than cockroaches. I worked as a travelling bard and storyteller, and recycled classic stories while trying to entertain over-muscled drunks in taverns. If you happen to visit that world and run across an oral retelling of Captain Nemo fighting Moby Dick while fleeing the French Revolution, now you know why. And the war that did get off the ground was absolutely not my fault. The Fae were involved too, and *they* were the ones who set off the Gullinbursti Bomb. I was just an unfortunate bystander.

THE LIGHT-HOUSE
BY EDGAR ALLAN POE

Another one that I had trouble getting hold of was Poe's *The Light-House,* after the author's demise. And the version I was after was the completed work, a full novel, unlike the unfinished version found in some worlds. Poe had been quite a famous writer during his lifetime in this world, though he still had problems with drinking and gambling. He'd lived in the American Confederate Empire, as it was called there, and his wife had been a practitioner of the local folk magics. While sorcery worked on that world and was a major subject in universities, most of the Fae in that world were over in Europe, so at least I didn't have them to worry about. The problem here was that there was supposed to be a cryptogram concealed in the book. It was one of those "solve the puzzle and you shall receive my accumulated wealth" scenarios, which led to copies of the book being very scarce (it had only been published as a limited edition, too). And several secret societies or obsessive treasure-hunters had made finding them even harder. I ended up being chased through the local woods by a large number of magically transformed killer cats, and having to dive into the lake to avoid them, and then crawling out on the other shore and being mistaken for a drowned ghost . . . Not one of my more triumphant episodes. And not my favourite way to spend Halloween.

THE TALE OF LOYAL HEROES AND RIGHTEOUS GALLANTS
BY SHI YUKUN

A year later, I was sent to acquire a copy of *The Tale of Loyal Heroes and Righteous Gallants* — a transcription of oral performances by the storyteller Shi Yukun. It was one of those books that show up in rather a lot of worlds, but this particular one was unique — it went on for a hundred chapters longer than other versions. The world where the book was based was quite peaceful, which made a nice change. It was ruled by the Chinese Empire, and there wasn't much magic or much technology, but there was a lot of trade. I had to establish an identity as a foreign student, travel halfway across China by slow train, and get a place at the university at Ch'ang-an in order to have access to the university library. This was where the only known copy of the full original was stored. I then spent a solid three months sneaking in by night and copying the manuscript by hand, and I only had to dodge the guards a few times. It wasn't a time-sensitive mission, and this way I could leave the original there. It was quite an enjoyable assignment. I even managed to get some studying done. My life isn't *all* running around and screaming, you know.

LADY CATHERINE'S DENIAL
BY JANE AUSTEN

Finally, there's one mission that I remember particularly due to the book itself. I'm not saying that the world wasn't interesting — it had high technology, moderate chaos levels, cloned dinosaurs, et cetera. But, more importantly, this was the only world on record where Jane Austen had gone on to write whodunits. Naturally I was briefed to retrieve the entire set. The hardest to find was her final book, *Lady Catherine's Denial:* the manuscript had vanished with Austen's death. I managed to trace it to the private estate of a mad scientist in Wales. (I'm not saying that all mad scientists read Jane Austen, but a surprising number of the ones that I've met do.) Annoyingly, he was the sort who fills his private park with carnivorous cloned dinosaurs to ensure privacy. I had to sneak in via an underground passage, from a disused local coal mine. Even then I was captured and almost ended up as an experimental subject. (Of course I escaped. I'm writing this, aren't I?) I still have a copy of the book on my own shelves, if you're interested. It starts with the murder of Lady Catherine de Bourgh . . .

LEGENDS OF THE LIBRARY

In the Library one hears plenty of stories about "the monster that lives in the basement" or "the Librarian who tried to find the oldest book in the Library and was never seen again" or "the time someone tried climbing out of one of the windows — that lead to nowhere." Typical urban legends — well, Library legends. Then there are the more classical ones. The sort that have a Librarian lost in the deepest part of the Library. She might come into a room containing a circle of ornate chairs, with sleeping knights in armour seated upon them, where a mysterious voice says to her, "Has the time come yet?" And she says, "No, go back to sleep," and then runs away, and she can never find the room again. This is a typical folktale of the Sleeping King and his Warriors type — whether about Arthur, or Barbarossa, or whatever.

But there are other stories.

They say that a Librarian once saw someone's cat squeezing through a corner between two shelves. (Some of the older Librarians have pets. Some of the pets can be a little strange.) So he pulled out some books to check behind them and found a crack in the wall. And since it was a brick wall, and he was a curious man, he levered out more of the bricks in an attempt to find out what was behind the wall. He found a vast echoing darkness, the air dry and unmoving, so pitch-black that even shining a torch into the void illuminated nothing. Being a halfway sensible man (a fully sensible man wouldn't have removed those bricks in the first place), he didn't try lowering himself down into it on a rope or anything like that, and he put the bricks back in place. But before doing that, he wrote a note on a piece of paper, suggesting that if there was anyone out there, he'd like to talk, and he threw the note into the darkness before sealing up the crack.

When he returned to his rooms, he sat down with the book he'd been reading earlier that day and tried to relax. But when he turned to the correct page, his bookmark had been replaced with something else — with the note that he'd thrown into the darkness. The paper was now brittle with age and dust, and written on the bottom in the Language was, **Not yet, I think.**

AN INTERVIEW WITH THE AUTHOR

Genevieve Cogman has written some wonderfully entertaining fiction, set within incredible new worlds. We wanted to find out a bit more about Genevieve's writing, her characters, and the origins of these worlds. Genevieve was kind enough to indulge our bookish curiosity — and please find our interview below.

Q. If you could choose one thing from Irene's world and bring it to ours, what would it be and why?

A. My first thought would be, the entire Library, but that's probably a bit excessive! So I'll settle for a login to the Library email system so that I can start accessing their most tempting files.

Q. How do your plots come together? Do ideas strike you while you travel to work, or in the supermarket? Or do

ideas actually emerge as you sit at the keyboard?

A. I think it was Agatha Christie who once said that the best time for planning a book is when you're doing the dishes. I find that ideas can come at any time — but rarely arrive at a convenient moment, such as when I'm actually sitting in front of the computer and ready to use them. This is why I often have a number of scribbled notes to hand by the time I get to the computer. I sometimes jot down particularly brilliant lines (!) that I don't want to forget (or at least lines that seem brilliant at the time — they don't always look as good a few hours later). I do even have ideas when I'm working at the day job. However, fortunately for my characters, I have yet to inflict on them any of the diseases or injuries I read about while at that job.

Q. George R. R. Martin talked about writers being either architects or gardeners — in terms of either planning ahead or rather letting the plot grow. Would you class yourself as one or the other, and if so, why is that?

A. I'd class myself as a gardener, but the sort who lays out the flower-beds before starting. I have an idea of what's going to happen, and a rough draft of the plot. I'll also have marked out stages such as "in this bit, Irene does X and acquires bit of information Y." But at that point I haven't necessarily worked out the full details of how she comes by that knowledge. And I may have other bursts of inspiration which develop in the process of writing, or characters who are supposed to be one-offs but end up making multiple appearances during the course of the novel. And then again, there are the parts of the plot which go something like this: "At this point Irene stages a brilliant escape attempt, but I haven't yet worked out how she does it — research this bit more." This can result in the whole metaphorical garden having to be redug. Still, it's all worth it if it makes for a better story . . .

Q. When a Librarian uses "the Language," it has all kinds of magical effects on the world. Do you have a favourite use of this Language in either *The Invisible Library* or *The Masked City*? And if so, what makes it special?

A. I think my favourite use of the Language is in *The Invisible Library,* when Irene commands the stuffed animals in the museum to animate and attack the werewolves.

It's baroque and dramatic and probably expends more energy than some other things she might have tried, but it was just such fun to write.

Q. Librarians have the mark of the Library tattooed on their backs. What does this look like exactly?

A. It's a rectangle of black script across the back, about a foot across, below the shoulder-blades. It's low enough that Irene can get away with a moderately off-the-shoulder dress! There's also a cartouche around it, providing a bookish framing device. Anyone looking at it who wasn't a Librarian would see Irene's name (or whichever Librarian's name it was) in their own native language. It can't be covered with make-up or dye, so Librarians tend to be careful in their choice of clothing. There are rumours that the cartouche around the Librarian's name is actually microscopically compressed script which goes into great detail about the Library. But you know how rumours are . . .

Q. I love Irene's dry wit and calm ability to rise to any (most!) occasions. Was she inspired by any other charac-

ters in fiction, or did she emerge fully formed?

A. I would like to think that she's mostly original, but probably I've unconsciously borrowed bits here and there. She definitely owes a debt to Lois McMaster Bujold's heroines. I also see her as having a certain resemblance to John Steed, from the classic TV series *The Avengers,* in terms of her polite manners and unscrupulous nature. (Kai gets to be Emma Peel.)

Q. Where does Irene's name come from? Is there a story behind that?

A. Irene is a lifelong admirer of Sherlock Holmes, and of the Conan Doyle stories in general, and named herself after the notorious adventuress Irene Adler (to Sherlock Holmes, always *the* woman) in a fit of enthusiastic obsession. These days she's much more embarrassed about it.

Q. What other authors have influenced you, in terms of writing these "Library" books?

A. Quite a few that I can think of straight away, and probably even more that I can't think of offhand but that if you pointed them out to me, then I'd go, "Of course, I should have thought of so-and-so." The first names that come to mind are Ursula Le Guin, Terry Pratchett, Diane Duane, Sir Arthur Conan Doyle, Barbara Hambly, John Dickson Carr, Umberto Eco, Roger Zelazny, Michael Moorcock, and Louise Cooper . . . Plus I owe a debt to classic television such as *Doctor Who* and *The Avengers* — and to kung-fu and wuxia movies.

Q. How long does a Librarian have to serve in the field as a Librarian spy before they can lord it over the juniors as a senior Librarian, posted to the Library itself?

A. Usually Librarians work in the field until they're too old or too severely injured to be able to handle the physical side of the job competently. This generally means working till they're in their sixties or seventies. Some even stay in the field for longer, if they really take to the world where they're living and working. But such Librarians tend to be "Librarians-in-Residence" who've put great time and effort into their cover identities. Some of them even choose to die a comfortable natural death in a world that they've grown to love. Others make their eventual retreat into the Library. Then they can finally settle down to read all the books they've collected, study the languages they've wanted to learn, write critical comparisons of books from different worlds, argue with their colleagues . . . oh, and mentor the juniors too.

Q. What goes into the education of a good Librarian spy?

A. Languages are very important. A Librarian who speaks (and reads and writes) multiple languages is very useful to the Library, as they can be sent on a much wider range of missions than a monolingual spy. General physical health, martial arts skills, and great marksmanship are all useful — as is the ability to run fast when needed. A good Librarian is expected to be able to be diplomatic where necessary, and to be able to blend in under most social circumstances. Some Librarians like to train their protégés in spycraft and wetwork (assassinations, etc.), plus strategy and tactics. Others encourage their juniors to learn skills like lock-picking, burglary, fast-talking, and the art of the con. The oldest Librarians, the ones who never leave the Library, teach less immediately useful skills such as art theory and literary criticism. They are also always ready to discuss their favourite works of literature and talk about how much tougher it was in their time.

The perfect Librarian is calm, cool, collected, intelligent, multilingual, a crack shot, a martial artist, an Olympic-level runner (at both the sprint and marathon), a good swimmer, an expert thief, and a genius con artist. They can steal a dozen books from a top-security strongbox in the morning, discuss literature all afternoon, have dinner with the cream of society in the evening, and then stay up until midnight dancing, before stealing some more interesting tomes at three a.m. That's what a perfect Librarian would do. In practice, most Librarians would rather spend their time reading a good book.

Q. Other than books (I know, what else is there but books?!), what might be a sought-after delicacy for the discerning Librarian?

A. Some sort of stimulant, for those long nights with an enjoyable read, whether it's tea, coffee, chocolate, cognac, or absinthe . . . Irene prefers coffee, with brandy for those moments when one really needs a slug of brandy. She hasn't yet developed an educated taste for coffee, but she does prefer the good stuff to the cheap stuff. Bradamant likes cocktails, but would rather have them bought for her than shake them herself. Coppelia takes her coffee very black, with a lump of muscovado brown sugar, producing something so richly bitter-sweet that it curls the toes of the casual drinker.

Q. Finally, the love of books and libraries comes across in every page of your work. Is there a particular library that is special to you, or is there one you'd still love to visit?

A. I have memories of libraries from all the places that I've lived, but I think one of my most special memories is the library from my old school — Christ's Hospital. I was one of the pupil librarians who used to help keep the books in order, and I used to spend a lot of my spare time there. I remember the bay windows in the main fiction section, and the light slanting through them in the afternoon. The heavy old wooden tables and chairs. The card-index. (This was over twenty years ago.) The side door leading to the old Dominions Library where a lot of the reference works and older books were stored, where it was always quiet. There were paintings and curtains and so on, but it's the wooden floors and shelving that I remember, dark and old and heavy, and the books themselves.

Of course, it may all be different now, but memories are an alternate world of their own.

ABOUT THE AUTHOR

Genevieve Cogman started on Tolkien and Sherlock Holmes at an early age, and has never looked back. But on a perhaps more prosaic note, she has an MSc in Statistics with Medical Applications and has wielded this in an assortment of jobs: clinical coder, data analyst, and classifications specialist. Genevieve Cogman previously worked as a freelance role-playing game writer, and her hobbies include patchwork, beading, knitting, and gaming. She lives in the north of England.

The employees of Thorndike Press hope you have enjoyed this Large Print book. All our Thorndike, Wheeler, and Kennebec Large Print titles are designed for easy reading, and all our books are made to last. Other Thorndike Press Large Print books are available at your library, through selected bookstores, or directly from us.

For information about titles, please call:
  (800) 223-1244

or visit our Web site at:
  http://gale.cengage.com/thorndike

To share your comments, please write:
  Publisher
  Thorndike Press
  10 Water St., Suite 310
  Waterville, ME 04901